DATE WITH THE EXECUTIONER

1817. Dawn breaks on a summer's day in Chalk Farm, London, and the scene is set for a duel between a lady's two ardent admirers. Paul Skillen has been teaching Mark Bowerman how to shoot properly, and although he is not sanguine of his chances, stands as his second. Although the duel is broken up, the passions behind the duel seem to spill out into the full light of day when Bowerman is stabbed to death in a stranger's garden. Paul and his twin Peter are determined to see justice done and are soon enmeshed in a spider's web of inheritance, treachery and fraud.

DATE WITH THE EXECUTIONER

DATE WITH THE EXECUTIONER

by

Edward Marston

Magna Large Print Books
Long Preston, North Yorkshire,
BD23 4ND, England.

British Library Cataloguing in Publication Data.

A catalogue record of this book is
available from the British Library

ISBN   978-0-7505-4542-6

First published in Great Britain by Allison & Busby in 2017

Published in Large Print 2018 by arrangement with
Allison & Busby Ltd.

Magna Large Print is an imprint of Library Magna Books Ltd.

Printed and bound in Great Britain by
T.J. (International) Ltd., Cornwall, PL28 8RW

CHAPTER ONE

1816

Putney Heath was the chosen location for a death. At that time of the morning, it was deserted. A breeze was making the grass ripple gently. The two coaches arrived at dawn, emerging out of the shadows into the first light of day. They rolled to a halt on either side of the clearing, hidden from sight by the encircling foliage. There was a sense of secrecy vital to the enterprise. Duels were illegal. Those involved were risking punishment. That was why they'd come so far out of the city. Like Leicester Fields, Chalk Farm and Wimbledon Common, the place was a popular choice. Swords had clashed there many times and pistols had often been discharged in anger. Blood had irrigated the Heath. Deaths had occurred in the questionable name of honour.

Paul Skillen had had misgivings from the start about the issuing of the challenge. He was acting as second to Mark Bowerman, who was so incompetent with a pistol in his hand that he'd come to Paul for lessons in how to shoot straight. Bowerman was a fleshy man in his early forties, blessed with wealth enough to live in comparative luxury for the rest of his days. Yet he was prepared to take part in a duel against an adversary who, even at first glance, held many advantages. Paul had urged his friend to extricate himself somehow from the situation but Bowerman would not hear of it. That would not only smack of cowardice, it would lose him the love and respect of the woman he adored. The duel, he insisted, was over an affair of the heart. Having once fought in a similar contest, Paul understood how he must be feeling. The difference was that Paul was an expert with any weapon, whereas Bowerman was clumsy and inexperienced. What drove the latter on was a passion that blinded him to doubt and danger.

'I'll die sooner than yield her up to *him*,' he vowed.

'That would be a poor advertisement for my skill as an instructor,' said Paul, wryly. 'My chief aim is to keep you alive.'

'You've nothing with which to reproach yourself. Nobody could have taught me so much in so short a period of time.'

'Follow my orders to the letter and you may yet survive.'

'I'll do more than that,' said Bowerman with a surge of bravado. 'I mean to kill him for his insolence.'

He glared across at his opponent. Stephen Hamer was a tall, lithe, handsome man of thirty with impeccable attire and an air of supreme confidence. Paul could see that he was extremely fit. The man was at once relaxed yet eager for action. After glancing at Bowerman, he whispered something to his second then sent him across to his opponent.

'He's coming to ruffle your feathers,' warned Paul.

'Then he's wasting his time,' said Bowerman.

'Hold your tongue and let me give him his answer.'

'I'll do my own talking, if you don't mind, Mr Skillen.'

When the second reached them, he gave a polite nod of greeting. He was a thickset man in his late thirties, well dressed and well spoken.

'Good morning to you both,' he said, politely. 'We had not expected you to turn up, Mr Bowerman, so you deserve congratulations, if only for that. We all know that this is an unequal contest. During his time in the army, Captain Hamer won several shooting contests and more than one duel. He bade me tell you that he has no wish to kill you and offers you the opportunity to withdraw before your fate is sealed.'

'Never!' cried Bowerman.

'You would, of course, have to render an abject apology and give your word as a gentleman that you'll cease to bother the lady forthwith.'

'Miss Somerville is *mine*. I'm here to defend her from that vile rogue.'

'Is that the message I am to carry back with me?'

'It is,' said Paul, stepping in to get rid of the man before Bowerman lost the remains of his self-control. 'Away with you, sir, and take your insults with you.'

With a gracious smile, the man turned on his heel and went quickly away.

'Ignore him, Mr Bowerman,' said Paul. 'He was sent to vex you.'

'Hamer will be made to pay for that.'

11

'It's essential that you remain calm and col-
lected.'

But there was no chance of that. Bowerman
was throbbing with fury. Hamer, by contrast, was
laughing happily with his second. It was as if the
whole event was a joke to them. Paul feared the
worst. The information that Hamer was an army
man was unsettling. Both of the duellists had
taken the precaution of bringing a surgeon with
them but it was clear to Paul that it was Bowerman's who would be called upon.

When the light had improved enough, the pre-
liminaries began. The referee, a short, squat man
with a rasping voice, called the combatants to
order. It was too late to turn back now. Bowerman
seemed to realise at last the scale of his task.

'If, so be it, there *is* a mishap,' he said, grabbing
Paul by the wrist, 'I beg of you to tell the lady
that I showed courage.'

'You have my word, sir, though I hope such
tidings will be unnecessary. In your own interests,
I urge you to put Miss Somerville out of your
mind. The only person who matters to you at this
moment is the one intending to shoot you.'

The advice helped to steel Bowerman. Pulling
himself to his full height, he marched bravely towards the referee. The rules of the contest were
recited, the box opened and the duelling pistols revealed. Hamer indicated that his opponent should
have first choice of weapon. After dithering for a
moment, Bowerman snatched up a pistol. Paul
watched helplessly from the sidelines. Beside him,
his valise already wide open, the surgeon was
poised to run to Bowerman's assistance. Neither

of them gave him an earthly chance of winning the duel because he was up against a proven marksman. They were being forced to witness an execution.

At the referee's command, the two men stood back to back then walked the requisite number of paces before turning and raising their pistols. Paul closed his eyes and waited for the gunfire. Instead, he heard loud, warning yells and the sound of many feet. Over a dozen men had suddenly materialised out of the bushes to interrupt the duel and to arrest everyone present. Paul recognised the man in command of them instantly. It was Micah Yeomans, a big, hulking man with unsightly features and gesticulating hands. The Bow Street Runner was in his element, enforcing the law by stopping the duel at the crucial moment and relishing the fact that he'd caught one of his sworn enemies. As the duelists were relieved of their pistols, Yeoman ambled across to Paul and grinned malevolently.

'Good morning,' he said, gloating. 'I've got you at long last. Am I talking to Mr Peter Skillen or to Mr Paul Skillen?'

Paul beamed at him. 'Why not hazard a guess?'

CHAPTER TWO

When the news came, they were in the shooting gallery. Gully Ackford, the big, broad-shouldered former soldier who owned the place, had just finished teaching someone the rudiments of boxing. Peter Skillen, as tall, lean and well-favoured as his twin brother, had spent two hours giving fencing lessons. Both men were glad of a respite. It was, however, short-lived. Their leisure was interrupted by Jem Huckvale, who flung open the door and darted into the room.

'You'll never guess what's happened,' he said, breathlessly.

'I'm afraid that I will,' said Peter with a sigh. 'My brother took his impulsive client to Putney Heath and is bringing his corpse back to the city.'

'You're quite wrong.'

'Are you telling me that Mr Bowerman actually *won* the duel?'

'It never took place,' said Huckvale.

'Why not?' asked Ackford. 'Bowerman would not have run away from the contest. There was far too much at stake for that. Did his opponent fail to appear?'

'They both turned up and, according to Paul, the duel was about to start when they were interrupted by Micah Yeomans and his men. Everyone was arrested and taken off to face the chief magistrate.'

14

Peter and Ackford were startled by the information. The diminutive Huckvale enjoyed his brief moment as the bearer of important tidings. As a young assistant at the gallery, his life consisted largely of doing chores and running errands. It was good to be the centre of attention for once.

'How did you come by this news, Jem?' asked Peter.

'I chanced to meet one of the Runners, Chevy Ruddock. He was there when they jumped out of the bushes on Putney Heath. Ruddock was crowing about the fact that Paul was dragged back in handcuffs. So I ran straight to Bow Street to find out the details.'

'What did you learn?'

'All that there was to learn,' replied Huckvale. 'The parties involved in the duel were bound over in the sum of four hundred pounds each and a figure of half that amount has been set on those in attendance – including Paul.'

'I'll get over there and bail my brother,' decided Peter. 'He'll have moaned about the handcuffs but this might be the best possible outcome. Intervention by the Runners has saved Mr Bowerman's life. In Paul's opinion, the poor fellow was about to commit suicide.'

'Then he's been very lucky,' said Ackford. 'He's been given the chance to repent of his folly in issuing such a bold challenge.'

'I just hope that he'll seize that chance, Gully, but I harbour grave doubts. Mr Bowerman is in the grip of an obsessive love that shields him from any acquaintance with reality. So deep is his

15

devotion to the person in question that he'll take on any rivals for her affections.'

'Only a remarkable creature could inspire such feelings.'

'Mr Bowerman described her as a jewel among women.'

'Is he an authority on the fairer sex?'

'Far from it,' said Peter. 'The only member of it he's really known is the wife to whom he was happily married. Her untimely death devastated him. He was still mourning her when Miss Laetitia Somerville came on the scene. Mr Bowerman told Paul that she'd resuscitated him.'

'Is the lady aware that he was about to fight a duel?'

'Oh, no – she'd have been horrified.'

'I don't blame her,' said Huckvale.

'What's the point of being given a new life if he's ready to throw it away so recklessly? Some women,' Peter went on, 'might be excited at the thought of two men fighting over them but, I suspect, Miss Somerville is not one of them. That is why Mr Bowerman and his adversary went to some lengths to conceal the truth from her.' He moved to the door. 'But I must be off. Paul will be chafing at the bit.'

After a flurry of farewells, Peter let himself out. Ackford turned to Huckvale.

'There's something you didn't tell us, Jem.'

'Is there?'

'The duel was a closely guarded secret. Only a handful of us knew of it.'

'That's true.'

'Then, how on earth did the Runners catch wind

of the event?'

Huckvale gulped. 'I forgot to ask that.'

It was a question that still vexed Paul Skillen and Mark Bowerman. Awaiting their release, they were alone in a private room at the Bow Street Magistrates' Court. The handcuffs had been removed and Paul was rubbing his sore wrists.

'This is Hamer's work,' said Bowerman, sourly.

'I think not.'

'Fearing that I'd kill or wound him, he made sure the duel was stopped.'

'Whatever else you can accuse him of,' argued Paul, 'it is not cowardice. When you issued your challenge, it was promptly accepted and Captain Hamer made no attempt to withdraw. He was incensed when the Runners appeared out of nowhere this morning.'

'So was I, Mr Skillen.'

'It was not in his interests to halt the duel.'

'Yes, it was. His nerve failed him at the last moment.'

'That was patently not the case. The Runners were in hiding before we even got there. They had advance notice of time and place. Hamer must be absolved of complicity. He was not responsible in any way.'

'Why are you taking *his* part?' protested Bowerman. 'You are *my* second.'

'I am, indeed, and my prime commitment is to you. That is why I view the interruption – annoying as it was in some respects – as an unexpected bonus.'

'Bonus!'

17

'You are still alive, sir. For that, I am eternally grateful.'

'I was prepared to surrender my life.'

'You've been spared that unwise gesture,' said Paul. 'The sensible thing is for you and Captain Hamer to settle your differences with a handshake, then each of you can go his separate way.'

'Am I hearing you aright?' asked Bowerman, spluttering. 'You're counselling me to forget that Stephen Hamer has designs on the woman I love? That's shameful advice, Mr Skillen, and I reject it forthwith. The issue is quite simple. One duel has been prevented. Another must be arranged.' His eyes blazed. 'You'll understand why I'll employ a different second next time.'

'That's your privilege, sir.'

'I need someone who knows what it is to risk *everything* for a woman.'

'Oh, I've been in that position, I do assure you, and I found true happiness as a result. But that's an irrelevance. Consider this, Mr Bowerman,' he added, solemnly. 'What will Miss Somerville think when she hears that you came perilously close to sacrificing yourself on her behalf?'

'I hope that she will think well of me.'

'The lady would prefer you to be alive. You're no use whatsoever to her when you're dead.'

Bowerman smiled fondly. 'That is where you are mistaken.'

'What do you mean?'

'It's none of your business, Mr Skillen.'

Before Paul could question him, there was a tap on the door and it opened to admit his brother. Bowerman had met Peter at the gallery but he

18

still marvelled at the uncanny likeness between the twins. He kept looking from one to the other.

'Good day to you, sir,' said Peter. 'I'm sorry to find you in such unhappy circumstances.'

'They are only temporary, Mr Skillen,' said Bowerman, airily. 'I will be out of here in no time at all.'

'My brother can leave immediately. I've arranged for his bail.'

'Thank you,' said Paul.

'This whole affair can now be forgotten, I hope.'

'Then you hope in vain, I fear.'

'You do, indeed,' said Bowerman, thrusting out a defiant chin. 'I will never let the matter rest until I have killed Stephen Hamer and rescued a dear lady from his unwanted attentions. Mark my words, gentlemen, I am resolved to see this dispute through to the bitter end. It can only be terminated by a death.'

After what they saw as a minor triumph, the Runners adjourned to the Peacock Inn, their unofficial headquarters. Micah Yeomans was soon quaffing a celebratory pint with Alfred Hale, his closest friend. After years of humiliation at the hands of the Skillen brothers, they were delighted to have got their revenge on one of them.

'He didn't like being handcuffed,' said Hale. 'Nobody else was.'

'I reserved that treat for Paul Skillen.'

'He was only the second.'

'I don't care if he was a casual bystander, Alfred. I wasn't going to miss the chance to make him suffer. He was at the site of an illegal duel.'

'I'd have been inclined to let it go ahead.'

'We have to enforce the law, Alfred.'

'We haven't always done so,' Hale reminded him, 'especially where we've been paid to look the other way. Everyone knows that duelling is a tradition among the nobs. It wasn't all that long ago that Viscount Castlereagh, our esteemed foreign secretary, fought a duel against Mr Canning, who is now in the same Cabinet. Would you have dared to interrupt that?'

'No,' admitted Yeomans, 'I'd have had more sense than to interfere. I fancy that Mr Canning still rues the day it happened. All that the foreign secretary lost was a button from his coat whereas Mr Canning was wounded in the thigh.'

'So why do we ignore *some* duels and prevent others from taking place?'

'The chief magistrate had a letter imploring him to take action. That's why we were dispatched to Putney Heath before dawn. And the effort was well worth it,' said Yeomans, chuckling. 'Paul Skillen fell into our hands.'

They clinked their tankards then drank deep.

A solid individual of medium height, Hale was dwarfed by his companion. Yeomans was not only a man of daunting bulk, he'd acquired strong muscles during his years as a blacksmith. The few criminals brave enough to tackle him were still licking their wounds. As the leading Bow Street Runners, they had built up a fearsome reputation in the capital. What irked them more than anything else was that it was overshadowed all too often by the achievements of Peter and Paul Skillen.

'It's a pity we didn't catch the *two* of them today,' said Yeomans, punching his chest with a fist before releasing a belch. 'I'd have found an excuse to keep them behind bars for a whole night. That would have brought them to heel.'

'It might have done the opposite,' said Hale.

'*We* are charged with policing London, not them. We have the legal right and the proper experience. The Skillen brothers have neither of those things.'

'Yet they do have an amazing record of success, Micah.'

'They've been lucky, that's all.'

'And clever, let's be honest.'

'Paul Skillen won't be feeling very clever after being arrested today. We taught him a lesson,' said Yeomans, complacently. 'As a result, he and that odious brother of his will steer well clear of us. From now on, we won't even get a glimpse of them.'

When the gardener arrived early that morning, he sensed that something was wrong. Though nothing was visible to the naked eye, his curiosity was aroused. He began a systematic search of the whole area, looking at flower beds, shrubs, bushes and trees, and even peering behind the statuary. His instinct was finally rewarded when he reached the arbour. Seated on the wooden bench was a stranger, a gentleman of middle years, apparently asleep. His hat lay on the ground as if tossed there uncaringly. The gardener cleared his throat noisily but it produced no reaction at all. Trying to wake him up, he shook the man vigorously but all that

21

he succeeded in doing was to make him roll off the bench completely. Only then did the dagger embedded in his back come into view. It was surrounded by a large bloodstain.

Mark Bowerman had warned that the dispute could only be resolved by a death. His words had been prophetic.

CHAPTER THREE

Eldon Kirkwood was a small man who wielded a large amount of power. As the chief magistrate at Bow Street, he was an expert on the nature and extent of crime in London. Those who cowered before him in court braced themselves for the tartness of his strictures and the severity of his punishments. He could be neither bribed nor deceived. Anyone who tried to intimidate him got especially short shrift; Kirkwood used the extremity of the law to pound them into submission. Yet it was not only the criminal fraternity, who feared him. The Runners were equally afraid of the peppery magistrate. When his summons reached Micah Yeomans, therefore, he responded at once and took Alfred Hale speedily along to Bow Street. Still panting from the race to get there, the two men stood before his desk to await orders.

'Foul murder has been committed,' he told them.

'That's nothing new,' muttered Hale.

'Be quiet!'

'Yes, sir.'

'Don't speak until you have something worth-while to say.'

'No, sir.'

'And the same goes for you,' said Kirkwood, flicking his gaze to Yeomans. 'I have important details to impart. Listen to them very carefully.'

'We will, sir,' said Yeomans.

The chief magistrate was crisp and concise. He explained that the murder victim had been found in the garden of someone else's house. A dagger had pierced his heart. The name of the dead man was Mark Bowerman.

'We arrested him only yesterday,' said Hale.

'You also arrested the person he was about to face in a duel, one Stephen Hamer. He must be your prime suspect. Unable to kill his enemy on Putney Heath, he obviously resorted to another method of attack. Captain Hamer needs to be arrested and interrogated.' He held out a sheet of paper. 'Thanks to the fact that he came before me yesterday, we have his address. Hunt him down.'

'We'll do so immediately,' said Yeomans, taking the paper from him.

'What if it's not him, sir?' asked Hale.

'Then it will be someone set on by him,' insisted Kirkwood, 'and that makes him culpable of homicide. It's as plain as the nose on your face, Hale. By some means or other, Hamer was determined to murder Bowerman. Instead of being shot in the chest, the victim was stabbed in the back.'

'I agree with your deductions, sir,' said Yeomans, obsequiously. 'It has to be Hamer. He was furious when we robbed him of the chance to shoot Mr Bowerman in that duel. It took two men to hold him.'

'I was one of them,' said Hale. 'He's a strong man.'

Yeomans straightened his back. 'I'm stronger.'

'There's no question about that, Micah.'

'Use that strength of yours to overpower the fellow and bring him to justice,' said Kirkwood. 'We must act swiftly before he has the chance to go to ground.'

'Leave it to us, sir,' said Yeomans, leading Hale out.

'I'm right behind you, Micah,' said the other, trotting after him.

As soon as they got outside, they paused to exchange a few unflattering remarks about Kirkwood. Much as they loathed him, they had to respect his authority. They were grateful to be given the opportunity to impress him for once. No difficulties could be foreseen by Yeomans. The main suspect in a murder case had just been served up to them on a plate.

'I wish that all crimes were so easily solved,' he said, airily. 'It would make our job a lot less problematical. The beauty of this one is that we won't have the Skillen brothers getting under our feet.'

'That's true.'

'They'll see what *real* policing can achieve.'

'Suppose they get to hear what's afoot?'

Yeomans was dismissive. 'There's no chance of that happening,' he said, curling a lip. 'We'll have Captain Hamer in custody before word even reaches them that Mr Bowerman is dead.'

It was a hollow boast. Peter and Paul Skillen had already been told of the murder and were hearing the salient details. Seated in the back room at the shooting gallery they listened intently to Silas Roe, the victim's butler. Deeply upset by the fate of his master, Roe was on the verge of tears throughout. He was a gaunt, grey-haired old man who'd been with Bowerman for many years and been fiercely loyal to him and to his late wife. Holding his hat in both hands, Roe bent his head and accepted what he saw as his share of the guilt.

'I should have insisted,' he said, apologetically. 'When the message came yesterday evening, Mr Bowerman was so pleased that he left the house at once. It wouldn't have taken long to send for a carriage but he was too eager to be off. He didn't tell me where he was going but I could guess who'd sent the letter.'

'Was it Miss Somerville, by any chance?' asked Paul.

'It was, sir. The paper had her fragrance. He was at her beck and call.'

'You sound as if you were very unhappy about that.'

'It's not my place to be happy or unhappy, sir. I was there to do anything I was asked and to ... keep a watchful eye on my master.'

'How did you first hear of the murder?' said Peter.

'The gardener who discovered the body came knocking on our door. He'd found Mr Bowerman's visiting card in his pocket so he ran straight to the house to break the terrible news. It hit me

25

like a thunderbolt, sirs, I don't mind admitting it.'

'What was your master doing in that garden in the first place?'

'That's the mystery, sir. To my knowledge, he'd never been anywhere near that house. As it happens, the property was empty, awaiting the arrival of new tenants. The gardener had been asked to carry out his duties as usual.'

'We'll need to speak to him,' decided Paul.

'I thought you might,' said Roe. 'I got his name and address for you.'

'Who reported the crime?'

'I did, sir. I went to Bow Street in person. That was after I'd been to the garden to verify what had happened, of course. I wouldn't believe that the master was dead until I'd seen proof with my own eyes.'

'Did you search him?' asked Peter.

Roe became defensive. 'I felt it was my duty.'

'That wasn't a criticism. I just wondered if you found the letter that had summoned him there in the first place.'

'It's exactly what I was looking for, sir, but it wasn't there. That was the strange thing. I knew he took it with him because I saw him put it in his pocket. The killer must have removed it.'

'Why would he do that?'

'I don't know.'

'Was anything else missing from Mr Bowerman's pockets?' said Paul.

'No, sir, there wasn't. Nothing else had been touched – including his purse.'

'Theft was not the motive, then.'

'Something else impelled the killer to strike,' said

Peter. 'He could have been exacting revenge, for instance, or settling an old score.' He turned to Roe. 'It was very sensible of you to come to us.'

'Mr Bowerman spoke so highly of you,' said the old man, addressing Paul, 'that I felt obliged to come here. He had great faith in you, sir.'

Paul shrugged. 'I'm sorry I wasn't there to protect him.'

'I feel the same. I'll never forgive myself.'

'The obvious suspect is his opponent in the duel,' suggested Peter.

'I agree, sir.'

'I fancy that you're both mistaken there,' said Paul.

'Are we?' said Peter.

'Stephen Hamer had his faults, I daresay, but he's no back-stabber. He was an army man. He'd want the satisfaction of looking Mr Bowerman in the eyes before shooting him.'

'You met the fellow, Paul. I didn't. I accept your judgement.'

'My master said he was a fiend in human form,' said Roe, bitterly.

'That would be going too far,' said Paul. 'What I saw during my brief acquaintance with him was an arrogant dandy who'd brush people brutally aside if they stood between him and his ambitions. Hamer would have welcomed a second duel and ensured that it was decisive.'

'Did you ever meet the man, Mr Roe?' asked Peter.

'No, sir, and I had no wish to do so. What he did to my master was nothing short of torture. It was painful to watch.'

Peter had heard most of the details from his brother. In the wake of his wife's death, Mark Bowerman had largely withdrawn from society. The couple had been childless so he had no other family members living in the house. Fearing that he might turn into a hermit, a friend had invited him to a dinner at which he'd first met a young woman named Laetitia Somerville. In spite of the age gap, there'd been an instant attraction between them. It was not long before Bowerman formed a real attachment to her. He'd confided to Paul that he intended to propose marriage and that she'd already given him indications that she'd willingly accept the offer. Before the relationship could develop to that point, however, another admirer suddenly appeared and – with no encouragement at all from Miss Somerville – began to make overtures towards her. It was too much for Bowerman to bear. Haunted by the prospect that his happiness would be snatched away from him, he'd challenged the interloper to a duel. It was a matter of honour.

Silas Roe added some information that was new to the brothers.

'There were things I kept from Mr Bowerman,' he confided. 'He had enough preying on his mind as it was. So I dealt with the other matters and told the rest of the staff to say nothing to the master.'

'What sort of things are you talking about?' asked Paul.

'It started with trespass. I heard someone walking in the garden at night. I frightened him away but he was back after a few days. This time he pushed a bench into the pond. I kept vigil after that and there was no trouble for a week. Then a trellis was pushed over and flower beds were trampled. I must have dozed off,' said Roe, 'because I didn't hear a sound.'

'They sound like acts of provocation,' said Peter.

'Yes, sir, they were, and Captain Hamer was behind them.'

'Do you have any proof of that?'

'No,' admitted the other, 'but I'll wager anything that it was his doing.'

'It was kind of you to protect your master like that.'

'As it was,' said Paul, 'he didn't need any more provocation. Hamer's arrival was sufficiently aggravating in itself. When he saw how distressed Miss Somerville was by the man's pursuit of her, Mr Bowerman confronted him.'

The brothers were grateful that Roe had come to the gallery. Sad to hear of his master's death, they were at the same time intrigued by the mystery surrounding it. Having been so closely involved with the man, Paul felt that he had a responsibility to look more closely into the circumstances of his murder. He thanked the old man for coming and assured him that he'd take on the investigation. Relieved to hear it, Roe gave him the name of the gardener who had found Bowerman's corpse and the address of the house where he stumbled upon it. The butler then took his leave.

Something puzzled Peter. He scratched his head.

'You never actually met Miss Somerville, did you?'

'No,' replied Paul, 'but I saw her clearly through

29

Mr Bowerman's eyes.'

'They were somewhat blinkered by desire, I suspect.'

'She is, reportedly, a very beautiful woman.'

'That's what interests me,' said Peter, thoughtfully. 'On one side, we have a jaded widower of middle years with – according to you – little physical appeal; on the other, there is a handsome former soldier who could cut a dash in any hostess's ballroom. In every way, the two men are unequal. Why did this fabled beauty favour Mr Bowerman when a much younger suitor was at hand?'

Bond Street was a fashionable promenade for the beau monde, a long strip of exclusive shops known for the quality of their stock and the steepness of their prices. The Runners had no time to stare in the windows or to mingle with the throng. Their destination was a neat double-fronted house in a side street off the main thoroughfare. Stephen Hamer's house suggested money and good taste. Having come with the prospect of arresting a murderer, Yeomans and Hale were dismayed to discover that Hamer was not only absent but that, according to the servant who answered the door, he had spent the night in St Albans. Since he was due back later that morning, the Runners decided to wait. They were conducted into the butler's pantry and asked to make themselves comfortable.

Hale was worried. 'If he's been away from London all night,' he said, 'he couldn't possibly have carried out the murder.'

'Yes, he could,' said Yeomans. 'To begin with, we only have the word of his servant that he went to St Albans. That could well be an alibi devised by Hamer to throw us off the scent. And even if he *did* go there last night, he could have stabbed Mr Bowerman before he left. I think we're sitting in the home of a killer, Alfred.'

'That's only supposition.'

'It's common sense. He wanted the man dead.'

'Then why bother to go to all the trouble of a duel?'

'It was a more formal way of committing murder.'

'I'm not convinced, Micah.'

'Well, I am and – more to the point – so is the chief magistrate.'

'It won't be the first time we've arrested the wrong man.'

'Rely on my instinct. Has it ever let us down before?'

The truthful answer was that it had but Hale lacked the courage to say so. Yeomans had a scorching temper when roused. It was safer to pretend to agree with him. The other Runner therefore kept his doubts to himself.

'What about the lady in the case?' he asked.

'What about her?'

'She may well be unaware of the murder of Mr Bowerman. I think that she has a right to be told at the earliest opportunity.'

'We'll call on her when we have Captain Hamer in custody.'

'Suppose that he resists arrest?'

Yeomans smirked. 'One punch will take all the

31

fight out of him.'

The wait gave them time to slip out of the pantry and take a peep at the drawing room. It was high-ceilinged, well proportioned and filled with exquisite furniture. What commanded their attention was the portrait of Hamer above the fireplace. Dressed in the uniform of the Royal Horse Guards, he looked proud, haughty and resolute. When they eventually heard the clatter of hooves outside the window, they went quickly back to the pantry. It was not long before Hamer was admitted to the house by his servant. Dressed in his riding attire, he sailed into the room, whip in hand. It was clear that he'd ridden some distance. There was thick dust on his boots and coat, and perspiration on his face. He looked from one to the other with contempt.

'There's no duel to prevent this time,' he said, pointedly.

'We're here on a related matter,' explained Yeomans. 'Sometime yesterday evening, Mr Bowerman was murdered. We have reason to believe that you were responsible for his death.'

'That's a monstrous allegation!'

'We must ask you to accompany us, sir.'

'The pair of you can go to the Devil!'

'Now, now,' cautioned Hale, 'respect our position. As Runners, we have a legal right to make an arrest.'

'On what possible evidence are you making it?'

'You had good reason to kill Mr Bowerman,' said Yeomans.

'I had an excellent reason but I would only have considered taking his life in the course of a duel.

I'd never shoot him otherwise.'

'He was stabbed to death, sir.'

'There you are, then. Isn't that irrefutable proof that I'm innocent of the charge? I didn't even know *how* he died. Can you really imagine someone like me resorting to a dagger? It's unthinkable. When he challenged me to a duel,' said Hamer, 'I gave him the choice of weapons – pistols or swords. Those are the weapons of a gentleman. Since neither of you will ever aspire to that status in society, you won't understand the rules by which we operate.'

'*Our* rules are much simpler,' said Yeomans, stung by the insult. 'When a crime is committed, we arrest the culprit.'

'Then go off and find him, you oaf.'

'We already *have*, Captain Hamer.'

The Runner glared meaningfully at him. His companion, however, was already wavering. Hamer's indignant denial had the ring of truth. Having arrested many villains in the course of his work, Alfred Hale had seen how they usually reacted. Most of them protested their innocence but few had ever done so with such blazing sincerity. He remembered the portrait above the fireplace. Could such a heroic individual stoop to a callous act of murder? It seemed impossible.

After a long, bruised silence, Hamer mounted his defence. He spoke slowly, as if talking to people of limited intelligence.

'When I left Bow Street yesterday morning,' he explained, 'I came straight back here and made arrangements for my trip to St Albans. I set off just after noon. The person whom I visited will tell you the time of my arrival and the length of my stay with him. I'll happily furnish you with his name and address. Since his family was there at the time, you'll have five other witnesses who will swear that I've been telling you the truth. At what time was Bowerman killed?'

'It was ... sometime in the evening,' said Yeomans, uncomfortably.

'I have a very long reach,' said Hamer, 'but even my arm is not able to touch London from St Albans. Where did the murder take place?'

'It was in the garden of a house near Cavendish Square.'

'I have neither friends nor acquaintances in that part of the city and, hence, no reason whatsoever to visit it. How am I supposed to have gained access to the place?'

'A resourceful man like you would have found a way in.'

'We are now in the realms of complete fantasy,' said Hamer with a sneer. 'Do what you foolishly assume to be your duty, if you must, but remember this: there is such a thing as wrongful arrest. Consequences will follow.'

Yeomans hesitated. Increasingly edgy, Hale turned to his friend.

'What are we going to do now, Micah?' he whispered.

CHAPTER FOUR

As he set off to find the lady in question, Paul Skillen had no clear idea of what to expect. Laetitia Somerville was patently a striking young woman. If she could arouse the affections of men as diverse as Mark Bowerman and Stephen Hamer, he reasoned, she had to be a person of rare qualities. During their time together at the shooting gallery, Bowerman had rhapsodised about her and, crucially, provided Paul with her address in case he was shot to death in the duel against his rival. Judged by its nondescript exterior, the house in Green Street was unremarkable. When he was invited in by a servant, however, he found himself in a dwelling of overwhelming charm and with a pervading air of prosperity. The place was so bright, well appointed and filled with delicate colours that Paul felt embarrassed at being the bearer of bad news. He would be besmirching a miniature paradise.

Shown into the library, he was struck by its faint whiff of perfume and by the number of poetry books on the shelves. He was not alone for long. Laetitia appeared magically in the doorway. Paul was momentarily dumbfounded. Since he lived with Hannah Granville, the most talented actress in London, he was accustomed to being alone with a gorgeous woman, but Laetitia's beauty was of a totally different order than that of his beloved.

While Hannah's arresting good looks could enchant a whole audience for hours on end, Paul was now within feet of an altogether more subdued, almost shy, private beauty. Laetitia was small, slim and graceful with a face of elfin loveliness framed by fair hair that hung in ringlets. She had a demure quality entirely lacking in the actress. She was followed into the room by a maidservant acting as a chaperone.

After an exchange of greetings, she waved him to a chair and perched on one directly opposite. Her sweet smile was evidence to Paul of her complete ignorance of the duel and the fate of one of those involved. He chose his words with care.

'I come as a friend of Mr Bowerman,' he began. 'He held you in the highest regard, Miss Somerville.'

'His devotion to me is very flattering.'

'He was distressed to learn that he had a rival suitor.'

'If you are referring to Captain Hamer,' she said, softly, 'then you should know that I would never accept him as a suitor. We were friends in the past but those days are ... long gone.'

'Yet he boasted to Mr Bowerman that the two of you were intimates.'

Her eyes flashed. 'That was unworthy of him and wholly untrue.'

'It caused great upset.'

'I shall apologise to Mr Bowerman on the captain's behalf.'

'That ... won't be possible, I fear,' said Paul.

'Why not?' There was a long pause. Her voice now had a tremor. 'I repeat my question, Mr

Skillen,' she went on, '*why* will it not be possible?'

'It's ... difficult to explain.'

'Answer my question, please.'

'Miss Somerville –'

'Come, sir. Say what you have to say and don't prevaricate.'

Paul took a deep breath before speaking. 'It's my painful duty to pass on sad tidings,' he said. 'They concern Mr Bowerman.'

She was on her feet at once. 'Has something happened to him?'

'I'm afraid that it has.'

'Then please let me hear what it is. Don't keep me in suspense.'

Paul got up slowly from the chair. 'Yesterday morning,' he said, gently, 'Mr Bowerman took part in a duel with his rival.'

'Heavens!' she exclaimed. 'What madness has seized him? He'd be no match for Captain Hamer.'

'Fortunately, the duel was interrupted by Bow Street Runners.'

'Thank goodness for that! He was rescued from certain death.'

'He met it elsewhere,' said Paul, moving closer to her. 'Sometime during yesterday evening, Mr Bowerman was, it appears, in receipt of a letter ostensibly sent from you.'

'But I never wrote any letter to him. I swear it.'

'Someone did, Miss Somerville, and its contents were such that he left the house at once in his haste to reach you. His body was found early this morning in the garden of a house near Cavendish Square. Mr Bowerman, I regret to tell you, had been stabbed to death.'

'No, no,' she cried, grabbing him by the coat. 'Tell me it's not true.'

'I wish that I could.'

'Mr Bowerman and I were about to be...' She shook her head in disbelief. 'He was *murdered?* That dear, kind, considerate man was killed?' Paul nodded. 'Who could *do* such a dreadful thing? The very thought is unbearable.'

Her face had crumpled and her whole body was trembling. After putting a hand to her throat, she swooned. The maidservant cried out in alarm. Paul was quick enough to catch Laetitia before she hit the floor.

Jack Linnane, the gardener, was a short, stout, round-shouldered man in his fifties with a ragged beard and eyes that were half obscured by bushy eyebrows. He was pulling out weeds when Peter Skillen arrived at the house and let himself in through the unlocked garden gate. Linnane straightened.

'This is private property, sir,' he warned.

'I've not come to trespass. I simply want information.'

Peter introduced himself and explained that he'd been given details of what had happened by Silas Roe, servant to the murder victim. Linnane brightened at once. He was ready to talk to anyone who was determined to solve the crime. The story he told was virtually the same as the one passed on by Roe but there were some new details as well. He'd been gardener there for years. Most of the houses nearby were owned by families who lived there on a permanent basis. This one, Linnane told him, had been occupied by a series of short-term tenants. Whether or not anyone was in residence, he was paid to keep the garden in good condition. After looking around, Peter praised him for his thoroughness.

'Show me where you found the body,' he asked.

'I told you, sir,' said Linnane, pointing a finger, 'it was over there.'

'Show me *exactly* where it was.'

'Why?'

'It may be of help to me.'

Linnane did as he was told, even sitting down on the spot on the bench where he'd found Bowerman. Shielded from the rest of the garden by trellises covered with trailing plants, the arbour was a natural suntrap. Immediately behind the bench was a low privet hedge. When Peter stood behind the seated gardener, he realised how easy it would have been for the killer to put an arm around the victim's neck before thrusting a dagger between the wooden uprights. In the struggle, Bowerman's hat would have been knocked off and landed on the ground where the gardener found it.

'This is a nice spot,' observed Peter.

'Best part of the garden, sir,' said Linnane. 'When I've finished my work for the day, I always sit here and smoke a pipe.' He chuckled. 'It does no harm if I have ten minutes thinking I own the house.'

'Who *does* own it?'

'I don't know, sir. I just do what the agent tells me.'

'You have a key to the garden, obviously.'

'It's all I have. I've never been in the house itself. Everything I need is out here. I can draw water from the well. I keep my tools locked in the outhouse.'

'It's a stout door in a high wall,' said Peter, looking at the gate. 'It would be difficult to get in here without a key. I'll need to speak to the agent to find out how many keyholders there are.'

'Nobody ever touches *my* key,' affirmed Linnane. 'I look after it carefully.'

'And so you should.' Peter glanced up at the house. 'Before I let myself into the garden, I went to the front door. It was securely locked and there was no sign of a broken window. Nobody forced their way into the property.' He turned to the gardener. 'Has anyone else been here to question you?'

'No, sir, they haven't.'

'They will. The Runners will certainly call at some point. When they do, will you pass on a message to them, please?'

'Yes, sir, I'll do so gladly.'

'Tell them that my brother and I are delighted to be working with them again.'

'Is that all, sir?'

'Oh,' said Peter, smiling, 'that will be more than enough.'

After weighing up the possibilities, Yeomans decided that he'd rather face the wrath of the chief magistrate than worry about the threat made by Stephen Hamer. Since he was at least flirting with the possibility that the man might not, after all, be guilty of the murder, he refrained from actually handcuffing him. He simply arrested Hamer and, after delivering a lacerating tirade, the latter agreed to go with them. They rode to Bow Street in the same jolting carriage. Not a word was spoken during the journey. The atmosphere was tense and Hale writhed in discomfort. Accustomed to manhandling dangerous villains, he was virtually paralysed while seated opposite the fuming Stephen Hamer. All three of them went into the chief magistrate's office. In less than ten minutes, one of them came out alone. Those who remained were given a verbal whipping.

'The pair of you are complete idiots!' snarled Kirkwood. 'What on earth possessed you to arrest Captain Hamer?'

'We were only obeying your orders, sir,' said Yeomans.

'The fellow was obviously innocent of the charge.'

'*You* were the one who said that he was guilty, sir,' recalled Hale. 'You told us it was as plain as the nose on my face.'

'I merely said that there was a faint likelihood that he *might* be involved. I was assuming – foolishly, as it transpired – that you and Yeomans would exercise discretion. Clearly, that was beyond your meagre capacities.'

'We're sorry, sir.'

'Didn't you *listen?* Didn't you hear what Hamer said? He has reliable witnesses who place him in St Albans at the time when the victim was murdered.'

'He could still have instigated the crime, sir,' said Yeomans. 'It was a point that *you* made when you sent us off to apprehend him.'

'I was mistaken,' said Kirkwood, 'and I knew it the moment he stepped into this office. He was enraged and rightly so. Didn't you stop to wonder why?'

'Nobody likes to be arrested, sir.'

'We didn't make a forcible arrest, Micah,' Hale reminded him.

'He behaved as if we had.'

'That was not the reason for his fury,' said Kirkwood. 'What upset him was not so much the fact that he was under suspicion. It was because he'd been robbed of the opportunity to kill Bowerman in a second duel. The real target of his ire was the man who wielded that dagger. Captain Hamer's rival may have been removed but *he* was not responsible for his death. That rankles with him.'

'Why didn't he tell us that?' asked Hale.

'You shouldn't have *needed* telling. It was writ large all over him.'

'All *I* saw was a very angry man.'

'Now you mention it, sir,' said Yeomans, hoping to curry favour, 'there was a strange tone to his protests. He behaved as if something very precious had been stolen from him. It was clever of you to identify it.'

'I prefer action to congratulation,' said Kirkwood with vehemence. 'I want proof that you have one functioning brain between the two of you. Hamer can be eliminated from the investigation. Find the *real* killer.'

'Yes, sir.'

'Have you visited the scene of the crime?'

'No, sir.'

'Do so immediately.'

'Yes, sir.'

'Question the gardener who found the body.'

'We will, sir.'

'Have you been to Mr Bowerman's house?'

'Not yet, sir.'

'Seek out Roe, the butler. When he reported the crime, he left only the bare details. Ask if his master had any enemies.'

'Yes, sir.'

'What of the lady at the eye of this little hurricane?'

'Are you referring to Miss Somerville, sir?'

'Who else, man? It was she who unwittingly caused the duel to take place.'

'We ought to speak to her, Micah,' said Hale. 'She might not even know that one of her suitors has met a gruesome end.'

'There's one more thing,' Kirkwood told them.

'Yes, sir. We need to have handbills printed.'

'I will take on that task, if only to ensure that it's done properly. You must do something that should already have been done and that's to examine the corpse. Search for clues. That dagger is one of them. It may be distinctive enough to be recognised. If so, a description of the murder weapon could be included in the handbill. Above all else,' said the chief magistrate, raising his voice, 'act with more celerity.'

'We already did that, sir,' confessed Yeomans, 'and we are rightly chastised for doing so. We apprehended Captain Hamer too hastily.'

'That's not why I'm advocating urgency.'

'Isn't it?'

'Mr Bowerman was a wealthy man. There'll be a large reward offered for information leading to the arrest and conviction of his assassin. You both know what happens when money is at stake.'

'Peter and Paul Skillen will come sniffing, sir,' said Hale.

'We'll not be deprived of our lawful prize this time,' vowed Yeomans.

'Then get out there and vindicate your reputations,' said Kirkwood, opening the door wide. 'Don't come back until you have redeemed yourselves by solving this crime promptly and leaving the Skillen brothers trailing impotently in your wake.'

'Yes, sir,' they said in unison before scuttling through the open door.

Paul Skillen was caught in an awkward situation. As he was lowering Laetitia Somerville gently to the floor, a manservant, alerted by the chaperone's cry of alarm, burst into the room. What he saw was a stranger bending over his employer as if about to molest her. In his eyes, it was a picture that told its story all too clearly. Without hesitation, the servant grabbed Paul and tried to drag him away. Since he was a strong young man, there was a fierce struggle. Paul's explanation of what had happened went unheard. All that the servant wanted to do was to defend Laetitia and overpower a man he thought was her assailant. It took Paul a couple of minutes to shake him off then stun him with a blow to the jaw. By that time, Laetitia's eyelids were starting to flutter.

'What happened?' she murmured.

44

'I brought some dire news, I fear,' said Paul.

She saw the manservant. 'What are *you* doing here, Robin?'

'Misconstruing what occurred, he bravely came to your assistance. I'd be grateful if you'd tell him I did not assault you in any way.'

'No, no, of course you didn't. Stand off,' she told the man as he moved forward to grapple with Paul once more. 'Mr Skillen was no threat to me. He kindly brought me tidings he felt I had a right to know. That was why I collapsed. The shock was too much for me.' She tried to move. 'Could you help me up, please?'

Paul and the manservant lifted her carefully to her feet. Robin was anxious.

'Would you like me to call a doctor?' he asked.

'No, no, there's no need for that. Thank you, Robin,' she said, dismissively. 'You may go now. It's quite safe to leave me.'

'Call me, if you need me.'

Staring resentfully at Paul, he rubbed his chin as he backed out of the room.

'I remember it all now,' said Laetitia, sitting down. 'You told me that Mr Bowerman had been ready to fight a duel with Captain Hamer but that it was interrupted. Later that evening...'

Her eyes moistened and she bit her lip. When Paul tried to put a consoling arm around her, she raised her palms and he backed away. He could see the anguish distorting her features. Eventually, she regained her composure.

'What must you think of us?' she said, apologetically. 'You come here out of the goodness of your heart and what happens? I collapse at your

45

feet and my servant starts beating you. By any standards, that's poor hospitality.'

'What happened is understandable, Miss Somerville.'

'I think you deserve an explanation.'

'Are you sure that I'm not intruding?'

'No, no, not at all – do sit down again, please.'

'Thank you,' he said, lowering himself onto a chair beside her.

Laetitia needed a few moments to gather her thoughts. Paul waited patiently until she was ready. Her voice was heavy with grief.

'Mr Bowerman and I had become close friends,' she said, measuring her words. 'I'm sure that he has told you what aroused his interest in me. It's only fair that you should look at the attachment from my side as well. Beauty is both a blessing and a curse, Mr Skillen. It is pleasing to look at in a mirror but it can excite the wrong feelings altogether in others. Suffice it to say that I have had far too many self-proclaimed admirers nursing improper thoughts about me. Such treatment makes one wary and not a little cynical.'

'I know someone in the identical predicament,' said Paul, thinking of Hannah. 'Being pursued by over-amorous gentlemen is a constant problem.'

'That is what set Mark ... Mr Bowerman, that is, apart from the pack. He didn't try to harass, trick or entrap me. He offered me true love and devotion. It was wonderfully refreshing. I'd never met anyone so considerate and undemanding.'

'I formed the same view of Mr Bowerman.'

'The more I got to know him, the closer I was drawn to him. Yes, he was somewhat older than

46

me but that meant he had wisdom and maturity. They are qualities I greatly appreciate. When he touched very lightly on the possibility of a betrothal, I was thrilled by the notion. It was only a matter of time before he'd have found the words and the courage to seek my hand.' Her body sagged. 'It will never happen now.'

'You meant everything to him, Miss Somerville.'

'I like to think so.'

'I am quoting his exact words.'

After nodding her thanks, she took out a handkerchief and dabbed at her eyes. Since she seemed to have got over the immediate shock of Bowerman's murder, Paul probed for information about his rival.

'You said earlier that Captain Hamer had been a friend in the past.'

'He was more of an acquaintance, really,' she said, evasively, 'but he did engage my interest at first, I must admit. He was handsome and daring and had fought in the Peninsular War. Any woman would be impressed by that.'

'You've no need to justify it.'

'He pursued me for some time, then he ... disappeared. Soon after that, I was introduced to Mr Bowerman and the captain faded in my memory. Then, out of the blue, he appeared on my doorstep and declared his love. I did my best to send him on his way but he was very persistent.'

'That's why Mr Bowerman challenged him to a duel.'

'It's the *last* thing he should have done,' she wailed.

'What will happen if Captain Hamer comes

47

calling again?'

She was decisive. 'He'll find my door slammed shut in his face.'

After plying her with more questions, Paul rose to leave.

'One last thing,' he said, casually. 'You mentioned that he fought in the Peninsular War.'

'That's right. Captain Hamer was in the Royal Horse Guards. He was immensely proud of the fact that he saw action at the battle of Fuentes de Oñoro. He boasted about it every time he gave me one of the souvenirs he'd brought back from the war.'

CHAPTER FIVE

The friendship between Charlotte Skillen and Hannah Granville was an example of the attraction of opposites. When she first saw the actress onstage, Charlotte had been dazzled by her histrionic skills. A career in the theatre was something she could never have aspired to herself because she had neither the talent nor the temperament. Nor could she ever have entered into the liaison outside marriage that Hannah enjoyed with Paul. Though she'd worried about it at first, Charlotte had come to accept that her brother-in-law had the right to live the kind of life he chose and, if it involved cohabitation with a famous actress, then he should be supported rather than condemned. Her husband, Peter, took the same view.

Though they had little in common, the two women got on extremely well together. Both were attractive, intelligent and in their late twenties but there the similarity ended. While Charlotte was reserved and thoroughly respectable, Hannah had the surface hardness necessary in such a competitive profession. She was loud, exhibitionist and volatile, having none of her friend's equanimity. Whenever she visited the house, she was struck by its atmosphere of calm.

'I love coming here, Charlotte,' she said with an extravagant gesture. 'It's a haven of peace in a war-torn world.'

'Thankfully, hostilities against the French have ceased.'

'I was speaking of the daily battles I have to fight to get my way.'

'Is the theatre quite such a contest of strength?'

'It is when rehearsals are going badly,' replied Hannah, 'and they reached their nadir today. That is why I flounced out and sought your company. You are so consoling, Charlotte. I love Paul to distraction but, when I most need his support, he becomes argumentative. Peter is an altogether more placid individual. Be grateful that you are not married to his brother.'

Charlotte suppressed a smile. There had, in fact, been a time when Peter and Paul had both sought her hand in marriage and she had been forced to choose between them. She had never for a moment regretted her decision. Even though he could never bring the same wild excitement as his brother, Peter offered a stability that was more suited to Charlotte's needs and

49

personality. She was relieved that Paul had never told Hannah about his earlier pursuit of her. It might well have compromised the warm relationship she now shared with the actress.

'What is the problem with the play?' she asked.

Hannah groaned. 'If I gave you chapter and verse,' she said, 'we'd be here until Doomsday. It's all so lowering.'

'Are you rehearsing a tragedy or a comedy?'

'You may well ask, Charlotte.'

'What is its title?'

'The Piccadilly Opera.'

'There will be music and singing, then.'

'Very little of either,' said Hannah with disgust. 'It's an opera with no arias, a tragedy with no suffering and a comedy without the slightest hint of true wit.'

'Heavens!'

'It's exasperating.'

'Who wrote this perverse play?'

'Ah!' cried Hannah with a harsh laugh. 'There you have it. His accursed name is Abel Mundy and he shouldn't be allowed within a hundred miles of a public stage. The man is an abomination. He is the kind of playwright I detest most.'

'And what kind is that?'

'A *live* one.'

They were seated in the drawing room. While Charlotte remained in her chair, however, Hannah felt the need to rise to her feet from time to time in order to express herself with more force. Charlotte was happy for her to do so. She was relishing a performance for which most people would have to pay.

'Give me a dead author before all else,' said Hannah, warming to her theme. 'His plays will have survived the test of time and have proven merit. Shakespeare is a case in point. An actor himself, he knew what actors needed. He gave them roles that stretched them to the limit of their art. And there are many others whose contribution to the annals of drama I value greatly. Their chief appeal, however, is that they are no longer alive to *interfere*. Abel Mundy, alas, does nothing else.'

'Why, then, did you agree to take part in *The Piccadilly Opera?*'

'It was the biggest mistake of my career.'

'Did you not see the play in advance?'

'I was merely given a description of it by the playwright and – since he was so pleasant and plausible at our first meeting – I placed my trust in him. There were, of course, temptations offered by the manager. One was financial but that was the least of my considerations. What persuaded me to accept the role was the promise that I could choose the next three plays in which I was to appear. Needless to say,' she went on, 'the first was *Macbeth.*'

'Your performance of Lady Macbeth was well received in Paris. What other English actress could play the part in French, as you did?'

'It's impossible to name one, Charlotte. But you see my dilemma. I go from the heights of *Macbeth* to the depths of *The Piccadilly Opera.*'

'Is there no way to withdraw from the play?'

'Not without a financial penalty and severe damage to my reputation. The truth of the matter is that I bought a pig in a poke.'

'What, then, is the solution?'

'I came here in the hope that *you* could tell me that. Your advice is always so sensible. I've come to a dangerous point in my career, Charlotte,' said Hannah, one hand on her heart. 'Do I revoke my contract altogether or do I grit my teeth and risk derision in this theatrical catastrophe?'

Peter Skillen moved to the window so that he could examine the dagger in the best light. It was a long, narrow-bladed weapon and, now that the blood had been wiped from it, it was glinting.

'It was made in Toledo,' he said.

'How do you know?' asked his companion.

'Toledo steel is the finest in the world. That was known as long ago as Roman times. Their armies chose Toledo blades above any other. As it happens,' Peter went on, 'I once had a rather memorable encounter with a dagger just like this.'

'Really?'

They were in the room in the morgue where the body of Mark Bowerman lay on a slab. Peter had only glanced at the corpse when the shroud was pulled back. He was less interested in the victim's wound than in the weapon used to kill him. He could feel its perfect balance. The stringy old man beside him was one of the coroner's assistants, charged with cleaning and preparing the cadavers for burial. Sensing a story, he pressed for details.

'Are you telling me that someone tried to kill you with a Toledo dagger?'

'He tried and he almost succeeded, my friend.'

'When was this?'

'It was during the war with France,' explained

Peter. 'My work often took me to Paris and, on one occasion, someone decided to make it my last possible visit there. Fortunately, I'd been warned of his intentions. When he tried to strike, I was ready for him.'

'A weapon like that could cut you to shreds.'

'It most certainly could.'

'How did you escape, Mr Skillen?'

'I didn't elude the dagger completely,' admitted Peter, indicating his shoulder. 'I still carry a vivid memento of it. As to the circumstances, I'm not able to recount them. I'm just grateful to be alive.'

It had not been Peter's only brush with death. Because he spoke French fluently, he'd been employed as a spy during the war and made frequent trips to the French capital. It was a hazardous period of his life and, though it had been quite exhilarating, he was relieved when it was all over. At the same time, he liked to think that he'd made a small but useful contribution to the war effort. The scar on his shoulder was a stark reminder of the days when he'd been in almost continuous jeopardy. Conscious of the agonies Charlotte had endured while he was away, he had been even more attentive to her since his return.

After turning the dagger over in his hand, he handed it back to the assistant.

'The one consolation, I suppose, is that death would have been almost instantaneous,' he said. 'Mr Bowerman would not have suffered.'

'It's his wife and family who'll do the suffering, sir.'

'Mrs Bowerman died some years ago. They had no children.'

'There'll still be relatives to mourn him.'

'I'm sure there will be.' Peter looked at the dagger once more. 'It's curious, isn't it?'

'I've never seen a weapon quite like it, sir.'

'That's what puzzles me. It's so individual. You'd have thought the owner would prize it. Instead of that, he left it buried in someone's back. Most killers would have taken it away so that it could be used again,' said Peter. 'In this case, however, it was deliberately left behind. I'm intrigued to find out why.'

When she left the house in a hackney carriage, Hannah was grateful that she'd sought advice about the quandary in which she found herself. While she had not been able to solve the actress's problem, Charlotte had managed to soothe her and offer much-needed sympathy. Having arrived there in a state of outrage, Hannah departed in a far more tranquil frame of mind. Paul Skillen had brought many wonderful things into her life and his sister-in-law was amongst the best of them. Charlotte could do what Paul himself could not and that was to view a situation coolly and dispassionately. Unlike Hannah, she would never act on impulse. The actress was unable to emulate her because she was the slave of an ungovernable spontaneity. It was one of the qualities that had first attracted Paul to her.

Should she honour her contract or refuse to perform in a play she felt so unworthy of her? There was no simple answer. Taking part in *The Piccadilly Opera* might well be injurious to the reputation she'd so assiduously built up, yet turning her back on a commitment she'd undertaken would not endear her to any theatre manager. They'd hesitate to employ an actress who'd behaved in such a cavalier fashion. Since she'd signed a contract, there'd also be legal repercussions, not to mention the substantial loss of money that was involved. Either course of action was perilous. Hannah felt trapped.

She was still deep in thought when she reached the home she shared with Paul. As she stood on the doorstep, waiting for a servant to admit her, she was wholly unaware of the angry pair of eyes trained on her from the other side of the street. The door was opened and Hannah disappeared. Only then did someone emerge from their hiding place and glare at the house with undisguised hatred.

Jack Linnane was wheeling a barrow when the Runners came in through the garden gate. Because they strutted towards him with an air of importance, he took against them at once. Peter Skillen had been polite and friendly towards the gardener. The Runners, by contrast, were brusque and demanding. It was almost as if he was being treated as a suspect himself. After brief introductions, Yeomans told him that he wanted truthful answers and complete cooperation. Linnane provided both under duress. He showed them where the murder had taken place and responded, albeit reluctantly, to the questions fired at him in quick succession by both men. Yeomans was not satisfied. Because the gardener was slow of speech, he felt the man was misleading them. He grabbed

Linnane by the scruff of his neck and shook him.

'Did you really *find* the dagger in the victim's back?' he yelled. 'Or did you put it there yourself?'

'No, no, sir,' protested the other. 'I'd never seen the man before.'

'I think you're lying.'

'It's not him, Micah,' said Hale.

'He's got such a villainous look about him.'

'That doesn't make him the killer. If he wanted to stab someone to death, he'd do it in a dark alley and relieve him of his purse. When the crime was reported to Bow Street, it was made clear that Mr Bowerman's purse and watch were still on the body. What could this man hope to *gain* from the murder?' He waved a hand. 'Let him go, Micah. He's innocent.'

'I still have doubts, Alfred.'

Nevertheless, he released the gardener who retreated a few steps. Hale contended that only a fool would invite Runners to investigate a crime that he'd just committed and the gardener was not that stupid. After a short argument, Yeomans finally accepted that Linnane had not been involved in any way. They gave him no apology for treating him so roughly. As he and Hale headed for the gate, the gardener called out to them.

'One moment...'

Yeomans turned. 'Yes?'

'I'm to give you a message,' he said.

'Who asked you to do that?'

'It was a gentleman, sir.'

'What was his name?'

'Mr Peter Skillen.'

Hale groaned. 'Has *he* been here?

'Yes, sir.'

'What was the message?'

'I was to say how much he was looking forward to working with you again.'

The Runners froze, exchanged a look of horror then stalked out.

Linnane felt so pleased to have thoroughly upset them that he sat in the arbour and rewarded himself with a pipe of tobacco.

Back at the shooting gallery, the brothers met up to exchange information. Gully Ackford was fascinated by what they'd so far unearthed. He showed particular interest in the murder weapon.

'It has to be one of Hamer's souvenirs from the Peninsular War,' he said.

'Not necessarily,' warned Peter.

'You heard what Paul discovered. Hamer was in the habit of giving Miss Somerville gifts he'd brought back from Spain and Portugal. And what is a soldier most likely to bring back? I can tell you that from my own experience. I brought back things I picked up on the battlefield.'

'Captain Hamer is hardly likely to have given Miss Somerville a dagger.'

'I'm not suggesting that he did. He kept it and used it to kill Mr Bowerman.'

'I disagree,' said Paul.

'It's too big a coincidence.'

'Hundreds of soldiers must have brought back a dagger like that one. It's not unique, by any means. And I refuse to believe that Hamer would stab a man he could easily kill in a second duel.'

'One of us must go and see him,' said Peter.

'I'll take on that office. Miss Somerville furnished me with his address.'

'You told us that she never wanted to see him again.'

'I can reinforce that message for her,' said Paul, firmly. 'I'd like the opportunity to learn a little more about Hamer.'

'There's one easy way of doing that,' suggested Ackford.

'Is there?'

'Yes, Paul. We can ask a favour of your brother.'

Peter was surprised. 'I know nothing whatsoever of Hamer.'

'Perhaps not, but you have a means of gaining intelligence. After all the work you did for the Home Secretary, he's indebted to you. I'm not simply thinking of your work as a spy in France. It was not all that long ago that you solved a mystery at the Home Office itself. Call on Viscount Sidmouth. A man in his position will have ready access to the War Office. He simply has to tell one of his minions to look into the regimental history of the Royal Horse Guards with reference to the name of Captain Stephen Hamer.'

'That's a brilliant notion, Gully.'

Ackford grinned. 'I have them from time to time.'

'He clearly painted a self-portrait of a hero when he first courted Miss Somerville,' said Paul. 'How true a representation was that?'

'Between the pair of you, you should be able to find out.'

'Right,' said Peter to his brother. 'You tackle Hamer and I'll repair to the Home Office. I'm

58

quite sure that Viscount Sidmouth will help us.'

Before they could leave, the door opened and Charlotte came in.

'I'm sorry that I'm late,' she said, 'but I had a visitor as I was about to leave the house. Paul can guess who it was.'

'Yes,' he said, 'it was Hannah. I told her to speak to you about the problem.'

'Thank you for having so much faith in me. I'm not sure I was altogether worthy of it. I know nothing at all about the way that the world of theatre operates.'

'You'd give her uncritical support, Charlotte. That's what she needed.'

'May we know what all this is about?' asked Peter.

'Hannah is grappling with a difficult problem,' explained Charlotte. 'She's reached a turning point in her career.'

'Put succinctly,' said Paul, 'she wants to murder a man by the name of Abel Mundy.'

Lemuel Fleet was known, paradoxically, for his slowness. Short, plump and in his fifties, he looked as if he carried the worries of the world on his shoulder, bearing down on him so hard that the fastest speed he could manage was a laboured trudge. Whenever he made the slightest physical effort, his flabby face would glisten with perspiration and the wig that covered his bald pate would shift to and fro from its mooring. While his body was sluggish, however, his mind could move like lightning and it was often required to do so. As manager of the Theatre Royal, Drury Lane, he had the immense responsibility of helping to entertain London and he knew only too well how fickle audiences could be. One mistake in the choice of a drama or the casting of a central character and they would howl the play off the stage, forgetting the endless delights he'd offered them in the past. A single failure could eclipse fifty successes.

When he called on Hannah Granville, he was carrying a sheaf of plays under his arm. The additional weight made him sweat more obviously than usual. Though she agreed to speak to him, Hannah laid down the rules at the outset.

'Do not *dare* to ask me to apologise to that man,' she declared.

'It would never occur to me to do so.'

'If an apology is in order, he should be making it to *me*.'

'You're being unkind to Mr Mundy,' he said, shuffling the plays. 'He came to us with the highest recommendation.'

'From whom, may I ask?'

'Theatre managers in different parts of the country.'

'It arose purely from their relief at having got rid of the fellow,' she said, acidly. 'Did any of them ever put *The Piccadilly Opera* on their stages?'

'Of course not, Miss Granville, that was new-minted for you. What they did present was *The Jealous Husband*, *The Provok'd Wife*, *Love's Dominion* and *The Fair Maid of Marylebone* – all of them triumphs written by Abel Mundy. And there are three others here from his talented pen.' He set the plays down on the table. 'I've brought copies of them for you to peruse.'

'I am grateful to you, sir. We are always in need of paper kindling for the fire.'

'Read them, I beg you. They are proof positive of his rare talent.'

'Oh, he does have a rare talent, I grant you that. Unfortunately it's for writing tedious drivel. His plot is ridiculous, his characters have no depth and the dialogue suggests that English is a foreign language to him. I am used to playing in the greatest dramas ever written, Mr Fleet. You are asking me to appear in one of the worst.'

'That's a harsh judgement, Miss Granville.'

'Whatever made you commission this dross?'

'I was inspired by the quality of his earlier plays,' he said, indicating the pile. 'And when he told me that *The Piccadilly Opera* would be his finest work, I was quick to seize on it for my theatre.'

'And *now?*' she asked, pointedly. 'Did he deliver what he promised?'

'Not exactly ... but the work still has merit.'

'I've been unable to detect it.'

'Let's not argue over that,' said Fleet, attempting a benign smile that somehow degenerated into a leer. 'I come as a peacemaker. There must be a way out of the impasse.'

'Yes – you must release me from my contract.'

'That's out of the question. You are the toast of London, Miss Granville.'

'I was when I last trod the boards at your theatre,' she said, tossing her head. 'I had Mr William Shakespeare to thank for that. All that Mr Mundy will do is drag me down to his own banal level. I'll not bear such disgrace, sir.'

'We *need* you,' he cried.

'Then change the play.'

'Don't even suggest it, dear lady!'

'Bury this one before it buries both of us.'

'The piece does have *some* virtues.'

Sensing that she had the upper hand, Hannah delivered her ultimatum.

'Make your choice, sir. Either Mr Mundy goes – or I do.'

He was quivering with fear. 'You can't mean that.'

'I stand by what I say. Send that charlatan on his way or I'll quit the company forthwith. But let me warn you of one thing, Mr Fleet. Offer the leading role in *The Piccadilly Opera* to someone else and there's not an actress in the whole realm who will lower herself to accept it.' Grabbing the plays, she thrust them violently back into his hands. 'Take this offal away before its stink pervades the whole house!'

CHAPTER SIX

Peter Skillen was glad of an excuse to visit the Home Office. Apart from anything else, he knew that he'd receive a cordial welcome. He'd not only undertaken many assignments during the war at the Home Secretary's instigation. In its wake, Peter had also unravelled one plot to assassinate Viscount Sidmouth and another to kill the Duke of Wellington. As a result, both men had written effusive letters of thanks to him. As he approached the building, he remembered the hidden secrets he'd earlier found inside it. Peter was in search of another secret now.

Three people were waiting impatiently to see the Home Secretary and they were annoyed when Peter's name was enough in itself to move him to the front of the queue. Sidmouth even opened the door of his office in person, stepping out to shake the visitor's hand.

'Do come in,' he invited. 'You're most welcome.'

'Thank you, my lord,' said Peter, stepping into the room.

'It's always a pleasure to see you, Mr Skillen. Everyone else brings me problems. You alone trade in solutions.'

'I've come in search of one this time, my lord.'

'To what does it pertain?'

'It relates to a brutal murder.'

'Take a seat and tell me all.'

They settled down opposite each other and Peter told his tale. As usual, he was concise, articulate and free from pointless digression. Sidmouth listened intently. He was a tall, slim man in his fifties, visibly worn down by the cares of state but retaining a quiet dignity. Earlier in his career, he'd been prime minister but had not excelled in the role, acting, as he did, in the long shadow of Pitt the Younger to whom he was often compared unfavourably. Even when ridiculed mercilessly by word and by caricature, he'd somehow maintained his composure. Peter admired him for that.

'Well,' said Sidmouth, sitting back, 'it's a desperately sad story. I can't pretend that I believe a duel is the most civilised way to resolve an argument. If we all reached for a weapon every time someone irritated us, the population of this country would soon be halved.' He gave a dry laugh. 'Yet one has to be impressed by the unexpected bravery of this Mr Bowerman in challenging a man who's made a profession out of bearing arms.'

'It was an unfair contest from the start.'

'Did your brother make no effort to avert it?'

'Paul did everything in his power, my lord, but Mr Bowerman was adamant.'

'He seems to have been a decent, upstanding gentleman who was given a glimpse of happiness that helped him to shake off his erstwhile gloom. The lady herself must be in despair.'

'My brother said that she swooned on receipt of the news.'

'It's a blow from which she may never recover,' said Sidmouth, seriously, 'but I sense that you came in pursuit of something. This gruesome narrative was the preface to a request, was it not?'

'It was indeed, my lord. We seek more information about Captain Hamer. He arrived out of nowhere to interrupt the burgeoning romance between Miss Somerville and Mr Bowerman. Where had he been until then? The War Office will have a record of his service to the regiment. In brief, what sort of soldier was he?'

'That's a very reasonable enquiry, Mr Skillen.'

'Will you be able to oblige me?'

'I'll do more than that,' said the other, reaching for his quill and dipping it in the inkwell. 'I'll draft a letter this very minute and you shall bear it to the War Office in person. Leave it there and await developments.'

'That's very kind of you, my lord.'

'You once saved my life, Mr Skillen. Writing a letter is the least I can do for you in recompense. As soon as I get a reply, I'll communicate the information at once. Will that content you?'

Peter got up. 'It will, indeed.'

'I can, however, forewarn you of one thing.'

'What's that?'

Sidmouth looked up at him. 'All that you will learn from the War Office,' he said, 'is that Captain Hamer was an exemplary soldier. We are talking about the Royal Horse Guards, remember. They expect the highest standards of their officers.'

A duel of another kind was troubling Lemuel Fleet. Though the enmity between his playwright and his leading lady had only sparked a war of words so far, he feared that in time they might resort to more dangerous weapons. After a lifetime in the theatre, he'd met many oversensitive authors and tempestuous actresses but none as determined to have their respective way as Abel Mundy and Hannah Granville. Neither of them showed the slightest inclination to compromise. The play had been advertised and substantial interest had been aroused. Fleet shuddered at the thought that *The Piccadilly Opera* might have to be cancelled.

Having tackled Hannah, he'd been shaken by her ultimatum. To keep her, he had to get rid of the play altogether. That was unthinkable. In the vain hope that Mundy might be amenable to a suggestion or two, he called on the playwright at the house where he was staying throughout rehearsals. When the manager was shown into the room, Mundy leapt to his feet and ran across to him. He was a tall, angular man in his forties with a scholarly appearance.

'Have you seen that raving she-devil?' he demanded.

'I've not long left her.'

'Did you give her my stipulations?'

'Not exactly, Mr Mundy–'

'I'll not budge an inch. I hope you told her that.'

'Miss Granville understands your position.'

'I'm not sure that she does,' said Mundy. 'She needs to be reminded that without people of my profession, unlettered hoydens like her would have no work.'

Fleet adjusted his wig. 'That's grossly unfair, sir,' he said, trying to assert his authority. 'She is neither unlettered nor a hoyden. Miss Granville is an actress capable of the most taxing roles. During her season in Paris, she played Lady Macbeth in French.'

'It's a language more suited to her excitability.'

'As for having to rely on men who follow your calling, I have to correct you. If every living playwright were to die this instant, the theatre would still thrive because we would be able to call on its rich heritage. Given the choice, I might as well tell you, Miss Granville would be happy to spend her entire career performing plays written two hundred years ago by the Bard of Avon.'

'Then perhaps you should remind her that Shakespeare had an advantage that we who follow him do not. He wrote exclusively for *male* actors,' said Mundy, 'and did not have to put up with the tantrums of hysterical women.'

Feeling that he'd scored an important debating point, he sat down with his arms folded. Fleet was a tolerant and forgiving man, making him a rarity in a contentious profession, but even he could not bring himself to like Abel Mundy. While he was ready to boast about his own talent, Mundy showed scant respect for that of other people. As far as he was concerned, actors were like toy soldiers taken out of a box and told where to move and what to say. In short, they were totally in his control. He denied them any right of protest. Mundy believed that they should be so grateful to take part in one of his dramas that they would succumb willingly to any of his requirements. Someone like Hannah Granville, who challenged him outright, was anathema.

'I believe that she is susceptible to reason,' said Fleet, forcing the lie out between clenched teeth. 'I am hoping that you may feel able to meet her halfway, so to speak.'

'I have no wish to meet that screeching shrew *anywhere*.'

'Miss Granville has legitimate grievances with regard to your play.'

'Oh,' said Mundy, nastily, 'so you've taken *her* side, have you?'

'I am completely impartial, sir. My only concern is to put something on the stage that is at once entertaining and uplifting. *The Piccadilly Opera*, I believe, is both of those things, once a few minor modifications have been made.'

Mundy stiffened. '*Modifications*, Mr Fleet?'

'Let's call them refinements.'

'I don't care what you call them. They are wholly unnecessary.'

'Miss Granville disagrees.'

'The lady is disagreeable by nature.'

'She has a large following, Mr Mundy.'

'As do I,' retorted the other, nostrils flaring. 'My play, *The Provok'd Wife*, was the talk of Bristol.'

'Provincial success is no guarantee of general approbation here in the capital. London audiences are harsher critics. Many plays that have won plaudits in places like Bristol, Bath and Norwich have shrivelled into miserable failures when put to the test here. I am not saying that your work will suffer the same fate,' he went on, quickly. 'It has enormous promise. But you are unknown here, Mr Mundy. That is why I engaged Miss Granville. Her name adds lustre to any play.'

'Unhappily, that is *all* it adds. Her real gift is for subtraction. When she speaks my lines, she takes away their poetry and their pathos. She robs my work of all the elements that give it truth and vitality.'

'You exaggerate, sir.'

'And what about *her?*' demanded the other. 'She goes through life in a veritable cloud of hyperbole.'

'One must make allowances for Miss Granville.'

'Upon my word, I'll not make a single one!'

'Then we are surely doomed,' said Fleet, removing his wig to scratch his pate. 'You wish for her to be removed from your play and Miss Granville urges with equal passion for the summary withdrawal of *The Piccadilly Opera*.'

'That's a scandalous idea!'

'Your own solution is just as impractical.'

'Get rid of that damnable harpie and all will be well!'

'If only it were that simple. Consider my dilemma. I have undertaken to offer drama that will please the palates of the most discerning audience in the world. Together, you and Miss Granville might conjure up something magical. Apart, you will only create a disaster. Is that what you and she *really* want to do? Is it your joint endeavour to crucify me in public and bring my theatre to its knees?' He replaced his wig and struck a pose. 'Come to composition with the lady,' he urged. 'Find a means of working harmoniously together or *The Piccadilly Opera* will never leave the pages on which it was written.'

While Alfred Hale was still looking at the corpse with intense curiosity, Micah Yeomans was examining the murder weapon. The coroner's assistant took the opportunity to display his knowledge.

'It's a Toledo blade, sir.'

'How do you know?'

'I recognise it by its quality. Roman soldiers did the same. That's why they chose Toledo steel for their swords.'

'You seem well informed.'

'I am only passing on what the other gentleman told me.'

Yeomans glowered. '*Other* gentleman?'

'Yes, sir, he called here earlier – a Mr Skillen.'

'He's done it yet again,' complained Hale. 'Whether it's Peter or Paul, they always seem to know something that we don't.'

'Those confounded brothers should have been

strangled at birth,' said Yeomans, vengefully.

'Why do they always hold the whip hand over us, Micah?'

'I'll snatch it from them and use it to flay them alive!'

'Then you've more courage than sense. I've seen them in action. It would be madness to take on either of the Skillen brothers. With sword, pistol or bare fists, they are invincible.'

'Then we'll have to choose some *other* weapons, Alfred.'

'What do you mean?'

'We are upholders of the law,' said Yeomans, grandiloquently. 'It's high time we let the two of them feel its full force.'

With a sudden downward jab, he left the dagger embedded in the table on which the body lay. It was still vibrating as they left the room.

'They *arrested* you?'

'Yes, they did, then the dolts accompanied me to Bow Street as if I was the lowest criminal.'

'This is insupportable, Stephen.'

'I made that point in the choicest language I could find.'

'Could they really imagine that you'd ever stab a man in the back?'

'Patently, they could.'

'Then they don't know the Stephen Hamer that I do.'

'Thank you.'

Rawdon Carr had been his second at the ill-fated duel, an old and trusted friend to whom he often turned for advice. They were in Hamer's house,

70

looking back over recent events. Carr was furious that the Runners had dared to suspect Hamer of murder and urged him to institute legal action. They were still discussing its nature when a servant knocked on the door and opened it.

'You have a visitor, Captain Hamer,' he said.

'What's his name?'

'Mr Paul Skillen.'

'It's the fellow who acted as Bowerman's second,' said Hamer, puzzled. 'What can he possibly want with me?'

'At least he won't have come to arrest you,' said Carr. 'He discharged his duties well on Putney Heath. Have him admitted.'

Hamer gave a signal and the servant disappeared. Seconds later, he conducted Paul into the room then left all three men together. After formal introductions, Paul was invited to sit down.

'I'd prefer to remain standing, if you don't mind,' said Paul.

Carr smiled. 'That sounds ominous.'

'I came to deliver a message to the captain.'

'Then let's hear it,' said Hamer.

'Miss Somerville wishes you to know that she has no wish ever to see you again. She requests that you make no attempt to call on her because you will not be allowed inside her house under any circumstance.'

'And *this* is the message she asked you to communicate?'

'I may have paraphrased her words.'

'Why did she choose *you* as her intercessor? You don't even know her.'

'It fell to me to break the news of Mr Bower-

71

man's death to her,' explained Paul. 'It caused her untold anguish. When I asked about you ... Miss Somerville said that the door would be slammed in your face.'

'That doesn't sound like Laetitia,' said Hamer.

'Indeed, it doesn't,' agreed Carr. 'It's far too unladylike. You misheard her, Mr Skillen. Such sentiments could never be expressed by her.'

'I promise you that they were,' said Paul, stoutly. 'But that's not the only reason that brought me here. I wanted to speak to Captain Hamer about his time in the Peninsular War.'

Hamer became wary. 'Why the devil should you want to do that?'

'I've known many soldiers in my time and – to a man – they like to collect trophies from their victories. The souvenirs usually comprise uniforms, hats, flags or, more often, perhaps, enemy weapons.'

'Damn your effrontery, Mr Skillen!'

'Are you saying that you did *not* forage on the battlefield?'

'Oh, Captain Hamer came back with a whole arsenal of weapons,' said Carr, laughing, 'but, frankly, that's none of your business.'

'It might be if the collection included a dagger made of Toledo steel and having a decorative handle.'

'I think it's time that you left,' said Hamer, forcefully.

'Evidently, you've not seen the murder weapon that took Mr Bowerman's life. It was such a dagger as I've described. It crossed my mind to wonder if it had once belonged to you.'

Hamer took a menacing step forward. 'Mind what you say, Mr Skillen.'

'It's a simple question,' said Paul, holding his ground.

'Are you going to leave or must I throw you out bodily?'

'I wouldn't advise the latter course of action, sir. I'm no defenceless opponent like Mr Bowerman. Even with my tuition, he could never have won a duel. The odds were stacked too overwhelmingly in your favour.' He drew himself up. 'The situation is very different now.'

Hamer looked as if he was about to attack Paul but something held him back. His cheeks reddened and his jaw muscles tightened. There was sheer malice in his eyes but there was also a hint of respect as well. They stood there in silence for several minutes. When Hamer turned sharply away, Paul knew that he'd won the confrontation.

'Remember what Miss Somerville said,' Paul reminded him.

'Get out of my house!'

'Good day to you, sirs.'

'And to you,' said Carr, cheerfully.

Turning on his heel, Paul left the room and could soon be heard opening the front door of the house. Carr had viewed it all with mingled interest and amusement but the visit had left Hamer fuming.

'Do you *have* such a weapon, Stephen?' asked his friend.

'As a matter of fact, I do,' replied the other, 'but I was not going to tell that to him. I can't believe the infernal cheek of the man. He was lucky that

73

I didn't knock him to the floor.'

'The luck may have been yours. Had you attacked him, I might now have been helping *you* up from the carpet. Mr Skillen is no mean adversary. He has the look of a fighting man to me.'

'I should have refused to see him, Rawdon.'

'But the fact is that you did and, as a consequence, I'm curious. If you have a dagger of the kind described, I'd be most interested to look at it.'

'You've seen my collection before.'

'Yes, but I did so without any particular weapon in mind – there are so many to choose from, after all. Things have changed now.'

'Oh, well,' said Hamer, reluctantly, 'if you must…'

'It's an odd coincidence if the murder weapon is identical to yours.'

'There won't be the slightest resemblance between them.'

He led his friend out and along a corridor to the rear of the house. Producing a key from his pocket, he opened the door of a room and stood back so that his friend could go in first. Carr entered what was, in effect, a small military museum. Filled with weapons of every description – from foreign as well as British armies – it also had an assortment of uniforms, hats, boots, gloves and medals. A large telescope interested Carr enough to make him handle it for a moment.

'It's French,' said Hamer.

'Nobody would have parted with this easily. It's an expensive instrument.'

'I had to kill its owner to get it.'

'What about the rest of these items?'

'Spoils of war.'

Carr replaced the telescope on a table. 'What about the dagger?'

'It's over here,' said Hamer, leading him to a glass-fronted cabinet. 'As you see, it's a large and varied collection. The one that Skillen referred to is right here at the front of the...'

Words ran dry and he simply gaped. Opening the cabinet, he took out the weapons one by one until they were all side by side on the table. Carr was concerned about his reaction.

'What's the trouble, dear fellow?'

'It's not here, Rawdon.'

'Are you quite certain that it *was* here?'

'Yes, of course.'

'One of the servants might have absent-mindedly moved it.'

'They wouldn't *dare.*'

'Then it's somewhere else,' said Carr, looking around.

'It's gone, I tell you. It's been *stolen.*'

'But that's impossible.'

'So I thought, Rawdon, but I was wrong. This room was not as secure as I intended. Since the dagger is not here...' He shook his head in disbelief. 'Then it might have been the murder weapon, after all.'

'Let's find out at once,' urged his friend. 'If Skillen can get access to Bowerman's corpse, then so can we. I'll bear you company. This is mystifying.'

Peter Skillen returned to the gallery to find his wife seated at the table, writing something in a large notebook. It contained a record of all the

75

cases in which they'd been involved over the years. Kept scrupulously up to date, it had details of every criminal who had ever crossed their paths. In some cases – if Charlotte had actually seen the person – there would be a rough portrait of him or her. The record book was an invaluable source of information and it was only one of many initiatives that she'd introduced. She gave her husband a welcoming smile and he responded with a kiss.

'Did you manage to see the Home Secretary?' she asked.

'I did more than that, Charlotte. He was so eager to help me that he dashed off a letter there and then. I've just come from delivering it to the War Office.'

'It pays to have friends in high places.'

'I *earned* his friendship, my love – and you know how.' He sat opposite her. 'But what's all this fuss about Hannah's latest play? Can she really have murder on her mind?'

'It's becoming something of an obsession, Peter.'

'Who exactly is Abel Mundy?'

'If you listen to her, he's the most black-hearted villain Hannah has ever met. She called him a freakish monster germinated outside lawful pro-creation.' Peter laughed. 'It's not a cause for glee,' she said, reprovingly. 'I had to endure almost an hour of her diatribes. The situation is intractable.'

'There's always a way out of a dilemma.'

'Not if both parties are obdurate.'

'Give me the full details, my love.'

'That would take far too long. All you need is the essence.'

But there was not even time for Charlotte to

76

reveal that. Before she could utter another word, the door was flung open and a dozen men charged into the room on the heels of Micah Yeomans. Peter and his wife jumped to their feet.

'This is very uncivil of you,' he protested.

'Civility has to go by the board when a crime has been committed,' said the Runner. 'We've had information that a wanted man is hiding here.'

'That's arrant nonsense.'

'Harbouring a fugitive is against the law.'

'And that's precisely why we'd never dream of doing it. Everybody in this building has a legal right to be here.'

'We'll need to make sure of that,' said Yeomans, turning to his men. 'Search every nook and cranny of the place. Flush him out of his lair.'

The members of the foot patrol who'd come in support charged off to begin their search, making as much noise as possible and causing as much disruption.

'I will complain to the chief magistrate,' said Peter, angrily. 'It's wholly unwarranted.'

'Complain, if you must, Mr Skillen, but I would have thought you'd like to keep well away from Mr Kirkwood. You were before him only yesterday.'

'That was my brother, Paul.'

'Really?' Yeomans gaped. 'I could have sworn that *you* were Paul.'

'That's not the only mistake you've made today.'

'We are acting on reliable information, sir.'

'I beg leave to doubt that.'

'If the rogue is here, my men will find him.'

'You should mention this incident the next time you talk to the Home Secretary,' said Charlotte

77

to her husband. 'He can overrule the chief magistrate with ease.'

'Viscount Sidmouth is wedded to law and order,' said Yeomans, pompously, 'so do not think you can frighten me by waving his name in the air like a banner. We came to smoke out a villain and that's what we will do.'

The next moment, there was the sound of a fierce struggle as several feet clattered down the staircase. Loud protests were filling the air.

'That sounds like Jem,' said Charlotte, going through the open door.

Peter followed her and was horrified to see Jem Huckvale being manhandled down the stairs by Alfred Hale, Chevy Ruddock and two other men. Small but powerful, Huckvale was wriggling like an eel. They had difficulty holding him.

'We caught him, sir,' said Ruddock, breathlessly. 'This is the man we were after. I'd recognise him anywhere. He stole a leg of mutton in the market this very morning.'

'I haven't left the gallery,' cried Huckvale.

'It's true,' said Peter. 'Jem lives and works here. He's being arrested for a crime he couldn't possibly have committed.'

'Besides,' added Charlotte, 'he's the most law-abiding person. Release him at once, Mr Yeomans. You have the wrong man.'

'We'll see about that, Mrs Skillen.' He nodded to the others. 'Take him out.'

Still protesting his innocence, Huckvale was more or less carried out.

'I understand your game,' said Peter, coldly. 'Because we have more success at solving crimes

78

than you do, you try to frighten us by raiding our premises. As you well know, Jem is no thief. You'll soon have to release him.'

'In that case,' said Yeomans, beaming, 'we'll have to raid the gallery again, won't we? And we'll keep on doing it until we catch the man we're after. He's here somewhere. I sense it.'

He walked jauntily out of the building.

CHAPTER SEVEN

On the journey to the morgue, Stephen Hamer sat in the carriage bristling with an irritation tempered by perplexity. He was utterly baffled. Someone appeared to have stolen an item from his collection of weapons. The discovery came only a day after the duel in which he'd been involved had been rudely interrupted. How could anyone enter his house so easily and walk away with a prized dagger? Who could have learnt of the duel and alerted the Runners? Were the two incidents the work of the same person? If so, had he also been the killer of Mark Bowerman? It seemed very likely.

One question dominated: where *was* the villain?

'I share your concern,' said Carr, patting his friend's knee. 'Somebody is one step ahead of us and that's vexatious. We need to track him down.'

'I agree, Rawdon, but how do we do that?'

'Let's start with the dagger. It may have gone missing but that doesn't mean it has to have been the murder weapon. You're not the only soldier to bring weapons back from the Peninsular War. London is probably awash with them.'

'There's only one that matters to me,' said Hamer, grimly.

'After we've established if it was or wasn't used to kill Mr Bowerman, I suggest that we pay a visit to the gentleman's house. We need to find out where the attack took place and what Bowerman was doing there in the first place. There will be an investigation into the murder but – from what you tell me of the Runners – it would be foolish to place any trust in them.'

'They're imbeciles. It's no wonder that crime is so rampant in the capital. If they are the only means of enforcing the law, then malefactors will continue to run riot. Look for no help from the Runners.'

'We'll act without them, Stephen. They may, of course, object.'

'A fig for their objections!' exclaimed Hamer with an obscene gesture.

The carriage rolled to a halt and they got out in turn. Once they'd identified themselves at the front door, they were taken to the room where Bowerman's corpse was kept. Herbs had been sprinkled to ward off the stink of death but it still invaded Carr's nostrils and he began to cough. More accustomed to the abiding reek of decay, Hamer was untroubled. During his days in uniform, he'd become habituated to endless casualties on the battlefield. After a brief examination of the cadaver, he asked to see the murder weapon. As he retrieved it from a drawer, the assistant passed on some information.

'It's made of Toledo steel,' he said, handing it over. 'That's the finest there is, sir. As a matter of fact–'

'Stop blathering,' snapped Hamer, interrupting him. He turned the dagger over to examine it from every angle. 'I know all about Toledo steel.'

'Well?' asked Carr. 'Is it yours?'

'It is,' confirmed the other.

'How can you tell?'

'I recognise one of my weapons when I see it, Rawdon.'

'Then how did it end up in Mr Bowerman's back?'

'That's what I intend to find out.'

'I'm afraid that you can't keep that dagger,' said the assistant, extending a hand. 'It's evidence in a case of murder. You can reclaim it when the crime is solved.'

Reluctant to give it back, Hamer eventually did so, warning the man to take good care of it. He then asked if the Runners had been there.

'Oh, yes, sir,' replied the other. 'I had a visit from Mr Yeomans and Mr Hale but they were not the first to come. A younger gentleman called before them. He was the one who told me about Toledo steel.'

'What was his name?' asked Hamer.

'Mr Skillen.'

'Why is *he* poking his nose into this affair?'

'He was Bowerman's friend,' said Carr, not realising that it was Peter Skillen who'd been there rather than his brother, 'and, like any decent man, he wishes to know who committed the murder. If

81

you'd been the victim, I'd have done the same. In fact, I wouldn't have rested until I'd learnt the full truth.'

They left the building and paused outside the door. Hamer was rancorous.

'We don't want Skillen getting in our way,' he said.

'I concur.'

'He's not like those bumbling incompetents who decided that *I* was the killer. Skillen is more intelligent, for a start.'

'He's more intelligent and, I'd venture, more resolute.'

'We must find a way to frighten him off.'

'He won't be frightened easily,' said Carr, thoughtfully, 'so it might be better simply to divert his attention. I'm sure we can devise a means of doing that.'

The moment he stepped across the threshold, Paul knew that he was in a house of mourning. It was a palatial residence that reflected the character of its late owner. The well-stocked library, the plethora of fine artwork and the selection of musical instruments told of a cultured man. Shown into the drawing room, Paul was able to view the striking portrait above the mantelpiece.

'That was the *first* Mrs Bowerman,' explained Silas Roe in a voice hoarse with grief. 'A happier couple never existed. They were ideally suited.'

'And yet he was prepared to embark on a second marriage.'

'That's true.'

'How did that come about?'

'I can't give you precise details, Mr Skillen. It was not my place to pry. The master was an intensely private man. I respected his privacy.'

'Someone must have introduced him to Miss Somerville.'

'That would be Sir Geoffrey Melrose.'

'How did he come to know the lady?'

'I have no idea, sir.'

'Was he a close friend of Mr Bowerman's?'

'He called here occasionally,' said Roe, 'and very few people did that.'

'Your master confided to me that he first saw Miss Somerville at a dinner party. Presumably, Sir Geoffrey Melrose was the host.'

'That's my understanding.'

'And, I daresay, you noticed a change in Mr Bowerman.'

'Indeed, we did,' said the butler, failing to keep the disapproval out of his reply. 'We were all very much aware of it.'

Paul questioned him for some time and was disappointed to learn that Roe had no idea of Sir Geoffrey's London address. On another front, too, he was thwarted.

'You told me that, on the day of the murder, Mr Bowerman received a letter.'

'Yes, sir, it was from Miss Somerville.'

'How could you be certain of that?'

'Her correspondence always had a pleasing aroma.'

'Did you actually see the handwriting?'

'I saw it and recognised it, Mr Skillen.'

'So you'd seen examples of it before, obviously.'

'Yes, sir.'

'Given the strength of feeling he clearly had for the lady,' said Paul, carefully, 'he'd certainly have kept her billets-doux.' Roe nodded. 'Might I see them, please?'

'I'm afraid not, sir.'

'Do you know where they are?'

'Yes, I do.'

'All that I ask is to have a quick peep at them.'

'That will not be possible,' said Roe, firmly.

'But they may contain valuable clues helpful to my investigation.'

'It was private correspondence, sir. Nobody will ever see it.'

'I was hoping for more cooperation from you, Mr Roe.'

The butler straightened his back. 'I know where my duty lies, sir.' He regarded Paul quizzically. 'May I ask if you are married, sir?'

'As it happens, I am not.'

'But there is a lady in your life, I dare swear.'

'There's a very special lady,' confirmed Paul.

'Then ask yourself this, Mr Skillen. How would *you* feel if a stranger was allowed to read letters sent by her for your eyes only?'

'I'd feel very angry.'

'You'd have every right to be so, sir,' said Roe. 'I'm sorry to turn down your request but perhaps you'll understand why now.'

Paul accepted that the butler was protecting the privacy of his late master and he admired him for that. He was about to put more questions to him when the doorbell clanged. Voices came along the corridor and Paul identified one of them at once. As the Runners came into the room, he spread his arms in a mock welcome.

'Ah,' he said, grinning mischievously, 'you've got here at last. Speed was never your forte, Mr Yeomans, was it?'

'That's the third time in a row,' said Hale. 'Garden, morgue and here – he always gets there first.'

'Someone has to show you the way. Though I have to correct you with regard to the morgue – it was my brother, Peter, who went there.'

'You've no business being under this roof,' said Yeomans, features twisted into an ugly scowl. 'I must ask you to leave.'

'I'll go in my own good time.'

'You'll not tarry when you hear what happened at the shooting gallery.'

Paul tensed. 'Why – what have you been up to now?'

'We've been doing our duty and upholding the law,' said Hale. 'When we had reports of a fugitive at the gallery, we descended on the place and searched it.'

'There are no fugitives there, man!'

'Yes, there was. We found him skulking upstairs and arrested him. His name is Jem Huckvale and we've a witness who will depose that he saw the little wretch steal a leg of mutton.'

'Jem is no thief!' yelled Paul. 'He's as honest as the day is long.'

'He's cooling his heels in Bow Street,' said Yeomans, enjoying Paul's discomfort. 'It's not like you to consort with criminals, Mr Skillen.'

'This is an example of pure spite. It's an act of shameless retaliation.'

'Our job is to clean up the streets of London.'

'Then you might begin by rounding up all the villains who pay you to ignore the way they make their living. Everyone knows how corrupt you are. How dare you accuse Jem Huckvale of a crime when the pair of you flout the law every day.'

'Do you want to end up in the same cell as your friend?' taunted Yeomans.

'I want him released immediately.'

'You're in no position to make demands, Mr Skillen.'

'We have a very good lawyer,' said Paul, warningly.

'Then he's going to be extremely busy in the future.'

'Why do you say that, Mr Yeomans?'

'I have a strange feeling that we'll get other reports of fugitives going to ground in your gallery,' said the Runner, 'don't you, Alfred?'

'Oh, yes,' agreed Hale. 'You're going to be seeing a lot of us, Mr Skillen.'

As he left the room, their sniggers followed him all the way to the front door.

True to her profession, Hannah Granville was bereft when she had no audience. With only the servants in the house, she felt that any performance she gave was bound to be unappreciated. She therefore hired a carriage to take her to the gallery where she could be assured of a sympathetic hearing. On her way there, the driver obeyed her instruction to take her past the Theatre Royal, Drury Lane, so that she could feast her eyes on a place that had been instrumental in advancing her career in the past. It had become, to some extent, her spiritual home and she drew strength simply from looking at it. As the carriage drove on, however, other thoughts flooded into her mind. Having been an inspiration to her, the Theatre Royal might now become a scaffold on which her reputation could die. Thanks to Abel Mundy, her long years of toil and dedication would be meaningless. She was facing execution.

Arriving at the gallery, she told her friend how concerned she was.

'Why don't you talk to the manager again?' advised Charlotte.

'I've already done that. He called on me earlier.'

'Had he spoken to Mr Mundy?'

'I'm not sure if he had the opportunity to speak,' said Hannah. 'When he came to me, Mr Fleet was like a beaten dog. When he left me, he was going to confront Mundy once again. At their first meeting, that ogre made excessive demands.'

'Your own have not exactly been marked by restraint,' said the other, gently.

'They've been calm and sensible, Charlotte.'

'That's a matter of opinion.'

'All I ask is the removal of this hideous man and his hideous play.'

'And what is to replace them?'

Hannah tossed her head. 'Who cares?

'*Everyone* cares,' said Charlotte, reasonably. 'The manager cares because his livelihood is threatened, you care because you require a play commensurate with your talent and the audience cares because it has been starved of the pleasure of seeing Hannah Granville onstage for a while and wants to welcome their favourite actress back. Then, of course,' she went on, 'there is the rest of the company to consider. What is *their* opinion of *The Piccadilly Opera?*'

'That's irrelevant. My opinion is the only one that matters.' Charlotte was about to point out that her friend was being rather selfish when they heard feet running down the corridor. The door opened and Paul came into the room. Hannah instinctively threw herself into his arms.

'Thank God you've come, Paul! I need you.'

'What are *you* doing here?' he asked.

'We've been discussing Hannah's latest play,' said Charlotte.

'Let's put that aside for a minute.'

Hannah stamped a foot. 'I won't have it put aside for a single second.'

'Something of more immediate importance has come up, my love,' he said, planting a consoling kiss on her forehead. 'I've just heard some disturbing news from Yeomans. Is it true that Jem has been arrested on a trumped-up charge?'

'Yes,' replied Charlotte.

'He must be set free at once.'

'Peter is already taking care of that.'

'Apparently, the Runners intend to raid the gallery again.'

'Gully is considering measures to prevent that. It may even be necessary to close the place for a few days.'

'I wish someone would raid the Theatre Royal,' said Hannah, petulantly, 'and arrest Abel Mundy for breaking all the laws of drama. *The Piccadilly Opera* is an act of criminality in itself.'

'With respect,' said Paul, gently squeezing her

arm, 'Jem's situation is more critical than yours. If it were proved – by means of arrant lies – that Jem *did* steal a leg of mutton, it would be the end of him. At best, he'd face transportation; at worst, he'd be given a death sentence.'

Hannah was for once forced to think about someone else's plight.

'Is it really that serious, Paul?'

'It could be.'

As it happened, Peter Skillen did not have to invoke the name of the Home Secretary to secure the release of his friend. When Jem Huckvale was taken to Bow Street, the chief magistrate heard the details of the case in the privacy of his office. Since he was the supposed witness to the crime, Chevy Ruddock gave his testimony, saying that he'd seen Huckvale sneaking away from the market with the mutton tucked inside his coat. It did not take long for Eldon Kirkwood to dismiss the case on the grounds of insufficient evidence. Much as he regretted doing so, he ordered Huckvale's release. Peter had brought a spare horse to Bow Street. Riding side by side with his friend, he expressed his sympathy.

'I'm sorry that they picked on you, Jem,' he said. 'Paul and I were the real targets. We were lucky that the chief magistrate is so meticulous. He soon found holes in the witness's testimony.'

'I was scared,' admitted Huckvale. 'I thought I was done for. And I was shocked that Chevy Ruddock could tell such barefaced lies.'

'He was suborned. You could tell that.'

'I've always thought he was the best of the

Runners. He's a decent man at heart. When he tried to keep watch on Paul, I pushed Ruddock in the Thames. There were times when I regretted that. Today, I wished I could do it all over again.'

'He'll think twice before he arrests you again.'

'How many times must it have happened before?' asked Huckvale.

'What – someone bearing false witness?'

'Yes, Peter.'

'It does happen occasionally, I fear.'

'If Mr Kirkwood had believed him, I might have...'

'You might have suffered the fate of other innocent victims,' said Peter, finishing the sentence for him. 'Fortunately, the chief magistrate is not easily fooled. Ruddock will get a roasting for what he did.'

'Mr Yeomans is the real culprit.'

'That fact won't go unnoticed.'

'Is he going to keep on raiding the gallery?'

Peter grinned. 'I have a feeling that he might be dissuaded from pursuing that particular line of attack on us,' said Peter. 'He'll get more than a rap on the knuckles from Mr Kirkwood.'

Heads bowed and cheeks red, Yeomans, Hale and Ruddock stood in front of his desk like three felons awaiting sentence in court. They were united by a collective sense of shame. The chief magistrate kept them waiting for a few minutes and let his fury simmer. When he suddenly rose to his feet, they took an involuntary pace backwards.

'Who was the author of this travesty of justice?'

he demanded.

'I was, sir,' confessed Yeomans, 'but it was no travesty. We did have legitimate grounds for suspicion. Ruddock *did* actually witness the theft of that leg of mutton.'

'It's true,' said Ruddock. 'I'd swear it.'

'And the thief looked uncannily like Huckvale.'

'I'd swear to that as well.'

'It was Chevy who set us in motion,' said Hale, attempting to shift the blame to their younger colleague. 'If he hadn't reported what he'd seen, the arrest would never have taken place.'

'Be quiet, Hale,' ordered Kirkwood. 'In my view, you are all equally culpable. I have three observations to make. First, when you saw the crime taking place, why didn't you arrest the thief on the spot?'

'I tried to do so, sir,' said Ruddock, 'but he ran off. I gave chase and would certainly have caught him had not his accomplice, lurking outside the market, tripped me up. I still have the bruises from the fall.'

'Don't expect sympathy from me.'

'No, sir.'

'Second, all this happened a week ago.' He transferred his gaze to Yeomans. 'Why did it take you seven days to arrest the man Ruddock claims to have seen at the market?'

'We've been very busy, sir,' said Yeomans.

'A case like this should have taken priority.'

'We realise that now.'

'If Huckvale *had* been the thief, he'd have had a whole week to leave the city and hide somewhere well beyond your grasp. Strike while the iron is hot. That's my rule. When you suspect someone, arrest him immediately.'

'We usually do, sir.'

'Third – and this is a damning indictment of your behaviour – the butcher whose mutton was stolen reported the theft. I took the trouble to look at the record and read what he said. All that Ruddock saw of the man was his back as he fled the scene. The butcher, on the other hand, was face-to-face with him. Do you know how he described the malefactor?'

Yeomans ran his tongue over dried lips. 'No, sir.'

'He said that the man was tall, skinny and rat-faced.'

'Huckvale is skinny, sir.'

'And he's rat-faced as well,' added Hale.

'That's why I was convinced it was him, sir,' explained Ruddock.

Kirkwood narrowed his lids. 'How could you confuse a tall man with a very short one?' he asked. 'Or are you going to suggest that Huckvale has lost six or seven inches since the crime? Is this the effect that eating a leg of mutton has on a man? His body shrinks in size? Is that your claim, Ruddock?'

'No, sir,' said the other, meekly.

'What about you two?'

'No, sir,' said Yeomans.

'No, sir,' said Hale.

At least we're all agreed on that,' said Kirkwood. 'I put it to you that you used this alleged sighting of a thief in the market as a pretext for raiding the shooting gallery where Huckvale works. While there, Mr Skillen assures me, you made an alarming amount of noise and caused actual damage to the property. And all of this was done in the search for a tall, skinny, rat-faced man who was not even on the premises. Is that an accurate account of today's farcical intervention?'

'We went there with the very best of intentions, sir,' said Yeomans.

'You went there to cause havoc and to upset the Skillen brothers.'

'That was not our primary purpose.'

'You also threatened further raids on the gallery.'

'It's the only way to keep them under control, sir. They are a nuisance and are already impeding the murder investigation.'

'Then the best way to establish your superiority is to solve the crime ahead of them. How can you do that when you waste time descending on their premises and seizing an innocent man? Mr Bowerman's killer must be caught but, I'll wager, the last place you're likely to find him is at the gallery.'

'We've made progress to that end, sir.'

'What end?'

'The hunt for the killer,' said Yeomans. 'We called at the victim's home.'

'Not before time, I may say!'

'His butler told us something of what lay behind the duel with Captain Hamer. And we were given a much deeper insight into his master's character.'

'Did the butler have any idea who might have murdered him?'

'None, sir. Mr Bowerman was a man with no known enemies.'

'What about Captain Hamer? He qualified as an enemy.'

'That's precisely why we arrested him.'

'Yes,' said Kirkwood, cynically, 'it was another of your blunders. Try to arrest people who will actually *remain* in custody, not those we have to set free with abject apologies for your over-exuberance. I suppose that I should be thankful you didn't accuse the captain of stealing a leg of mutton as well.'

'It couldn't have been him, sir,' Ruddock put in, helpfully. 'He's too handsome to be called rat-faced.'

'Going back to the murder victim,' said Yeomans, 'we feel that we can see the path that the investigation must follow. As a next step, we must introduce ourselves to Miss Somerville.'

'You should already have done that. It's what I advised.'

'We'll go there at once, sir.'

'I must first extract a promise from you.'

'You shall have it, sir.'

'Whatever else you do,' said Kirkwood, scornfully, 'don't arrest the lady as well. In fact, don't arrest *anybody*. Your record in that regard has been lamentable. Gather evidence as patiently as you can and try, I beg of you, to be tactful for once. Mr Bowerman was on the brink of proposing marriage, you tell me. That being the case, Miss Somerville must be looked at as a grieving widow. Tread very carefully. She will be fragile.'

Seated on the ottoman in her boudoir, Laetitia Somerville untied the pink ribbon around the letters she'd received from Mark Bowerman and began to read them in chronological order. It had been a slow courtship at first but had soon picked up pace. The letters became longer and increasingly affectionate. They were infused with a tentative passion that matured into something far stronger. Written by a man who'd never expected to find love again, each one marvelled at his good fortune in meeting her. It was impossible not to be touched by the poignancy of it all. He was not simply dead, Bowerman had been cruelly murdered. What troubled Laetitia most was that a missive, allegedly written by her, had been used as the bait. Who had committed the forgery and how could they possibly have known it would entice him out of the safety of his house? Impelled by the hope of seeing her again, Bowerman had answered the summons and gone to a designated place where someone lay in wait for him.

Having read the correspondence in its entirety, Laetitia got up abruptly and took all but the final letter across to the little fireplace. Tossing them into the grate, she set them alight and watched the thwarted ambitions of Mark Bowerman going up in smoke. When she returned to the ottoman, she picked up his last communication to her and read it with a smile of satisfaction.

CHAPTER EIGHT

Hester Mallory arrived at the bank just before it was closing. The chief clerk tried to turn her away, suggesting that she might return on the following day, but the manager then caught sight of her. Leonard Impey had always had an eye for a pretty woman and he was momentarily startled. Hester was far more than pretty. Still in her early thirties, she had a beauty and sophistication that would turn heads anywhere. Acting as her chaperone was a young, pallid manservant. Dismissing his clerk, the manager introduced himself and shepherded the visitors into his room. When he closed the door behind them, he felt a thrill at the fact that they were in private together. Her companion was invisible. Hester's attire, bearing, graceful movement and soft voice made her thoroughly enchanting.

Offered a seat, Hester lowered herself into a chair. Impey hovered around her. He was a plump man in his fifties with a flabby face and overlarge lips. Gazing at her over the top of his spectacles, it was all he could do to stop himself dribbling with pleasure.

'How may I be of service to you, Miss...?'

'It's Mrs Mallory,' she replied. 'Mrs Hester Mallory.'

'Welcome to our humble bank.'

'Thank you, Mr Impey. It was recommended to me as the most trusted institution of its kind in

96

the whole of London.'

'That's praise indeed, Mrs Mallory. May I know who spoke of us in such fulsome terms?'

'I can do more than that,' she said, opening her bag. 'I have a letter of introduction from him. I'm sure that you remember Mr Jacob Picton?'

'How could I forget such a distinguished gentleman? We were fortunate to do business with him for many years. How is Mr Picton?'

'Read what he says and all will be explained.'

Taking out the letter, she handed it over to him. Impey retreated to his desk and sat down to peruse the missive. Picton had invested heavily in property in the capital and, when more houses came on to the market, he'd borrowed money from the bank to purchase them. His record of success was almost unrivalled. Rental income alone allowed him to live in luxury in Mayfair. It was only when his health began to fail that he sold off much of his property empire and moved to a country estate in Hampshire.

'Mr Picton speaks well of you,' said Impey, reading the letter and recognising his old friend's distinctive calligraphy. 'You and your husband are neighbours of his, I see. Is Mr Mallory travelling with you?'

'No, Mr Impey, my husband rarely stirs from the country, but I felt that it was time I stayed here for a while to rub off the rust a little, so to speak. I do have another purpose for the visit, as it happens.'

'Do you?'

'My husband will soon be celebrating his fiftieth birthday and I am going to give him a gift that he has sought ever since we met.'

'What might that be?'

'Why, it's a portrait of his dear wife, of course.'

He tittered. 'I should have guessed.'

'It's long overdue.'

'And is Mr Mallory aware of your plan?'

'That would spoil the surprise,' she said, laughing gaily. 'I've been in secret correspondence with an artist who has a reputation for portraiture. According to Mr Picton, he's without compare. Unfortunately,' she added, with a wry smile, 'artists of that kind tend to come at a high price.'

'I'd be surprised if he charged you a single penny,' he said, gallantly, 'for he'll realise what a privilege it will be to have you as a client.'

'It's kind of you to say so, Mr Impey!'

'He'll have the pleasure of looking at you for long periods.'

'I hope they're not too long, sir. I am very restive.'

Impey stood up to lean across the desk and return the letter. She gave him a smile of thanks before popping it into her bag. Having felt jaded after a long day's work, he was refreshed. He was also anxious to help a potential client.

'What exactly has brought you to us, Mrs Mallory?'

'I merely wanted to introduce myself,' she explained, 'and to establish trust between us. You need to know something of me before any transaction can take place and I, in turn, wanted to find out if Mr Picton's high opinion of this bank was justified.'

'That's a wise precaution.'

'It's one that I always take.'

'If you have any questions about the way that we operate, I'll be happy to answer them. I think you'll find that we've maintained the high standards noted by Mr Picton. Do please give him my regards when you're next in touch with him.'

'I'll certainly do so.'

Hester studied him carefully as if trying to weigh him up. Feeling a trifle uncomfortable under her scrutiny, Impey resumed his seat. When her appraisal was over, she gave him a reassuring smile.

'I can see that you're a man with financial acumen,' she said, approvingly.

'It's an essential quality for a bank manager.'

'You are far too experienced to take a new client at face value.'

'That's quite right.'

'Then let me ask you this, Mr Impey...'

Yeomans and Hale could still hear the chief magistrate's invective ringing in their ears. What they'd conceived of as a clever ruse to keep the Skillen brothers at bay had rebounded against them. Their prisoner had been released and they'd been roundly chastised. As they approached the house where Laetitia Somerville lived, they felt hurt and badly misunderstood.

'I still think it was a clever idea of yours, Micah,' said Hale.

'It gave them a fright and taught them we'll stand for no interference.'

'Mr Kirkwood doesn't appreciate us.'

'We must force him to do so, Alfred.'

'And how do we do that?'

'For a start,' said Yeomans, 'we must make the

most of this visit. Leave me to do the talking to Miss Somerville. I have a way with distressed ladies. I know how to calm them. When we leave here, we must have a lot of new evidence to impress the chief magistrate. It's the only way to win back his good opinion of us.'

'But I don't think he ever *had* a good opinion of us.'

'He knows our true value.'

Yeomans pointed at the bell and Hale stepped forward to ring it. When the door opened, a man-servant looked at them enquiringly. Explaining who they were, Yeomans asked to see Miss Somer-ville.

'I'm afraid that won't be possible, sir,' said the man.

'Is the lady not at home?'

'Miss Somerville is here but she's taken to her bed. She's left orders that she wishes to see nobody – nobody at all. Good day to you.'

Before they could stop him, the servant shut the door. Hale was despondent.

'Everything is going wrong for us today.'

Yeomans bit back an expletive. 'We'll be back,' he vowed.

Gully Ackford was delighted that Jem Huckvale had returned to the gallery and greeted him with a warm embrace. He treated Huckvale like a son and had schooled him in all the disciplines that were taught there. Though he looked small and almost puny, Huckvale was a difficult opponent in a boxing ring and several clients preferred to seek tuition from him. Ackford took his young friend away to offer solace after the fright of his arrest. Peter and Paul were left alone. Conscious that Hannah would be in the way, Charlotte had accompanied her back to the house. The brothers were therefore able to talk in private at last. After exchanging their respective news, they discussed their strategy.

'One problem is solved,' said Peter. 'After today's little episode, we needn't fear another raid from the Runners. Gully can take down the barricades.'

'He was relieved to hear that.'

'What will you do next, Paul?'

'I'd like to track down Sir Geoffrey Melrose. As the person who invited Mr Bowerman to a dinner party at which he met Miss Somerville, he'll be able to tell us something valuable about both of them.'

'How will you go about finding him?'

'I have friends in high places,' said Paul.

Peter laughed. 'The only reason you know them is that they frequent *low* places. Your years of wild abandon have finally come in useful, Paul.'

'Half the nobility love to gamble. It may well be that Sir Geoffrey is among them. At all events, I'm certain that one of the acquaintances I made during my time at the gaming tables will be able to tell me how I can get in touch with him.'

'Won't he come forward of his own volition when he hears of Bowerman's death?'

'That depends on whether or not he lives in London, Peter. If he resides in the country, it may be some time before he finally hears the news. And it will not bring him to *our* doors. Sir Geoffrey is more likely to seek out the Runners.'

'There is a simpler way to locate him.'

'Is there?'

'Why not approach Miss Somerville? If he knew her well enough to invite her to a dinner party, Sir Geoffrey will be part of her circle. Ask her for his address.'

'I thought of that but decided against the idea. There's something about Miss Somerville I find slightly disquieting and the annoying thing is that I've no idea what it is. Besides, since she's now in mourning, she may be distressed to hear that we are looking into her past, as it were.'

'That's a valid point.'

'What will you be doing, Peter?'

'I've been thinking about the house where the murder occurred,' said his brother. 'Why was Mr Bowerman lured there and how did the killer know that it would be unoccupied? More to the point, how did he get into the garden in the first place? The house must be rented by an agent. I'll seek him out.'

'I'll be interested in your findings.'

'What I'll be interested in is what the War Office can tell me about Captain Hamer. We mustn't forget him, Paul.'

'He won't *let* us, I promise you.'

'You had your doubts about him and your judgement is always sound.'

'Hamer worries me. At the very time when Mr Bowerman was about to propose marriage to Miss Somerville, he came back into her life. It was almost as if he responded to a cue.'

'There's another reason to distrust the man,' said Peter, taking a letter from his pocket. 'This arrived earlier. It was sent by the man I met at the mortuary.'

'What does it say?'

'The dagger that killed Mr Bowerman *did* belong to Hamer, after all.'

Evening found the two of them at Rawdon Carr's club in Pall Mall. While Carr was relaxed, however, Stephen Hamer was tense and preoccupied. His friend nudged him.

'You haven't touched that excellent glass of port.'

'It must have been someone from my army days,' said Hamer.

'Are you still obsessed with that dagger?'

'Who else would know that I possessed it?'

'*I* did, your servants did and, I daresay, you showed your collection to the occasional visitors. Why look to the army for a culprit?'

'I made enemies, Rawdon.'

'We all do that, sometimes without even knowing it.'

'These enemies bear grudges. I wounded one of them badly in a duel and I seduced another one's mistress. They'd both have cause to strike at me.'

'Then why haven't they done so before now?'

'I don't know.'

'And how would they have been aware that Mr Bowerman even existed? You can discount your former comrades, Stephen. The person we're after, I fancy, is closer to home. Have you had to get rid of any servants recently?'

'I have, as a matter of fact. A man called

Grainger had to be dismissed.'

'What was his offence?'

'He questioned a decision of mine. I had him out of the house in minutes.'

'Then he's a much more promising suspect.'

'Grainger wouldn't *dare* to steal anything from me.'

'He dared to challenge your authority.'

'That's true...'

'And since he lived under your roof,' said Carr, 'he'd know all about your collection of weapons and where to find the key to the room where it's kept. As for information about Bowerman, he could easily have gained that by listening outside a door. We discussed the duel at length.'

Hamer shook his head. 'Grainger was dismissed over a week before we knew that there would *be* a duel. He couldn't possibly have heard of Bowerman, still less planted a dagger in his back. No, it has to be someone else.'

'You've been brooding on it ever since we examined the body.'

'A shot between the eyes would have been a kinder death for him.'

Carr smirked. 'Since when have you discovered the concept of kindness?'

'Someone is trying to implicate me in a murder, Rawdon. I resent it.'

'I don't blame you.'

'I want to use that dagger of mine to slice off his balls and gouge out his–'

'Keep your voice down,' said Carr, cutting in. 'I don't need to know the gory details. The first step is to identify the man and any confederates who may have been involved. I was hoping we might learn something useful by calling at Bowerman's house earlier on but the visit was fruitless. All that the butler could tell us was where the murder took place.'

'He told us something else as well.'

'Did he?'

'Yes – Paul Skillen had been there.'

'He's an enterprising young man. We must be equally enterprising.'

'You said that we ought to divert his attention.'

'The matter is in hand. Shall I tell you what I've done?'

Smiling complacently, Carr drained his glass in one satisfying gulp.

There were two of them. It was well after midnight when they arrived. Each of them carried a sledgehammer. While one man attacked the front door of the shooting gallery, the other pounded away at the rear entrance to the premises. The locks soon burst apart. The men were not done yet. Each had brought a snarling dog on a thick leash. The animals were released into the gallery and went racing around the building, barking madly and searching for prey. There was pandemonium.

Huckvale was awakened by the first hammer blow. The second violent thud made him leap out of bed and rush to open the window but he could see nothing down below in the darkness. Grabbing one of the swords he used for instruction, he came out on to the landing with the intention of descending the stairs to see what was causing the noise. The baying of the dogs and the sound of their paws on the wooden steps changed his mind instantly and he retreated to the safety of his bedroom, slamming the door behind him and bemused by what was happening.

Ackford, by contrast, assessed the situation quickly. They were under attack. Roused from his slumber, he took down the loaded musket that hung on his wall and left his room purposefully. Though he could only see blurred outlines of the animals, he knew that they had to be destroyed before they could sink their jaws into him. He shot the first one dead then used the stock of the weapon to knock the other one unconscious. Sword in hand, Huckvale emerged from his room to see the two carcases on the floor.

'Where did they come from?' he asked.

'Fetch a lantern. We'll have to make some repairs.'

'Someone must have knocked down the door.'

'Arm yourself with a pistol. It may be needed.'

When the lantern was alight, they went downstairs and examined the damage. Outside both broken doors was a dog leash. Once he was certain there was no danger, Ackford put his musket aside.

'Take the horse and ride to Peter's house.'

'He'll be fast asleep, Gully.'

'So were we until a few minutes ago. Peter needs to be told. He's used to being woken up at all hours.'

'What about Paul? Shall I rouse him as well?'

'My guess is that he's still awake. With a woman like Hannah beside me, I know that I would be.

Paul can wait until morning. His brother is the one we need.'

Paul and Hannah were, in fact, still wide awake and had not even retired to bed. They had spent hours discussing a plea from Lemuel Fleet when he'd called at the house for the second time. The manager had implored Hannah to attend a rehearsal the following day, assuring her that the playwright would not be present so they could talk openly about the defects in his play. He stressed that there were other people in the company and that their views ought to be taken into account.

'I'm not going,' said Hannah, reaching her decision.

'I believe that you should.'

'You don't have to act in that dreadful play.'

'If I was contracted to do so,' said Paul, 'then I'd honour that contract.'

'Don't talk to me about honour,' she cried.

'You have a legal obligation, Hannah.'

'Where in the contract does it oblige me to speak atrocious lines and sing appalling ditties? *The Piccadilly Opera* is beneath me. I was beguiled into agreeing to act in it. Mr Fleet misled me completely.'

'The manager is a reasonable fellow. Discuss changes with him.'

'I demand to change the whole play.'

'That's no basis for a proper discussion.'

'Do you *want* me to be pilloried?' she howled, jumping to her feet. 'Are you pleased at the thought that I'll be jeered until the audience flees the theatre in disgust? Have you no pity on me?'

'I have the greatest pity,' said Paul, enfolding her in his arms, 'but I also have faith in your powers as an actress. You can make the most banal lines sound like the work of a Marlowe or a Shakespeare. And when you sing, the silliest of ditties become arias from Handel. There's no risk whatsoever of derision, Hannah. You sprinkle magic on every play in which you appear.'

Hannah was sufficiently mollified to let him kiss her. She even agreed to sit down again. The manager's second visit had given her food for thought. She had no quarrel with Fleet himself and every reason to deal kindly with a man who'd given her so much help and support. Hannah felt sorry that she'd sent him off twice with a flea in his ear. He deserved better. At the same time, however, she resolved that she was not going to appear in what she considered to be a threadbare play written by an egregious playwright. Simply by letting her pour out her heart, Paul had been helpful. Hannah saw that it was unkind of her to keep him up any longer.

'Let's go to bed,' she suggested.

'I'm not sharing it with a third person,' he warned.

'What do you mean?'

'When I get between the sheets, I don't want to find that you've invited Abel Mundy to join us. Leave him downstairs, Hannah. We've talked about him enough. I'm not going to let him come between us. Is that agreed?'

She kissed him full on the lips. Paul had his answer.

Peter Skillen did not mind in the least that he'd been pulled from his bed in the dead of night. If there was a crisis at the gallery, he wanted to be there. After saddling his horse, he galloped off with Huckvale trying to keep up with him. By the time they got to their destination, Ackford had tied up the unconscious dog and already repaired the broken doors. They could offer stiffer resistance if attacked by a sledgehammer now. As a precaution, Ackford had also reloaded his musket and kept it within reach. Having heard Huckvale's account of what happened, Peter heard a more measured description of events from Ackford.

'Who was responsible for the attack?' asked Peter.

'Jem has a theory,' said the older man.

'Yes, I know. He thinks that the Runners are to blame.'

'It's their revenge,' argued Huckvale. 'They were livid that I couldn't even be held in custody for a while. I wouldn't be at all surprised if Yeomans and Hale were swinging those sledgehammers.'

'I would,' said Peter. 'They'd never stoop to anything like this.'

'I disagree.'

'Peter is right,' said Ackford. 'The Runners might ruffle our feathers but they'd stop well short of launching an assault on the gallery. It was lucky that I had my old Brown Bess musket when I met those dogs. It's the one I first fired at the Battle of Yorktown when I was a raw recruit in the British army and it probably saved my life. If I hadn't dealt with those ravening curs, they'd have torn me to bits. This is not simply a matter of damage to property. It was a case of attempted murder. Yeomans and Hale would never condone that.'

'So who would?' asked Huckvale.

'I wish I knew, Jem.'

'Is it someone we helped to put in gaol? Did one of them ask their friends to attack us out of spite? Is that what happened?'

'It's possible,' said Ackford, pensively.

'It's more than possible, Gully.'

'What's your opinion, Peter?'

'It *could* be connected to some villain we put behind bars,' conceded Peter. 'Most of them threaten to get even with us one day. But I incline to the view that that's not the case here. The key lies in the timing.'

'That's why I thought it was the Runners,' said Huckvale. 'They boasted about making our lives more difficult – and then *this* happens.'

'Something else has happened, Jem. A blameless man was stabbed to death because he had the misfortune to fall in love with a beautiful woman. She already had an admirer and he's the person we should start looking at.'

'Captain Hamer?'

'He resents the fact that Paul is investigating the murder. My brother had a frosty reception when he called on the man. The one thing Hamer knows about Paul is that he works here at the gallery and taught Mr Bowerman how to fire a pistol. It's a natural assumption on Hamer's part that my brother also lives here. I think that tonight's ugly business was a warning. It was telling my brother to stop trying to find Mr Bowerman's killer.'

'Nobody can stop Paul from doing what he

thinks is right,' said Ackford. 'As for frightening him off, the attack will only make him more determined to press on. And the same goes for the rest of us.'

'Perhaps I should have brought Paul here as well,' said Huckvale.

'I told you it was unnecessary.'

'Let him have his sleep, Jem,' said Peter. 'I'll speak to my brother first thing.'

'He'll be very angry. He doesn't have your self-control, Peter. When he hears what happened here, he'll fly into action.'

'My feeling is that Paul will reach exactly the same conclusion as me. Captain Hamer is behind this attack. The burning question is this: how do we respond?'

After a night of heavy drinking at Carr's club, Stephen Hamer had reeled home and been put to bed by the servants. He lapsed into a deep sleep and might well have stayed in bed for hours had he not heard – or thought he'd heard – a persistent whining outside the front door of the house. As he occupied the front bedroom, he was closest to the noise. Hamer tried to ignore it but it was impossible. There was a note of pain and pleading that eventually forced him to investigate. Pulling himself out of bed, he padded across the room and drew back the curtain. It was sometime after dawn and there was enough light for him to see clearly. What he saw directly below the window made him gasp.

Two dogs were on the ground. One was so motionless that it looked dead. The other had his legs tied together and wore a muzzle that restricted him to the piteous whine. Hamer remembered something that Rawdon Carr had boasted about the previous evening. It had involved two dogs.

Stomach heaving, he began to retch.

CHAPTER NINE

Leonard Impey always arrived early at the bank in the morning so that he could supervise its opening. Because he was anticipating the return of Hester Mallory, he turned up with a decided spring in his step. They'd had a most satisfying discussion on the previous day and he felt that he'd convinced her to do business with his bank. He had not relied entirely on the letter of introduction she'd brought from a friend. As with every new client, he'd asked a series of searching questions. All of them had been answered in a way that reassured him. He felt that it would be a pleasure to serve Mrs Mallory and tried to think of ways that would prolong her visit to his office. As each of his employees arrived, he took the opportunity to step outside the building and look up and down the street, even though the bank would not actually be open for almost an hour. His behaviour did not escape the notice of the others and they traded sly giggles. All of them had seen the woman when she'd first arrived and been struck both by her evident charm and by its effect on the manager.

When the last member of his staff came in, Impey seized the chance to slip once more out of the bank. The chief clerk appeared at his shoulder.

'Are you looking for someone, sir?' he asked.

'No, no,' replied the other. 'I just wanted some fresh air.'

'Does that mean you're not feeling well, Mr Impey?'

'I feel perfectly well.'

'I'm glad to hear it, sir. Do you have any specific orders for me today?'

'As a matter of fact, I do,' said Impey. 'You saw Mrs Mallory visit us yesterday. If she's decided to do business with us, she could be an important client. When she returns, have her shown into my office immediately.'

Paul Skillen had been horrified to hear of the attack on the gallery and, as his brother predicted, he singled out Stephen Hamer as the likely culprit. It was his idea to leave the two dogs outside the man's front door, giving him a shock and letting him know that he'd been identified as the culprit. When Peter called on him for the second time that day, his brother's fury had not subsided.

'We should have smashed down the doors of *his* house and let in a whole pack of wild dogs,' said Paul, vehemently. 'Gully and Jem might have been seriously hurt.'

'Luckily, they weren't.'

'We have to fight back somehow, Peter.'

'We did that when we left the dogs outside his home.'

'It's not enough. I'll go and confront him this morning.'

'You've a more pressing duty before you do that,' said his brother. 'Thanks to one of your acquaintances from that gambling hell you once patronised, you know where Sir Geoffrey Melrose may be found. Unfortunately, he's not here in London at the moment. Ride out to his estate and pass on the bad tidings about Mr Bowerman. It's likely that he's unaware of the murder. His reaction to the news will be interesting.'

'He'll be upset. He was a friend of Mr Bowerman.'

'We need to know the nature of that friendship.'

'Very well,' said Paul, 'but we mustn't let Hamer off the hook.'

'I couldn't agree more.'

'I'll call on him at once.'

'No, Paul, I can do that. While you visit Sir Geoffrey, I'll go to Hamer's house and take him to task for what occurred last night. As it happens, I have another reason for meeting the fellow.'

'Have you?'

'Yes,' said Peter, 'someone brought a letter from the Home Secretary earlier this morning. It contained the reply that he got from the War Office.'

'What did it say about Captain Hamer?'

'See for yourself.'

Taking a letter from his pocket, he passed it to Paul. He was amused to see his brother's eyes widen in amazement as he read the contents.

'I was as surprised as you are,' said Peter.

'I suppose that I shouldn't have been. This is typical of Hamer. I'd love to see his face when

114

you wave this under his nose. It will take the swagger out of him.' After finishing the letter, he handed it back. 'Watch out for that friend of his, Rawdon Carr. He's the oily devil who acted as second at the duel and tried to make Mr Bowerman tender an apology in exchange for his life. Carr is one of Hamer's hangers-on.'

'I'll give the two of them your regards, Paul.'

'I'll still want to meet them face-to-face.'

'You can do that when you've spoken to Sir Geoffrey. Find out if he was deliberately playing the matchmaker when he invited Mr Bowerman and Miss Somerville to dinner.'

'I'll also ask him why he thought that two such different people would ever be attracted to each other.'

'There's no accounting for taste, Paul.'

'I learnt that when I first met Hannah. She seemed hopelessly beyond my reach. I was ensnared at once but it never crossed my mind for a second that I'd have the slightest appeal for someone like her. Miraculously, I did somehow.'

'I still can't understand it,' teased Peter. 'Being serious, there's something I must ask on Charlotte's behalf. She spent a fair amount of time yesterday listening to Hannah's woes about this play she's acting in. Charlotte wants to know if any decision has been made.'

Paul rolled his eyes. 'Thankfully, it has.'

'Has she pulled out?'

'No, she eventually agreed to attend a rehearsal this morning. It took me hours to persuade her to do that. The theatre is her lifeblood. When she meets the other actors again, she'll be among friends. It might help to soften her stance against Abel Mundy.'

'Is he really the fiend she describes?'

'Hannah calls him the Prince of Darkness.'

The rehearsal got off to a promising start. The moment that Hannah entered, the rest of the cast rose to their feet and gave her a spontaneous round of applause. She was touched and even permitted a few welcoming kisses on her cheek. Simply being back in the theatre was a tonic for her. It brought her fully alive. Lemuel Fleet was at her elbow immediately, thanking her profusely and promising her that alterations and additions would be made to *The Piccadilly Opera*.

'There *are* parts of the play that will pass muster,' he said.

She arched an eyebrow. 'I've never seen any of them.'

'You look upon it with a jaundiced eye, Miss Granville.'

'Not to mention a queasy stomach,' she added, raising a laugh from the others. 'But you may be right, Mr Fleet. Perhaps I am being too critical. No play is entirely beyond redemption. All that this one needs is a change of title, a change of plot, a new cast of characters and, above all else, a skilful playwright.'

'Mr Mundy may yet rise to that level.'

'He has a desperately long way to go.'

Fleet changed his tack. 'Let us at least rehearse the first scene.'

'It's too flat and leaden,' she claimed.

'That's why I've decided to open with a fanfare.

It will secure the attention of the audience and prepare them for your entrance. There are several other points in the text where I've introduced additional music.'

'Will there be songs worth singing?'

'We will lose those in the play and replace them with ones that will meet your approval. I want more jollity and sprightliness in the performance. Do you hear that, everyone?' he went on, raising his voice. 'Let a sense of enjoyment fill the theatre.'

'It's to be a real comedy, then,' she observed. 'That will be an improvement.'

There was general agreement. Unlike Hannah, most of the cast were not in constant demand so they had to suppress any mutinous feelings about a play. If any of them were singled out as being in any way rebellious, they would be viewed askance by theatre managements. Forced to hold their tongues, they were delighted to have a mouth-piece in Hannah. She was able to point out the many shortcomings of the play that they'd all discerned. It turned her into their heroine.

The rehearsal began and there was a new feeling of optimism. Scenes that had hitherto been limp and tedious now became brighter and more entertaining. There was a laughter that had never existed before. In spite of her objections, Hannah found herself relishing the experience of being back onstage again. The new songs she was given to sing made her even happier. All of the changes enhanced the play beyond measure. There were moments when she actually forgot how much she hated *The Piccadilly Opera*. The amended version made it almost presentable.

117

The euphoria could not last. Without warning, the joyful mood was shattered. Unbeknownst to anyone, Abel Mundy had walked in. Transfixed by what he saw, it took him minutes to find his voice. He used it to emit a high-pitched scream of rage.

'Stop, stop, stop!' he demanded. 'What are you doing to my play?'

'We've made a few slight changes,' said Fleet, 'that's all, Mr Mundy.'

'You've savaged my work.'

'It's what it required,' said Hannah, boldly. 'We put some life into it.'

'This is all your doing, Miss Granville,' said the playwright. 'I write a serious drama and you turn it into an inconsequential little squib. You could never reach the heights that my work demands.'

'Now, now,' said Fleet, jumping in before Hannah could reply. 'Let's keep the debate on a friendly level. Hot words leave bad feelings in their wake.'

'So do incompetent plays like this one,' murmured Hannah.

'I'll brook no insults,' howled Mundy.

'Then you'll best leave while you may, sir, or I'll tell you what I really think of this dull, dreary, lifeless piece of theatrical mediocrity that dares to call itself a play.'

'This is insufferable!'

'The door is behind you, Mr Mundy.'

'There'll be repercussions from this.'

'Yes, we'll finally have something worth performing.'

'That's enough!' yelled Fleet, removing his wig

and throwing it to the floor. 'This is disgraceful behaviour. Differences of opinion should be settled in private. A true compromise can only be reached if there is moderation on both sides.'

'Look for no moderation from me,' said Hannah, pointing at Mundy. 'I only have to see that hideous visage and I begin to feel sick. Look at him, everyone! What you see before you is the death's head of British drama!'

It was her last jibe and it struck home. Before she could add even more abuse, the quivering playwright swung round and ran out as if something had just set fire to his coat-tails. There was an ominous silence.

Fleet retrieved his wig. 'The rehearsal is over,' he growled.

In response to the summons, Rawdon Carr rode quickly to his friend's house. The first thing he saw on arrival was the gardener, loading a dead dog into a barrow before wheeling it around to the rear of the property. A servant came out to take care of his mount. Carr went into the house and found Hamer in the dining room, seated at the table with a half-empty decanter of claret in front of him.

'I've just seen someone wheeling a dead dog into your garden,' said Carr.

'He's going to bury it.'

'Whose animal was it?'

'Yours, Rawdon.'

'Don't be absurd!'

'You hired those two men to release dogs into that shooting gallery. What you just saw was one of the animals. I had the other put down as well.

Its whining was giving me a headache.'

'I'm not sure that I follow you, Stephen.'

'He *knows*.'

'Who are you talking about?'

'Skillen knows that we were responsible for last night's attack.'

'But that's impossible.'

'Is it?' asked Hamer. 'Then perhaps you'll explain how the two dogs were dumped outside my front door, one of them shot dead and the other trussed up. They were left there by Paul Skillen. The message was unmistakable.'

'I see,' said Carr, wincing. 'That is unfortunate, I grant you. My intention was to give him such a fright that he'd stop getting in our way.'

'He's much more *likely* to get in our way now, Rawdon.'

'That's not necessarily the case. Besides, Skillen has no proof whatsoever that we were in any way involved. If he challenges us, we simply swear that we had no part in the business.'

'What if the men you hired were caught?'

'They weren't, I assure you. I paid half their fee in advance so that I'd have confirmation that the job was done before they had their money in full. They said that it all went as planned.'

'Finding two dogs outside my house this morning was not part of the plan,' said Hamer, sourly. 'The sight of them almost made me puke.'

'I'm sorry about that.'

'Now you can see why I sent for you.'

'I can, Stephen, but we have nothing to worry about. Skillen has made a wild guess that we arranged that attack. We simply deny the allegation.

I'll say that we spent most of the night at my club before rolling back to my house. The notion of setting a pair of dogs on him would never occur to us.'

'It occurred to *you*, Rawdon.'

'They'll never know that.'

Carr took the wine glass proffered by a servant. He poured himself a generous amount from the decanter then had a first sip of it. Hamer remained anxious.

'Cheer up, man!' said Carr, patting his shoulder. 'Brace yourself. You've faced enemy soldiers in battle. Why are you so upset by a couple of mangy dogs?'

'How would *you* like to see them outside your front door?'

'Frankly, I wouldn't.'

'We've been found out,' stressed Hamer. 'That could be awkward.'

When the doorbell rang, he sat up with a start. Carr was unperturbed.

'It's probably not him, Stephen. It's just a tradesman calling.'

'Then why has he come to the *front* door?'

'Stay calm. There's no need for concern.'

'I sincerely hope that you're right.'

They drank their wine and Hamer relaxed slightly. Moments later, there was a tap on the door and it swung open to reveal a servant.

'A Mr Skillen is asking to see you, sir.'

'Tell him I'm not at home,' said Hamer, tensing.

'No, don't do that,' advised Carr. 'That will only strengthen his suspicions. Let's face him together and send him packing.' After thinking it over,

121

Hamer gave an affirmative nod. Carr took over. 'Show the gentleman in.'

The servants withdrew and Carr moved to stand behind his friend. It was a matter of seconds before Peter was escorted into the room. When the servant left this time, he closed the door behind him. Peter looked from one to the other.

'You are Mr Carr, I presume,' he said, directing the question at him.

'Heavens!' exclaimed the other, 'you have a very short memory, Mr Skillen. We shook hands on Putney Heath but two days ago.'

'You are mistaken, sir.'

'Have you taken leave of your senses?'

'They are in excellent condition, Mr Carr. Let me introduce myself properly. My name is *Peter* Skillen. The person who acted as Mr Bowerman's second was my brother, Paul.'

'Your *twin* brother, I see,' said Hamer, staring at him.

'I'm here in Paul's stead.'

'Then you must meet Captain Hamer,' said Carr, indicating his friend.

Peter pretended to look around. 'I see nobody of that name in this room.'

'He sits before you.'

'That's not *Captain* Hamer,' said Peter, levelly. 'It's Lieutenant Hamer.'

'Confound you, man!' cried Hamer, getting to his feet. 'I'll have you know that I was a captain in the Royal Horse Guards. The Blues are one of the finest regiments in the whole world. We fought at Waterloo.'

'Your regiment distinguished itself at Waterloo

and it has my admiration and gratitude for doing so. But you were no longer a member of the regiment at that point in time, were you, Lieutenant?'

'*Captain* Hamer, if you please.'

'Show my friend due respect,' insisted Carr.

'He doesn't deserve it. As you well know, Lieutenant Hamer was court-martialled for conduct unbecoming an officer. He was drummed out of the regiment before it got anywhere near Waterloo.'

'Where the devil have you got these disgraceful lies?' demanded Hamer.

'They came to me via the Home Secretary,' said Peter, easily. 'As a favour to me, he made contact with the War Office and enquired about your military career, such as it was. In claiming to have been a captain, you're acting fraudulently.'

'We don't have to endure this nonsense,' said Carr. 'Be off with you, sir.'

He moved forward to touch Peter but saw the look in his eye and pulled back.

'I'm staying until I've said my piece,' asserted Peter. 'My first question is this. Posing as a captain, you fought a duel ostensibly for the hand of Miss Somerville. Is the lady aware of the deception you practised?'

'Mind your own business,' snarled Hamer.

'Is the regiment itself aware of what you've been doing in its name?'

'Don't answer that,' counselled Carr. 'He's trying to goad you.'

'The former Lieutenant Hamer doesn't need any goading, if you ask me,' said Peter. 'He's almost straining at the leash. On the subject of leashes,' he continued, 'what's happened to the two dogs we left outside your front door?'

'They've been buried,' grunted Hamer.

'But one of them was still alive.'

'He was shot.'

'That's poor reward for what he did at your behest. He and his companion ran all over the gallery. If it hadn't been for the quick thinking of my friends, someone could have been seriously injured, perhaps even killed.' He leant forward. 'Being guilty of attempted murder is far worse than conduct unbecoming an officer.'

'Get out!'

'Or was it *you* who hired those men to batter down the doors?' asked Peter, turning on Carr. 'Your friend gives the orders and you run the errands.'

'Be quiet!' yelled Carr, shaking with righteous indignation. 'You know nothing about us. We were not party to any attack on the shooting gallery. If you want the real culprits, look elsewhere.'

'I don't need to,' said Peter, coolly. 'They stand before me.' He turned to Hamer. 'My brother learnt something very interesting yesterday. The dagger that killed Mr Bowerman belonged to you. Is that true?'

'It might be,' admitted the other, 'but I never put it there.'

'We're resolved to find out who did use it,' declared Carr, 'no matter how long it takes us.' After taking a deep breath, he resorted to an attempt at charm, smiling warmly and speaking softly. 'Come, sir, we should not be enemies. We want the same thing as you and your brother and that's to catch the killer. That is where our energies are directed. Someone stole that dagger from here in order to embarrass the captain ... my good friend, Stephen Hamer, that is. We should be combining resources and working together. The Runners will never find the villain in a month of Sundays. It therefore falls to us to do so.'

'Then you must work on your own,' said Peter, with biting contempt. 'We don't make common cause with a blatant liar like former Lieutenant Hamer and his pet monkey.'

'I'm nobody's monkey!' cried Carr.

'I speak as I find, sir.'

'Take care, Mr Skillen, I warn you.'

'How many dogs do you intend to set on the gallery next time?'

'We haven't a clue what you're talking about,' said Hamer, dismissively, 'so we'll thank you to stop making unsubstantiated allegations.'

'I endorse what the captain says,' added Carr.

'Except that he never attained that rank,' Peter reminded him. 'Since you've issued a warning to us, I'll reply with one of our own. My brother and I will carry out an independent investigation and, if you try to hamper us in any way, Paul and I will come looking for you. Is that plain enough for you, gentlemen?'

He had the satisfaction of seeing both men shift their feet uneasily.

When a couple of hours had passed, Impey began to give up hope that she would come. Though Mrs Mallory had expressed a desire to transact business with his bank, she admitted that she intended

125

to speak to other banks before she committed herself. Impey came to suspect that she'd been offered a more cordial welcome or better terms elsewhere and reproached himself for not impressing her the previous day with his eagerness to serve her. Another hour dragged by and he accepted defeat. Then, out of the blue, she turned up with her chaperone and was shown in by the chief clerk. Impey was on his feet at once, holding the chair until she sat in it and pouring out a veritable flood of niceties. Having sent the clerk out, he enjoyed once more the frisson of pleasure at being so close to Hester Mallory.

'I thought you had deserted us,' he said, hands fluttering.

'Not at all, Mr Impey – I had other bank managers to visit, that is all.'

'Yet you've come back to us.'

'Nobody was able to accommodate me with the same readiness as you.'

'Any friend of Jacob Picton's will get preferential treatment here. Now,' he continued, sitting behind his desk, 'you said that you were in need of money to engage the artist who is about to paint your portrait.'

'That's true and, of course, I will need expenses while I'm here in London.'

'What is the total amount that you require, Mrs Mallory?'

'I feel that a thousand pounds will cover all eventualities.'

'I can authorise a loan at a very reasonable rate of interest.'

'Your trust in me is heartening, sir, but I'd like to

126

offer additional proof that I am a bona fide client. As well as the letter from Mr Picton,' she said, taking a document from her bag, 'I have a bond for £2500, in Mr Picton's name, to offer as security for the loan.' She got up to pass it to him. 'The important thing is that my husband must know nothing of the portrait I intend to give him as a birthday gift. When he receives it, of course, he will be overjoyed and will reimburse Mr Picton without delay. I am sorry that a certain amount of deceit is involved but Mr Mallory deserves a complete surprise. He has been the dearest of husbands.'

'As well as the most fortunate,' said Impey, venturing a compliment.

She smiled. 'Thank you, kind sir.'

'I can see that you and Mr Picton have been co-conspirators.'

'None of this would have been possible without his assistance and advice.' She stood up. 'But you'll need time to study the bond before you advance any funds. I'll come back this afternoon.'

'No, no,' he said, 'there's no need for that. Give me a moment to examine it then I will open the safe myself and take out the specified amount. My only concern is that you should be leaving here with such a large amount of money. This is a very dangerous city, Mrs Mallory.'

'I have a carriage waiting outside.'

'That's very sensible of you.'

'We are all too aware of possible jeopardy,' she said. 'It's the reason my husband will never allow me to travel with money or with jewellery. Highwaymen will have no rich pickings from me. All I brought of real value was the bond and that is useless to any gentlemen of the road.'

'You and Mr Mallory have behaved very sensibly.'

'We always look ahead. It is an article of faith with us.'

Charlotte Skillen had been alarmed when they'd been roused from their beds with the information that the gallery had been attacked. Peter had gone to inspect the damage and returned to tell her that everything was now under control. Nevertheless, it was only when she went there later that morning that she was persuaded the building now had stouter defences. Ackford had mended the doors and Huckvale fixed large brackets to the jambs so that he could slot in some thick planks of wood.

'We've done everything but install a portcullis,' he said.

'You've done well, Jem,' said Charlotte. 'It must have given you a terrible shock, having two large dogs running up the stairs to attack you.'

'It did. They sounded as if they wanted to eat us alive.'

'This is very upsetting. First, we have the Runners bursting in and arresting you. Then we have last night's attack. What next?'

'Whatever it is,' promised Ackford, 'we'll be ready for it.'

'And where will the trouble come from?'

'It won't be from the Runners, I'll wager.'

'Gully is right,' said Huckvale. 'In raiding the gallery, they went too far. They'll have been given a stern reprimand by the chief magistrate. Chevy

Ruddock may get more than a rebuke.'

'So I should hope, Jem.'

'Peter is still certain that Captain Hamer insti-gated last night's assault. That's why he and Paul took those dogs to his house. Oh,' she went on, 'I shouldn't be calling him a captain any more. The Home Secretary had word from the War Office and passed it on. It turns out that Hamer never rose to the rank of captain and he was dismissed from the regiment after a court martial.'

'That tells us a lot about his character.'

'If he's a disgraced soldier,' said Huckvale, 'he could have been Mr Bowerman's killer, after all.'

'I doubt that, Jem.'

'Why?'

'It looks as if he's joined the hunt for the killer. That's what prompted last night's crisis. Hamer wants Peter and Paul out of the way so that he can have a clear field. If he solves the crime, he can claim the reward. Bills have been printed and posted up everywhere. Whoever catches the assassin stands to make a lot of money.'

'We can use it to repair the gallery properly,' said Charlotte. 'Peter and Paul have set their minds on apprehending the man who murdered Mr Bowerman.'

'Hamer is going to have serious competition.'

'It won't only come from Peter and Paul,' Huck-vale pointed out. 'You're forgetting the Runners.'

'They're too slow.'

'They do solve *some* crimes. Give them credit for that.'

'I will,' said Ackford, 'though some of their so-called successes come about because of all the informers they retain, most of them seasoned rogues. No, Micah Yeomans will do his best but he'll always be trying to catch up with Peter and Paul. Hamer is the problem. We can ignore the Runners.'

Having been turned away the previous day, Yeomans and Hale called at the house again that morning. Given the same message that Miss Somerville was not to be disturbed, they camped on her doorstep and vowed to wait there until she was ready to admit them. It was noon when Laetitia finally relented and had them shown in. Removing their hats, they entered the house respectfully. Wearing a black velvet dress and an expression of deep sadness, she was seated on the edge of a sofa. Yeomans introduced himself and his companion. Her only response was a slight movement of her head. Hale felt that they were intruding on her grief.

'Perhaps we should come back another time,' he whispered.

'We've waited long enough already,' said Yeomans.

'Miss Somerville may not be in a fit state to answer questions.'

'She's as eager as we are to see this murder solved.' He took a step towards her. 'Isn't that true?'

'Yes, it is,' said Laetitia. 'I want to see Mr Bowerman's killer hanged.'

'We'll find him for you,' said Yeomans.

'Thank you.'

'But we'll do so much quicker if we have a little

130

help from you.'

'How can I possibly be of assistance?'

'You knew the gentleman – we did not.'

'That's true.'

'What manner of man was he, Miss Somerville?'

'He was the most wonderful friend I've ever had,' she said, dabbing at a tear with her handkerchief. 'I've lost a rare jewel among men in Mr Bowerman. He changed my life when he came into it. How I shall manage without him,' she added, voice cracking, 'I simply don't know.'

'You have our sympathy.'

'Yes,' said Hale, 'we're sorry to bother you in your bereavement.'

'It is, however, necessary,' said Yeomans. 'Tell us a little more about Mr Bowerman. Take your time and go at your own pace. There's no hurry,' He took out a notebook. 'When and where did you first meet? How close were you and he? How did you feel when Captain Hamer turned up as if he had a claim on your affections?'

After waving them to some chairs, Laetitia spoke slowly and with great emotion. She talked about the fateful dinner party at which she'd first encountered Bowerman and how there'd been an immediate affinity between them. The courtship, she hinted, had been gentle and unforced. At no point was there any threat to their happiness. She admitted to being startled by the sudden reappearance of Stephen Hamer and insisted that she no longer considered him to be a friend, still less a suitor. When Yeomans asked her if Hamer should be viewed as a suspect, she shook her head

131

firmly. She had no doubt whatsoever of his innocence.

'Do you have any idea who did murder Mr Bowerman?'

'No, I don't, Mr Yeomans.'

'Did he ever talk about his enemies?'

'How could he when he had none? Nobody could dislike Mark ... Mr Bowerman, I should say. He was such a thoroughly decent man in every way.'

'We've known other thoroughly decent men who've been murdered,' said Hale, darkly. 'On closer examination, they turn out to be less angelic than they're painted.'

'That's clearly not the situation here,' said Yeomans, nudging him into silence. 'If he had no enemies, we must search for a motive other than simple hatred. One look at you, Miss Somerville, and a motive suggests itself at once. Someone coveted you so much that he could not bear the thought of a rival.'

'Mr Bowerman had no rival,' she declared. 'I discouraged all other attentions offered to me. There is no jealous lover.'

'What about Captain Hamer?'

'He belonged to my past.'

'You might say that. He believed otherwise.'

'I left him in no doubt about my feelings,' she said with a touch of irritation. 'Of one thing you may be absolutely certain, Mr Yeomans. It is quite *impossible* for me even to consider a closer union with Captain Hamer.'

CHAPTER TEN

Paul Skillen had always scorned danger. Whatever circumstances arose, he never considered risk. He preferred to plunge straight in and get the best out of an experience. It was the same when he went on a journey. Travel outside London exposed everyone to untold hazards and – on the basis that there was safety in numbers – most people chose to ride by coach or be in convoy with others. True to character, Paul went alone even though the journey to Eltham took him through open countryside at several points. Were he to encounter trouble, he was relying on his skill with sword and pistol to carry him through. As he set off, the steady, unvarying canter of his horse gave him a feeling of invincibility.

On his way to the country residence of Sir Geoffrey Melrose, he was able to enjoy the changing landscape around him and let his mind play with the possibilities surrounding the murder. Were they in search of one man or a gang? Who was capable of forging a message from Laetitia Somerville so cleverly that it achieved its object? Having pored over her letters for hours like the devoted suitor he was, Mark Bowerman would have known every detail of her calligraphy. Yet he'd somehow been deceived. Paul was convinced that the letter was the work of a woman, someone who was familiar with Laetitia's hand. The forger, he concluded, either had to be someone in her circle or someone who had been close to her but was now estranged. He needed to speak to Laetitia again.

What had the killer gained from the murder? That's what puzzled him. Significantly, no money was stolen from the victim and Paul could still not see what had been gained by his death. In the course of their time together, he'd got to know Bowerman well. The man was honest, well educated, invariably pleasant and, by nature, remarkably inoffensive. Nothing about him invited dislike, let alone hatred. It was ironic that, having taken part in a duel where he could easily have been shot dead in the chest, he was instead stabbed in the back during what he believed to be a rendezvous with the woman he intended to marry. Why had that particular house been chosen and who selected the garden as the murder scene?

One possible explanation surfaced: Bowerman had not been the prime target at all. The killer was really intent on hurting Laetitia Somerville and the best way to do that was to snuff out her hopes of marriage. Her new suitor was seen as dispensable. He had to die in order that she would suffer or, in time, be available for the killer himself. It might be that Bowerman had no enemies but she certainly did. Laetitia had told him that beauty could be a curse at times. Many men must have sought her hand or lusted after her body. Was one of them ready to commit murder in order to remove an obstacle?

Having stopped at a village inn to take refreshment and rest his mount, Paul climbed into the saddle again. It was not long before he returned to his meditation. Preoccupied as he might be, however, he was still alert to danger. When he came over a hill and saw a copse ahead of him, he noticed a beggar sitting beside the road with his back against a tree. Though the man seemed to be alone, Paul sensed that he might have an accomplice or two. Vigilance was paramount. As he got closer, therefore, he studied the man and looked at the branches of the tree beneath which he sat. There was a moment when the beggar adjusted his position and glanced upwards. Paul was quick to interpret the situation. They – at least two of them – were waiting for a lone and unwary traveller. Giving no indication that he suspected a trap, he kept his horse going at the same pace.

The beggar rose to his feet and stood in the road. He cupped his hands to plead for money. Slowing to a trot, Paul pretended that he was going to stop. He knew what was coming next. The beggar would grab the bridle and the man in the tree would drop down on Paul. In the event, they were out of luck. When the beggar tried to stop the horse, Paul kicked him so hard under the chin that he broke the man's jaw. Before the accomplice could leap down from the tree, he was shot in the arm. Paul then used the butt of his pistol to knock down a third man who came running out of the copse. Kicking his mount into a canter, Paul went on his way, leaving the robbers to lick their wounds and rue their misfortune.

'All I require is the name.'

'I'm sorry, Mr Skillen, but I'm unable to help you.'

'Is it a state secret?'

'All details of our property are confidential.'

'That garden was the scene of a murder,' said Peter, angrily. 'Doesn't that make a difference?'

'No, sir, it doesn't. We have our rules. I'd lose my position if I broke them.'

'Can't you see how *important* this information is?'

'We must protect the anonymity of our clients.'

Peter had to control the urge to strike the man. They were in the office of the agent responsible for letting the house but he refused to say who actually owned it. He was a tall, lean, sallow man in his forties with a face so nondescript that Peter would never remember a single feature of it when he left the building. The agent's manner shifted annoyingly between condescension and unctuousness. Expecting cooperation, Peter was frustrated by the man's attitude.

'Supposing that you owned the property, sir,' said the agent.

'I don't understand.'

'How would *you* like it if we released your name and address to anyone who walked in here and asked for it? Most of our clients use this agency because we have a reputation for keeping secrets. Wouldn't you be offended if we betrayed you?'

'The only thing that offends me is your attitude.'

'I can't help that, sir.'

'If I obtained a warrant, you'd have to surrender the details.'

'Do you have such a warrant?'

'At the moment, I don't.'

'Then you have no legal right to inspect our files.'

'I simply want one name.'

'It makes no difference.'

Peter looked around the room. It was neat, tidy and purely functional. Beside the large, long table were a series of locked cabinets. Inside one of them, he thought, was the information he needed. He looked at the window. It was small in size but a man could still squeeze in through it. There were two locks on the door and a grille that could be pulled down outside it. The agency was well protected.

'Is there anything else I can do for you, sir?' asked the man, rubbing his palms together as if trying to warm them. 'Are you interested in renting a property?'

'Yes,' said Peter, 'as a matter of fact, I am.'

'Which part of London do you favour?'

'The one we've just been talking about.'

'We have three available houses in that area.'

'I already know the property I'd like to rent.'

The agent opened a sheaf and took some pages out of it, laying them down on the table with a flourish. He let his finger trail across them.

'Take your pick, Mr Skillen.'

'I've already made my selection and it's not one of these. I want the house where someone was murdered.'

'I've told you before. You're too late. New tenants are due to move in next week. They have a year's lease.'

'That's a pity,' said Peter, bitterly. 'If I occupied the property, I might actually get to know who owns it.'

Known for her patience and tolerance, Charlotte Skillen was fast approaching the point where one or both would give way. Hannah Granville had come to the gallery straight from the abandoned rehearsal. As before, she listed all of the play's faults and all of the playwright's failings. In the exchange with Abel Mundy, she boasted, she had been the clear winner and been supported by the rest of the cast. There was no hint of sympathy for the doomed manager. Charlotte felt impelled to point that out.

'One is bound to feel sorry for Mr Fleet,' she said.

'He is to blame for this whole imbroglio.'

'The manager acted in what he conceived of as the best interests of his theatre, Hannah. That is why he chose you as his leading lady.'

'I have no quarrel at all with *that* choice,' said Hannah. 'It's his selection of the play that is the point at issue.'

'You insisted on the right to have three choices against the one exercised by Mr Fleet.'

'That was a fair exchange.'

'It may appear so to you,' said Charlotte, softly, 'but it looks different to the unbiased observer. That's not to say I don't support you in every way,' she went on, 'but many people would not. They'd argue that you gained far more than the manager. As for the dispute, their advice would be that you and Mr Mundy should look for an amicable compromise.'

'*Amicable!*' exclaimed Hannah. 'You are asking

me to be amicable towards that excrescence?'

'You've often worked before with people you detest. You've told me about them many times.'

'That was in my younger days when I was forced to do what I was told. I've outgrown that phase of my career. Fame gives me privileges. One of those is to appear in roles that allow me to dazzle an audience.'

'Regardless of the play, you'll always do that.'

'Not if I am shackled to *The Piccadilly Opera*.'

'Let's go back to the start,' suggested Charlotte. 'When the manager first described the plot to you, what was it that aroused your interest? I know that you hate every word of the play now but that wasn't the case beforehand. Something must have pleased you. What was it?'

Hannah relented. Having poured out her woes to Charlotte once again, she felt that her friend had been forced to listen to the harangue long enough. It was time to be reasonable. Concessions had to be made.

'The plot did have some value,' she confessed. 'Though it had elements both of *The Beggar's Opera* and of *The Duenna*, it also had traces of originality. What it did not have was the genius of a Gay or a Sheridan to develop them. My role, as it was described to me, had a surface attraction. I was to be the only daughter of a wealthy man determined to marry me off to a repulsive old lecher with whom my father did business. What I yearned for instead as a husband was a handsome young artist with all the qualities a woman could desire but with little money and no real prospects of acquiring any.'

'So you had to choose between obedience to your father and love?'

'What would *you* have done, Charlotte?'

'I'd have eloped with the handsome young artist.'

'That's exactly what I do in the play. In fact, it's the best moment I have. Once we think we're safe, we sing a duet that will bring tears to the eyes. Unfortunately, we've been betrayed. I am dragged back home and my lover is wrongfully imprisoned as a punishment. Luckily, he finds a friend in the prison chaplain, the only other decent man in the play. The chaplain has an important role. As for me, Esmeralda, how do I escape from a lewd old man and rescue my beloved from the cell he shares with the dregs of London life?'

Hannah went on to describe the twists and turns of a plot that had a lot of comic scenes to add spice and humour to the play. Without realising it, she was actually talking with a degree of enthusiasm about it. In getting her to accept that *The Piccadilly Opera* had some appealing features, Charlotte had done what she intended. She'd calmed her friend down and made her assess her position anew.

'*That's* how I was hoodwinked,' said Hannah.

'A presentable plot is no trick. It's true that some of it is plundered from better playwrights but you've often said that plagiarism is rife in the theatre.'

'It's true. Shakespeare stole his plots without blushing.'

'Then Mr Mundy can't be blamed for doing the same.'

'Don't couple his name with that of a master

dramatist. Shakespeare could spin straw into gold. Mundy can only do that in reverse.'

'What will happen next?'

'That's no longer my concern. I've washed my hands of the enterprise.'

'How will Mr Mundy feel about that?'

'He'll be distraught, Charlotte.' She struck a pose. 'Without me, there'll *be* no performance of his play.'

Marion Mundy was a chubby, plain woman with an abundance of curly red hair and an unswerving loyalty to her husband. She'd shared his recurring setbacks in finding a market for his plays and consoled him as the letters of rejection – some of them harsh to the point of studied cruelty – quickly piled up. During moments when even his steely confidence began to bend, she was there to praise him and stiffen his resolve to pursue a life in the theatre. When at last he was given his opportunity, she sat proudly beside him at the first performance of his first play. It had its obvious faults but it managed to please an audience in York. The applause validated Abel Mundy. In his view, and that of his wife, he'd joined the theatrical elite.

From that moment on, his progress was slow but steady. Each new play was met with unstinting praise from his wife and he drew great strength from that. As he achieved more success and his reputation spread, they knew that it was inevitable that his work would eventually move from the backwaters of the provinces to one of the great theatres of the capital, buildings where the finest playwrights and actors had left vivid memories still hanging in the air. Mundy longed to be mentioned in the same breath as the titans of his profession. Marion loved being mentioned as his wife.

Returning from the rehearsal, he had a face like thunder. She was on her feet at once to wrap her arms around him and ease him down onto the sofa. Sitting beside him, she removed his hat and saw the perspiration on his brow.

'You've been running, Abel,' she said.

'I could not get away from the accursed place quick enough.'

'What happened?'

'It's too painful to relate.'

'Did it involve that hateful woman again?'

'It *always* involves Miss Granville.'

'Why will she not recognise your talent as a playwright?'

'She is too busy admiring herself in a mirror.'

'Did she dare to abuse you again?'

'Yes, Marion,' he replied, 'and she did so in front of the whole company.'

'That's unforgivable. Miss Granville should be dismissed at once.'

'I've urged that solution on the manager time and again.'

'What's his reply?'

'He is bound hand and foot, contractually.'

'It's she who should be bound hand and foot,' she said with sudden intensity, 'and then thrown into the Thames with a ship's anchor attached. Miss Granville should be shunned by respectable society,' she continued. 'It's an established fact that she lives in sin with a man.'

142

Mundy was about to point out that most of the actresses of his acquaintance shared a bed with a man who was not their husband. He'd met two of them who were the discarded mistresses of the Prince Regent and one who'd enjoyed a brief flirtation with no less a person than the Duke of Wellington. Moral standards were more fluid in theatrical circles. While he told his wife many things about his dealings with the acting profession, he concealed far more.

'I won't let you be treated like this, Abel,' she declared.

'What can you possibly do, my love?'

Marion tightened her fists until her knuckles turned white.

'I don't know as yet but ... I promise that I'll think of something.'

Sir Geoffrey Melrose was a big, broad-shouldered man in his sixties with ruddy cheeks that dimpled when he laughed. If he was staying at his country residence, he loved to go for a ride first thing in the morning before galloping back to the house. Only the most inclement weather could prevent him from taking his favourite exercise. When he returned after a stimulating hour in the saddle, one servant came out to take care of his horse and another to receive his hat and his riding crop. The second man had news for his master.

'You have a visitor, Sir Geoffrey,' he said.

'Splendid! Who is it?'

'The gentleman's name is Mr Paul Skillen.'

'It's not a name with which I'm familiar. What's his business with me?'

143

'He refused to divulge it, Sir Geoffrey.'

'A touch of mystery, eh? I like that.'

He walked into the hall, went along a corridor and swept into the drawing room with a smile of anticipation. Paul rose to his feet immediately and introduced himself. Sir Geoffrey was hospitable.

'Sit down, dear fellow, do sit down. Have you been offered refreshment?'

'No, Sir Geoffrey, I haven't.'

'Then you must let me repair the lapse immediately. If you've ridden here from the centre of London, you'll need something to revive you.'

'I require nothing, I do assure you.'

'Then perhaps you'll tell me what's brought you to my door?'

'I have sad tidings to pass on, I fear.'

Sir Geoffrey's dimples vanished. 'Whom do they concern?'

'It's Mr Bowerman.'

'Why, what's old Mark been up to? He has no cause for sadness. The lucky devil is likely to marry one of the prettiest fillies you've ever seen. Had I been twenty years younger, I'd have been his jealous rival. Mark Bowerman must be bursting with joy. What's all this about sad tidings?'

'Mr Bowerman is dead, Sir Geoffrey.'

'*Dead?* But he was a picture of health when I last saw him.'

'He did not die by natural means,' said Paul, quietly. 'I regret to inform you that he was murdered.'

Sir Geoffrey was so shocked that he collapsed into an armchair. A look of sheer despair covered his face. The news had silenced him completely

144

so Paul went on to explain what exactly had happened, starting with a description of the duel. The other man had great difficulty matching what he was hearing to a friend for whom he had a deep affection. He was torn between anguish and incredulity.

'Mark tried to fight a duel?' he asked with a mirthless laugh. 'The fellow didn't know how to hold a pistol, let alone fire one. It was madness for him to challenge anyone. No disrespect to your tuition, Mr Skillen, but it would take you six months at least to get him to a point where he was even competent. Poor, dear, kind, blameless Mark!' he sighed. 'What have you done to deserve this? Who could dislike you so strongly that he was moved to sink a dagger in your back? It's beyond belief.' After struggling with grief for a few minutes, he suddenly looked up. 'What about dear Miss Somerville?' he asked. 'Does she know about this?'

'I had to apprise her of the situation,' said Paul. 'The lady was stunned.'

'I don't blame her. Well, what a turn of events this is! Thank you so much for taking the trouble to bring the news to me.'

'I'm not simply here as a messenger, Sir Geoffrey. I intend to find the man who killed Mr Bowerman. To that end, I'd be grateful for some help from you.'

'I don't see what help I can possibly give you, Mr Skillen, but I'm at your service, nonetheless. Ask me whatever you wish.'

Long after she'd departed, Leonard Impey was

still savouring the experience. Hester Mallory had not only returned to transact business with his bank, she'd stayed for half an hour to converse with him. A customer who had an appointment with him was forced to wait while the manager revelled in the privacy of his office. When she'd eventually departed, Impey escorted his new client all the way to the waiting carriage, opening the door for her and assisting her into the vehicle with a gentle hand under her elbow. The fleeting moment of contact was exhilarating.

Back in his office, he'd showered the other client with apologies for making him wait, then discussed the loan that was requested. Much later, when he was alone again, Impey had another visitor. The chief clerk knocked on the door and entered without waiting for an invitation. He was carrying something in his hand.

'I've been looking at this bond, sir,' he said, worriedly. 'You deposited it in the safe when you took out some money for Mrs Mallory.'

Impey was tetchy. 'You had no reason to look at it.'

'I was only following your advice, sir. You've always insisted that, where a major transaction is involved, a second pair of eyes is recommended.'

'Perhaps I did say that, but you should have asked my permission first.'

'I'm sorry that I didn't,' said the clerk, 'and even sorrier that you didn't let me examine the document before you advanced the cash. I might have saved you from a rather embarrassing situation.'

'What do you mean?'

'Given the faith you so clearly placed in Mrs

146

Mallory, I hesitate to suggest this, sir...'

'Don't beat about the bush, man,' said the manager, irritably. 'I'm a busy man. Say what you have to say then leave me alone.'

'The bond is not genuine, Mr Impey.'

'Don't talk nonsense. I've been through every line with great care.'

'Then perhaps I should remind you that I dealt with Mr Picton for many years. I got to know him extremely well. There is no way that he would have sanctioned a bond of this kind. I'm surprised that you missed this blatant error, for instance,' he went on, putting the document in front of the manager and jabbing a finger at a particular point. 'Do you see what I mean, sir?'

Snatching up the bond, Impey looked at the wording indicated. Doubts began to form and swiftly turned into fears. He'd given a stranger one thousand pounds from the safe and helped her into the carriage so that she could take the money away. The colour drained from his face and the authority from his voice.

'It's a forgery,' he croaked.

Hester Mallory sailed into the room with a smile of triumph.

'How did you get on at the bank?' asked the man.

'That fool of a manager would have given me twice the amount.'

Opening her bag, she took out the banknotes and threw them high into the air so that she could stand in a veritable blizzard of paper. Hester laughed.

'I'll try that other bank tomorrow,' she decided.

Joining in the laughter, the man swept her up in his arms.

'This deserves a celebration,' he said and he carried her quickly upstairs.

Sir Geoffrey Melrose talked at length about his late friend with an affection edged with sorrow. All that Paul had to do was to listen and toss in the occasional question. At the root of the relationship with Mark Bowerman there was a family connection. Sir Geoffrey was uncle to Bowerman's wife. Belonging to the same club, the two men saw a lot of each other until the unexpected death of Lucy Bowerman. As a result, her husband had become something of a recluse and Sir Geoffrey was one of the few people who could tempt him out of his self-imposed exile from society.

'When you got to know him,' he recalled, 'Mark was a delightful companion. He was witty, intelligent and interested in politics. We talked for hours on end. I fancy that I was his only contact with real life.'

'How did he come to meet Miss Somerville?' asked Paul.

'It was completely by accident.'

'You didn't deliberately bring them together, then?'

'Dear Lord – no! That's not what happened at all.'

Sir Geoffrey went on to explain his own routine. Crippled with arthritis, his wife rarely left their country estate but she insisted that he went up to London on a regular basis to enjoy seeing his friends. Mark Bowerman was one of them. Though he didn't confide his plan to Lady Melrose, he hit on the idea of holding a dinner party at his London address for some male friends and a group of beautiful young women. With a disarming smile, Sir Geoffrey warned Paul not to misunderstand the situation. His female guests had not been professional sirens, hired for the occasion and prepared to be compliant. They were all eminently respectable and were simply there to adorn the room and lighten the conversation. The dinner party, Sir Geoffrey said, had been an unqualified success.

'Laetitia Somerville was a gorgeous creature but too serious-minded for my taste. To be candid, I preferred one of the others. A serious thought had never passed through her brain, God bless her.' He quickly wiped the broad grin from his face. 'Not that anything untoward happened between us, of course. She was far too young and I was far too married. In any case, it was not that kind of occasion.'

'Did Mr Bowerman and Miss Somerville have the opportunity to speak alone?' asked Paul.

'No, we all stayed together in the dining room. In fact, Mark hardly said a word to Laetitia. He was mesmerised by her. As soon as the guests departed, he demanded to know how he could get in touch with her.'

'Did you give him her address?'

'I'd have given him the address of anyone who cheered him up so much.'

'He told me that she had a resemblance to his first wife.'

'That's true. Lucy was a beauty as well.'

'Did you ever see him and Miss Somerville together again?'

'No,' said Sir Geoffrey, 'but I was hoping to do so at their wedding. That was an event that even Lady Melrose would insist on attending. Alas, it was not to be!'

'Thank you,' said Paul, getting to his feet. 'That was enlightening. You've been more helpful than you know.'

'I'm glad to hear you say that.'

'There is one favour I'd like to ask. Could you possibly provide me with the names of all the people who were at that dinner party you gave?'

As he considered the request, Sir Geoffrey's eyebrows formed a chevron.

'I'm not sure that I can,' he said at length.

Charlotte was still dazed by her latest visit from her friend. Hannah Granville had talked at her for the best part of an hour. When her husband returned to the gallery, Charlotte was grateful for his welcoming kiss.

'Thank you, Peter,' she said, 'I needed that.'

'Don't tell me that Hannah's been chewing your ear off again.'

'*Somebody* has to listen to her.'

'Why must it always be you?'

'There's yet another crisis, Peter. Suffice it to say that the chances of the play actually being performed are very slim. Still,' she continued. 'What's your news?'

'I was baulked.'

'Didn't they tell you who owns the property

where the murder occurred?'

'The agent refused to do so.'

'Then he was withholding what might be valuable evidence.'

'I made the point very forcefully. That garden was no random choice. The killer selected the venue on purpose.'

'Is there no way of identifying the owner?'

'Oh, yes,' said Peter, blithely. 'I'll get the information tonight.'

'But you just told me that the agent refused to give it to you.'

'There's more than one way to skin a cat, Charlotte.'

'You don't mean...?' He gave a nod. 'But that's illegal.'

'If it's the only way to get what we need, so be it.'

'I don't want you taking any risks, Peter.'

'It will be something of a squeeze to get into the building but I think that I can manage it. On the other hand,' he went on as an alternative popped into his mind, 'it would be even easier for my accomplice.'

'Who do you mean?' Peter looked up at the ceiling. 'Jem?'

'He'd be ideal. Jem is small enough and nimble enough.'

'Be careful, Peter. We don't want him to have another brush with the law. The Runners would dearly love to have a legitimate reason to arrest Jem.'

'They won't get the chance, my love. He'll be in and out of there in a flash. Besides, the Runners have something far more important to worry about than a case of trespass. Micah Yeomans has a murder to solve.'

As they stood on the Thames embankment, the Runners discussed ways of trying to appease the chief magistrate. All their efforts had so far been frustrated and they were stung by the realisation that Peter and Paul Skillen were moving faster than them.

'How do they do it?' asked Hale. 'They're always ahead of us. I felt sure that we'd be the first to call on Miss Somerville but one of them had already been to the house. In fact, he broke the news of the murder to her. *We* should have done that, Micah.'

'Be quiet.'

'Why didn't we?'

'I'm thinking,' said Yeomans. 'We need to hobble the Skillens.'

'We tried that when we raided the gallery.'

'There has to be a subtler way.'

Hale pondered. 'We could always get Chevy to keep an eye on them,' he said after a short while. 'He could lurk outside the gallery.'

'No, he'd only give himself away. When we asked him to keep Paul Skillen under surveillance, the idiot finished up down there in the Thames.' He spat into the river. 'Besides, he can't tell the difference between the two brothers.'

'Neither can I, if I'm honest.'

'It's easy,' said Yeomans. 'One is right-handed and the other is left-handed.'

'Which is which?'

'Peter is right-handed.' He scratched his head.

'Or is that Paul?'

They began to stroll meditatively along the embankment, searching for a way to advance their own investigation at the expense of the one being pursued by their rivals. Hale offered a few suggestions but they were hastily dismissed by his colleague. It was Yeomans who finally believed that he'd espied a way to seize the advantage.

'The duel,' he said, coming to a halt. 'We're forgetting the duel, Alfred.'

'But it never took place.'

'Exactly.'

'I don't understand.'

'We are privy to information that the Skillen brothers don't have.'

'Are we?'

'How did we know when and where the duel was to take place?'

'An informer gave us the information.'

'That's our starting point,' argued Yeomans. 'We must find the informer. I'll wager that we'll get a lot more evidence that way. It's somebody who *knows* all the people involved and who had a motive for preventing that duel.'

'You're right, Micah. How do we find him?'

'We don't, Alfred.'

'But you just said that he might be the key we needed.'

'Try listening properly,' said Yeomans, giving him a shove. 'I didn't mention a man at all. The one thing we do know about our informer is this: it was a woman.'

CHAPTER ELEVEN

When Paul eventually arrived at the gallery, they were all keen to know what he'd found out in Eltham. Since Jem Huckvale was busy teaching someone the fundamentals of swordsmanship, only Peter, Charlotte and Gully Ackford were left to form an attentive audience. While the men were amused by his treatment of the robbers who'd lain in ambush, Charlotte was concerned.

'Supposing there were more of them? You might have been hurt.'

'As you see,' said Paul, stretching his arms, 'there's not a scratch on me.'

'Are you going to tell Hannah about this encounter?'

'No, Charlotte, I'm not.'

'What's the reason for that?'

'There are two reasons, actually. First, Hannah is not in a listening mode. All she wants to do is to talk about this latest play of hers. It's been a source of friction with the manager ever since she agreed to act in it.'

'The friction continues,' warned Charlotte. 'Hannah walked out of a rehearsal today after a fierce argument with the playwright.'

Paul grimaced. 'That means I'll hear all the gruesome details.'

'What's the second reason?'

'I don't wish to upset her. When she first realised

what a hazardous life Peter and I lead, I almost lost her. It's far better if I keep the truth from Hannah. For instance, she knew nothing about the duel.'

'In your place, Peter would have told me everything.'

'That's because I can trust you not to try to stop me,' said Peter. 'Hannah is different. She'd be more fearful.'

'Go on with your story, Paul,' suggested Ackford. 'What sort of man was Sir Geoffrey Melrose and did you learn enough to make the journey worthwhile?'

'Oh, yes,' replied Paul, 'I did.'

He went on to describe Sir Geoffrey and the life that he led in the country. It was very different to the time he spent in the city. Freed from his disabled wife, the man was a bon viveur who spread his wings wide. Of his fondness for Bowerman, Paul had no doubt. It had been a deep and lasting friendship. He'd been interested to discover more about the man for whom he'd acted as a second. What Paul was less certain about was Sir Geoffrey's account of the fateful dinner party. The older man had claimed that he couldn't remember how the women came to be invited and he only provided the name of one male guest.

'What's he trying to hide?' asked Ackford.

'I don't know,' said Paul.

'Do you think he deliberately arranged for Mr Bowerman to meet Miss Somerville? Is that what happened? Was he playing Cupid?'

'He swears that he'd never met her before.'

'Yet he obviously knew the sort of woman who could attract Bowerman. It was one who reminded him of his first wife.'

'Sir Geoffrey said that that was an agreeable coincidence.'

'It doesn't sound as if he's been entirely truthful with you, Paul,' said his brother. 'He wanted to give the impression of helping you while holding some of the information back.'

'I got one name out of him, Peter. Before I track down the man, I want to pay a second visit to Miss Somerville. I've lots of questions for her. For a start, I'd like to see if her memories of the dinner party chime in with those of Sir Geoffrey.' He turned to his brother. 'What will you be doing, Peter?'

'Jem and I are going to break the law,' said the other.

'Then be very careful.'

'It won't take long, Paul.'

Before he could explain what he was planning to do, Peter was interrupted by a sharp knock on the door. He opened it to find a man standing there with a letter in his hand. He held it up.

'I'm to deliver this to a Mr Peter Skillen,' he said.

'Who sent it?'

'I've come from Mr Impey.'

'Then it's important,' said Peter, taking the missive from him. 'Come in a moment. When I've read this, you can take back my reply.'

He stood back to admit the man then walked to a corner of the room. Unfolding the letter, he read the single sentence that it contained.

'You won't need to give him my reply,' he said to the man. 'I'll deliver it in person.' He turned to the others. 'Mr Impey needs help. He wouldn't

156

summon me unless it was very serious. I'll have to go to the bank immediately.'

Notwithstanding the setback following their first visit there, the Runners decided to call at Stephen Hamer's house for the second time. When they were invited in, they had to face some stinging invective both from Hamer and from Rawdon Carr. They withstood it with fortitude. As it eventually died away, Yeomans tried to mollify the two men with an apologetic shrug.

'You are right to criticise us, gentlemen,' he said. 'We acted too quickly and too unwisely. I'm hoping that we can put that mistake behind us.'

'Have you come to make another one in its place?' asked Hamer, cynically.

'We've come to ask for your help, sir.'

'First, you arrest, me and now you have the gall to court me.'

'You want the killer as much as we do, Captain Hamer.'

'You're wrong. We want him far more. For you, he's simply one more villain out of the many you've pursued during your career. For me, this is a very personal matter.'

'It's true,' added Carr. 'That's why we don't want the Skillen brothers to be the first to unmask him. The killer is a prize we reserve for ourselves.'

'But it's our duty to arrest him,' said Hale. 'We're Runners.'

'You've barely learnt to *walk* properly, man, let alone run.'

'Insults will get us nowhere,' cautioned Yeomans. 'Mr Carr has just given us another reason for cooperation. We share a mutual dislike of Peter and Paul Skillen. They have been a nuisance to us for many years – nay, "nuisance" is too mild a word. The Skillens have been a positive menace.'

'I can see why,' agreed Hamer. 'We, too, have had our problems with them.'

'They need to be controlled, that's all,' said Carr.

'It's a question of working out how best to do that.'

'We tried and failed,' admitted Hale.

'The more obstacles you can strew in their path,' said Hamer, 'the better. But what's this talk of cooperation? How can you possibly help us, Yeomans?'

'We can help each other,' replied the Runner.

'How do we do that?'

'We go back to your dispute with Mr Bowerman. You and Mr Carr went to Putney Heath in the firm conviction that the duel would take place. Correct?'

'Yes, that's correct.'

'Everything was about to go as planned,' said Carr, 'when you and your cohorts suddenly jumped out of the bushes.'

'Do you know *why* we did that, sir?'

'Someone betrayed us.'

'We can't wait to get our hands on him,' said Hamer, malevolently. 'If you know his name, we demand that you release it.'

'The letter that reached us was unsigned,' Yeomans told them. 'One thing, however, was unmistakable. It was not written by a man at all. The hand was clearly that of a woman. Now, gentlemen,' he went on, 'can either of you suggest who that woman might be?'

Hamer and Carr stared at each other in surprise.

Peter Skillen was no stranger to the bank. He and Paul had had many commissions from Leonard Impey, most of them involving either the transfer of large sums from one place to another or the recovery of stolen money. Banks were natural targets for robbers. Runners like Yeomans and Hale derived a comfortable income from London banks, which retained them as guards at certain times every month. Country banks were especially vulnerable and Runners were often paid to pursue those who'd robbed them. Like many other bank managers, Impey had learnt that the Runners had severe limitations. Effective at frightening potential thieves away, they were less reliable when investigating more complex cases. Because of their superior rate of success, Peter and Paul were therefore often in demand. They were deemed to be more intelligent, resourceful and, crucially, more honest.

As he entered the bank, Peter saw a smile of gratitude light up the gloomy countenance of the chief clerk. Peter could see he was needed. Shown into the manager's office, he shook hands with Impey.

'Thank goodness you've come, Mr Skillen!'

'There was a faint whiff of desperation about your summons,' said Peter.

'We've had a minor calamity.'

'If it was an armed robbery, I trust that none of your employees was hurt.'

'It was not an *armed* robbery,' said Impey with bitterness. 'If anything, it was a case of theft by *disarming*. Take a seat and you shall hear what happened.'

When they'd both settled down, Impey gave a full account of the forgery. He didn't spare himself. He confessed that he'd been cunningly wooed by Mrs Mallory and that he'd been tortured by regret ever since. He heaped praise on his head clerk for exposing the fraud and wished that he'd had the sense to have the man present during the discussions with their new client. His narrative ended with an apology.

'I should have listened to your advice, Mr Skillen.'

'It's a simple precaution,' said Peter. 'As soon as a complete stranger, however attractive, presents you with a bond or comes in search of a substantial loan, it's sensible to check their credentials. If they claim to be newcomers to the capital, get someone to confirm that the address they've given you for their stay here is a correct one. I guarantee that you'll find the hotel whose name was given to you by this Mrs Mallory will have no record of her as one of their guests.'

'We've already established that fact.'

'But you did so *after* the event. The damage was already done.'

'You've no need to censure me,' said Impey. 'I've scourged myself soundly, I promise you. When I think how easily I was deceived, I ache all over. This will cast a dark shadow over my future here. Unless we can somehow recover the money, I will face demands for my resignation. You've

160

saved me before,' he went on, extending his arms in a plea, 'do so again, I implore.'

'I'll do what I can, sir.'

'Is there a glimmer of hope that you will succeed?'

'Oh, yes,' said Peter. 'Mrs Mallory – or whatever her real name is – may have used her charms to obtain money by forgery but she's also left a firm imprint on your mind of what she looks like. You'll be able to give me a very accurate description of the lady and so, I fancy, will your chief clerk.'

'She was unforgettable, Mr Skillen.'

'It will be easier to trace someone who is so distinctive.' He took out a notebook. 'Paint a portrait of Mrs Mallory for me.'

Impey winced at the mention of a portrait. It had been one of the many lies that he'd accepted without question. Shamefaced and embarrassed, he gave a detailed picture of her, drawing attention to her voice and deportment. Peter noted everything down carefully.

'What is your first step?' asked the manager, anxiously.

'It's to issue a warning, sir. I am not free to devote all my time to this case because I am already involved in the pursuit of a man wanted for murder. But I will do my best to deal with both crimes in parallel. You will simply have to be patient.'

'I know that forgery is a lesser crime than murder but my future is at stake here. Yes, it was my own fault, I admit that freely. I just ask that you show some pity and understanding.'

'There is one thing I can do immediately,' said

161

Peter, rising to his feet. 'I'll go to the Bevington Hotel.'

'But we already know that Mrs Mallory is not staying there.'

'She may well have done so in the past, sir. Why settle on that particular hotel if she was not familiar with it? If she *has* used it before, they will certainly recognise her from the description you've given to me.'

'That's true, Mr Skillen.'

'The other avenue open to us, of course, is Mr Picton. How could the lady have a letter purportedly written by him if she didn't have some contact with the man? Correspondence of some sort must have passed between them.'

'I never thought of that.'

'Out of courtesy,' Peter told him, 'Mr Picton ought to be made aware of the way that his name was misused. He'll be very annoyed.'

'He'll be very annoyed with *me*, I know that.'

'I'd suggest that he be allowed to see the forged bond.'

'Yes, yes,' said Impey, opening a drawer in his desk. 'I have it here.'

'Of equal interest to Mr Picton, of course, is the letter of introduction he is supposed to have drafted, but I daresay that Mrs Mallory was careful to retain that.'

'She was, Mr Skillen.' Coming around his desk, he handed over the bond. 'Thank you so much for responding to my call. You've already given me some comfort.'

'When you spoke of the lady,' remembered Peter, 'you spoke of her dainty feet. No matter how dainty, they'll have left large footprints for me to follow. And there may be another source of comfort for you, sir.'

'I'm in sore need of it.'

'You will not be the only victim of her guile.'

'What makes you think that?'

'We are dealing with a greedy woman,' said Peter. 'If the bond had been for a much smaller amount, your chief clerk would not have been quite so suspicious. Mrs Mallory's demand was excessive. And since she was given money so willingly by you, she'll go in search of other amenable bank managers.'

When she heard that Paul Skillen had called on her again, Laetitia Somerville was eager to see him and to hear if his investigation had borne fruit. She therefore had him shown into the drawing room where she was reclining on a sofa. Head bowed in grief, Laetitia was wearing her black dress.

'I'm sorry to intrude, Miss Somerville,' he said, gently. 'I know that you're not in the mood for visitors.'

'I'm not in the mood for anything at the moment, Mr Skillen.'

'I wish that I was able to bring you good news for a change. While I'm still bent on locating the man who killed Mr Bowerman, I have no real progress to report.'

'He *must* be caught and hanged,' she said.

'He will be. I give you my word.'

'Thank you, sir. I have every faith in you.'

'What I can tell you, however, is that the inquest will take place tomorrow. I was told of the arrangements just before I came here.'

She was flustered. 'Am I expected to be present?'

'That won't be necessary.'

'There's nothing I'd have to say.'

'Nobody will call upon you.'

'I'd find it too distressing to bear, Mr Skillen.'

'Then you must stay away. It will, perforce, be a relatively short event. The coroner's verdict is easy to predict. Mr Bowerman was killed by a person or persons unknown.'

'*Someone* must be called to account,' she insisted.

'They will be.'

He looked at her more closely. Sorrow had veiled her beauty, aged her visibly and left a rather unprepossessing visage in its place. Her eyes were dead, her cheeks hollowed and the corners of her mouth turned down. Paul compared her unfavourably with Hannah Granville. Whatever the situation, she never lost her essential loveliness. If she was angry or sad, excited or passive, her beauty continued to dominate. Indeed, when her temper flared and her eyes blazed, she was at her most alluring.

'May I ask if Captain Hamer has been in touch with you?' he said.

'I've not heard a word from him.'

'Not even a letter of condolence?'

'He knows that my door is barred to him.'

'We've been finding out curious details about him,' said Paul. 'It turns out that he never held a captaincy and, after a court martial, he was ejected from his regiment.'

She sat up in astonishment. 'Where did you

learn this?'

'It came from the most reliable source – the War Office.'

'Well, well,' she said, 'that does come as a shock. Are you certain of this?'

'I am, Miss Somerville. Something about the fellow struck a jarring note.'

'Then I'm glad I've done with him.' She appraised him for a moment. 'You are a clever man, Mr Skillen. You are also very thorough.'

'It's a tool of my trade,' he explained. 'There's something else you should know about the former Lieutenant Hamer.'

'What is it?'

'He's trying to scare me away.'

Paul told her about the raid on the gallery and how he was convinced it was the work of Hamer and Carr. Having confronted them, he was certain that they'd make another attempt to hamper his investigation. Listening carefully to every word, Laetitia was especially interested to hear that he had a twin brother.

'To whom am I speaking at the moment?' she asked.

'I'm Paul Skillen.'

'How can I be sure of that?'

'My brother had no dealings with Mr Bowerman. He was a client of mine who became a good friend. Peter never even met him.'

'Yet he's prepared to search for his killer.'

'In an emergency like this, we always help each other.'

'That's ... reassuring to know,' she said, slowly.

'At the moment, of course, it's *your* assistance

I seek.'

She drew back slightly. 'What can *I* possibly tell you?'

'You can explain how you came to meet Sir Geoffrey Melrose.' He saw the confusion in her eyes. 'You surely remember him, Miss Somerville. I met him myself this morning. Sir Geoffrey is a man who makes a lasting impression. It was at his dinner party that you first met Mr Bowerman.'

'Of course,' she said, recovering quickly. 'I did meet him but it was only on that one occasion. All I recall of that dinner is the fact that Mark came into my life. That blotted everything else out.'

'How did you come to be invited to Sir Geoffrey's house?'

'As it happens, I went there with a friend.'

'May I ask his name?'

'It was a woman friend,' she said.

'Could you provide me with her name and address?'

She was guarded. 'Why should you wish to speak to her?'

'I'd like to hear her memories of that dinner party as well.'

'That may be difficult,' said Laetitia. 'Some time ago, I heard that she'd moved to France and was seriously ill. She may not still be alive.'

Irritated at first that the Runners should dare to call on them, Hamer and Carr were glad that they'd spoken to them. They'd learnt that Yeomans and Hale were not the complete buffoons they'd imagined. They had a good record of arrests and – judging by the quality of their apparel – they

166

contrived to make policing the city a lucrative task. Their antipathy towards the Skillen brothers had pleased Rawdon Carr. He wanted to know everything they could tell him about the way their rivals operated. In particular, he'd wanted to know what their weak points were. Hamer, on the other hand, was still trying to digest the information that a woman was responsible for the abandoned duel. As soon as their visitors had left, he rounded on Carr.

'Did you hear what they said? We were thwarted by a woman.'

'All that we know, Stephen, is that a woman wrote the letter. The most likely thing is that it was dictated to her by a man.'

'Why do you say that?'

'What better way to hide his identity?'

'A man could easily have scrawled the details in such a way as to disguise his hand completely. No, Rawdon, we made a startling discovery today. If for nothing else, I'm grateful to the Runners for that.' His brow wrinkled in thought. 'Who could it possibly have been?'

Carr smirked. 'There are rather too many suspects,' he said. 'You've seduced and cast aside any number of women since you came to live in London. One of them wanted to get even with you.'

'But how could she possibly know about the duel?'

'Vengeful women will go to any lengths, Stephen. You should know that by now. The arrangements were secret but someone might have passed on the details if offered enough money. That would be my guess. One of your mistresses is

167

behind this. She chose her moment with care.'

'But what did she stand to gain?'

'What women always crave. They want satis-faction.'

'I can't see that anyone would be satisfied with merely disrupting an event like that. The one explanation is that it was an admirer of Bower-man, desperate to stop me putting a bullet inside his stupid head.'

'Yes,' said Carr, 'that's a possibility as well. In fact, now that I think about it, that may be a more convincing answer.'

'What about the murder?'

'No woman was capable of that, Stephen. It was a task for a man.'

'Yet a woman was involved. Bowerman was tricked by a letter that seemed to come from Laetitia.'

'In that case,' decided Hamer, 'we are looking for *two* women – one who cared enough for Bowerman to save him and another who wanted him dead. How could such a dry and humourless fellow interest two passionate women? It's be-yond my comprehension.' About to walk across the room, he came to a dead halt. 'There is *one* person capable of forging a letter, of course...'

'You can rule *her* out at once.'

'She's a malicious little bitch.'

'There's just one problem,' said Carr. 'Rumour has it that she's been struck down by a malady and is unlikely to recover. Besides, she moved to Paris months ago so we can definitely leave her out of our list of suspects.'

The Bevington Hotel was a relatively small but luxurious establishment in Park Lane. As soon as Peter laid eyes on it, his spirits rose. If he was visiting a large hotel with a multitude of guests moving in and out all the time, the woman he was tracking could have been lost in the crowd. There was no danger of that at the Bevington. When he spoke to the manager, he explained that he was acting on behalf of the bank.

'We've already had someone here on the same errand,' said the man.

'Not quite,' corrected Peter. 'He was asking if a Mrs Mallory was staying here. My question is somewhat different. I'd like to know if someone currently posing under that name ever stayed as a guest at your hotel.'

'When would this be, sir?'

'How good is your memory?'

'I flatter myself that it's extremely good.'

The manager was an unusually tall, thin, pale-faced man with an almost patrician air about him. Resenting his condescension, Peter nevertheless needed his help so he forbore to confront the man.

'Let's look back over the last year, shall we?' he said.

'A lot of people have stayed here during that time, Mr Skillen. I can't pretend to remember each and every one of them.'

'This lady would assuredly stay in the memory.'

'Under what name was she supposed to be a guest here?'

'That's what I'm endeavouring to find out.'

Peter went on to give him the description of her that he'd got from Impey. He emphasised the woman's unassailable buoyancy and the quality of her attire. Something of a dandy himself, the manager seized on the details of her appearance.

'I do believe I recall the lady in question,' he said.

'What was her name?'

'My memory is sound, sir, but it is not encyclopaedic. While her name escapes me, her reason for staying here does not. She was a guest for a few days before going on to Ascot.'

'That would mean she stayed here last June.'

'I can give you the exact date, if you wish.'

'I'd be most grateful.'

Peter followed him into the reception area and waited while the man went behind the counter and turned back the pages of a ledger. When he came to the relevant place, he ran his finger down the list of names.

'Here we are,' he said. 'I've found her for you.'

'Was she staying here as Mrs Mallory?'

'Oh, no,' replied the other.

'Then what name *was* she using?'

The manager looked up at him. 'Miss Arabella Kenyon.'

Unable to placate the playwright, Lemuel Fleet decided against another futile appeal to Hannah Granville. He employed a different tactic altogether and caught Charlotte by surprise. When he turned up unexpectedly at the gallery and introduced himself, she was taken aback.

'Have you come for lessons in fencing, boxing, archery or shooting?' she asked in wonderment.

'I'd love to be proficient in all of them,' he said, grimly, 'then I'd be able to kill the pair of them in

170

four different ways. Let me explain, Mrs Skillen. That is your name, I believe?'

'It is, sir.'

'I've heard it often on Miss Granville's lips and, I gather, her beau is your brother-in-law. I need to speak to one or both of you.'

'Then you'll have to settle for me,' said Charlotte. 'Paul is not here and, in any case, is not able to prevail upon Miss Granville.'

'What about you?'

'I might have marginally more influence, Mr Fleet.'

'That's why I came. Talking to Mr Mundy is like banging my head against a brick wall. Talking to Miss Granville is akin to putting it inside the mouth of a lion.'

'You've no need to recount what happened today, sir. I already know.'

'What you heard was wildly prejudicial.'

Charlotte smiled. 'I allowed for that, sir.'

'In brief, the situation is this...'

Fleet spoke slowly and painfully. What Charlotte heard was a version of events that differed considerably from the one that her friend had given her. Entirely new facts emerged. Hannah, it transpired, had been a destructive force from the very start. She had two of the actors dismissed from the company – one man, who kissed her in the course of the play, had bad breath; the other, who tried to kiss her in the dressing room, had bad judgement. There was an endless litany of complaints. Hannah wanted this scene removed from the play and that song inserted in its place. She'd quarrelled with the costume designer.

She'd insulted one of the stage hands. When he got on to Abel Mundy, the manager was able to reveal a catalogue of crimes. He accepted that he was at fault in putting actress and playwright together. They were archetypes of incompatibility.

When he paused for breath, Charlotte offered a comment.

'Miss Granville is my friend,' she began, 'but I can't defend some of the behaviour you've described. What I can suggest, Mr Fleet, is that her outbursts are symptoms of the fact that she is very unhappy.'

'Does that give her licence to make us all suffer?'

'No, it doesn't.'

'Then why has she turned into the company tyrant?'

'That may be overstating the case,' said Charlotte, reasonably. 'When she arrived at the rehearsal today, she was given a rapturous welcome.'

'The ovation was a sign of the sheer relief we all felt.'

'When did you first engage her, Mr Fleet?'

'I'm beginning to wish that I'd never done so, to be honest.'

'It was two years ago, wasn't it? Hannah was in *The School for Scandal*.'

'And she was magical,' he said.

'Did you have trouble from her in rehearsals?'

'We had none whatsoever.'

'Did she scatter insults wherever she went?'

'No, Mrs Skillen, she spread compliments far and wide.'

'What of the playwright? Did they come to blows?'

172

'Miss Granville adored Sheridan,' he said, 'and he worshipped her. It was a marriage of true minds in every sense. That's what made it a pleasure to employ her.'

'She is still that same talented actress,' Charlotte pointed out. 'Hannah has not lost one jot of that magic you noted. She's simply unable to bring it to *The Piccadilly Opera* because she thrives on enthusiasm and this play fails to enthuse her.'

Lemuel Fleet was struck dumb by her articulate comments. He'd come to appeal to Charlotte to intercede with Hannah on his behalf. Where he could only offer threats or concessions to the actress, a close female friend might be more persuasive. Charlotte's analysis of the problem was impressive. Though she understood little of the workings of the theatre, she sensed the emotional turmoil in which Hannah was caught up. Fleet dared to hope that he might have found an emissary.

'Could I ask a very special favour of you, Mrs Skillen?'

'I'm honoured that you deigned to approach me, sir.'

'I'd be prepared to offer you a fee.'

'It would only be returned,' she said, firmly. 'If I can help in any way, I'll be happy to do so but I'll not take a penny.'

'You're my one hope of salvation.'

'Then it's only fair to warn you I've so far failed to make Hannah view the situation in a more impartial way.'

'Would you try to do so again?'

'I'd try anything to bring peace and harmony,

173

Mr Fleet.'

'Then you have my undying thanks. We *need* Miss Granville as a ship needs a mainsail. It may be that this vessel does not have the high quality to which she is accustomed but it is still sea-worthy. Convince her of that and all will be well.'

'I can make no promises.'

'None will be demanded, Mrs Skillen. You spoke of peace and harmony. Having listened to you, I'm confident that both can be restored.'

Hannah Granville was more restless than ever. Nothing could divert her or hold her attention. She had tried resting on the bed, reading a novel, singing her favourite songs and accompanying herself on the piano. She soon lapsed back into a deep misery. What she wanted most was Paul's company because he was the only person who could raise her spirits. Unfortunately, he had commitments elsewhere. It might be hours before she saw him again. Bored, sulking and rudderless, she walked to the front window and stared out.

Seconds later, the glass was shattered by a stone.

CHAPTER TWELVE

Tiny shards of glass were scattered across the room. Several of them hit Hannah's body but it was the few that struck her face that threw her into a panic. As she felt blood trickling down her cheeks, she let out a hysterical scream. It brought the servants running to see what the trouble was. Hannah was quivering all over.

'I might have been *blinded!*' she cried. 'I could have been disfigured for life.'

'Come away from the window,' advised one of the women, leading her into the hall. 'It will be safer out here.'

'I can feel blood. Have I been scarred for life?'

'There are only a few scratches, Miss Granville.'

'It feels as if my whole face is on fire.'

'What happened?'

'Someone threw a stone at the window.'

'It might not have been aimed at you, Miss Granville. Whoever threw it might not even have known you were in the room.'

'They saw me,' insisted Hannah. 'When I stood in the window, it suddenly burst into smithereens. Someone was trying to kill me.' She shrank back. 'What if they're still there?'

'I don't think they will be.'

In fact, the manservant had already run out into the street in search of the assailant. He looked up and down but saw nobody at all. He came back into the house.

'They've gone,' he announced. 'It may have been children, having fun.'

'Fun!' exclaimed Hannah, dabbing at the wound. 'Is this their idea of fun? It's deplorable. A person can't even look out of a window with impunity.'

'I'll clear up the mess in the drawing room,' he volunteered.

'Thank you, Dirk,' said the servant who still had a supporting arm around Hannah. 'Why don't we go into the dining room, Miss Granville? You'll be perfectly safe in there.'

'I don't think I shall ever feel safe in this house again.'

She allowed herself to be led into the other room. Breaking away from the servant, she went straight to the mirror that hung over the mantel-piece to examine her face. Still in shock, she was horrified to see three red scratches on one cheek. Blood had only oozed from one of them but that was enough to alarm her.

'How do you feel now, Miss Granville?' asked the servant, solicitously.

'I feel dreadful,' she replied, dabbing at the blood with a handkerchief.

'I'll ask someone to go to the houses opposite and ask if there are any witnesses to what happened. It must have been horseplay of some kind. I can't believe that anyone would deliberately try to harm you.'

'Oh, yes, they would,' said Hannah, calming down sufficiently to make a considered judgement. 'I think I know who hurled that stone at me.'

'Who was it?'

'It's a nasty, vicious man named Abel Mundy.' Pulling a face, she put the handkerchief to her cheek again. 'It *stings* so much.'

'Would you like me to send for a doctor?'

'Yes, I would.'

'I'll get someone else to look after you.'

'No, no, I'm much better now. Fetch the doctor

and don't worry about looking for witnesses. Mr Mundy hurled that stone. I'll wager anything on it.'

The servant headed for the door. 'I'll be as quick as I can.'

Left alone, Hannah inspected herself in the mirror yet again. One of the shards had grazed her cheekbone. When she saw how close it had been to her left eye, she shuddered. An actress lived by her looks. The partial loss of her sight and the ugliness of a damaged eye would spell ruin for her. That had been his intention, she believed. Mundy was not simply trying to frighten her, he wanted to drive her from the stage altogether and he might well have succeeded. Caught up in her plight, she didn't hear the sound of approaching hooves. Hannah was still staring into the mirror when the door opened and Paul rushed in to throw protective arms around her.

'I've just heard what happened,' he said.

'It was terrifying, Paul. The glass went everywhere.'

Holding her at arm's length, he scrutinised her. Dozens of shards had lodged in her dress but he didn't notice them. His gaze was fixed on the facial wounds and the specks of glass stuck in her hair.

'What happened?' he asked.

'Mr Mundy watched me standing in the window and threw a stone.'

'Did you actually see him?'

'No,' she admitted, 'but who else would do such a thing? He's so obsessed with getting his play on the stage that he's trying to force me out of the company for good. I could have been *killed,* Paul.'

'I don't think your life would have been in danger,' he said, 'but your career might have been. This is appalling, Hannah. If Mundy is responsible for this, he'll finish up behind bars and I'll be the one to put him there.'

'Don't leave me just yet,' she begged, clutching at him.

'I'll stay as long as you wish.'

'I've sent for a doctor but you're the best medicine. I feel better already.'

'Do you feel able to tell me in detail exactly what happened?'

'No,' said Hannah, nestling against his chest. 'To tell you the truth, I want to forget all about it. You've no idea how utterly defenceless I felt.'

They stood together in silence for several minutes. Paul could feel her heart still racing. Chiding himself for not being there to look after her, he realised that he had to balance her needs against the murder investigation that was taking up so much of his time. Paul was not entirely convinced that Mundy had been the culprit but he wasn't going to upset her by disagreeing with her claim. All he wanted was to comfort and reassure her.

When she came into the room, Charlotte Skillen dispensed with greetings.

'Your front window has been smashed,' she said, then noticed the tiny wounds, 'and what on earth have you done to your face, Hannah?'

On the principle that the bank manager was in dire need of some support, Peter Skillen returned to Impey's office and told him what he'd found

178

out. The manager was gratified that he'd taken the time to make initial enquiries and was interested to hear that the woman who'd persuaded him to advance one thousand pounds against a bond worth over twice that amount had been in London before. She'd been calling herself Miss Arabella Kenyon on that occasion but was now operating under the guise of a new name. Peter made a suggestion.

'The lady can change her identity as easily as she can change her hat,' he said. 'It would be a kindness to your rivals if you warned them to be on guard against her. You may not wish to help people with whom you're in competition, of course. I'm not sure what the protocol is in your profession. But I feel sure that Mrs Mallory is not here to make one strike before fleeing the city. That warning would be appreciated by people in your position.'

'Quite so, Mr Skillen.'

'Does that mean you *will* spread the word?'

Impey sat back in his chair and breathed in deeply through his nose. There was a problem, he realised. In warning other bankers that there was a forger at work, he'd be admitting that he'd been taken in by her wiles. People might thank him for alerting them but they would also laugh up their sleeves at the thought that Leonard Impey, one of the most experienced bank managers in the city, had been swindled and humiliated by a scheming woman. In the banking community, he'd be ribbed about it for months afterwards. He reached his decision.

'I'll think about it,' he said, evasively.

'*You* would be glad of such a warning, sir.'

'That's true but there are other factors to consider here. Apart from anything else, it might be entirely in vain. Having made a killing here, Mrs Mallory may have left London altogether. In fact,' he continued, trying to persuade himself as well as Peter, 'that's her most likely course of action. If she was here last June, she might well have played the same trick on another bank before going on to Ascot to place some of her ill-gotten funds on the horses. That is the way she works, I believe. Her method is to hit and run. Though the manager in question refused to make it public, she probably swindled another bank last year before disappearing. This year it was our turn. Thank you for your good counsel, Mr Skillen, but I'd prefer to keep our troubles to ourselves. No other bank is in danger. Mrs Mallory is too wily to take risks.'

Had he seen her at that moment, Impey might not have recognised her as the woman whose forged credentials had deceived him. A totally different dress and the careful application of cosmetics had changed her appearance markedly. The dark, curly wig and the wide-brimmed straw hat with its explosion of feathers completed the transformation. When she walked into the bank, even wearing a veil, she was the immediate cynosure. There was a sense of style and wholesomeness about her that was captivating. The manager noticed it at once. Emerging from his office, he first glanced then stared with unashamed curiosity. She glided across to him.

'Mr Oscott?' she enquired, sweetly.

180

'Yes, that's me.'

'I had a feeling you were the manager. You have an air of seniority. I've come for my appointment, Mr Oscott.'

'Then you must be...'

'That's right,' she said. 'My name is Kenyon – Miss Arabella Kenyon.'

He offered her a polite bow and inhaled her bewitching perfume.

'This way, please,' he said, indicating the door. 'Come into my office, Miss Kenyon. We have a lot to discuss.'

Charlotte's arrival was timely. While the incident had disturbed her, she was by no means persuaded that Abel Mundy was the person who'd thrown a stone at the window. At Hannah's instigation, Paul was ready to ride off at once to challenge Mundy but he had no idea where the man was lodging. Charlotte stepped in to suggest that he should first go to the manager. He could report what had happened and, if Fleet felt a visit to the playwright was justified, get the address from him.

'What if he refuses to give it?' asked Hannah.

'I think that's highly unlikely,' said Charlotte. 'He'll be as keen to know the truth about the incident as we are.'

'We already *know* the truth. It was Mundy's doing.'

'I still think there's some doubt about that,' said Paul.

Hannah shot him a look. 'Are you disagreeing with me?'

'I'm merely suggesting that we should get more

181

evidence of his involvement before we accuse him. Don't worry, Hannah. If he's the culprit, he'll be made to pay handsomely for it. I can promise you that.'

'Challenge him to a duel.'

'This can be settled by lawful means.'

When Paul went out into the hall, Charlotte walked after him so that she could have a private word with her brother-in-law. She looked over her shoulder to make sure that Hannah was not listening.

'Be sure to tell Mr Fleet that I'm here.'

'Why should I do that?' asked Paul.

'It's exactly what he requested. Having failed to make any headway with the two warring parties, he came to the gallery and, as a last resort, sought my help. Mr Fleet thought that another woman might have more influence over Hannah.'

'That was a wise move.'

'We shall see.'

'You can talk to Hannah in a way that none of us can.'

'I can only do my best. As for the broken window, I'd absolve Mr Mundy of the charge. He may be angry with her but he's not given to hasty action or he'd have taken it before. Were he caught committing such a crime, he'd be liable for arrest.'

'He'd get a beating from me beforehand,' said Paul. 'Like you, however, I don't think he'd be stupid enough to do anything so rash.' He kissed her on the cheek. 'Stay with Hannah and try to soothe her. Mr Fleet made the right choice when he came to you. *The Piccadilly Opera* may yet survive.'

182

Laetitia Somerville was inhospitable when she heard that the Runners had decided to call on her again. She asked for them to be turned away but they were too stubborn. Yeomans warned that they would stay outside the front door all night, if need be, because they had important information to pass on to her. At length, she capitulated and had the two of them let in.

'I was hoping that you'd show me more consideration,' she told them. 'You must have met many people who've suffered bereavement. It's a time when tact and forbearance are required. The last thing you should do is to call unbidden at people's houses.'

'You have our apologies,' said Yeomans.

'I said that we shouldn't bother you,' Hale put in.

'At least one of you has some sensitivity,' observed Laetitia.

'Now, what's this news you insist on passing on to me?'

'The inquest into Mr Bowerman's death is tomorrow.'

'Is that your pretext for coming here?'

'We thought it would interest you, Miss Somerville.'

'It does, sir, but it comes too late to be a surprise. Mr Skillen told me of it some hours ago. If that's all you have to say, I bid you farewell.'

'Paul Skillen was here *again?*' asked Hale in agony.

'He, too, has a good reason to catch the killer.'

'He may have a reason but he has no legal right.

183

We *do*, Miss Somerville.'

'And how much evidence have you gathered?'

'Ah, well...'

'It's slow work,' said Yeomans, uneasily, 'but we have made some advances. We're expecting help from Captain Hamer and Mr Carr.'

'I'd rather you didn't mention his hateful name,' she said, turning her head away. 'If the captain hadn't chosen to make an unheralded reappearance, then Mr Bowerman and I would be making preparations for our wedding. Instead of that,' she said, wistfully, 'he will be visiting a church for his funeral.'

'We share your dismay.'

'Do you want the details of the inquest?' asked Hale.

'No, I do not,' she said, brusquely.

'But you could give your testimony.'

'There's nothing I can say that will have any bearing on the murder of someone who was precious to me. I'd rather remember Mr Bowerman as the person who gave my life a sense of purpose. An inquest would only distress me.'

'They always bore me,' admitted Hale.

'It's your choice, Miss Somerville,' said Yeomans. 'Have you had any further thoughts about who might be responsible for the murder?'

'No, I have not.'

'Is there anyone who would have resented the idea of you getting married?'

'I'm not going to discuss my private life with you,' she said, haughtily.

'But, without realising it, you may be able to give us some guidance.'

184

'The thing is this, Miss Somerville,' said Hale. 'You already know that a woman is involved because she sent Mr Bowerman a summons in your name. What you don't know, perhaps, is that the information we had about the duel was also in a woman's hand.'

'Can you suggest who she might be?' asked Yeomans.

'No,' she said, face impassive.

But her brain was whirring away.

Lemuel Fleet was surprised when Paul arrived at his house and disturbed when he heard about the injuries sustained by his leading lady.

'How badly was she hurt?' he asked. 'Will she have to withdraw?'

'By the grace of God, the wounds were superficial, but they could easily have caused permanent damage to Miss Granville's face.'

'It's an omen. This play is doomed.'

'Forgive me, Mr Fleet,' said Paul, forcefully, 'but my only concern is for Miss Granville's safety. That's more important than any play.'

'Bills have been printed, tickets have been sold.'

'That's not the point at issue.'

'It is in my opinion.'

'Then you have clearly not reached the same conclusion as Miss Granville. Had you done so, you'd realise that there was no prospect whatsoever of a single performance of the play taking place.'

Fleet gulped. 'The lady surely doesn't think that...?'

'Oh, yes, she does.'

'But that's inconceivable, Mr Skillen.'

'There's been bad blood between her and Mr Mundy from the start.'

'Regrettably, that's true, but he'd never do anything like this.'

'He's already done it,' said Paul. 'According to Miss Granville, he's been throwing metaphorical stones at her since they first met. Today, she believes, he resorted to a real one.'

'That's fanciful. Mundy would be cutting his own throat. Without her, there'd *be* no play. I could never conjure an actress of her stature out of the air. Mundy knows that. He has to find a way to work with Miss Granville and vice versa.'

'That fantasy seems a long way off at the moment.'

Paul admitted that he, too, had doubts that the playwright was in any way culpable. He told Fleet that it was his sister-in-law's idea that he should first make contact with the manager in order to get Mundy's address.

'I'm indebted to the lady,' said Fleet, 'and I'd be grateful if you'd tell her that. Had you gone straight to confront Mr Mundy at his lodging, this whole business could have got dangerously out of hand. By coming here, you've at least had the time to review the situation with a degree of calm.'

'I may appear calm,' warned Paul, 'but I'm seething with anger. Miss Granville is very dear to me. If someone threatens her in any way, they'll have to answer to me. Mr Mundy may be innocent of the charge – that's yet to be proven, in my view – but somebody hurled that stone and I will hunt him down.'

'I'll gladly join you in that hunt, sir.'

'He's all *mine*, Mr Fleet.'

'I, too, have a score to settle with the villain. That stone may have been thrown at Miss Granville but it's an indirect attack on *me*. Without her, the play perishes.'

Paul chided him for taking such a selfish attitude, arguing that his major concern should be for Hannah rather than for the financial difficulties he might suffer as a result of cancellation. Fleet was duly humbled. He had the sense to realise that Paul was a possible ally. Being so close to the actress, he could apply even more pressure on her than his sister-in-law. What he could not do, however, was to speak to her as another woman. That was why Charlotte's help was vital as well. In order to get a compromise, the manager needed both her and Paul.

'Let's first call on Mr Mundy together,' he said. 'There's no deceit in him. He's a man who wears his heart on his sleeve. When we tell him of this incident, we'll know immediately if he was behind it by his reaction.'

'It may even induce some sympathy in him for Miss Granville.'

Fleet was pessimistic. 'That's too much to ask.'

Back at the gallery, Peter was explaining to Jem Huckvale what they had to do. He'd even drawn a rough plan of the building and marked the window through which he believed the younger man could easily crawl. In the time he'd worked and lived at the gallery, Huckvale had done a wide variety of things but the overwhelming majority of them had been perfectly lawful activities. Having to commit a crime worried him.

'What if I'm caught?' he asked.

'There's no chance of that, Jem.'

'Being hauled off to Bow Street is not very nice. Last time, they had no reason to take me there. This time, they would.'

'Yeomans and Hale will be nowhere near the place we're going to,' said Peter, confidently, 'because it would never occur to them to ask why the murder took place where it did. While you're getting hold of a piece of crucial information, they will be chasing their own tails somewhere else.'

'I'm still not happy about it.'

'You've nothing to fear.'

With a consoling arm around his shoulders, Peter reminded him how many much more hazardous things he'd done in the past. Compared to those adventures, the burglary would be swift, silent and without danger. Though Huckvale was not entirely convinced, he would never turn down the opportunity to work alongside Peter and his brother. Theirs was a world of excitement and that was irresistible.

It was evening now and the gallery was closed. Peter promised that he'd return at midnight to collect Jem for their nocturnal outing. Waving goodbye, he let himself out of the building. A figure hurried up to him. Though light was fading, Peter was able to recognise Silas Roe at once. The butler was animated.

'I'm so glad to find you,' he said, grabbing Peter's arm. 'I was hoping against hope that you'd still be here.'

'Why is that, Mr Roe?'

'I've brought some news for you, sir. When you came to the house, the information was not then in my possession. It is now.'

'Before you go any further,' said Peter, raising a hand, 'I should tell you that I'm not *Paul* Skillen. I'm his brother, Peter. We did meet when you first came here.'

'I remember. I thought I was seeing double.'

'Paul is not here at the moment and I have no idea where he is.'

'Oh, that's disappointing.'

'Are you so anxious to make contact with him?' Roe nodded. 'Then perhaps you can tell me what this latest news is. If it has a bearing on our investigation, then I'm eager to hear it. I can pass it on to Paul when I see him.' Roe looked uncertain. 'Clearly, it's something of great importance. We don't want to be discussing it out here in the street. Why don't we step back inside the gallery? We can talk in relative comfort there.'

Fleet was glad that he'd be present when Paul and the playwright met so that he could act as a buffer between them. Determined to avenge the woman he loved, Paul was likely to take a more combative approach towards Abel Mundy. An argument might easily flare up. Even if Mundy had no connection with the smashing of the window, blows might be exchanged. Each one would be felt by the manager. When they reached the house, Fleet was on tenterhooks, appealing to Paul to hold his peace.

189

'Let me do the talking, Mr Skillen.'

'If he threw that stone, I'll say what I have to say with my fists.'

'No, no – anything but that, please!'

'Ring the bell,' ordered Paul. 'I want to meet the man who's caused Miss Granville so much pain and anguish.'

Fleet did as he was told. A servant answered the door and they were admitted to the hall. Marion Mundy received them in the drawing room. Having met the manager before, she gave him a guarded welcome. He introduced Paul as a friend of Hannah Granville. The woman's face darkened instantly.

'We need to speak to your husband, Mrs Mundy,' said Fleet.

'It's on a matter of the utmost urgency,' added Paul.

'I'm sorry, but he's not here,' she said.

'Where is he?'

'My husband is where he always goes at this time of the day, Mr Skillen. He's in church. In fact, he's been there for well over an hour.'

If Mundy had been in church that long, Paul reasoned, he couldn't possibly have thrown a stone through his front window. On the other hand, the wife was only telling them what she believed. The playwright might have cut short his devotions for once and slipped across to Paul's house to lurk outside it.

'We'll wait until he gets back,' said Paul.

The Peacock Inn was as busy as usual that evening but they had no difficulty finding a table.

Yeomans had such physical bulk and such a daunting reputation that other patrons would always make way for him. Quaffing their pints, he and Hale sat in a corner and discussed what the day had brought them.

'I can see why Bowerman was attracted to her,' said Yeomans before releasing a sly belch. 'Miss Somerville would warm any man's bed.'

'She's well beyond our reach, Micah.'

'Thought is free.'

'Something about her worries me,' said Hale. 'Why is a woman like that not married already? And when she does finally choose a husband, why pick on someone like Mr Bowerman?'

'He's rich and respectable.'

'I think she'd set her sights a little higher than that.'

Yeomans beamed. 'On someone like me, you mean?'

'No – on a rich, respectable man with a title.'

They were still enjoying their beer when Chevy Ruddock walked into the pub.

He was a lanky young man with a willing heart and a face that seemed to sprout a new wart or pimple every month. Proud to work with the two leading Runners, he was ruthlessly exploited by them. He hurried across to their table.

'You sent for me, Mr Yeomans.'

'We have an assignment for you,' said the other.

'I'm ready, sir.'

'We had thought to give you the task of watching the Skillen brothers.'

'Oh no,' pleaded Ruddock, 'I've tried doing that before. Keeping an eye on Paul Skillen was

191

like trying to hold an eel with a pair of soapy hands. It's not a job for one man but for twenty.'

'We can't spare that many from our foot patrol,' said Hale.

'So you'll be shadowing someone else,' explained Yeomans. 'You're to stick to him like a limpet even if it means staying up all night.'

'My wife won't like that, sir. She misses me.'

'We all have to make sacrifices.'

'Who do you want me to follow?'

'It's that man we arrested at the duel – Captain Hamer.'

'Then you must think he's still the main suspect.'

'No, you nincompoop – he's not the killer. I'm hoping that he'll lead us to the man so that we can apprehend him. Captain Hamer is set on revenge. It's not because of any love he had for the victim. If we hadn't stopped him, he'd have shot Bowerman dead on Putney Heath. Someone else killed him instead and that rankles with the captain. His pride was hurt badly.'

'I see,' said Ruddock. 'I'm to stay on his tail because you and Mr Hale have no means of tracking down the killer yourselves.'

'No!' yelled Yeomans. 'That's not the case at all.'

'We've picked up his scent already,' lied Hale, 'but the captain has advantages that we lack. The killer, we believe, is someone who is – or used to be – in his circle. Though he's refusing to admit it, he already has ideas of who it might be. Follow him and he'll lead us to the prize. We then jump in ahead of him and make the arrest.'

'I like the plan,' said Ruddock.

'While you're at it, look out for that friend of his, Mr Carr. They're often together. Between them, they'll soon identify the man we want.'

'There's just one thing, sir...'

'Yes?'

'What if Peter and Paul Skillen catch the man before us?'

'What if I hit your head with this tankard?' asked Yeomans, raising it high. 'Do as you're told, man, and stop trying to think on your own. It will addle your brain and make your prick turn blue.' He took a notebook from his pocket. 'I'll write down Captain Hamer's address for you,' he said. 'And while I'm doing that, you can order a pint apiece for the two us. Go on – do something useful for once.'

When he returned home and found his wife absent from the house, Peter knew exactly where to find her. He rode straight to Paul's house. Surprised to see no light in the front room, he was even more taken aback by the sight of the planks of wood in the window frame. Even in the poor light, he could see pieces of glass all over the ground. Let in by a servant, he found Charlotte in the dining room with Hannah. While the latter had largely recovered from the incident in the drawing room, she still bore the marks of it on her cheek. Grateful to see her husband, Charlotte gave him a brief account of what had happened. It was then embellished by Hannah who still held to the notion that the person who'd hurled the stone at her was Abel Mundy.

'Where's Paul?' asked Peter.

193

'He's gone to pound Mr Mundy into oblivion.'

'Yet he has no proof that the playwright is the culprit.'

'I don't need proof,' said Hannah. 'I feel it in my bones.'

'How long ago did Paul leave?'

'It was well over an hour or more,' replied Charlotte. 'Even though he went to see Mr Fleet first, I'd have expected him back by now.'

'I hope he's learnt who was behind this dreadful attack on Hannah.'

'It *has* to be Mundy,' asserted the actress. 'Who else has a reason to hate me?'

'Nobody – you are universally loved.'

She pointed at her face. 'Not when I look like this.'

The front door opened and they heard voices in the hall. All three of them rushed out of the room to greet Paul, asking what he'd found out. When he'd established a degree of calm, he took them all back into the dining room and made them sit down around the table. Hannah frothed with impatience.

'Has he been arrested and put in chains yet?' she demanded.

Paul shook his head. 'No, my darling, he has not.'

'But he committed a terrible crime.'

'*Someone* did but I'm satisfied that it was not Mr Mundy.'

'Don't believe a word he said.'

'It was his wife who did most of the talking,' explained Paul. 'What none of us knew is that Mundy is a deeply religious man. He attends church every day. His wife is the daughter of a country vicar and as devout as her husband. At a time when the window was broken, Mundy was in church. I know that for a fact because I took the trouble to go there. He was in conversation with a priest. They were discussing theological niceties.'

Hannah was deflated. 'And he'd been there a long time?'

'Yes,' said Paul. 'Mrs Mundy spent time with him in church as well.'

'That means it must have been ... someone else.'

'Whoever it was, I'll catch him somehow. You have my promise. Meanwhile, I suggest that you keep away from the front window.'

Hannah was too distraught even to reply. Forced to accept that Mundy was not responsible, she had to accommodate the unsettling truth that someone else despised her enough to want to inflict injury. Seeing that the actress was in need of love and reassurance, Peter took his wife into the other room so that Paul was left alone with Hannah. They needed time together. Charlotte, meanwhile, told Peter about the plea from the theatre manager and how she'd done her best to talk Hannah round to the view that she had somehow to overcome her objections to the play and the playwright. It was well over a quarter of an hour before Paul joined them to say he'd persuaded Hannah to retire to bed. Peter seized his moment.

'Before you take her upstairs,' he said, 'I have important news for you.'

'What is it?'

'Mr Roe called to see you at the gallery. Disappointed that you weren't there, he instead passed on the information to me. It seems that he was rather more than a butler. He was the trusted friend and confidante of Mr Bowerman. He often dealt with his master's lawyer on his behalf.'

'Go on, Peter.'

'The lawyer came to visit the house today. He told Roe something that shook him. It appears that Mr Bowerman was so enchanted by Miss Somerville that he changed his will to make her the main beneficiary. In the event of his death,' said Peter, 'she was to inherit the bulk of his fortune. Don't you find that interesting?'

Along in her boudoir, Laetitia read his letter yet again then held it to her breast. It contained Bowerman's promise to amend his will in her favour. She knew that he would keep his word.

CHAPTER THIRTEEN

As he rode through the dark streets with Peter beside him, Jem Huckvale voiced his reservations. Having a great respect for the law, he was reluctant to break it.

'Is there no other way you can find out who owns that house?'

'No, Jem. The agent refused to tell me.'

'What about the neighbours? One of them might know.'

'All they know is that a succession of tenants

have stayed there. The gardener said the same thing. He hasn't a clue who actually owns the property because he's never met the person. He takes his orders from the agent.'

'I'm still unhappy about breaking in there.'

'You'll be in and out in a flash. You're not really *stealing* anything. You're simply there to get hold of something that should be public knowledge. Why is the agent being so secretive?'

'Perhaps it's what the owner wants.'

'That's all the more reason to discover his name.'

Huckvale remained uneasy. Though he knew that Peter would never willingly endanger him, he still feared that something could go awry with the plan.

'I won't know where to look.'

'The details we want are locked away in one of the cabinets.'

Huckvale was fearful. 'That means I'll have to cause damage.'

'There may be a way of opening the lock with a knife. It's a very simple design. I took note of that.' He reached out a hand to touch his friend's shoulder. 'Calm down, Jem. You're going into an office, not into a bank vault.'

On their way there, they passed the garden in which Mark Bowerman had been murdered and Peter felt a pang of sympathy for him. In all probability, the victim had never been to the house before. Bunkered by love, it had never struck him as odd that he'd been asked to meet Laetitia there rather than at her home. He'd gone to his death with a pathetic eagerness.

When they reached their destination, Peter first carried out a close inspection of the area to make sure that nobody was about. He then tethered the horses at the rear of the property and led Huckvale to the window he'd picked out.

'I'd never get through that,' whispered the other.

'Yes, you would.'

'It's too high up even to reach.'

'You can stand on my shoulders, Jem. Go in head first.'

'But how do I open the window?'

'You're being very awkward,' said Peter. 'Ordinarily, you'd never ask a question like that. You'd simply work out a way to do something and get on with it.' He undid his saddlebag and took something out. 'This is a jemmy,' he went on, passing the tool over to him. 'It will get you in through the window and, if you can't open the cabinet with your knife, then you'll have to force it open with this.'

'When I get inside, how will I see?'

'I'll pass you the lantern by sitting astride my horse.' Huckvale was still unconvinced. 'If it were not important, I wouldn't ask you to do this. Yes, breaking and entering is a crime but it pales beside murder. Inside that office is a piece of information that may help us to identify the killer. We need your help to find it, Jem. Don't let us down.'

'No,' said the other, committing himself at last, 'I won't.'

'Then climb on my back and stand on my shoulders.'

'I will.'

'Once you're inside, you're quite safe. There's

nobody else in the building.'

'What if somebody turns up out here?'

'I'll deal with that eventuality,' said Peter. 'Now let's get you in through that window. It will be child's play to someone as agile as you.'

Unable to sleep, Hannah lay propped up on the pillow. Paul was beside her but nothing he could say was able to take away her demons. She was afraid. Someone had tried to harm her, even to inflict permanent injury, and the most worrying feature of the situation was that it had not been Abel Mundy's doing. His proven innocence was like a physical blow to her and she searched for a means of involving him somehow in the attack on her. While he hadn't been responsible himself, she thought, he could easily have hired someone to loiter outside the house in the hope that she'd eventually appear in the window. That theory had a lot of appeal to her until she remembered that he'd been revealed as a man of Christian conviction. In response to her verbal assaults on him, he might revile her with words but that was all. Religion would hold him back from anything else.

Hannah had another enemy. The fact that he was unknown made him even more frightening. Would he strike again and, if so, where would he do it? It was unnerving. By virtue of her talents, she'd earned herself a vast number of admirers. Wherever she went, onstage or elsewhere, she was showered with praise. Hannah had been so accustomed to uncritical approval that she'd begun to take it for granted. It was one of the reasons for her feud with Mundy. He'd actually dared to criticise her performance. But the new development was a more sinister one. Someone reviled her as a person. He wanted blood.

'Try to get some sleep,' advised Paul.

'I daren't close my eyes.'

'You're in no danger when you're beside me, Hannah.'

'Then why do I feel so perturbed?'

'You have a vivid imagination, that's why.'

'Are these scratches imaginary?' she asked, pointing to her face. 'Did I dream up the pieces of glass in my clothes and hair? They were *real*, Paul.'

'I know, and I apologise.'

'Who is he?'

'I'll soon find out.'

'And why is he picking on me?'

'You're the most gorgeous woman in London,' he said, kissing her gently on the side of the head, 'and you have a legion of would-be suitors. It could be that one of them is unable to accept your rejection of him. In living with me, you exclude him from ever getting close to you. A rebuff like that would fester with some men.'

'That wouldn't make them turn on *me*,' she argued. 'You would surely be the target because you stand in the way of someone else's happiness. That stone would have been aimed at you, Paul.'

'There's merit in that argument,' he conceded. 'But I still refuse to believe that you could stir up real hatred in someone's heart. You're the kindest woman alive.'

'Abel Mundy hates me.'

'He dislikes you, Hannah, but he must respect your talent. And part of him must admire you as a woman.'

'Heaven forfend!'

'Under that crusty exterior, he's a normal human being. When he gazes at someone as dazzling as you, he's bound to look askance at that plain, homely, dull, unexciting wife of his. Anyway, enough of him,' he continued. 'Mundy was not to blame. That's certain. Is there anyone in the company who might wish to hurt you?'

'No, Paul, they've all been a delight to work with.'

'Then we must look elsewhere.'

'Where do I start?' she wailed. 'The very thought that he's still out there makes my stomach churn. To be honest, I'm terrified to leave these four walls.'

'But you must do so, Hannah. Don't let him see that he's frightened you. Be on your guard at all times, naturally, but don't let a stone through a window ruin your life. You're far too brave to do that, aren't you?'

'Yes,' she said with an attempt at firmness.

But, in the darkness, he could not see the naked fear in her eyes.

It was easier than Huckvale had imagined. Standing on Peter's shoulders, he jemmied open the window then went through it head first, curling up as he reached the floor and rolling forward like a ball. Peter lit the lantern and, by dint of mounting his horse, reached up to pass it through the window to his accomplice. Huckvale had another pleasant surprise. His knife unlocked the first cabinet without difficulty. Inside was a pile of ledgers. Holding one of them beside the lantern, he saw that it contained a list of the properties handled by the agency. He was about to search through them when he heard two sounds that made his blood run cold.

Peter reached up to tap on the window, a prearranged signal that somebody was coming. And Huckvale heard both horses moving away. Extinguishing the lantern, he crouched under the table in the dark and wished that he was still in bed back at the gallery.

Peter, meanwhile, was dealing with what might be an emergency. Hearing the approach of footsteps, he decided that the first thing he had to do was to lead the newcomer away from the building. He therefore took both horses around a corner and along a lane that ran between the houses. The footsteps behind him quickened and he was relieved that he'd only have to deal with one person. Finding a post to which he could tether the horses, he did so swiftly then dived into the doorway of a walled garden. Secure from sight, he waited.

The prowler was cautious. The footsteps slowed then stopped. Ears pricked, Peter listened for more sounds of movement. There were none. He came to believe that the stranger had backed off and gone on his way. It was only when he heard the sound of a leather strap being undone that he realised the man was very close to him, trying to open a saddlebag in search of booty. Peter came out of his hiding place at once, saw the hazy outline of the thief and flung himself at the man. While set on overpowering him, Peter was conscious that too much noise would only rouse people from their beds. He therefore clapped one hand over the man's mouth and used the other arm to drag him across to the wall.

The man responded by pounding away with both elbows and trying to shake Peter off but he was held too firmly. He was an older man in rough garb with a greasy cap that was knocked off in the struggle. Strong and determined, however, he bit Peter's fingers to make him pull his hand away from the mouth. A stream of expletives poured out, accompanied by the noisome stink of beer. Peter decided to end the brawl quickly. Grabbing the man by the hair, he smashed his head into the brick wall and sent blood cascading down his face. It took all the fight out of him. He was unable to do anything more than to flail wildly. When his head was banged against the wall a second time, he fell unconscious to the ground. Peter knew that they needed to complete their task and get away before the man woke up and started rousing the neighbours with a cry of rage. Valuable minutes had already been lost. There was no more time to waste.

He led the horses swiftly back in the direction from which they'd come, hoping that nobody else was abroad. A stray rider or pedestrian could ruin the whole enterprise.

Jem Huckvale was almost certain that he'd be caught. Someone had come. Peter might have been able to elude him but Huckvale was trapped. As soon as the open window was seen, his plight was settled. They'd know he'd entered the premises illegally. Being in the pitch-dark intensified his feeling of dread and vulnerability. He'd not only be caught, he'd have failed in his bid to get a telling piece of evidence. No magistrate would accept that he was committing one crime in order to solve a more heinous one. Huckvale had no legal right to be there.

When he heard knuckles banging on the window, his heart constricted. Someone had come in search of him. It was only when Peter hissed his name that he realised his friend was back. Huckvale leapt to his feet.

'Is everything all right?' he asked.

'It is now. Light the lantern again.'

'I haven't found what I'm after yet.'

'Keep trying,' said Peter. 'And please hurry up.'

Huckvale did as he was told. With a glow in the lantern once more, he went through the first ledger but found it unhelpful. He therefore pulled out the drawer again and saw that there were three others in there. Which was the one he needed? Or did he have to open one of the other drawers? Peter had assured him he'd be in and out in a matter of minutes. It already seemed like an hour.

He began to leaf through the pages as if his life depended on it.

Hannah Granville was too tired to stay awake yet too anguished to fall asleep. The only way that Paul could persuade her to drift off was to promise a search of the exterior house where, she feared, someone was waiting for a second opportunity to injure her. As soon as he got out of bed, her eyes closed and her breathing changed. By the time he eased the bedroom door gently open, she was already slumbering.

In his opinion, the search outside was a pointless exercise. The person who'd aimed the stone at Hannah had disappeared at once. Knowing that the whole house would now be on guard, he would not return. Paul nevertheless honoured his promise. He peeped out through windows in unoccupied rooms upstairs, then he went slowly down the steps. Expecting to find nothing at all threatening, he was alerted by the clip-clop of a horse. The noise took him quickly into the drawing room. Though most of the window was boarded up, some panes had been untouched by the stone. Paul was therefore able to see out. What he could discern in the gloom was a sturdy figure dismounting from the horse and creeping up the path towards the house.

Paul ran quickly into the hall and grabbed his sword from its scabbard. There was a slight rustling noise as something was pushed under the front door. Pulling back the bolt, he flung the door open, put a bare foot on the crouching man's chest and pushed him to the ground. Before the visitor could move, the sword was at his throat and Paul loomed over him.

'Who the devil are you?' demanded Paul.

'It's me,' said Peter, holding up both arms in surrender. 'It's your brother.'

Paul lowered the weapon. 'What are you doing here?'

'I was trying to leave a message without disturbing you. I had no idea that you were lurking behind the front door. You gave me a real fright.'

'*You* were the one who alarmed *me*,' said Paul, reaching out a hand to help him to his feet. 'Why on earth are you abroad in the small hours?'

'Jem and I have been at work.'

'Ah, yes, I'd forgotten. You wanted to break into that office.'

'That's exactly what happened.'

'Did everything go well?'

'The burglary was not without incident,' said Peter, retrieving his hat from the ground. 'Poor Jem reckons that his heart stopped at least four times.'

'And did you get what you were looking for?'

'I got rather more than that, Paul. My intention was simply to find out who owned the property and to see if he had any connection to the people with whom the murder has involved us.'

'What did you discover, Peter?'

'That house – or garden, to be more precise – was not chosen purely by accident. It was singled out.'

'Who actually owns the property?'

'Stephen Hamer.'

When his servant opened the bedroom curtains that morning, Hamer saw that light rain was falling out of a leaden sky. He ignored the weather. He was simply grateful that there were no dogs left outside his front door. It was an image printed indelibly on his brain. It reminded him that the Skillen brothers could not be intimidated. There'd always be reprisals. What he didn't notice from his bedroom was that someone was watching the house from a vantage point across the road.

An hour later, after he'd had his breakfast, Hamer had a welcome visitor. It was Rawdon Carr, the friend on whose advice he'd so often relied. When a servant had relieved the newcomer of his wet cloak and hat, Hamer conducted Carr into the drawing room.

'The Skillen brothers worry me,' he confessed.

'I'm still trying to find a way to get them off your back, Stephen.'

'Don't let it require dogs next time.'

'As it happens, it did cross my mind to use two terriers by the name of Yeomans and Hale but they'd never get the better of the brothers. They've tried before. The only use they have for us is as scavengers, gathering up evidence from that army of informers they keep. We can look for nothing more from the Runners.'

'They think they're in partnership with us, Rawdon.'

'Let them. When the time comes, we'll spurn them like mistresses who've outlived their usefulness and become tiresome.' He grinned. 'That's a situation we both know well.' He peered at the bags under his friend's eyes. 'You look as if you've hardly slept a wink.'

'I haven't.'

'Who was the lucky lady this time?'

'There isn't one.'

'It's not like you to take a vow of celibacy, Stephen.'

'I kept coming back to the same question. Who is doing this to *me*?'

'You do have a habit of making enemies,' said Carr, 'most of them female, I grant you, but there

207

are probably men with long memories as well.'

'It has to be someone close to me, Rawdon.'

'Or someone who *was* close at one time. That brings us back to your spent mistresses. None of them went willingly. Didn't the last one assault you?'

Hamer laughed. 'She punched me hard,' he said, 'and I rather enjoyed that. A woman roused is always a joy to see. I took her back to bed for an hour then sent her on her way for good. Though she pretended to go quietly this time, the little baggage stole a silver salver from the dining room. I let her keep it as a souvenir.'

'Perhaps she stole a Spanish dagger as well,' suggested Carr.

Hamer's laughter died out at once. It was something he'd never considered. When he thought about his relationship with the woman, he realised how much she must have learnt about his life and circumstances. She'd been particularly keen to find out how wealthy he was. In fact, it was her wish to convert a fleeting romance into a marriage that convinced him to get rid of her.

'Did you ever confide in her?'

'No, Rawdon, that was not why the affair blossomed.'

'Was she ever in this house when you were absent?'

'As a matter of fact, she was.'

'There you are, then – she could have done some prying.'

'I expressly forbade it.'

'When the cat's away...'

'She wouldn't have *dared*.'

'A desperate woman would dare anything, especially if she has designs on becoming Mrs Hamer. She'd certainly find a means of getting into that collection of weapons you hold so dear. We know she had a thieving instinct because she filched your salver. *That's* who got hold of the dagger, Stephen,' said Carr, decisively. 'What's her name?'

'Miss Eleanor Gold.'

'Find her quickly and shake the truth out of her.'

'Not so fast,' said Hamer, 'you're leaping to conclusions like a master of hounds going over a five-barred gate. It was not a long attachment. She'd only have been left alone in this house two or three times.'

'Once was enough.'

'If she'd taken that dagger, she'd have tried to use it on me.'

'Miss Gold might have done something far more subtle,' Carr pointed out. 'She could've used it *against* you and left you to face the consequences.'

'I'm sorry, Rawdon, but there's a fatal flaw in your argument. Bowerman was not struck down anywhere. He was stabbed to death in a property that I own. Eleanor could never have known it belonged to me.'

'Her accomplice might have done so.'

'What accomplice?

'I'm talking about the one who committed the murder, of course. A lot of forethought went into the plan. Bowerman was killed to throw suspicion on to you and a house you owned was chosen as the venue for the crime. Two enemies are in league against you,' said Carr, 'and only one of them wears a petticoat.'

'I refuse to believe it of Eleanor.'

'Soft-heartedness doesn't become you, Stephen.'

'She was fiery but not capable of plotting against me.'

'Then she was recruited by a man. He's the real villain.'

'I wonder...'

'Where is Miss Eleanor Gold now?'

Hamer was dismayed. 'I have no idea, Rawdon.'

'Then I suggest we find out – very quickly.'

When he called at the house, Lemuel Fleet did so with great trepidation. Hannah Granville needed to be handled with great tact at the best of times. In the wake of the attack on her, he suspected, she'd be in a state of constant turbulence. He was wrong. Much to his relief, he found her subdued and, for once, almost reasonable. Their discussion took place in a room at the rear of the house because she refused to enter the drawing room again.

'How are you, Miss Granville?' he asked.

'I'd rather not talk about the incident, if you don't mind.'

'Mr Skillen spoke of scratches to your cheek. I see no sign of them.'

'They are still there, Mr Fleet, but I choose to hide them.'

'And are you reconciled to the idea that Mr Mundy was not responsible for throwing that stone at the window?'

'I'm more than reconciled,' she said, quietly. 'I feel slightly abashed that I raged at an innocent man. That doesn't mean I'm ready to overlook all the insults he's directed at me,' she continued, 'but I no longer accuse him.'

'Is it permissible to pass on his best wishes to you?'

'I'd rather not hear his name at all, if you don't mind.'

'Then I might as well leave now,' he said, getting up.

'No, no, sit down again, please. There are things we must talk about.'

He resumed his seat. 'How can I do without mentioning his name?'

'You've spent your working life accommodating headstrong actresses, Mr Fleet. Accommodate *my* whims, please.'

'I've done rather a lot of that recently,' he murmured.

'What guarantees can you offer me?'

'I can offer you none with regard to ... the gentleman who remains nameless.'

'That's not what I'm worried about,' she explained. 'In view of what happened, this house is my fortress. I'm afraid to stir outside it. What guarantees can you give me of my safety?'

'You shall have as many bodyguards as you wish. As well as looking after you during rehearsals, they'll convey you to and from the theatre.'

'Thank you. I needed that reassurance.'

'Does that mean you *will* return to the company?'

'It means that I will not rule it out, sir.'

Fleet smiled. 'I never hoped for the slightest concession from you.'

'Nor have you got one,' she said. 'If I'm to resume my painful acquaintance with *The Piccadilly Opera,* it is there that the concessions have to be made.'

'You have an unexpected ally, Miss Granville.'

'Is that really so?'

'Were I not forbidden to do so, I would tell you the lady's name.'

'Then I encourage you to do so,' said Hannah, curiosity taking over. 'You refer to Mrs Mundy, I take it. It's the husband I abominate. I feel nothing but sympathy for a wife who is yoked to such a burden for the rest of her life. What did Mrs Mundy say?'

'She was profoundly sorry to hear of your plight. The first thing she did was to offer up a prayer for your recovery. The lady is not so wedded to her husband that she is entirely blind to his failings. She has a vastly higher opinion of his play than you do, perhaps, but she's ready to admit its occasional inadequacies.'

'They are not *occasional,* Mr Fleet.'

'Please don't deliver another diatribe, Miss Granville.'

'I wasn't going to. Before I can think of returning to the fold, there is an urgent question to be answered.'

'What is it?'

'Since *he,* it transpires, is not bent on harming me, then who *is?*'

Now that she'd rallied visibly, Paul Skillen felt able to leave her alone at the house. He had enquiries to make elsewhere. When he'd called on Sir Geoffrey Melrose, the man's memory had been strangely uncertain regarding the dinner party he'd once given at his town house. While readily confirming that Mark Bowerman and Laetitia Somerville had been present, he could only supply Paul with one other name. It was that of Rollo Winters, described by Sir Geoffrey as a politician of sorts and a decent fellow to boot. Paul deduced that the two men were old cronies.

Having been told that Winters called at his club every morning at the same time, Paul made sure that he arrived there shortly after. There was no need for any introductions. Winters was already expecting him because he'd received notice of it. Paul could see that Sir Geoffrey had warned his friend not to be too forthcoming. Rollo Winters was an impressive man, tall, well proportioned and with more than a little of his earlier good looks. There was an almost noble quality about him. His long black locks were tinged with grey and his face deeply lined but he seemed far too sprightly to be the sixty-year-old proclaimed on his birth certificate.

'Good day to you, Mr Skillen,' he said with bogus jocularity. 'Sir Geoffrey has told me a little about you and your quest. I'm not sure that I can help you.'

'It depends on how retentive your memory is.'

'Oh, it's very retentive. That's essential in a politician. You have to remember an interminable number of names and be able to relate each one to the way they vote and the company they keep. You must never speak out of turn among fellow politicians. That could be fatal. Memory is your saviour.'

'Does it only operate in the House of Commons, Mr Winters?'

'I see what you're getting at. You refer to dinner parties.'

'I refer to one in particular, sir. It was at Sir Geoffrey's house.'

'Then a problem raises its head at once, Mr Skillen. When he is here, Sir Geoffrey often has dinner parties. You might say that it's a way of life for him. He's never happier than when entertaining friends. I've been to so many of the gatherings that I have difficulty separating them.'

'This one involved a gentleman named Mr Bowerman. After the death of his wife, he shunned society. Simply getting him to the table was an achievement in Sir Geoffrey's eyes. Since he only made that single appearance, your retentive mind *should* remember Mr Bowerman.'

'Indeed, I do. He was rather too shy and desiccated in my view. All that he did was to stare fixedly at the ladies present – one lady, actually – and contribute nothing whatsoever to the prevailing hilarity.'

'Let's talk about that one lady, if I may,' said Paul. 'Her name was Miss Laetitia Somerville.'

'Was it?' asked the other in mock surprise. 'I believe you're right. The truth is that I never remember the names of the fairer sex. Their faces, bodies and carriage are engraved on my mind for ever but, since they're of no political significance, I treat them as the pleasing and decorative objects that they are.'

'Had you met Miss Somerville before?'

'Unhappily, I had not.'

'Do you know how she came to be there?'

'Sir Geoffrey must have invited her.'

'I'm wondering if she came at *your* behest, Mr Winters.'

'That's very flattering,' said the other with a chuckle, 'but it's not true. When you reach my age, alas, beautiful young women don't flock to join your circle. A young man like you, however, is in a different position.' Closing one eye, he regarded Paul with the other. 'If you want to know who took her to the dinner party, why don't you approach the lady herself?'

'I've already done so, sir.'

'What was her explanation?'

'She went along at the invitation of a female friend.'

'Then that's your answer. Why bother me?'

'I was not entirely persuaded by her claim. Also, I thought you could tell me a little more about the occasion.'

'What is there to tell?' asked Winters with a grin. 'It was a typical dinner party thrown by Sir Geoffrey. The food was delicious, wine flowed freely, the ladies sparkled and the only thing that impaired the general gaiety was that gloomy individual, Bowerman. We just ignored him and revelled into the night.'

'Yet he was the one who gained the real prize,' said Paul. 'Having met Miss Somerville, he developed an interest in her that burgeoned until it reached the point where he wooed and won her over.'

'I'd never have thought him capable of it.'

'Appearances can be deceptive.'

215

'Oh, you don't need to tell me that,' said Winters, chuckling again. 'When I look at the benches opposite me in the Commons, I see rows of serious, upright and apparently respectable men. In reality, of course, many of them are rogues, charlatans, certifiable idiots and seasoned adulterers.' He put a hand to his chest. 'I am none of those things, by the way.'

But Paul had already made his appraisal of Rollo Winters. Beneath his affability was a calculating politician who'd learnt to keep intrusive questions at bay. It was evident that he remembered the dinner party extremely well and could, if he desired, have listed the names of everyone present. In doing that, however, he would have revealed the real nature of the event. It was not simply a gathering of like-minded friends. The women were expected to be more than merely decorative. Paul recalled that Bowerman had told him that Laetitia stood out from the other women because she didn't flirt or giggle drunkenly. Quiet and dignified, she'd never let her guard down. Bowerman had admired her for that.

'It's almost noon,' said Winters. 'Can I offer you refreshment of some sort?'

'No, thank you,' replied Paul.

'I only come fully awake with that first brandy. Don't you need something to brace yourself against the demands of the day?'

'I like to keep my head clear, Mr Winters.'

'Alcohol sharpens the brain, take my word for it.'

'Then why did it deprive you of the details of a dinner party you once attended? The wine may have flowed yet the memory was dulled.'

Winters scowled. 'You're not a member of this club, Mr Skillen,' he said, crisply. 'If you don't leave immediately, I'll ask the steward to throw you out.'

Paul smiled. 'I'll gladly take my leave of you.'

As he stood up, he caught sight of someone out of the corner of his eye. The man came in through the door, stopped and went straight out of the room again. When he turned around, Paul saw that there was nobody there.

CHAPTER FOURTEEN

In spite of his antagonism towards her, Abel Mundy had a vestigial sympathy for Hannah Granville. When he'd first heard what happened, he felt sorry for her and not a little relieved that she'd survived the attack more or less intact. Had she been seriously injured, she'd have been unable to appear in his play and the production would have had to be abandoned. Without her, it could not take place; even with her, unfortunately, its chances of being performed remained slim. Mundy had been shocked that a rehearsal should be held without his knowledge and that radical changes were made to his work. Fleet had done his best to soothe the irate playwright and to convince him that alterations were unavoidable. After staring into the abyss of possible cancellation, Mundy finally accepted that *The Piccadilly Opera* at least ought to include proper arias to justify its title. Without them, his play might vanish altogether without trace. Given the torment it had caused to everyone involved, no other London theatre would touch it. Lemuel Fleet was his only hope.

Since there had to be cooperation on his part, Mundy decided to go to the theatre and discuss the situation with the manager. Before he did so, he went into the drawing room to tell his wife what he was going to do. He found her on her knees in prayer in front of the small crucifix they'd put up on the mantelpiece. It was not unusual to see her in such a position. They said prayers together every night beside the bed before they got into it. What made a difference this time was the fact that she remained in an attitude of submission for much longer than usual. It was several minutes before she finished. Becoming aware of her husband, Marion rose to her feet immediately.

'I'm sorry,' she said. 'Were you waiting to tell me something?'

'Yes, my dear, I was. I'm going to see Mr Fleet to seek a compromise.'

'Then my prayers have been answered.'

'Yet you were the one who said that I shouldn't change a syllable of the play.'

'That was before Miss Granville was almost blinded. I've been tortured by the thought of what might have happened to her. You'd have lost the chance of seeing a play of yours at the Theatre Royal, perhaps, but you'll go on to write others that will grace the stage there. In her case,' she said, 'she'd have lost both her eyesight and her whole career. Miss Granville would never be able to act again.'

'God bless you, Marion. You have a tender heart.'

She thrust out her jaw. 'It can be a block of ice, if necessary.'

'This latest crisis has rightly melted it,' he said. 'As a gesture of compassion to Miss Granville, I'll allow more music in my play. Whether or not that concession will be enough to pacify her, only time will tell.'

'Would you like me to come with you, Abel?'

'No, I must deal with Mr Fleet man to man.'

'Don't give way too easily.'

'I won't, my dear. He'll have to beg me.'

They walked to the front door together and she opened it for him before she accepted a kiss on the cheek. Something had clearly touched her.

'I was too harsh on Miss Granville,' she admitted. 'When I heard that she was cohabiting with a man, I was very scathing. I still condemn it strongly, of course. It's sinful behaviour. Yet somehow I found myself warming to Mr Skillen when he leapt so promptly to her defence.'

'It's no more than *I* would have done had *you* been in trouble, my dear.'

'That's my argument. He acted like a loving husband.'

'She's his paramour.'

'I'm not denying that, Abel.'

'That should tell you the sort of woman she is.'

'All that I wish to say is that Miss Granville is fortunate to have such a man at her side. Not that I'm condoning what they do,' she added, quickly. 'It's wrong before the eyes of God and anathema to both of us. But we mustn't sit in judgement on her private life. It behoves us to remember that *she* is the key to the future of your play.'

Peter felt that Jem's nocturnal antics had provided an intriguing clue to the crime. If a property owned by Stephen Hamer was specifically chosen as the murder scene, then he was either involved or someone was trying to put him in an awkward position. Should the Runners learn what Jem Huckvale had found out, they'd use it as another excuse to arrest Hamer. Because he was convinced that Hamer had not committed the crime, Peter would never inform Yeomans of their discovery in the agent's ledger. Paul agreed with his brother that the former soldier must have an enemy trying to wreak some sort of revenge. They could only guess what prompted it.

Having made a valuable contribution to the investigation, Peter felt able to take time off in order to render some assistance to the bank. He therefore rode in the direction of Epping Forest in search of Jacob Picton. A valued customer of the bank, the man would be aghast at the news that his name had been used to defraud the institution. Peter was hoping that he might be able to explain how a young woman was able to forge both a letter and a bond in his name. Like his brother, he set out alone on his horse. When he saw a coach going in the same direction, however, he was quick to ride behind it for safety.

Leonard Impey had told him that Picton was a prosperous man but Peter was unprepared for the size of his residence. Set in an estate of untold acres, it was imposing. Simply to maintain the extensive formal gardens, a large staff would have been needed. To run a house that large with its classical portico and its arresting symmetry, an even larger number of servants would be engaged. Picton shared his abode with a wife, four married sons and a confusing litter of grandchildren. Family friends were also staying there. Generous to a fault, Picton spread his bounty freely.

When Peter arrived, the butler did not immediately let him into the house. Stray callers were discouraged. Only when the name of the bank was mentioned was Peter allowed in. He was escorted along a wide corridor decorated with marble statuary and shown into the library. It was immense. A quick inventory of the shelves told him that Picton was a man of Catholic tastes. There were books on every subject under the sun with a special place reserved for tomes about architecture. He was just about to examine one of them when Jacob Picton came in.

'Mr Skillen?' he asked.

'Yes, sir – I'm very pleased to meet you.'

'I'm told that you're an employee of the bank.'

'I don't actually work there,' said Peter, 'but I've been retained by Mr Impey a number of times when there's been suspicious activity.'

'Is that what's brought you here – criminal behaviour?'

'Unhappily, it is.'

Picton was an old man bent almost double by age. Propped up by a walking stick, he shuffled across the room and lowered himself into a chair. Peter noticed the blue veins on the back of the man's skeletal hands. His long, snow-white beard was supplemented by wispy hair and by the tufts that grew in his ears. While his body was in decay, however, his faculties were undiminished.

'Why have you come to me, Mr Skillen?'

'First, let me show you this, sir,' said Peter, handing him the bond. 'We believe it to be a forgery and need you to endorse that view.'

Spectacles dangled on a ribbon around Picton's neck. He had some difficulty fitting them onto his nose. When he'd done so, he examined the document and emitted a growl of displeasure.

'Where did this come from?'

'They were presented to the manager by a Mrs Hester Mallory.'

'I know nobody of that name.'

'Is it a forgery?'

'It's a very clever forgery,' said Picton, squinting at it through his spectacles once again. 'I might almost have written this myself. The woman has copied my hand perfectly. What betrays her is a grammatical solecism of which I'd never be guilty. That's why I can say categorically that this is a fake bond.'

'Thank you for confirming it, sir.'

'Though I'm known for my generosity, I'd never advance an amount of that size to a total stranger.'

'I'm not sure that that's how she could be described, Mr Picton.'

'You think it was somebody I *know?*'

'It's certainly someone who knew you,' said Peter. 'At the very least, Mrs Mallory had access to correspondence of yours and an awareness of your dealings with the bank. Both letter and bond were sufficiently convincing to take in Mr Impey and he is not a gullible person.'

'How much money did he advance?'

'It was all of one thousand pounds.'

Picton clicked his tongue. 'That was uncharacteristically rash of him.'

'The lady seems to have been extremely plausible.'

'Feminine wiles are at play here, Mr Skillen. Had a man presented this bond to him, the manager would have needed more proof of his veracity before he handed over so much. I'm disappointed in him.'

'Mr Impey is very disappointed in himself, sir.'

'When you return to the bank, you can bear a letter to him from me. This time it *will* be genuine and not very pleasant to read.' He let the spectacles fall from his nose. 'I know what you're going to ask me. You want me to identify this lady posing under the name of Mrs Mallory. Describe her for me.'

Peter repeated what he'd been told by Impey, recalling the impression she made on first acquaintance. He also pointed out that she'd arrived just before the bank was about to close.

'That was deliberate,' he concluded. 'Mrs Mallory gave the manager very little time to question her. Having used your name as an endorsement, she promised to return on the following day.'

'Why didn't Mr Impey subject this bond to closer scrutiny?'

'He saw no reason to do so.'

'Impey should have done that as a matter of course.'

'Luckily, his chief clerk had doubts.'

'I'm glad that someone did. I find it very unsettling that my name was used.'

'That's why I wanted you to know what had happened.'

'What action have you taken on the bank's behalf?'

Peter told him of his visit to the hotel where Mrs Mallory claimed to be staying and how he'd learnt that, even though she was not a guest at the time, she had been in the past. On that occasion, she'd employed a different name. When he told Picton what that name was, the old man's eyes kindled.

'Miss Kenyon, was it?' he said. 'I knew her as Edith Loveridge...'

When he heard the carriage draw up outside the house, he went to the window and saw her getting out and paying the driver. Moving quickly into the hall, he opened the front door and gave her a welcoming embrace before whisking her into the drawing room. He was eager to learn her news.

'How much did you get this time?'

'This manager is rather more careful than Mr Impey,' she said, 'and requires time to consider the transaction. No matter, I had him dangling like a fish on a line. In due course, I vow, we'll get every penny requested.'

Chevy Ruddock was unhappy. He hated surveillance work. When he'd had a similar assignment, he thought it would be a feather in his cap but that hope soon perished. Given the task of watching a brothel in Covent Garden, he'd spent interminable hours at his post and suffered all kinds of humiliation. It was the same on this occasion. On duty for the whole night, he'd been pestered by stray dogs, harassed by drunken oafs and soaked by the rain. The one consolation was that Yeomans had given him the use of a horse but it was never needed. Instead of passing the night with his wife in the comfort of their bed, he and the animal had stood together in mutual misery in the darkness. Ruddock was tired, bored and very wet.

Nothing of consequence had happened. Earlier that morning, Rawdon Carr had visited his friend then left. Though he made a note of the times of arrival and departure, Ruddock doubted that they would be of any significance. Hours rolled by. He was just about to drop off to sleep when there was some action at last. Stephen Hamer left the house and mounted the horse his servant brought out for him. He set off at a canter. Ruddock hauled himself into the saddle and went after him. His fear that he'd be noticed soon faded away. Hamer was riding with such urgency that he only had eyes for what lay ahead of him.

Eventually, he reached a fine house not far from Piccadilly and reined in his horse. A servant came out to take care of it and Hamer was admitted to the building. Ruddock dismounted, tethered his horse to a railing and studied the building. When someone emerged from a neighbouring house, he went quickly across to the man.

'Can you tell me who lives next door?' he asked, politely.

'Yes,' said the man, obligingly. 'It's a Miss Somerville.'

'Would that be Miss *Laetitia* Somerville?'

'Yes – do you know the lady?'

But Ruddock was already running back to his horse.

Paul called at the gallery at an ideal time. Gully Ackford and Jem Huckvale had just finished teaching their respective pupils and were having a rest. They were interested to hear Paul's latest theory. Having met both Sir Geoffrey Melrose and Rollo Winters, he had a clearer idea of what must have happened at the dinner party given by the former. It had not been an evening of intellectual debate. Sir Geoffrey and his friend were men of the world who took their pleasures where they found them or, in this case, where they set them up. Unencumbered by their wives, they wanted an evening of merriment that ended in the bedroom and they'd invited their guests accordingly. With the exception of Mark Bowerman, the men were of one accord; with the exception of Laetitia Somerville, the women were chosen because of their known readiness to acquiesce. Inevitably, Bowerman and Laetitia had been thrown together as the outsiders. That led Paul to one conclusion.

'Sir Geoffrey betrayed his friend,' he decided.

'Is that what he admitted?' asked Ackford.

'Oh, no, it was quite the reverse, Gully. He claimed to be acting in the spirit of true comradeship, rescuing Bowerman from his hermetic existence and introducing him to real life again. I fancy there was rather more to it than that.'

226

'I see what you mean, Paul.'

'He was invited for the sole purpose of meeting Miss Somerville.'

'Did the lady *know* it?' said Huckvale.

'I think she arranged it, Jem.'

'But she *wanted* to marry Mr Bowerman, didn't she?'

'She gave him reason to believe that she did,' said Paul, developing his theory as he went along, 'and she seemed genuinely distressed by his death when I first met her. Then we had the information that Bowerman's will had been changed recently in her favour. In one sense, therefore, his murder was actually good news for her.'

'Do you think she was involved in it?' asked Ackford.

'No, I don't. Miss Somerville was really shocked by it.'

'Then what exactly is going on?'

'I was going to ask the same question,' said Huckvale. 'It's all a bit confusing to me. From what you've told us, Mr Bowerman was a good man.'

'He was a person of great integrity,' said Paul. 'His one weakness was that he was somewhat unworldly and I certainly wouldn't have said that of Sir Geoffrey or Winters. 'What I'm coming to believe is this: Miss Somerville was looking for a wealthy man she could entrap and lead by the nose. I don't believe she ever intended to marry him. When he'd done what she really wanted and changed his will out of love for her, she was ready to dispose of him.'

'The duel,' said Ackford, smacking the table for

227

effect. 'Another suitor turns up and lays claim to her, more or less forcing Bowerman into challenging him. Hamer didn't arrive out of the blue at all. He was waiting until he was called.'

'That's the way my mind is working, Gully. There could be a conspiracy here. Once he'd served his purpose, Mr Bowerman was in the way. Hamer was summoned to kill him in a duel. It's so cruel,' said Paul. 'In trying to make Miss Somerville his wife, Mr Bowerman was unwittingly setting a date for his own execution. Instead of using a noose, however, Hamer was planning to shoot him dead with a duelling pistol.'

'That's not only cruel,' said Huckvale, 'it's wicked.'

'Hamer and Miss Somerville have been working hand in glove all along.'

'Yet you said earlier that she was shocked by Mr Bowerman's murder.'

'What shocked her was that it didn't take place on Putney Heath. That was the execution she'd ordered. Someone chose a different way to kill him.'

'Who was that, Paul?'

'Your guess is as good as mine.'

'And why was he stabbed in the garden of Captain Hamer's house?'

'He was only a lieutenant, Jem.'

'Oh, yes. I was forgetting. Your brother told us about that.'

'In answer to your question,' said Paul, 'I don't know. What I suspect is that someone wanted to settle a score with Hamer and Miss Somerville. Both of them were stunned by the murder and she couldn't suggest who might possibly have been responsible for it. Now,' he went on, 'I must get back to Hannah. As you'll have heard, she's a trifle upset at the moment.'

'Yes,' said Ackford, 'Charlotte told us a stone smashed your window.'

'I've got a crime right on my doorstep.'

'It's no worse than being attacked by two dogs in the middle of the night.'

'Yes, that must have been a rude awakening, Gully.'

'I was really shaken.'

'And so was I,' admitted Huckvale. 'It was far worse than being arrested by the Runners. They can bark very loud but at least they don't bite.'

Troubled by hunger pains, Yeomans and Hale repaired to The Peacock to enjoy a meat pie apiece and to wash it down with a pint of beer. It was not long before they were joined by Chevy Ruddock, still sodden and so exhausted that he couldn't complete a single sentence without yawning dramatically. Yeomans grabbed him by the neck and shook him like a rag doll.

'Wake up, man!'

'I'm tired, Mr Yeomans.'

'We've told you before. Runners never sleep.'

'Well, I do,' said Ruddock, unable to suppress the biggest yawn yet.

'What have you found out, Chevy?' asked Hale.

Ruddock fingered his shoulder. 'I found out that there's a hole in this coat where the stitching's come undone. I'll have to ask my wife to sew it up again. The rain kept seeping in through the hole. My shirt is wet through.'

'Forget about your shirt. What did you learn?'

'Captain Hamer stayed in all night – unlike me.'

'Were there any visitors?'

'Not until this morning, sir. Then that friend of his arrived.'

'Mr Carr?'

'That's the one. He has a very sharp tongue. He called me all sorts of vile names when we interrupted that duel.' He pulled a notebook from his pocket and flipped through the pages. 'He arrived at nine o'clock and left exactly thirty-five minutes later. The captain came to the door to wave him off.'

Yeomans contributed his own yawn. 'Is that all you found out?'

'Oh, no, I haven't come to the best bit yet.'

'What is it?'

'Captain Hamer left his house at' – he consulted his notebook – 'it was three minutes after two o'clock and he was in a hurry.'

'Did you follow him?'

'Yes, Mr Yeomans.'

'Where did he go?'

'It was to this house in a street off Piccadilly. I'd love to live somewhere like that. Agnes, my wife, would be so happy there. But it will never happen unless we get taken on as servants. We know our place.' Yeomans shook him again. 'Don't do that, sir. I have a job standing up straight. If you shake me again, I'll finish up on the floor.'

'Give us some useful *information*, man!'

'I wondered who lived there so I asked a neighbour.'

'And?'

'It was Miss Somerville's house.'

The Runners gazed at him in surprise and then, when they were confronted by another monstrous yawn from Ruddock, they turned to look at each other.

'I thought she hated the captain,' said Hale.

'She did, Alfred. She didn't even want us to mention his name.'

'Then why did she let him go into her house?'

'Perhaps he forced his way in.'

'Is that what happened, Chevy?'

There was no reply to Hale's question because Ruddock had just nodded off to sleep. Eyes closed, he stood there immobile with a seraphic smile on his face. It was removed by a kick on the shin from Yeomans. Coming awake with a start, Ruddock hopped on one foot while he rubbed his other leg.

'That hurt!' he complained.

'Then tell us what we want to know,' said Yeomans. 'Did the captain have a struggle to get into the house?'

'No,' said Ruddock, barely managing to keep his balance. 'He was let straight in. A servant came out to stable his horse for him. It was almost as if he was expected.' He stood on both feet again. 'I thought you'd like to know.'

'We're delighted with the news,' said Hale.

'Well done, Ruddock!' said Yeomans.

'This deserves a reward. You look as if you're starving. Take my seat and help yourself to what's left of my pie.' Hale got up from the table. 'I'll fetch you a tankard of beer to help it down.'

231

In the face of such kind treatment, Ruddock glowed. He'd done something to gain their appreciation at last. He was still grinning when he fell asleep again.

Lemuel Fleet had come so close to falling into a crater of despair that he felt it was only a matter of time before he finally toppled. His profession acquainted him with possible danger every day. When trying to set up a performance of a new play, so many things could go wrong. All of them had happened to *The Piccadilly Opera*. There was no affliction from which the play had not suffered. As it stood, it was wholly unfit for public consumption. Were he to put it in front of an audience, it might ruin his reputation irreparably. He knew to his cost how wild theatregoers could be. They insisted on value for money. Fleet was aware just how many riots had been started by discontented patrons over the years. On one occasion, when higher prices were introduced, there had been continuous rioting for all of sixty-six days until the management relented.

Loving the fabric of his theatre as much as its traditions, he was terrified of wanton destruction. A bad play with a half-hearted actress as its central attraction would provoke anger and violence. He was staring into the crater yet again.

'I wonder if I might have a word, Mr Fleet.'

'What's that?' He came out of his reverie to see his visitor. 'Why are you here, Mr Mundy? No rehearsal is called for today.'

'I wish to speak to you.'

'Yes, yes, come on in, please do.'

'You said that your door was always open.'

Fleet was staggered less by the playwright's arrival than by the unusual tone of his voice. It was soft, low and almost apologetic. He got up to bring Mundy fully into the office and eased him into a chair, taking the one opposite for himself.

'I've been talking things over with my wife,' said Mundy.

'I do the same thing myself.' Fleet gave a nervous laugh. 'I don't mean that I talk to *your* dear spouse, of course. I converse with my own. It often helps me to see things in a new light somehow. Does it have the same effect on you?'

'As a rule, it doesn't.'

'I'm sorry to hear that.'

'My wife, Marion, is my mainstay. Whatever course of action I take, she will always endorse without ever questioning it.'

'There aren't enough women like that about,' said Fleet.

'That, I should add, was until today. She did think for herself this time.'

'Oh?'

'Indeed,' said Mundy, 'she resorted to prayer beforehand so that she had divine authority for it. She pointed out that we have both been too ready to abuse Miss Granville when all that she wants is for my play to be seen at its very best. The attack on her has made us take a more understanding view of her.'

'Am I actually *hearing* this?' asked Fleet, close to delirium. 'Are you telling me that you approve of Miss Granville's suggested improvements?'

'Oh, no, they are far too comprehensive. I stand

by my right as the playwright to protect my work. I'll make changes after – and only after – reasonable discussion. In essence, I'm committing to finding a middle way between my own suggestions and Miss Granville's more savage approach to the text. Is that fair, Mr Fleet?'

'It's more than fair.'

'Will the lady herself take the same view?'

'We can but ask.'

'Then I urge *you* to do the asking. For some reason, I irritate the lady.'

'I simply can't understand why,' said Fleet, concealing the lie behind a broad smile. 'Once again, I am ready to act as a willing go-between.'

'Remember what the Bible says – "Blessed are the peacemakers"…'

'I think that we should bless your dear wife as well. Mrs Mundy may have found the way to save all our skins.'

Slipping quietly into the church, Marion Mundy walked down the aisle then stepped into a pew. She knelt down and went through the prayers that she routinely said every day. Her mind then turned to her husband. Secure in the house of the Lord, she prayed in earnest for the success of his play and for the removal of the incessant bickering that it had so far produced. She remained on her knees until the pain eventually forced her to get up.

'I'm worried, Laetitia.'

'It's not like you to lose your nerve.'

'I *haven't* lost my nerve,' retorted Hamer. 'I'll

face any kind of jeopardy without a shred of fear but I prefer it to be visible. That's what makes this situation so maddening. Things are happening out of sight.'

'We can deal with them.'

'You can't shoot at what you can't actually see.'

'I thought you might have worked out who is behind it all by now.'

'That's what I've been trying to do. Rawdon came up with the best suggestion. He wonders if it might be someone from whom I parted rather abruptly. The obvious name was Eleanor Gold.'

'Was she that pouting young woman with a high opinion of herself?'

'She was very appealing at first.'

'What happened?'

'I made the mistake of trusting her, Laetitia.'

'In what way?'

'Thinking it was safe to do so, I let her stay in the house when I wasn't there. Rawdon believes that she might have taken the liberty of reading your correspondence to me and of sneaking into my little museum. In other words,' said Hamer, 'Eleanor could have stolen that Spanish dagger of mine.'

'And if she read my letters to you,' said Laetitia with growing alarm, 'she'd have been aware of what we'd planned. She'd know, for instance, the exact time when the duel was taking place.'

'More importantly, she could have studied your hand carefully enough to forge a summons to that credulous fool, Bowerman. Yes,' he decided, 'I think we may be on the right track at last. Eleanor Gold and an accomplice are the villains.'

'Then it was stupid of you to let her get so close. Why didn't you just take what you wanted and throw her out?'

'She was very sweet, Laetitia.'

'She's sweet and murderous, by the sound of it.'

'Rawdon and I will find her,' he vowed. 'We just have to hope that someone else doesn't get to her first. If that happens, we're done for. Eleanor will be able to tell them how you tricked Bowerman into changing his will, then handed him over for me to kill in a duel. We must catch her *first*.'

'You'll have no competition from the Bow Street Runners.'

'I wasn't thinking of them.'

'Are you still concerned about the Skillen brothers?'

'They are the real problem,' he conceded. 'Rawdon tried to frighten them off but his plan was foiled. He's trying to devise another way of diverting them.'

'Then he needs to put it in place very soon.'

'I'd happily meet anyone in a duel but I'd think twice about it if the man with the other weapon in his hand was Paul Skillen. He's dangerous.'

'I agree with you, Stephen. He troubles me as well.'

'His brother is an equal threat to us.'

'Then we may have to get rid of both of them, permanently.'

'That won't be easy,' he said.

'Are you afraid of them?'

'No, of course I'm not, Laetitia. But I treat them with respect. When you signed the death warrant for Bowerman, you gave me an easy task.

I'd have shot him dead before he'd even pulled the trigger.' He pursed his lips. 'Killing Peter and Paul Skillen is a much more daunting task but it's not one from which I'd flinch. In fact, I think I'd relish it.'

She was merciless. 'If it needs doing, you and Rawdon must do it.'

Laetitia heard the clang of the doorbell and moved to the window. When she peered around the curtain, she saw Yeomans and Hale standing outside. She turned quickly back to Hamer.

'It's those damnable Runners again,' she said. 'They mustn't find you here.'

'I'll hide in there,' he said, moving towards the adjoining room.

'Don't come out until I call you.'

'Listen to what they want then send them quickly on their way.'

'Just go,' she urged, opening a door for him.

When Hamer had gone, Laetitia sat down again in a posture that suggested grief and remorse. She was still wearing the black dress and exuding a sense of irreplaceable loss. When the servant brought news of the visitors, she agreed to see them on the condition that they stayed only a short time. After passing on the message to the Runners, the servant ushered them into the room.

Yeomans came straight to the point. 'Where is Captain Hamer?'

'I beg your pardon,' she said.

'You told us that you detested the man.'

'And I do, Mr Yeomans. His name is abhorrent to me.'

'Then why did you let him into this house?'

237

'I'd never deign to do such a thing,' she said, hotly.

'Oh, yes, you would, Miss Somerville.'

'We had the captain's house watched,' said Hale, triumphantly. 'Earlier today, he was seen to leave his abode and ride straight here. One of your servants stabled his horse as if he was used to seeing Captain Hamer.'

'So I'll repeat my question,' said Yeomans, moving forward until he loomed over her like a huge, dark cloud. 'Where *is* he?'

CHAPTER FIFTEEN

Laetitia Somerville was rarely at a loss for words but she was groping in vain for them now. Their arrival and challenge was so unexpected that it took all the wind out of her. Maintaining her composure, she retreated into silence. It was soon broken. The door opened and Stephen Hamer charged angrily into the room.

'How dare you treat me like this!' he yelled. 'It's insulting. The chief magistrate will hear about it.'

'He will,' agreed Yeomans, 'and he'll praise us for exposing your lies.'

'Miss Somerville swore to us that she had no time for you,' said Hale, 'yet here you are, walking into this house as if you own it.'

'I have every right to a private life,' said Hamer with asperity, 'and so does Miss Somerville. What has this city come to when it condones the use of

Peeping Toms on innocent people?'

'We're not sure that you *are* innocent, sir.'

'I take the same view as my colleague,' said Yeomans, heavily. 'When a person tells us one thing then does completely the opposite, we grow suspicious.'

'The captain was allowed in for only one reason,' said Laetitia, regaining her confidence, 'and for one reason only. He'd written to me, asking for permission to apologise in person. Because he expressed his heartfelt sympathy for the death of Mr Bowerman, I agreed to see him.'

'It's true,' said Hamer, catching her eye and reading its message.

'It does not mean that we are now on terms of friendship,' she went on. 'I've made that crystal clear. I've accepted the apology but that's all I've done. From today onwards, the captain is not welcome within these four walls.'

'It's no more than I deserve.'

'And that's all you have to say, is it?' taunted Yeomans.

'Yes,' said Hamer, 'so you can get out right now.'

'We haven't finished yet, sir. If – as you and Miss Somerville claim – this was a brief visit to say that you were sorry, two questions arise. Thanks to a colleague of ours, we know the exact time when you were admitted to the house. It was over an hour ago. Does it always take you that long to offer an apology?'

'Don't be impertinent!'

'The second question is the important one. If you had a good reason for being here, why were

239

you hiding in another room so that we didn't see you?'

'If you are going to interrogate us like this,' said Laetitia, grandly, 'beware of the legal consequences. I retain one of the finest lawyers in the capital. If officers of the law step out of line, as both of you are now doing, he will have no compunction in having you dismissed.' She stood up to confront them. 'What did you do before you became a Bow Street Runner, Mr Yeomans?'

'I was a blacksmith,' he replied.

'It's an occupation more suited to a man of limited intelligence like yourself.' She turned to Hale. 'What about you?'

'I was a harness-maker,' said the other.

'So the pair of you worked exclusively with horses, did you? That will explain your total lack of manners. Dumb animals have no need of etiquette.'

'We're used to people sneering at us, Miss Somerville,' said Yeomans. 'It's usually a sign of their guilt.'

'Of what are we supposed to be guilty?' demanded Hamer.

'We think you are in collusion with each other.'

'That's nonsense!'

'You can rant and rave all you wish, sir. We see what you see.'

'Then arrest me yet again, if you dare, and do the same to Miss Somerville this time. Take us before the chief magistrate and justify your mistake. I've been to Bow Street before, please remember, and I walked away as the innocent man I was. You would have been duly admonished for your mistake. On this occasion, I'll warrant, your fate will be much worse.'

'Not to worry,' said Laetitia, 'there's always a call for good blacksmiths.'

'Harness-makers are also in demand,' said Hamer.

'Do as the captain suggests and arrest us.'

They had reached an impasse. The certainty with which the Runners had entered the house had begun to crumble slightly. Had they placed the wrong construction on the fact that Hamer had called at a house where he was supposedly unwelcome? Ruddock had noted how familiarly he'd entered the building. Was that what had actually happened? If not, thought Yeomans, at least they'd have someone to blame. Ruddock would always be their whipping boy.

For their part, Laetitia and Hamer were hoping that their outraged denials were enough to put the visitors to flight. News that one of them was under surveillance had been a profound shock and a reminder that they needed to take the utmost care. Having derided the Runners, they now realised that Yeomans and Hale were not as inefficient as they'd assumed. When they saw grounds for suspicion, they acted accordingly. As a result, they'd caused Laetitia and Hamer acute embarrassment.

The two parties faced each other. Nobody moved and nobody spoke. Minutes steadily accumulated. Hamer looked for signs of weakness in the Runners while they, in turn, watched for an opening they could exploit. It never came. The impasse was eventually broken.

'To use an army term,' said Hamer, 'I'd advise

241

a tactical retreat on your part.'

'We'd advise *you* to start telling the truth for once,' Yeomans retaliated.

'You have a warrant for our arrest?'

'No,' confessed Hale.

'Then it's time for you to withdraw.'

Though he was desperate to stay, Yeomans could find no reason to do so. Their mission had failed. He sought to win at least a token of gratitude from them.

'There was another reason why we came,' he said.

'Tell us what it is,' invited Laetitia, 'then get out of my house.'

'The inquest delivered its verdict.'

'It was exactly what we said it would be,' added Hale. 'It's recorded as a case of murder by a person or persons unknown.'

'Then get out there and catch them,' said Hamer. 'You won't find them here.'

'You heard Captain Hamer,' said Laetitia, reinforcing his command. 'He's given his word as a gentleman that he is innocent of the stabbing and I need hardly say that I, too, am wholly innocent of the crime. Your visit is therefore at an end. Please don't have the effrontery to come to this house again.'

After mumbling their apologies, the Runners crept out of the room.

When the letter arrived, Hannah read it with a mingled interest and distrust. Delivered by hand, it had been sent by Lemuel Fleet and told of the offer made by Abel Mundy. Hannah read it three times before she handed it over to Charlotte, who was seated at the rear of the house with her. Charlotte's response was more optimistic.

'This is good news, Hannah.'

'I wonder.'

'To some extent, it's an olive branch.'

'It's certainly not the surrender that I desire,' said Hannah. 'I am not only thinking of myself. I speak on behalf of the entire company.'

'I think they'd be cheered by the manager's letter. According to him, Mr Mundy is prepared to give ground.'

'Yes, but how much ground?'

'There's only one way to find out,' said Charlotte.

She was delighted that her friend had received encouragement at last. As well as reviving the hope that the play would be performed after all, it took Hannah's mind off the fear of another attempt to harm her. Dirk, the manservant, had been going out of the house regularly to make sure that nobody was watching for a chance to strike again. So far nothing remotely suspicious had been seen. While that had calmed Hannah, the letter had a less soothing effect on her altogether.

'His stipulation disturbs me, Charlotte.'

'Why is that?'

'Mundy insists that we discuss things together.'

'Isn't that the obvious thing to do?'

'Not when it forces me to look at that repulsive face of his.'

'Mrs Mundy doesn't find it repulsive.'

'That's neither here nor there,' said Hannah. 'If I'm honest, I'm afraid that the very sight of the man will make the hairs on the back of my neck stand up. I'll be in no state for the reasonable debate that Mr Fleet is suggesting.'

'The deadlock has to be broken somehow, Hannah.'

'Why must *I* make concessions?'

'All that the letter asks is that you recognise Mr Mundy's readiness to accept change and agree to search for a compromise acceptable to both of you. You're under no pressure to do anything that offends you.'

Hannah picked up the missive again but she had no time to read it again because Paul had just returned to the house. Coming into the room, he embraced Hannah then gave his sister-in-law a kiss.

'Dirk tells me that there's been nothing to report,' he said. 'It's as I thought. Nobody will dare to come back because they know we're on guard now.'

'Hannah's had a letter from Mr Fleet,' said Charlotte. 'He's calling a truce.'

'What does he say?'

'You can read it for yourself,' said Hannah, 'but only after you've told us where you've been and who you've seen. I'm not yet ready to make a decision about the play. In any case, it pales beside a murder investigation. What have you learnt?'

Paul told them more or less what he'd told Ackford and Huckvale at the gallery. He believed that the dinner party had been stage-managed in order to make possible a meeting between Bowerman and Laetitia Somerville. Who had actually devised the scheme, he was not sure, but Sir Geoffrey

Melrose and Rollo Winters had been willing accomplices. Now that the relationship had ended with Bowerman's murder, both men had tried to distance themselves from any guilt. The two women listened open-mouthed to the revelations.

'Miss Somerville is *capable* of such villainy?' asked Charlotte.

'Oh, I think she could do much worse,' said Paul. 'What now seems clear is that she and the so-called Captain Hamer are working together.'

'Does that mean they're lovers?'

'I'm not sure about that, Charlotte, but their guilt is incontestable.'

'Then they should be in custody,' said Hannah. 'Why don't you and Peter arrest them and take them before a magistrate?'

'It's too early for that. Lock them away and we might never find out who killed Mr Bowerman because they are the only people who can lead us to the killer. Someone is venting his spleen on them by trying to incriminate them. Frankly,' said Paul, 'I'm more eager to catch the man who *did* murder Mr Bowerman rather than those who plotted to have him shot dead in a duel. Once that's done, Peter and I can round up Hamer and Miss Somerville.' He looked at Charlotte. 'By the way, where is my brother?'

'He rode off to see someone who lives near Epping Forest,' she said, glancing up at the clock on the mantelpiece, 'but he should be back by now.'

Leonard Impey had feared the reproaches of his old friend and client and he had good reason to do so. What Peter brought back from his visit to

245

Jacob Picton was a letter of blistering criticism. It not only accused the manager of naivety and incompetence, it severed a relationship that had lasted for over thirty years. Impey collapsed into his chair and shrugged helplessly.

'It's all true, Mr Skillen. I deserve to be skinned alive like this.'

'Mr Picton did have *some* words of praise for you, sir.'

'Well, there's not one of them in his letter. What did he say?'

Peter told him of his visit to Epping Forest and how devastated the old man had been when he learnt what had happened. While he had never met a Mrs Mallory, he'd remembered an Edith Loveridge only too well. She'd wormed her way into Picton's social circle by means of a friendship with one of his daughters-in-law. They'd shared an interest in painting and, between them, produced a number of landscapes of the surrounding countryside.

'So she didn't come to London in search of an artist, as she claimed,' said Impey, sourly. 'Edith Loveridge, alias Arabella Kenyon, actually *was* one. But how could she forge Mr Picton's calligraphy so convincingly?'

'I asked him that,' said Peter.

'What was his explanation?'

'He wrote her a letter of thanks when she gave him a watercolour of the house. The painting impressed him and used to be on a wall in his study. As a result of my visit, I expect that it's been destroyed.'

'And was he absolutely *sure* that she's now

posing as Mrs Hester Mallory?'

'He was prepared to put his life savings on it, sir.'

'So before she deceived me, she insinuated herself into *his* affections.'

'Mr Picton never really liked the woman and, of course, he never advanced her any money. When I told him the name that she used in London, he was livid.'

'Why is that?'

'His wife's name is Hester.'

'It was very cruel of her to utilise it in such a way.'

'At least we know a lot more about her, sir.'

'But do you know enough to catch her yet?'

'I feel that I'm getting closer,' said Peter. 'That's all I can claim.'

Impey puffed his cheeks and went off into a world of his own. All that Peter could do was to wait. When the manager eventually came out of his daydream, he apologised profusely.

'I owe you profound thanks for finding out the truth, Mr Skillen.'

'I won't give up until I've caught up with the lady.'

'What about this murder enquiry in which you're entangled?'

'My brother has taken the lead there,' said Peter. 'I'll stay involved through him. As for the woman Mr Picton called "the fatal temptress", he had some advice.'

'It's in his letter. Since I'm such an easy prey to beauty, he urges me to retire.'

'That's a matter for you, sir. In the short term,

there's something you could do that might be of help to me. Warn the other banks that there's a viper in town.'

'You know quite well that I can't do that,' said Impey. 'If one makes a huge error of judgement, one doesn't want to advertise the fact to one's competitors.'

'That's not what you'd be doing, Mr Impey.'

'Yes, it is.'

'There's no reason why anyone should know what really happened in this office,' explained Peter. 'I'm not going to tell them that you were fleeced. My intention is to warn them that you were approached by a forger but that you were clever enough to discern the forgery. They'll look on you favourably, sir. You'll become something of a hero in the banking world.'

'Will I?'

'You'll also be making it more likely for the woman to be caught. If I pass on the warning to other managers, it may well be that one of them has been approached by her to transact business. Miss Kenyon wants to make as much money as she can before disappearing from the city. Let's prevent her from doing that.'

'Yes, but in a sense we'll be telling them a lie. I *was* fleeced.'

'It's a necessary deception,' said Peter, 'in order to save others. Members of the banking fraternity will thank you for alerting them and know what to do if Miss Kenyon or Mrs Mallory knocks on their doors. I urge you to let me raise the alarm, sir. You will stand to gain for it,' he pointed out. 'If I can catch this woman, you may well get your money back.'

Impey laughed with relief. 'Then do it, Mr Skillen. Do it instantly.'

Rawdon Carr was troubled by the news that his friend's house had been spied upon. Calling on Hamer that afternoon, he was told about the confrontation with the Runners. The accusation that they were in league together had been a sobering moment for them.

'That would have ruined everything,' said Carr, uneasily. 'How did you extricate yourselves?'

'We browbeat them,' explained Hamer. 'Between us, Laetitia and I reduced them to snivelling wrecks. We forced them to apologise and away they went.'

'Don't ignore the warning, Stephen. They caught you together. That's what alarms me. What if it had been someone else? Had the Skillen brothers linked you and Laetitia, *they* wouldn't have been put to flight quite so easily.'

'We realise that.'

'I suggest that the two of you keep well apart for a while.'

'We've already agreed to do that, Rawdon.'

'That's a sound decision,' said Carr. 'Stand by it.' He changed tack. 'Have you had any more thoughts about Eleanor Gold?'

'Indeed, I have. I've been trawling through my memories of her. At the time, of course, I was swept away by her charms – and they were considerable. I always knew that someone like her would have a colourful past. Eleanor was very experienced.'

'Then she'd have sensed that you were tiring of her.'

'That's more than possible.'

'So she might well have plotted her revenge. It looks as if it might have involved stealing that dagger.'

'I'm inclined to agree.'

'If *she* stole it, who actually used it?'

'I don't know, Rawdon. It can only have been one of her former conquests, I suppose. Living as a courtesan, she will have had dozens of admirers.'

'Did she ever mention their names?'

'Oh, yes. She sometimes teased me that, if she were not with me, she could still be enjoying the perquisites of being Sir James Babington's mistress. She made it sound like a life of endless indulgence. I had to remind her that Sir James lost a leg in a riding accident.'

'What was her response to that?'

'Eleanor said that his income of forty thousand pounds a year was adequate consolation and that it helped her to overlook his physical short-comings.'

'How did they part?'

'She always maintained that it was on the best of terms.'

'Then she could easily have gone back to him.'

'That's what I've been wondering,' said Hamer, running a hand across his chin, 'and there are a couple of other names that have popped into my mind.'

'Let's start with Sir James,' suggested Carr. 'I can make discreet enquiries about him. If he's recently acquired a new mistress, she might turn out to be Eleanor Gold. Ah, I see a problem,' he admitted. 'Would a one-legged man be capable of stabbing someone in the back?'

'Sir James is a politician. Back-stabbing comes naturally to him.' They traded a laugh. 'Seriously, he'd never do his own dirty work. He'd hire an assassin. But this is all conjecture. I can't be certain that he's in any way involved. Eleanor might have returned to someone else altogether. I can give you at least another four names.'

'We'll divide them up between us.'

'Thank you, Rawdon. You're always so helpful.'

'My motive is pure self-preservation,' said the other with a grin. 'I'm a partner in the enterprise. If you and Laetitia fall, then so do I.'

'Well, it won't be the Runners who bring us down. The people we must fear are these anonymous enemies who know far too much about us. That disturbs me. Then again,' he continued, 'we have Paul Skillen and his brother creeping up on us. I'd hoped you'd have dealt with them by now.'

'I promised to divert them,' said Carr, 'and I've kept my word.'

'What have you done?'

'You'll soon see, Stephen. The Skillens will no longer be a nuisance to us. They'll have an urgent problem to solve.'

Jem Huckvale was accustomed to dealing with a whole range of customers at the gallery, from nervous young men who wished to learn the noble art of self-defence to overconfident ones who felt they were expert swordsmen and who needed someone on whom to practise. Huckvale had even taught a woman how to handle a bow and arrow. When she was there, Charlotte handled all the bookings and recorded the names neatly in the ledger. Checking the list, Huckvale saw that his next task of the afternoon was an hour with one Mr Philip Needham, who wished for instruction in shooting. It was only when he actually arrived that it became clear that Needham was a man of the cloth. Of medium height, he was a solid individual in his thirties with a pleasant smile and a sense of other-worldliness about him. When he stepped into the shooting gallery, he answered the question burning its way into Huckvale's brain.

'Why am I here?' he said. 'That's what you wish to know. Why does a priest who abjures violence of any kind want to become proficient with a gun?'

'You wish to defend the church – is that it?'

'Metaphorically, I defend the church every day and I do so with a combination of faith and prayer. I was called, Mr Huckvale. Do you know what that means? I heard the voice of God one day and it drew me to labour unceasingly on His behalf.'

'Have you ever held a weapon before, Reverend?'

'I've held the Bible, the greatest weapon in the world against sin.'

'What about pistols?'

'They are foreign to me and I must learn to fire them. Every summer, you see, we hold a church fete and one of the events is a shooting match. It's won by the same obnoxious person time and again. My parishioners begged me to find someone to displace him as our champion.' He gave a bow. 'That honour falls to me.'

'Then I will do my best to turn you into a winner,' said Huckvale, 'though it may take several lessons to do so.'

'I'll come every day if necessary.'

Though he seemed an unlikely pupil, he was clearly dedicated. That would make the task much easier. Huckvale had taught far too many people who began with an enthusiasm that quickly diminished and made them half-hearted. Needham was acting out of commitment. The first thing he was taught was how to handle the weapon. Huckvale pointed out its constituent parts and warned him never to carry it with him if it was loaded. When Needham had memorised everything, his instructor turned to the target and explained how to hold the pistol straight. After loading the weapon, he fired it and hit the centre of the target.

Needham applauded him. 'That was magnificent.'

'I do it many times a day, Reverend. Practice makes perfect.'

'Then let me start practising at once. Please load it for me.'

Huckvale obeyed then handed him the pistol. Squinting at the target, his pupil planted his feet in the way he'd been told and extended an arm. On the point of pulling the trigger, he suddenly swung round and held the pistol against Huckvale's skull. His voice became harsher.

'May God forgive me for it,' he said, 'but I'm afraid that I've been lying to you. I can fire this as well as anybody, especially from close range. Please don't give me the opportunity to do it, Mr

Huckvale.' He nudged his prisoner. 'Start moving.'

'Where are we going?'

'We're leaving by the backstairs. I have a friend waiting for us outside.'

'Who *are* you?'

'No more questions,' said the other, jabbing him in the ribs.

'But I work here. I have other people to instruct.'

'I'm the one giving the instruction now,' said Needham. 'If you dare to call for help, it will be the last time you ever utter a single word. Do you understand?'

'You're not a priest at all, are you?'

'Be quiet and do as you're told.'

A second jab in the ribs hurt even more and made Huckvale wince. He was helpless. As long as the weapon was held on him, he was at the mercy of someone who was strong, ruthless and armed. Huckvale was pushed unceremoniously down the backstairs and along the corridor to the rear door. After the attack by the two dogs, it had been reinforced but it offered no protection now. Compelled to open it, Huckvale drew back the thick bolts then turned the large key. The door swung back on its hinges. Waiting for him outside, Huckvale saw, was a short, thickset man with a sack in his hand. It was the last thing the prisoner remembered because his head was struck hard from behind by the butt of the pistol and he fell forward into oblivion. He didn't feel the sack being put over his head or realise that the man outside the door picked him up with ease and slung him over his shoulder.

The carriage was only yards away. Huckvale

was bundled into it.

His visit to a third bank introduced Peter to Harold Oscott. The manager was a rotund man of middle years. Peter sensed that he was not entirely welcome. Whenever he'd called at the other banks to deliver his warning, he'd met with interest and gratitude. Oscott, however, had the look of someone who floated on a cloud of self-importance. The first thing he did when Peter was shown into his office was to consult his watch and shake his head.

'I can only give you two minutes, Mr Skillen,' he said.

'You might find that I require rather more than that.'

'I have appointments to honour. As it happens, there's a particularly important customer about to arrive.'

'He will be obliged to wait.'

Oscott spluttered. 'You can't come in here and tell me how to conduct business,' he protested. 'If you're from Mr Impey, as you claim, then you should confine your business to *his* bank.'

'I come in the spirit of fellowship, sir. Bankers should support each other.'

'We are rivals, sir. We thrive on competition.'

'Are you saying that you won't accept advice?'

'Not if it comes from Impey or any other manager. This bank maintains the very highest standards and has done so for many years. Our reputation speaks for itself. That is why we've been so successful under my aegis.'

'Mr Impey thwarted an attempt at fraud.'

255

'That's *his* concern.'

'It may also be yours, sir,' said Peter, annoyed by his peremptory manner. 'Other bank managers have been more receptive to what I have to say. That makes your attitude all the more surprising.'

'Good day to you, Mr Skillen,' said the other, looking at his watch again. 'Your time has run out. I need to speak to genuine customers.'

'One of them may try to defraud you.'

'Like others before them, all that they will do is to *try*. Nothing eludes me. I have a sixth sense where fraud and forgery are concerned. It's led to a number of arrests. I can do without your warning, sir. The door is behind you.'

'Then I bid you farewell,' said Peter, mastering his irritation.

He let himself out of the manager's office and walked to the main door. As Peter stepped out into the street, a carriage drew up outside. Glancing through the window, he could see the figure of a woman in a wide-brimmed hat. When she opened the door of the vehicle, however, he looked more closely. Everything about her suggested that she might be the very person about whom he'd attempted to talk to Oscott. She was young, shapely and excessively beautiful. There was a brimming confidence about her that alerted Peter. Oscott had spoken of a particularly important customer. Here, he surmised, she was.

Peter was in two minds. Part of him wanted to get out of her way in the hope that Hester Mallory or Arabella Kenyon would beguile the bank manager as skilfully as she'd enchanted Leonard Impey. Great satisfaction could then be drawn by Peter from the fact that Oscott had also been fleeced. Another part of him, however, urged him to strike while he had the opportunity. Left at liberty, she'd get away with the thousand pounds she'd extracted from Impey and whatever she conjured out of Oscott's safe. Peter decided to follow her into the bank so that he could challenge her there.

But the chance never came. The intense interest he'd shown in her had been noticed. The woman sensed danger at once. Instead of getting out of the carriage, therefore, she stepped straight back into it and a servant shut the door after her. She banged the roof of the vehicle and it set off down the street with the driver cracking his whip to demand more speed. Peter chased hard for some time but was unable to catch up with it. Cursing his luck, he stood on the pavement and panted from his exertions. When he got his breath back, he realised that he had one pleasurable duty to perform. He could return to the bank to inform Harold Oscott that the appointment with his important client had been abruptly cancelled and that the manager's fabled sixth sense had somehow detected nothing amiss about the lady.

Abel Mundy had learnt to rely on his wife over the years. Having no children, they'd been drawn ever closer together. What was remarkable about Marion Mundy was her ability to adapt to her husband's moods and needs. Most women brought up in a country vicarage would have looked askance at the whole business of theatrical presentation. In their opinion, it would have smacked of corruption and sexual licence. Those who flocked to watch plays, they believed, were as louche and venal as the people who actually appeared on the stage. It was a view supported by the stories of drunken brawls and riots that appeared in newspapers. Theatres were breeding grounds of danger.

When she'd first met Mundy, he'd been a devout young man of literary inclination. Poetry was his first love and she'd been wooed by his verses. While he'd made a living as a printer, he'd yearned for the status that came with being an author, wishing to write words himself instead of merely putting the work of others into print. Poetry had slowly given way to plays, initially of a strongly Christian character. His wife had been his only audience at first. In spite of her upbringing, she was slowly drawn towards the theatre and, when his first play was eventually performed in public, it was a moment of transfiguration for her.

'Miss Granville has at last agreed to meet me,' he told her.

'Thank heaven for that!'

'I'll need the patience of Job to contend with her.'

'Bear in mind what she's been through,' advised his wife. 'I think about it all the time. She was lucky not to be blinded. Deal gently with her, Abel.'

'I'll be gentle but firm, my dear.'

'Don't let her dictate. When all is said and done, it's your play.'

'What is left of it,' he said with a sigh. 'But all great works undergo a measure of rewriting. One must accept that. Even the Bard's plays have been amended over the years to suit the prevailing public taste. Nahum Tate's version of *King Lear*, for instance, has a happy ending.'

'I hope that the same can be said of your battle with Miss Granville.'

'She can be inspirational, there's no question about that.'

'Then she is privileged to work with an inspirational playwright.'

'Thank you, my dear.'

Mundy understood the significance of the meeting. It was a last chance to rescue his play. He therefore had to make the effort to bend a little. Whether or not the actress would do the same was an open question.

'You've come such a long way,' said Marion with pride. 'You're on the verge of fulfilling a life's ambition. Please don't fall at the final hurdle.'

'I won't,' he assured her. 'I feel that the storm is finally over.'

At the end of an hour of teaching someone how to fence with foil and rapier, Gully Ackford saw his pupil to the front door and waved him off. As one man left, another arrived for instruction in the boxing ring from Jem Huckvale. Inviting the newcomer in, Ackford called up the stairs for his colleague to come down. There was no reply. When he shouted even louder, the result was the same. It suddenly struck Ackford that, during the previous lesson, he'd heard very few shots being fired above his head. A lesson would normally be punctuated by gunfire. He ran quickly upstairs to the shooting gallery and found it empty. He made a quick search of the upper part of the building but saw no sign of Huckvale.

Ackford then heard a flapping sound. It seemed to come from the backstairs. Bounding down them two steps at a time, he saw that the rear door was ajar and was being blown to and fro by the wind. Since the invasion by the two dogs, they'd been very careful to keep the doors securely locked. Huckvale would never have dreamt of departing from the building that way without telling Ackford, and he would certainly never have left the door open. Huckvale had unaccountably disappeared. There was only one explanation.

He'd been kidnapped.

Bound, gagged and with a splitting headache, Huckvale lay in the dark and wondered where he could possibly be and how he could have got there.

CHAPTER SIXTEEN

After his adventures at one bank, Peter Skillen returned to the person who'd hired him so that he could deliver his report. Leonard Impey listened with an interest edged with disappointment. Hearing that the woman who'd comprehensively deceived him had made her escape, he sagged in his chair.

'So you missed your chance,' he groaned.

'I gave her an almighty fright, sir. That will slow her down. She knows that someone is on her tail now. I don't think she'll be unwise enough to venture into another bank for a while.'

'What about Oscott?'

'I had the pleasure of telling him that the woman had been ready to help herself to some of the bank's money with bogus documents. Since he'd already declared those documents to be legitimate,' said Peter, 'he was very embarrassed.'

'Then he'll know how *I* feel.'

'You actually *lost* money, sir. He didn't. When he realised just how close he'd come to doing so, he had the grace to thank me.'

'Did he apologise?'

'He mumbled a few words but that was all.'

'Oscott and I are two of a kind,' confessed Impey. 'We were taken in by the woman's appearance and never thought to ask what lay behind it.'

'She's a very striking lady. Most men would have been similarly impressed.'

'I'm not paid to be impressed, Mr Skillen. I was given the task of running this bank because of my ability to read people's characters. I completely misread hers. My only solace is that she worked her spell on Oscott as well.'

'He begged me not to divulge that information.'

'His secret is safe with me.'

'So,' said Peter, 'I feel we've made progress. I now know exactly what Mrs Mallory, or Miss Kenyon, actually looks like and I've protected other banks from falling victim to her. She'll be more cautious from now on.'

'So will I, Mr Skillen.'

'I was very sorry that she got away and my other regret is that I didn't see who her companion was. All I caught was a glimpse of a man who stayed in the carriage. It must have been her accomplice. My instinct was to let her get inside the bank before I moved in. Having apprehended her,' explained Peter, 'I could then have gone outside to arrest the man as well.'

'The pair of them should hang.'

'Forgery is no longer a capital offence, sir.'

'It should be.'

'All victims of it must feel that.'

'What will you do now, Mr Skillen?'

'I'll continue my search for her,' replied Peter, 'though I can only devote limited time to it. The main thing is that Mr Picton is now aware of her forging documents in his name. As a consequence, he supplied valuable information about her. I was lucky enough to be on hand to encounter her but she interpreted my curiosity only too well.'

'That's a pity.'

'Knowing she's at risk, she'll stay hidden for a while.'

'You've done well,' said Impey, opening a desk and taking out a pile of banknotes. 'Let me know how much I owe you for the time you've already given me.'

'I won't take a penny until she and her accomplice are in custody.'

'When will that be?'

'The sooner, the better,' said Peter. 'This has been a fascinating case but, with respect, it lacks the importance of a brutal murder. I'm hoping that Mrs Mallory will be caught in the very near future, enabling me to concentrate all my energies on the search for a killer and his female confederate.'

'So there's a woman at the heart of both cases, is there?'

'Unhappily, there is. Crime has an attraction for both genders. Men *and* women can labour under the illusion that it will bring them a fortune and cost them no pain. By the time they realise they were misled, they feel the full weight of the law.'

'When was this, Gully?'

'It must have been well over an hour ago.'

'What was Jem doing?'

'He was teaching someone how to fire a pistol.'

'Do we know the man's name?'

'We know the one he gave to us. It was Philip Needham. In retrospect,' said Ackford, 'it's likely to have been false.'

The first thing he did when he discovered Huckvale's disappearance was to send word to Paul Skillen, who responded to the call for help instantly. Having ridden at a gallop to the gallery, Paul was now standing with his friend in the courtyard at the rear of the property.

'Have you searched for any witnesses?'

'That's what I did until you got here.'

'Did anyone *see* anything?'

'Two people watched a carriage leave here in a hurry but they had no idea who was inside it. It's ironic, Paul. Dozens of people were around at the time yet not one of them was aware what was happening right under their noses.'

'Did you actually meet this Philip Needham?'

263

'No,' said Ackford, 'but Charlotte did. She put his name in the book so she'll be able to give us a good description of him. But why pick on Jem? He has no family from whom a large ransom can be demanded.'

'Money is not at stake here.'

'Then what lies behind it?'

'This is another ruse from Hamer and that friend of his, I fancy. Having failed with their first attempt, they're set on diverting us another way. While we're spending all our time looking for Jem,' said Paul, 'they'll have the field clear.'

'Not entirely – there are the Runners.'

'Oh, they can be outwitted without too much difficulty. We can't, Gully, so we have to be removed from the chase. Hamer and Carr are determined to be the first to lay hands on the people behind the murder.'

'Do they covet the reward money?'

'No, they're wealthy men in their own right. They're driven by rage that someone robbed them of their prize. Mr Bowerman should have been shot dead on Putney Heath, not murdered in the garden of a house owned by Hamer.'

'Do you think that they'll hurt Jem?'

'There's no need for that. They simply want to hamper us.'

'So where do we start looking?'

'First of all, I'll tell Peter what's happened. Then the two of us will pay the counterfeit Captain Hamer a visit. He was warned of the danger of upsetting us.'

'What about me, Paul?'

'You must hold the fort here.'

'But I want to join in the search. Jem would expect it of me.'

'He'll know that we won't let him down, Gully. Wherever he is, Jem won't be downhearted. He can trust in us to rescue him.'

Though his eyes gradually grew accustomed to the dark, Huckvale could still see very little. What he did realise was that he was in a coal cellar. There was dust everywhere. He also had a nasty taste in his mouth and surmised that the sack put over his head had once contained rotten potatoes. Struggling to piece together what had happened, all that he could recall was that the Reverend Philip Needham had tricked his way into the gallery then put a pistol to Huckvale's skull. Unable to feel the large bump on his head, he knew that it was there because of its insistent throbbing. His attackers had tied him up securely and made it impossible for him to make any noise beyond a muffled cry. And who, in any case, was likely to hear him? He was underground in a cellar that served equally well as a dungeon.

Huckvale was helpless.

Lemuel Fleet was banking heavily on the success of the meeting between the two antagonists. The last time they'd come face-to-face, he reflected, was when Abel Mundy had interrupted the rehearsal of a revised version of his play and exchanged abuse with Hannah Granville before making a hasty exit. At that point, the situation had seemed irrecoverable. What had changed everything was a stone hurled through a window at Hannah. Terrifying her, it had opened a well-spring of compassion in the playwright that Fleet didn't suspect was there. Both parties were therefore coming in a different frame of mind. Hannah had been chastened and Mundy was sympathetic towards her. It was a basis on which the manager felt that he could build.

There was a long table in his office. When the disputants arrived, he took care to seat them at either end and to put himself in the middle between them. Decanters and glasses had been set out. Hannah turned down the offer of a little wine but Mundy, unusually, accepted a glass of brandy to fortify him. Fleet talked in general terms about his plans for the rest of the season before turning to *The Piccadilly Opera*. He first invited each of them to make an opening statement.

Controlled and subdued, Hannah began with an apology for any hurt she'd caused the playwright by her unfair criticism of his work. She praised the aspects of it that she found most appealing and said that, in the interests of the whole company, she was prepared to be more tolerant of what she perceived as weaknesses. Mundy winced at the mention of weaknesses but he did not rush to the defence of the play. Instead he told her how sorry he and his wife had been to hear of the attack on her and he went on to say that it was a privilege to work with an actress who had no equal on the stage. He spoke with more caution than any real passion but he nevertheless managed to coax a slight smile onto her face.

So far, Fleet decided, it was going well. There was no hint of the pulsating hostility that had bedevilled their earlier conversations. Both were calm and respectful towards each other. It was the moment to reveal a bonus.

'I have been in communication with Benjamin Tregarne,' he said, pleased to see the looks of sudden joy on their faces. 'I took the liberty of showing the play to him and he was complimentary.' Mundy beamed. 'At the same time, he felt that it could be improved musically.'

'I accept that,' said the playwright.

'It's something I've advocated from the start,' added Hannah.

'At last,' said Fleet, 'we have something that unites us.'

Hannah did more than offer approval. Benjamin Tregarne had written some of the finest comic operas ever seen on the English stage. Now in his declining years, he didn't take on any more commissions for operatic work and confined himself to less taxing enterprises. To sing something specially composed for her by Tregarne was truly an honour in Hannah's eyes. By the same token, Mundy was thrilled to be associated with the renowned composer.

'Mr Tregarne feels that full-blown arias would be out of place,' Fleet told them, 'and he has suggested that, in their stead, he'd compose a series of ariettas to be placed throughout the play, mostly to be sung by Miss Granville. They would delight the ear and lift the whole performance immeasurably.' He looked from one to the other. 'Do we agree on that?'

'We do,' replied Hannah. 'Mr Mundy?'

'I couldn't be happier,' said the other.

'To secure Mr Tregarne's services is a coup on your behalf, Mr Fleet, but can he possibly compose the ariettas in time?'

'As it happens,' said Fleet, 'he has work in progress that he can adapt very easily to the demands of the play. It has everything we need. He played and sang one of the songs for me. It was exquisite. Needless to say, when his name appears on the new bills we'll have printed, there will be even more interest in the play.'

'That goes without saying,' said Mundy.

Hannah nodded. 'I've sung his songs before. They are magical.'

'I've made *my* attempt at improving the play,' said Fleet. 'Now it is your turn. Please state what you believe should be done in a polite and reasonable way.' He smiled at Hannah. 'Miss Granville.'

Opening her purse, she took out a sheet of paper and unfolded it.

'I have pared down my suggestions to a bare minimum,' she said. 'In essence, the play is too long and too mawkish.' Mundy gulped. 'I believe that we should omit the last scene in Act One and the first in Act Two. The duet in Act Three is slightly awkward to sing but it may be that Mr Tregarne can rescue it from its inherent infelicities. The ending, of course, needs to be given more drama and deeper emotion. Apart from that,' she went on, refolding the paper, 'I have no comments to make.'

Mundy was already puce with anger but he managed to contain it somehow. A celebrated composer had liked his play enough to provide ariettas for it, yet its leading actress was tearing it to pieces. Benjamin Tregarne had lit a fire of hope inside the playwright. Hannah had just extinguished it. Mundy needed a few moments to recover his equilibrium.

'What's your reply?' asked Fleet.

'It's this,' said Mundy, straightening his back and staring at Hannah. 'I might consider some of Miss Granville's unjustified scorn if she would stop pulling faces during the duet, waving her arms about so wildly in the prison scene and grinning at the audience throughout as if they've paid their money for the sole purpose of admiring her teeth. In short, she should *act* the part properly instead of distorting it into a travesty of the original.'

Hannah leapt up truculently. 'I cannot believe I'm hearing this.'

'You may hear a lot more, if you wish,' he said.

'Silence, silence,' implored Fleet.

'Are you going to let him launch such a vicious attack on me?' she cried. 'It's worse than being hit by a shower of glass.'

'You insulted me,' roared Mundy.

'It's no more than you deserved.'

'Your behaviour has been reprehensible from the first rehearsal.'

'And yours has been boorish,' she retorted.

'You poison everything you touch.'

'Then please come closer so that I can touch *you.*'

'Miss Granville,' cried Fleet. 'We are all friends here.'

'I'd never befriend a man of no discernible talent.'

'When I agreed to work with you,' said Mundy

with a sneer, 'I had to lower my standards considerably.'

'You don't *have* any standards,' snapped Hannah. 'I might have made the mistake of being in the wrong play, but you, sir, are in the wrong profession.'

'That's slander!'

'It's the truth.'

'I'll bring an action against you for defamation.'

'I'll bring one against you for brazenly impersonating a playwright.'

Once started, the argument quickly gathered pace and the insults became sharper and more personal. Perspiration glistening on his furrowed brow, Fleet begged them to stop but to no avail. All the bitterness that had been stored up on both sides now had an outlet. The manager was swept away by the surging torrent of abuse. When the two of them finally ran short of bile and of breath, Fleet spread his arms in supplication.

'What am I to tell Mr Tregarne?' he wailed.

Peter Skillen was outraged when he learnt that Huckvale had apparently, been abducted. Back at the gallery, he found his brother and Ackford still trying to work out how it must have happened. Peter had dismissed all thought of the murder investigation and of his work for the bank. The priority now was to rescue Huckvale and call someone to account for the crime. Since Paul was convinced that the kidnap had been ordered by Stephen Hamer, the brothers rode straight to his house. They were in no mood for social niceties. When a servant answered the door, they pushed past the woman and went straight into the drawing room. Hamer and Carr were having a private conversation when the brothers burst in.

'What the devil are you doing?' yelled Hamer, getting to his feet.

'We've come to ask you the same thing,' said Paul. 'We believe that our close friend, Jem Huckvale, has been abducted from the shooting gallery. You gave the order for the kidnap.'

'I deny it wholeheartedly.'

'When the dogs were let loose, they failed to serve their purpose so you tried another way to frighten us off.'

'Why should I do that?'

'Because there are things you don't wish us to find out,' said Peter. 'You also want to catch the man who killed Mr Bowerman before we do.'

'That much is true,' conceded Hamer. 'The rest is sheer nonsense.'

'Before we go any further,' said Carr with a smile, 'it would be a great help if you could please identify yourselves. I can't tell one brother from the other.'

'This is Paul Skillen,' said Peter, indicating his brother, 'and I am Peter. We speak with one voice about Jem Huckvale. Have him released at once.'

'But we've no idea where he is, dear fellow.'

'Mr Carr is giving you an honest answer,' said Hamer, backing his friend up. 'We had no part either in the attack on the shooting gallery or in this supposed kidnap. Why are you so certain that your friend has been spirited away?'

'The gallery is his home and place of work,' said Paul. 'Jem would never leave it without giving a warning beforehand.'

'Perhaps he just wandered off.'

'You obviously don't know Jem. He's very conscientious.'

'What was he doing before he disappeared?' asked Carr.

'He was giving instruction to someone called Philip Needham.'

'Do either of you recognise that name?' asked Peter. The two men looked blank and shook their heads. 'You may, of course, know him under his real name.'

'And what's that, Mr Skillen?'

'We don't know.'

Carr raised an eyebrow. 'There seems to be a lot of things you don't know,' he observed, drily. 'You don't actually know if your friend was abducted or not. You assume that the man who came for instruction gave a false name but you have no proof of that. The search for a culprit has, mysteriously, brought you to this door yet there are no two people less likely to hatch a kidnap plot than Captain Hamer and I. Why single us out? It's the wildest kind of speculation.'

'It's based on my estimate of your characters,' said Paul, levelly. 'You and Lieutenant Hamer – I refuse to give him a rank to which he's not entitled – are palpably unworthy of any trust. You lied about having those dogs unleashed at the gallery and you're lying about this.'

'Get out of my house before I horsewhip you!' shouted Hamer.

'You'd regret trying to do that.'

'My brother will only beat you to a pulp,' said

Peter, drawing a pistol. 'If you'd care to arm your-selves, we can step into the garden and settle our differences there.'

'Unlike the duel with Mr Bowerman,' said Paul, 'you'll have a more able adversary this time. Or are you too cowardly to accept the challenge?'

'Don't you dare accuse me of cowardice,' snarled Hamer.

'We've seen no signs of bravery in you.'

'Take that back, you rogue!'

Paul did not flinch. 'I take *nothing* back.'

Carr sounded a soothing note. 'Calm down, gentlemen,' he said. 'We are civilised human be-ings, not ruffians in a tavern who fight at the least excuse. Step apart from each other,' he urged, easing Hamer away from Paul. 'Something is missing here.'

'Yes,' said Paul, 'it's any semblance of honesty.'

'I was about to say that it was good manners, Mr Skillen. People don't usually enter someone else's house unless they are invited in. You came in by force. That was not only impolite, it was flirting with illegality.'

'We refuse to be fobbed off, Mr Carr.'

'Nobody is fobbing you off,' said the other. 'You have been allowed in to discuss the situation. We understand your anger. Your affection for your friend shines through and that's admirable. But before you hurl unjust accusations at us, there is something you should first have obtained – evidence.'

'We have the evidence of our own eyes,' said Peter.

'And of our own noses,' said Paul. 'This place

273

reeks of deceit and treachery.'

'I told you to leave,' warned Hamer.

'Where is Jem Huckvale being held?'

'I don't give a damn where he is – now out you go!'

On the point of grabbing Paul, he was stopped dead by the pistol held at his throat by Peter. Everyone froze in position and there was a long silence. Hamer did not budge. He met Peter's gaze without fear.

'Kill me, if you wish,' he said, 'but it will be in defiance of true justice. I did not order the abduction of your friend and I have no inkling where he might be. As God's my witness, I am innocent of the charge.'

The weapon suddenly felt extremely heavy in Peter's hand.

Though he was relatively small, Huckvale was strong and lithe. Unable to break clear of his bonds, or to bite through the gag in his mouth, he instead conducted a brief search of the cellar by means of rolling over and over on the floor. He soon came into contact with lumps of coal fallen from the large pile that occupied much of the space. His head was still pounding and ropes were biting into his wrists and ankles yet he managed a smile of sorts. The best way to move coal was with a shovel. There had to be one somewhere in the cellar. Huckvale started to roll with even more urgency.

When she left the theatre, Hannah craved re-assurance. Ideally, she wanted to go back to the house and fling herself into Paul's arms but she knew that he would not be there. The other person who'd offer her support and consolation was Charlotte, so she told the driver of the carriage to take her to the gallery. On the way there, she was smarting from what she felt was her maltreatment at the hands of Abel Mundy. Though his Christian beliefs held him back from using expletives, he'd nevertheless found words that could inflict deep wounds. As she recalled them, Hannah was affronted afresh. The carriage deposited her outside the gallery and she ran into the building. Flinging open the door, she dashed into the room used as an office, making Charlotte look up in surprise.

'What's happened?' she asked, getting to her feet.

'It was excruciating,' cried Hannah. 'I've just been through an unimaginable ordeal.'

Charlotte embraced her warmly then eased her gently into a chair. The tears came like a minor waterfall and all she could do was to wait for several minutes until Hannah had recovered enough to tell her friend what had befallen her. Nothing was left out of the narrative. She remembered each individual insult from the playwright. Reliving her ordeal brought on a fresh burst of tears at one point. Hannah then made an effort to sit up and regain her poise.

'He'll have to be dismissed,' she said.

'What about his play?'

'It ought to be destroyed, Charlotte.'

'Mr Fleet doesn't think so.'

'His judgement is abysmal.'

'Yet he thinks that you have no peer on the

English stage.'

'In that instance, his opinion is sound,' said Hannah, 'but his assessment of Abel Mundy is woefully awry. That man is impossible to deal with.'

'The meeting was not entirely a disaster,' argued Charlotte. 'When you heard that no less a person than Benjamin Tregarne would compose some songs for the play, you were delighted.'

'It's true. I was.'

'Mr Mundy was also pleased.'

'We both were, Charlotte.'

'There must have been a wonderful feeling of goodwill as a result.'

'There was, there was,' said Hannah. 'I was floating on air.'

'That was before you made your demands.'

'But they weren't demands. They were sensible suggestions to improve the play and rescue it from its banality. I was trying to *help*.'

Much as she loved her friend, Charlotte had pangs of sympathy for Mundy. It was clear that he'd been cruelly provoked. Before they could discuss the meeting any further, Gully Ackford came into the room. He saw that Hannah had been crying.

'I shed tears myself when I realised that he'd gone.'

'Who had gone?' asked Hannah.

'Jem has been kidnapped. Isn't that why you've been crying?'

'No, it isn't.'

'Hannah was involved in an argument at the theatre,' explained Charlotte.

'What's this about a kidnap?'

'Jem disappeared earlier on. Gully is certain he was abducted.'

'But why – and by whom?'

'We don't know, Hannah.'

'Paul thinks he has the answer,' said Ackford. 'He believes that Hamer is behind it. Peter and Paul went off together to confront him.'

'This is terrible,' cried Hannah. 'Why did you let me ramble on about *my* problems when this has happened? Why didn't you tell me, Charlotte?'

'You needed comfort.'

'I feel so guilty. All that I had to endure was someone losing his temper. Jem Huckvale is the victim of a dreadful crime. Oh,' she went on, 'do forgive me for my selfishness. I should be thinking about Jem.'

'We'll find him somehow,' said Ackford.

'Why was he abducted?'

'Someone wants to take our minds off Mr Bowerman's murder. I suppose that that's a good sign in a way.'

'A *good* sign!' exclaimed Hannah. 'How can you possibly say that?'

'It shows that we've made more progress than we thought. Our rivals are scared, Miss Granville. They're trying to shackle us.'

'Poor Jem! My heart goes out to him.'

'If anyone can find him,' said Charlotte, 'it will be Peter and Paul.'

'I hope they can find the man who kidnapped him as well,' said Ackford, teeth gritted. 'I'd like a word with him.'

'What did you call yourself?'

'The Reverend Philip Needham.'

The other man guffawed. 'You've never been inside a church.'

'He didn't know that.'

'You fooled him good and proper.'

'My orders were to get him out of the way. That's what we did.'

'And we got well paid for it.'

He jingled the coins in his purse. The two of them were in a tavern, drinking ale and congratulating themselves on their success. Jem Huckvale had been easily deceived and just as easily overpowered.

'Where did you get that name from?' asked the shorter man.

'Philip Needham? He was a real person.'

'And was he a real priest?'

'No, Nathan, he was a butcher. My parents wouldn't get their meat from anyone else. He was a big, red-faced man with a huge belly on him.'

'Talking of names, what's his?'

'Who?'

He held up the purse. 'I mean the gentleman who gave us this.'

'People like him don't have names, Nathan.'

'How did you find him?'

'I didn't – he found *me*.'

'What happens to the lad we left in the coal cellar?'

'Nothing – he stays there.'

'I thought we'd have to let him go in the end.'

'That was the idea, Nathan, and that's what I agreed to do. I was to wait for the word then release him. But there's no point now, is there?'

he said with a chuckle. 'We've been paid so we can forget all about Jem Huckvale. As far as I'm concerned, he can stay in that cellar and rot.'

He lifted his tankard and downed the remainder of his ale.

Fresh from another reprimand at the hands of the chief magistrate, Yeomans and Hale redoubled their efforts to solve the crime. Information came in from a variety of sources but it was difficult to link it into a coherent whole. One item did catch their attention. There was a report of unlawful entry into an agency dealing with rental property, much of it in the vicinity where the murder occurred. Though nothing appeared to have been stolen, they felt that it was worth investigating. The agent gave the Runners a frosty reception.

'It's no good coming after the event,' he said, spikily. 'We expect you to prevent crime from happening in the first place.'

'How did the burglar get in?' asked Yeomans.

The agent pointed. 'He climbed through that window.'

'How do you know?'

'It was still open when I got here later on.'

'Yet nothing was stolen, I hear.'

'That's not the point. Somebody was trespassing. It's a crime.'

Hale studied the window. 'It's very small,' he said. 'I wouldn't have been able to climb through it and you couldn't even get your head in, Micah.' He recoiled from his companion's punch then turned to the agent. 'Has anyone been showing an unusual interest in this place recently?'

'Oddly enough,' said the agent, 'there was some-one.'

'I don't suppose that you remember his name.'

'That's an offensive remark. I always remember names.'

'What was this man called?'

'Peter Skillen.' The Runners were astounded. 'I see that you know him.'

'We know him all too well,' said Yeomans. 'What did he want?'

'Mr Skillen was keen to know who owned the house where a murder took place a few days ago. I refused to give it to him. It's always been our policy to respect confidentiality.'

'How keen was he for the information?'

'He was extremely keen, not to say overeager.'

Turning slowly, Yeomans looked at the window. Hale read his mind.

'It wasn't him, Micah. Peter Skillen is agile but even he couldn't wriggle through a space like that.'

'I wasn't thinking about him, Alfred.'

'Then who *were* you thinking about?'

'Jem Huckvale.'

Hampered by the ropes and the darkness, he took a long time to find the shovel. In the course of the search, he created small clouds of coal dust, some of which got into his eyes. In the end, however, he rolled up against something hard and metallic. It was the shovel. Because his hands were tied be-hind his back, Huckvale had to wriggle into the most uncomfortable position in order to get close to the shovel. He felt the edges of the implement for the sharpest point. Then he put the rope against it and rubbed as hard as he could. It was slow, painful work and he could feel the circulation being cut off in his arms but he persisted until his strength was almost drained. Making one last effort, he exerted as much pressure as he could, then felt the strands burst apart at last. After tearing off the gag, he undid the ropes around his ankles. He rubbed his ankles and his wrists. Huckvale then felt the bump on his head gingerly.

With great difficulty, he hauled himself to his feet and rocked unsteadily for a few moments. When he was able to walk properly, he felt his way around the walls until he came to a door. Thrilled that he'd be able to escape, he turned the handle only to discover that the door was securely locked. His sense of triumph evaporated. His bonds might have been discarded, but he was still a prisoner. There was no way out.

CHAPTER SEVENTEEN

The brothers returned to the gallery to find that Hannah was still there with Charlotte. When Paul asked how the meeting with Abel Mundy had gone, the actress promised to tell him everything later on. Her predicament couldn't compare with the one in which Huckvale found himself. Hannah had been praying that no physical harm would come to him. Charlotte wondered about their visit to Hamer's home and, between them, they recounted in detail what had happened.

'They denied all knowledge of the kidnap,' continued Peter. 'For the first time since I had the misfortune to meet him, I actually believed Hamer when he said that he didn't know who'd seized Jem from here. There was a glimmer of sincerity in his eyes.'

'He's still involved somehow,' said Paul.

'We have to prove it.'

'Our main task is to find Jem quickly.'

'We can only do that if we track down his kidnapper.'

'I was hoping we could drag his name out of Hamer.'

'He wasn't the one who hired him, Paul,' said his brother. 'That's the kind of work Carr would have undertaken. He's the friend who runs errands for the captain.'

'Hamer's only a lieutenant.'

'Yet he did actually bear arms in battle. That's in his favour. And he did bring back military souvenirs from Spain. One of them killed Mr Bowerman.' He turned to his wife. 'You're the only person who actually met this Philip Needham. What sort of person was he, Charlotte?'

'He was a well-built, well-dressed man in his thirties, a little above my height. In some ways he might have been accounted good-looking. He seemed polite and reasonably well educated,' she said. 'And he insisted on having Jem as his instructor. That struck me as odd, considering that Gully is the expert with any guns. When I told him that, Mr Needham said that it was Jem or nobody.'

282

'Did he explain why?

'He claimed that a friend of his had recommended Jem.'

'Is that all you can tell us about him?' asked Paul.

'Well, no, as it happens, it isn't,' she said, recalling the meeting.

'Go on.'

'There was something vaguely familiar about him, Paul. I've been racking my brains trying to work out why that was.'

'Has he come to the gallery before?' asked Hannah.

'No, I don't think so.'

'How else can you have met him?'

'There's only one possibility,' said Charlotte, thinking hard. 'His was one of the countless faces I've seen at the magistrate's court. And the only reason I'd be there was that Peter or Paul must have arrested him at some time. Yes,' she went on with a growing certainty, *'that's* where it must have been. If so, we're in luck. I'll probably be able to tell you what Philip Needham's *real* name is.'

The unexpected visit of the two brothers had shaken him as much as it had annoyed him. Stephen Hamer needed two glasses of brandy before he calmed down. He turned angrily on Rawdon Carr.

'I asked you to get them out of my way,' he yelled, 'not set the pair of them on to me. Why did you have to arrange a kidnap?'

'It was the best way to distract them, Stephen. If they're spending all their time looking for their

283

friend, they're not going to trouble you.'

'But that's exactly what they did. They forced their way in here.'

'Yes,' said Carr, easily, 'and you got rid of them by giving them an honest answer. You *didn't* contrive the abduction. You had no part in it. Until they rushed in here, you had no idea what I'd done.'

'I do now,' said Hamer, ruefully.

'I deliberately held back the details of what I'd arranged by way of protecting you. When they stopped hectoring you, Peter and Paul Skillen had to accept that your answers were patently truthful. The first time you even knew of the kidnap was when they accused you of organising it.'

'In future, I'd like to know exactly what you do, Rawdon.'

'So be it.'

'It was galling to be made to feel at a disadvantage in my own home. From now on, tell me what you've been up to at every point.'

'Then I will,' said Carr with an emollient smile. 'You already know about this man Huckvale now. His disappearance will keep them preoccupied for days. For the rest, I've set in motion a search for Miss Eleanor Gold and for the other two ladies whose names you gave me. I have minions looking for them right this moment.'

'I've done the same with regard to the other couple of women.'

'You shouldn't be so prodigal, Stephen. I can make a mistress last a year or more. I get full value out of my investment that way.'

'My appetite is stronger than yours. I wear

284

ladies out.'

'You didn't wear Eleanor Gold out. She was eager to stay.'

'Her charms faded.'

'Throwing her out so roughly may have been a fatal error,' said Carr. 'You have to learn to be more considerate towards your conquests. If you treat them like mere whores, they nurse resentment.'

'Eleanor was certainly resentful. She's a real demon.'

'I look forward to meeting her when my men have found out where she is. Every new piece of information you give me about her makes me think she's the most likely person to be party to the persecution of you. We must locate her,' said Carr, 'and bewilder the Skillen brothers.'

'Paul Skillen is the worst of them. He's so tenacious.'

'Earlier today, I saw a good example of his tenacity. When I called into my club, I almost bumped into him.'

'Whatever was he doing there?'

'It was not difficult to descry his purpose,' said the other. 'He was talking to my old friend, Rollo Winters. I'm sure that you can guess what he was talking about.'

'It was that dinner party!'

'He's leaving no stone unturned, Stephen.'

'Laetitia told me that he's also been to see Sir Geoffrey Melrose.'

'Neither he nor Rollo will give anything away,' said Carr, confidently, 'but my point holds. Paul Skillen is obstinacy personified.'

'How do you know that it was Paul and not Peter?'

'You've seen them both together.'

'They're quite indistinguishable.'

'Not to my eye,' boasted his friend. 'Paul is the more flamboyant. That's how I identified him at the club. I was very careful not to let him spot me.'

'I'm glad of that, Rawdon. He knows too much about us already.'

'Well, he won't be in a position to gather any more information. I made sure of that. This friend of his, Jem Huckvale, is being hidden in a place that nobody would ever find. Skillen and his brother will spend *ages* looking for him.'

Newcomers to the gallery were always surprised to find a woman of Charlotte's appearance working there. Now in her thirties, she looked younger. She was intelligent, composed and beautiful. While she looked out of place, however, she fulfilled some important functions. In addition to helping to run the place, she had kept a record of every crime in which Peter and Paul had been involved as detectives. Most had been solved but there were occasional failures. If her husband and her brother-in-law were appearing in court to give evidence, she usually went along to watch the proceedings and to make notes about the defendant. Details of name, age, appearance and crime were duly entered in her record book and, if she had the time, she'd even include a rough sketch of the man or woman being convicted. It was through her sketches that she was now searching.

Two or three times, Charlotte stopped to scrutinise a particular face, trying to convert her deft lines into something of flesh and blood. While she pored over the table, the others waited expectantly. When she suddenly stood up, they thought that she'd found what she was after at last but it was a false hope. With a long sigh, she sat down and began to go through all the faces again.

'Have you found anyone remotely like him?' asked her husband.

'I've found at least two, Peter, perhaps more.'

'How recently did you actually see the man?

'Oh, it must be two years ago, at least,' she said. 'I remember thinking that he looked too law-abiding to be a villain.'

'You could say that of a lot of them,' interjected Paul. 'They cultivate an appearance of innocence that sometimes fools a magistrate.'

'It would never fool the *chief* magistrate,' said Peter. 'Mr Kirkwood has eyes like a hawk. He can see through people.'

'Here he is,' said Charlotte, tapping a page. 'I think it is, anyway.'

They gathered round and looked over her shoulder at the sketch. Hastily drawn, it had nevertheless caught the salient details of the man's face.

'Who is he?' asked Hannah.

'His name is Luke Swait. He's a bootmaker by trade. He was charged with receiving stolen goods but the case was dismissed for lack of evidence.'

'I remember him,' said Peter. 'He was well spoken and very plausible.'

'Do you have an address, by any chance?'

'No,' said Charlotte, 'but I made a note of where

you arrested him. It was in a tavern in Covent Garden called The Black Horse. It's probably one of his haunts.'

'Come on,' said Peter to his brother. 'Let's go there straight away.'

When they opened the door to leave, however, they found their way barred by Yeomans and Hale. The Runners stood there with folded arms.

'Where do you think *you're* going?' asked Yeomans.

'We're going to rescue a friend,' said Paul. 'He was kidnapped from here and we think we've identified the man involved.'

'We've come to speak to Jem Huckvale.'

'He's the person who's been abducted.'

'You're stopping us from catching the man responsible,' said Peter, irritably. 'In any case, why are you interested in Jem?'

'We've just come from an office that was burgled,' explained Yeomans. 'We were told that Peter Skillen – whichever one of you that is – went there to find out who owned the house where Mr Bowerman was murdered.'

'That's true. I did. I was turned away.'

'So you went back at night with Huckvale.'

'I did nothing of the kind.'

'He would have been small enough to climb through that little window,' said Hale. 'That was how the burglar must have got in.'

'London is full of people even smaller than Jem. Start questioning them. Our only concern at the moment is to rescue our friend. He could be in serious danger. Now, are you going to get out of our way or not?'

After a moment's token resistance, the Runners stood aside and the brothers ran out of the building. Yeomans and Hale went after them. If there was an arrest to be made, they intended to make it. And they were determined to accuse Huckvale of taking part in the burglary.

Huckvale tried his best to lever open the door with the help of the shovel but he could not get the edge of the tool into the tiny gap between door and jamb. All that he succeeded in doing was to expend a lot of energy and to bend the implement out of shape. After a brief respite, he sought to break the lock by smashing it with the shovel but it held firm. The real problem was that he couldn't actually see what he was doing so was unable to direct the blows accurately. He threw the shovel away in disgust and sat down on the dusty floor. Above him he could hear distant sounds of traffic as people moved freely about the street. Huckvale had shouted for help until his throat was hoarse. He was now aching badly and his hands were blistered.

Another idea then struck him. The coal must have been delivered from above through a hole. Somewhere in the dark ceiling would be a cast iron cover of some sort. All that he had to do was to find it. There was a problem. Even with the shovel fully extended, he could only just touch the ceiling. He prodded around until he heard a dull clang. While he'd located the cover, he couldn't push it with any force so it stayed firmly in place. The only way that he could get close enough to exert any force was to bring all the coal together in one pile. Ignoring the pain from his blisters, he therefore shovelled away for all he was worth, tossing the coal into the area directly below the cover. When he'd finished, he needed a few minutes to catch his breath.

Climbing onto the pile was hazardous. The first time he tried it, Huckvale slipped and fell, grazing his hands on the sharp pieces of coal and collecting a few bruises for good measure. But he was not deterred. He took more care as he picked his way up the pile for the second time. Coal shifted mutinously under his feet but he maintained his balance somehow. He also got the shovel fixed against the middle of the cover. With every ounce of his remaining strength, he pushed.

'Here we are,' said Swait, depositing two tankards on the table. 'Drink up.'

'It's my turn next,' said his friend.

'We can afford to drink for a week.'

Swait had a long, noisy sip of his ale then lowered himself onto his chair. Though the tavern was quite full, they managed to find a quiet corner where they could talk without being overheard. Swait was still enjoying the memory of how he'd tricked Huckvale at the gallery. His companion, however, was troubled by a twinge of compassion.

'I've been thinking, Luke...'

'What have you been thinking about?'

'It's that lad we locked in the coal cellar.'

'Best place for him, if you ask me.'

'Yes, but how will he get out?'

'I couldn't care less, Nathan.'

'It's dark down there and cold,' said the other.

'We ought to let him out at some point. He's tied up and can't move. If he's not released, he'll die of starvation, eventually.'

'Don't worry about that,' said Swait. 'We've finished with him.'

'But you were told to set him free when the word came.'

'Who's to know if we don't?'

'*I'll* know, Luke, and it'll be on my conscience.'

'If you work with me, you don't *have* a conscience.'

'I was ready to help you kidnap him but I'll not be a party to murder. That's what it'll be if we leave him down there.'

'Listen,' said Swait, pulling him close. 'This is the second time I've put work your way. When you knocked down the door of that shooting gallery and let the dogs in, you got paid more than you'd earn in months of selling vegetables in the market. You didn't have a conscience about that, did you?'

'No,' agreed his companion. 'I didn't.'

'Then why is this so different? You don't care if Huckvale is savaged by a dog yet you worry about him when he gets tied up in a dark cellar.'

'Nobody else knows he's down there, Luke.'

'Somebody will one day. When the weather changes and they need coal for a fire, somebody will find him. It's not our problem any more,' said Swait. 'Enjoy the money to the full. That's what I'm doing. What if he does die? Nobody will ever suspect us. We're in the clear.'

But even as he spoke, he saw a look of horror in the man's eyes as the latter noticed someone entering the tavern. Spinning round, Swait understood the reason for his friend's alarm. Yeomans and Hale, familiar figures to the criminal fraternity, were searching for someone and they had a third person with them.

It was Peter Skillen who spotted them first. He saw enough of Swait to recognise him from his wife's sketch and the man's reaction in any case gave him away. He and his companion leapt to their feet in a panic. Peter elbowed his way through the small crowd to get to them. While he tried to grab Swait, the Runners managed to intercept the other man before he could reach the back door. They quickly overpowered him. Peter, however, was having a struggle. He grappled with Swait until the latter shoved him hard and made him fall backwards over a stool, banging his head on the floor. In a flash, Swait ran to the rear exit and dashed out into a small courtyard, only to run straight into the arms of the waiting Paul Skillen.

'How did you get out *here?*' cried Swait in amazement. 'I just pushed you to the floor in the tavern.'

Paul grinned. 'Baffling, isn't it?'

Then he flung the man against a wall and felled him with a punch to the jaw.

On his way, Rawdon Carr made sure that he was not being followed. Having heard how Hamer's house had been watched, he was being even more cautious. Far too much information had already seeped out and that was disturbing. When he reached the house, he was admitted at once and taken into the drawing room. He whisked off his hat and gave Laetitia a token bow.

'Stephen sent me in his place,' he explained.

'It's good to see you, Rawdon. Do sit down.'

'Thank you.' He took the chair opposite her. 'I heard about the visit of the Runners. They're becoming a real nuisance.'

'They are indeed.'

'Stephen said that you browbeat them into making an apology.'

'It was the only thing we could do. We can't have them realising how close Stephen and I really are. That would spell danger for us all.'

'You're completely safe, Laetitia. Now that Bowerman is out of the way at last, you're a lady of leisure again. You don't have to pretend that you actually love that gullible fool now. After a decent interval, you can look for another likely victim to ensnare in the same way.'

'It was you who found Mark Bowerman for us, Rawdon.'

'I'm sorry that you had to put up with his tedious company for so long.'

'For all our sakes,' she said, 'I was prepared to do that. It was in the certain knowledge that he'd be shot dead by Stephen in a duel. That's what happened last time. You found the target, I brought him to the verge of a proposal of marriage and he kindly gave me proof of his devotion by amending his will in my favour. Just when he thought his happiness was about to be secured, I told him that I was being harassed by a former admirer. You know the rest.'

'Stephen killed him and we three shared the proceeds.'

'That's exactly what should have happened again.'

'I know it is.'

'Someone is toying with us, Rawdon. It makes me feel very uncomfortable.'

'We'll run them to earth, I promise you.'

'I keep coming back to the same name,' she told him.

'That's what I did at first, Laetitia,' he said, 'but it can't possibly have been her. Rumours of her illness were true, it seems. To put our minds at rest, I've made enquiries and learnt the truth. She died somewhere in France several weeks ago. We have to look at someone else.

'Stephen mentioned a woman named Eleanor Gold.'

'She is now our main suspect. I've instituted a search for her. She's angry enough with Stephen to want to inflict real harm on him and, if she's the beauty he described to me, Miss Gold would have no trouble finding an accomplice. It has to be her,' he declared. 'She was left alone in his house with access to his correspondence from you and to the room where he kept his military souvenirs. She would not only have been aware of the time and place of the duel,' he went on, 'but, if she'd been through his papers, she'd have known about the other property that Stephen owned. That's why she had Bowerman murdered there – to give Stephen a fright.'

'It gave us all a fright, Rawdon.'

'We'll get her, I swear it.'

Laetitia was reassured. She looked at him with a fond smile.

'Where would we be without you? she asked. 'You do so much for us.'

'Don't overestimate *my* contribution. You and Stephen do most of the work. I could never emulate your charms, nor could I be certain of killing a man in a duel. To be candid, I'd even have baulked at shooting as easy a target as Bowerman. I simply don't have Stephen's experience with a pistol in my hand.'

'You do more than your share, Rawdon, and we're deeply grateful.'

'Hearing you say that is enough reward in itself.'

They exchanged a look of mutual regard and he smiled sadly.

She became businesslike. 'There is another problem, of course. Paul Skillen must not be allowed to solve the murder before we do or he may learn some very sensitive secrets.'

'We'll get to the killer first,' he promised her, 'and shut his mouth for good. We'll deal with Eleanor Gold the same way. Being a woman won't save her life. As for Paul Skillen, he won't bother us again, Laetitia. I devised a plan to send him running around in circles. I arranged the kidnap of a close friend of his.'

It had taken him time and effort to shift the cover on the coal-hole. When he finally moved it enough to see daylight above, Huckvale was almost exhausted and dripping with sweat. Tossing the shovel aside, he was breathing stertorously. Though there was now an aperture through which he could escape, there was no way that he could climb up to it. What he could do, however, was to call for help. In the street above, he could hear hooves clacking, cartwheels turning and voices rising in argument. Gathering up his strength, he yelled at the top of his voice.

'Help! I'm down here!'

Nothing happened. Though he called out in despair a dozen times, nobody came to peer down into the cellar. So close to other human beings, he nevertheless began to feel that he would still be entombed indefinitely. He waited minutes before he was ready to shout again until his lungs and throat were on fire. This time, he accompanied his plea with a fusillade of coal, hurled piece by piece through the hole and into the street.

'Help!' he cried. 'I'm down here in the cellar.'

All of a sudden, he got a response that made him cry out with mingled joy and relief. The faces of Peter and Paul Skillen appeared above. Huckvale waved to them. When Peter saw his friend's dilemma, he lay face down on the ground and reached out his arm to its full extent. By standing on his toes, Huckvale was just able to grasp his hand. He was lifted slowly upwards and out of the cellar, emerging to find that Yeomans and Hale were there as well, each one holding a prisoner.

'Is that you, Jem?' asked Paul. 'You're covered in coal dust.'

'That's him,' said Huckvale, pointing to Swait. 'That's the Reverend Philip Needham, the bare-faced liar who kidnapped me.'

'The other man is his accomplice. Both of them are under arrest for the kidnap and my guess is that they may have had something to do with those two mad dogs let loose at the gallery one night.'

'We'll gct the truth out of them,' vowed Yeomans.

Swait gave a snort. 'We're saying nothing.'

'It was all Luke's fault,' said his accomplice. 'I wanted to have him released but Luke said we should leave him down there in the coal cellar to rot away. He's got no conscience but *I* have.'

'Your conscience didn't stop you from committing serious crimes,' said Peter. 'Who was your paymaster?'

'We don't know his name,' said Swait, sullenly.

'He's lying,' grunted Yeomans. 'But if he was planning to leave Huckvale trapped down there, then it's a case of attempted murder. Come on, Alfred. Let's take these villains where they belong.'

He and Hale marched the two prisoners off and left the brothers to console their friend. Huckvale shuttled between fear and delight.

'I thought I'd be left down there for ever.'

'You wouldn't have survived all that long without food,' said Peter. 'And if you were tied hand and foot, you'd have been in grcat pain.'

'I was, and my hands went all numb.'

'How did you get free of your bonds, Jem?'

'That was the easy bit,' replied the other. 'Getting the cover off was much harder. My arms are still aching.'

'Charlotte is the person to thank,' said Paul. 'When he came to arrange instruction, she met the man calling himself Philip Needham and fancied she'd come across him before. That gave us a vital clue.'

'How did the Runners get involved?'

'They came to the gallery to accuse you of burglary.'

Huckvale tensed. 'I *knew* I shouldn't have climbed into that place.'

'You committed no crime,' Peter assured him. 'On the contrary, you were helping to solve one by getting hold of an important piece of information. The Runners have suspicions but no evidence whatsoever to connect either of us with the burglary. If they challenge us again, deny their charge.'

'You need a bath,' said Paul, looking at his friend's black face. 'Let's get you back to Gully. He's been worried sick about you, Jem.'

Huckvale grimaced. 'I don't blame him,' he said. 'I was worried sick about myself.'

In all the time he'd been back in their accommodation, Abel Mundy had said no more than a few words. His wife didn't need to ask him what had happened. His expression and manner were eloquent. The attempted reconciliation had been a total failure. He and Hannah Granville were farther apart than ever. The only thing his wife could do was to put food and drink in front of him then stay discreetly out of his way. She was alone in the other room when he came in. Marion looked up from the Bible she'd been reading.

'I'm sorry,' he said, quietly.

'You don't have to say anything until you're quite ready, Abel.'

'I'm not sorry for what I said to her. Someone should have done it ages ago. Miss Granville is a tyrant. Give her full rein and she'll trample all over us. That's what she tried to do to me today and I refused to bow down before her.'

'I can see that tempers must have flared.'

'There was passion on both sides.'

'What about Mr Fleet?'

'He could do nothing, Marion. We were both out of control.'

'I'm so sad to hear that. Naturally, I take your side, Abel, but I did hope that you could moderate your demands and ... take a step or two towards her.'

'If I'd done that, I'd have been tempted to strike her.'

She was shocked. 'You'd never raise your hand to a woman!'

'I came close to doing so today,' he confessed, 'and I'm ashamed of it.'

'Do you think that Miss Granville will be ashamed in any way?'

'She's not capable of it. Other people are always in the wrong. It's never *her*.'

Marion Mundy wanted to offer him comfort but she couldn't find the words even though she'd been searching for them in the scriptures. Bible stories were shot through with anguish and disaster but she'd never found one that related to the work of a playwright. Creating a drama of high quality had taken her husband almost a year and there'd been endless revisions after that as he strove to make it sufficiently appealing to win the interest of Lemuel Fleet. Having his play praised and accepted in London had been the pinnacle for Mundy. The ensuing period of time was one of constant disappointment and regret. All the joy had been squeezed out of him like a wet rag.

The delicate hands doing the squeezing were, in his view, those belonging to Hannah Granville.

'What will you do now, Abel?'

'I don't know.'

'Would you like me to speak to Mr Fleet?'

'That would do no good.'

'Shall I try to reason with Miss Granville?'

'You'd only expose yourself to abuse and I won't allow that.'

'There must be *something* I can do, surely?'

'Just pray for me, Marion.'

'That's what I have been doing.'

'Pray for me and for my poor, dear, hapless play.'

Peter Skillen had decided to go to Bow Street to see what information he could glean from the two prisoners. It was left to Paul to take Huckvale safely back to the gallery. Both rode on the same horse. Jangled by the ordeal in the cellar, Huckvale was recovering quickly and blamed himself for being taken in so easily by someone masquerading as a priest.

'I should have known that he was an impostor.'

'You'll be more careful next time, Jem.'

'Working at the gallery used to be such a pleasure,' said Huckvale. 'Nothing ever went wrong. Yet in the last few days, it has. I've been charged with a crime I never committed, set on by a pair of angry dogs and kidnapped by two men who locked me up in a coal cellar. What's next?'

'Don't take it to heart,' said Paul. 'You suffered in a good cause. You're helping us to solve the murder of Mr Bowerman.'

'Am I?'

'That's why they abducted you. They know how much you mean to us. When *you're* in jeopardy, Peter and I won't rest until we've rescued you. While we're doing that, we can't be investigating the murder.'

They arrived back at the gallery to a cordial welcome. Though none of them was prepared to embrace him because of the filth on his clothing, Ackford, Charlotte and Hannah offered sympathy and kindness. They sat him down, brought him a glass of brandy and made much of him. It was rare for Huckvale to be the centre of attention and he savoured it. Charlotte produced her record book and showed him the sketch she'd once done of Luke Swait.

'That's him,' said Huckvale. 'That's the rogue who cozened me.'

'His days as a sham priest are over,' said Ackford. 'If he escapes the gallows, then he'll be transported for certain, and so will that friend of his.'

'Good riddance!'

'You, meanwhile, need a good bath and a long rest.'

'I'd be glad of the bath but I'm not going to rest. After what's happened, I'm eager to rejoin the search for the killer.' He indicated his apparel. '*He* did this to me. It was on his orders that I was knocked unconscious and thrown into that cellar. Whoever he is, he has a lot to answer for.' He took a sip of brandy and winced. 'I don't like the taste at all.'

'Drink it up,' advised Paul. 'It will do you good.'

'Then perhaps *I* should have a glass of it,' suggested Hannah. 'After my clash with Mundy, I'm in sore need of something to revive me.'

'Was the meeting with him a failure?'

'No, Paul, it was a catastrophe.'

'Whose fault was that, Hannah?'

'It was *his* fault, of course,' she said, annoyed that he should even ask the question. After a few moments of reflection, she made a slight concession. 'Well, he wasn't *entirely* to blame, perhaps, but he was the one who lit the fire in the first place. All that I did was to fan the flames a little.'

'I can imagine,' he said with a wry smile. 'But how do you feel now?'

'I feel desperately sad because the play will be abandoned.'

'I'm not thinking about that. I was wondering if you'd got over the shock of being hit by that shattered glass.'

'That's something I'll never forget until we find the culprit.'

'And we will, Hannah.'

'It's the one advantage of losing *The Piccadilly Opera*,' she said. 'I won't have to step onto a stage and be at the mercy of an unknown enemy in the audience. When I'm in the middle of a performance, I'm totally unguarded. He could do far more than throw a stone at me then. There,' she went on, turning to Huckvale, 'I'm doing it again. I'm going on about myself when I should be thinking about you, Jem. You've had far worse to bear than me. You must have thought you'd die down there in the dark.'

'I was afraid that nobody would ever find me,' said Huckvale.

'Well, we did,' added Paul. 'Not that we can actually recognise you. I've seen chimney sweeps with cleaner faces than you.'

'Time for that bath,' said Ackford, taking over. 'Off we go, Jem.'

Before they could leave the room, however, Peter returned. He looked grim and determined. They all gathered around to hear his news.

'Luke Swait couldn't give us a name,' he explained, 'because he was never told it. His paymaster was careful to give very little away. That said, I did eventually get a good description of the man out of Swait.'

'Did it sound like anyone we know?' asked Paul.

'Oh, yes, we've got to know him all too well.'

'What's his name, Peter?'

'It's the one I was expecting to hear,' said his brother. 'Mr Rawdon Carr.'

CHAPTER EIGHTEEN

As they marched into the chief magistrate's office, they did so without a shred of their usual apprehension because they had a triumph to report. Kirkwood looked up from his desk with weary cynicism.

'What setbacks have you come to relate?' he asked.

'We've brought nothing but good news, sir,' said Yeomans, brightly. 'To be honest, we feel that congratulations should be the order of the day.'

'That's right,' said Hale. 'We've made two important arrests.'

Yeomans nudged him. 'Let me explain, Alfred.'

'I'm sorry.'

'Remember your place.'

'I will, Micah.'

'I always take the lead.'

'When you two have finished arguing,' said Kirkwood, 'perhaps one of you would be kind enough to enlighten me. To what arrests do you refer?'

'We apprehended two men guilty of kidnap and other crimes,' said Yeomans, grandiloquently. 'Thanks to our quick thinking and prompt action, they were seized at The Black Horse in Covent Garden. Both men resisted arrest so we had to overpower them before dragging them back here.'

'What are their names?'

'One is Luke Swait, a bootmaker; the other is Nathan Cooper, a greengrocer.'

'And how did you find them?'

'It was by a combination of hard work and clever deduction, sir. We'd had our suspicions about them for some time. When we caught wind of the abduction, we knew that someone was in grave danger as a result so we moved swiftly to round up the malefactors.'

'That wasn't exactly what happened, Micah,' put in Hale.

'Keep out of this.'

'A certain amount of luck was involved.'

'Any good fortune we enjoyed was fully deserved,' said Yeomans, silencing him with a glance. 'Our experience at policing was the telling factor. That's why two villains are now languishing in custody and facing the prospect of transportation. In my view,' he added, voice deepening for effect, 'both of them should hang.'

'Oh,' said Kirkwood with light sarcasm, 'so you've promoted yourself to the magistracy now, have you?'

'No, no, sir, that would be presumptuous.'

'You'll need a far better knowledge of the law if you are to sit beside me.'

'I know my limitations.'

'We both do,' said Hale.

'In this instance, however, we feel that we surmounted them.'

'Let me recapitulate,' said Kirkwood. 'Suspecting these two individuals of various crimes, you heard of a kidnap and attributed it immediately to them. You therefore hastened to Covent Garden to make the arrests. Is that correct?'

'More or less,' said Yeomans.

'Do you have anything to add?'

'Only that we're proud to do our duty, sir.'

'What about you, Hale?'

'I agree with what Micah just told you, sir,' said Hale. 'It's an honour to uphold the law.'

'Then why can't you do it with at least a modicum of honesty?'

'We always do, Mr Kirkwood.'

'Honesty is our touchstone,' affirmed Yeomans.

'Yet your version of events is wildly at variance with the other one that I was given. Both accounts can't be right. What you clearly don't know,' said Kirkwood, 'is that Mr Peter Skillen gave me *his* report of what occurred.'

'Don't believe a word of it, sir.'

'He'll tell you anything,' warned Hale.

'*We* captured those two men.'

'Mr Skillen doesn't deny that you made the actual arrests,' said Kirkwood, 'but it was he who led you to the tavern where the two men were found. He, after all, had a personal interest in catching them because they'd abducted a close friend of his and left him trussed up in a coal cellar. It now transpires that Swait and Cooper were also responsible for knocking down doors and releasing two dogs at the shooting gallery in the middle of the night.'

'We were unaware of that, sir,' confessed Yeomans.

'You seem unaware of most things.'

'That's unfair. We made significant arrests.'

'Unfortunately,' said Kirkwood, 'you never got anywhere near their true significance because you never established who actually *paid* these ruffians. Mr Skillen clearly did. He was exuding quiet satisfaction. In essence,' he went on, 'this case has demonstrated why the Skillen brothers can out-think, outmanoeuvre and outrun you at every turn. Two prisoners are in custody and I applaud your role in putting them there. But you failed utterly to connect their activities with the murder of Mr Mark Bowerman. That is what Mr Skillen did and why he left here with such celerity.'

Yeomans gasped. 'He *knows* who hired those two rogues?'

'He's gone off to confront the man.'

'Who is he?' asked Hale. 'We must get to him first.'

'Yet again,' said Kirkwood, scornfully, 'you are

far too slow. Instead of deserving the name of Runners, you should have another appellation altogether. You and Yeomans are Bow Street Snails. You can only crawl while the Skillen brothers do the actual running.' Yeomans and Hale were thunderstruck. 'Don't just stand there like a pair of marble statues. Get after them!'

Hannah Granville had improved markedly. On the journey between the gallery and the house, she showed no sign of fear and didn't once look out of the carriage window with trepidation. Seated beside her, Charlotte was pleased that her friend was no longer frightened of her own shadow. In place of her normal garrulity, Hannah was also remarkably quiet, not to say contemplative. The ride was conducted in silence for the most part. Charlotte waited until they were safely inside the house before she made any comment.

'I'm so pleased that you've regained your confidence,' she said.

Hannah looked bemused. 'Have I?'

'You're refusing to let anyone unsettle you.'

'That's because I'm unsettled enough as it is, Charlotte. The truth of it is that I behaved atrociously at the theatre. Mr Fleet was begging us to find a middle way and I stayed rooted to an extreme position.'

'According to you, Mr Mundy did likewise.'

'That was only in response to the stance I took,' admitted Hannah. 'If I'd been less demanding and more persuasive, we'd never have been in this mess. Yes, *he* was to blame as well. What he alleged about my performance was unpardonable. I despise him for it. But I offended him deeply. I hurt his pride so much that his only defence was to denigrate my talent.'

'It's beyond reproach,' said Charlotte. 'Everyone accepts that.'

There was another sign of improvement. Without even thinking, Hannah had led the way into the drawing room, the very place where the window had been smashed only feet away from her. It held no terrors for her now. Beside the prospect of the cancellation of the play, it was now a minor consideration.

Through a part of the window not boarded up, Charlotte saw a carriage draw up outside and wondered who the visitor might be. It was Hannah who identified him first. As the waddling figure of Lemuel Fleet alighted from the vehicle, she braced herself for the inevitable.

'It's the manager,' she said. 'He's come to tell me that *The Piccadilly Opera* has been replaced by another play and that I've been replaced in the company.'

'He can't do that. You have a contract.'

'In behaving the way I did, I effectively renounced it.'

'It would be madness to dispense with you, Hannah.'

'He might think it a greater lunacy to retain my services.'

Charlotte stood up. 'Would you like me to leave you alone with him?'

'No, no, I may need your support.'

'I don't wish to be in your way.'

'Without you, Charlotte, I'd be lost.'

She reached out to take her friend's hand and pull her back down onto the sofa. The doorbell rang and Lemuel Fleet was soon ushered into the room. In sweeping off his hat, he dislodged his wig, pushing it forward so that it covered one eye. He quickly readjusted it. After an exchange of greetings, he was offered a seat.

'How are you, Miss Granville?' he enquired.

'I am not at my best, sir.'

'Yet you seem considerably more serene now.'

'That's the serenity of exhaustion, Mr Fleet. I am *so* tired.'

'Then I won't keep you long from your slumber.'

There was an uncomfortable pause. Charlotte tried to lighten the atmosphere.

'Would you like some refreshment?' she asked.

'No, thank you.'

'I know that I'm intruding but only at Hannah's insistence.'

'I've no objection to your presence, Mrs Skillen,' he said. 'Miss Granville has oftentimes told me how staunch a friend you are. This is a time when we all need to lean on our friends.'

'Break it to me, Mr Fleet,' said Hannah, unable to stand the suspense. 'If I am to be dismissed, do it swiftly and without malice.'

The manager was shocked. 'How can you even suggest such a thing?'

'It would be no less than justice.'

'I'm not here to dismiss anybody,' he told her, reaching into his pocket to take out a scroll. 'I came to deliver this for your consideration.'

'What is it?'

'It's one of the songs that Mr Tregarne has

309

composed for you. Strictly speaking, he did not have you in mind when he first worked on it but I think you'll find that it captures the mood perfectly in Act Five.' He handed her the scroll. 'Peruse it at your leisure. Do you have a piano here?'

'No, I don't.'

'There's one at our house,' volunteered Charlotte, 'and I'd be happy to accompany Miss Granville. But if this is a song for the play, are you saying that it might still be staged?'

'That's in the lap of the gods, Mrs Skillen. I say no more.'

He got up, bade them farewell and left the room. Hannah was motionless.

'Well, go on,' urged Charlotte. 'See what he brought for you. You have an opportunity to sing a new-minted song by no less a composer than Mr Tregarne. Every singer in the country will be green with envy.'

On his previous visit to the house, Peter Skillen and his brother had charged in without invitation. He was more patient this time. Arriving on his own, he asked the servant to tell her master that he'd called on a matter of urgency. After a long wait, he was allowed in. Stephen Hamer was alone in the room where he kept his souvenirs. Peter was shown in. There was a muted exchange of greetings.

'It seems that you've learnt some manners at last,' said Hamer.

'I've come with a simple request.'

'What is it?'

310

'I need the address of Mr Carr.'

'Why? What's your business with him?'

'I have to pass on some bad news,' said Peter. 'The two men he hired to abduct our friend are now in custody. As it happens, they were also behind the attack on the shooting gallery when the doors were battered down and dogs allowed in.'

'I've said before that I know nothing of that.'

'Mr Carr does. He paid them handsomely.'

'That's highly unlikely,' said the other, mustering some indignation. 'I've known Rawdon Carr for many years. He's a man of principle. If two villains are making allegations against him, I'd advise you to ignore them.'

'It may well be that Mr Carr is innocent of the charges. At all events, he deserves the right to defend himself against them. That's why I need his address. You are most welcome to accompany me, Lieutenant Hamer.'

Hamer winced. 'I was worthy of a captaincy,' he said.

'Your military career must bring you a lot of satisfaction,' said Peter, looking around the collection. 'It obviously meant a great deal to you. What a shame it is that you chose to throw it all away.'

'I fought for my country, Mr Skillen. It's more than *you* can claim.'

'That's debatable. For the record, I worked as an agent behind enemy lines for a number of years and was answerable directly to the Home Secretary. It was because of my relationship with him that I was able to obtain details of your

311

service record from the War Office.' He indicated a weapon in a glass case. 'I carried a pistol just like that,' said Peter, 'and I had a dagger similar to those on display here secreted about my person in case of emergencies. They often cropped up. In our different ways, Lieutenant Hamer, we *both* fought for our country.'

Hamer studied him with a grudging respect. He and Carr were up against a more formidable opponent than they'd imagined. His immediate problem was how to buy time in order to warn his friend.

'You have come to the wrong place, Mr Skillen,' he said. 'The truth is that I don't know where Mr Carr lives. He never stays anywhere long. He will rent a house for a few months then move to another temporary abode. There's a touch of the nomad about Rawdon Carr.'

'Then all you have to do is to name the company from whom he rents his houses. Is it the same agency as the one looking after that house of yours where the murder of Mr Bowerman occurred?'

'It could be,' muttered the other.

'Then why didn't you give him free access to it? If Mr Carr is such a revered friend, why didn't you offer him the empty property that you own? That's what I'd have done in your position.'

'You're not *in* my position, Mr Skillen.'

'I'm sincerely grateful for that, sir.'

There was a moment of high tension. Hamer bristled and Peter got ready to repulse an attack. In a room full of weapons, it would have been easy to reach out and grab one. That was exactly what Hamer seemed on the point of doing. What held him back was the discovery that Peter had worked as a British spy in France and must therefore have endured many hazards. Evidently, he would defend himself well.

'I'm afraid that I can't help you,' said Hamer at length.

'I had a feeling you'd say that.'

'As for these preposterous charges against my friend, I'd dismiss them out of hand. He would *never* be party to a kidnap.'

'You have a rather higher opinion of Mr Carr than I do.'

'He's stood by me through some very difficult times,' asserted Hamer, 'so I'm well aware of his strength of character. I'd trust him with my life.'

'Forgive me,' said Peter, 'but the only life that concerns me at the moment is that of our friend, Jem Huckvale, who was tied up in a coal cellar and could well have perished there – thanks to Mr Carr.'

'This is *nothing* to do with him.'

'We shall see.'

'You are relying on the word of two mendacious ruffians.'

'They're hoping to win favour by telling the truth for once,' said Peter. 'However, I can see that I'm wasting my time here. Since you seem strangely unaware of where your friend resides, we'll have to find his address by other means. Goodbye, Lieutenant.'

Turning on his heel, Peter walked to the front door and let himself out of the house. Hamer, meanwhile, was throbbing with anger. Going to the window, he watched his visitor mount his horse and ride away. Hamer rushed to the library, sat down at his desk and dashed off a letter before summoning a servant. He thrust the missive into the man's hands.

'Take this to Mr Carr immediately.'

As the man left the house at speed, he soon went past an alleyway without looking down it. The diminutive figure of Jem Huckvale stepped cautiously into view then set off in pursuit.

While his brother had gone to Stephen Hamer's house, Paul Skillen went in search of the same information at the home of Laetitia Somerville. Though he was admitted at once, he was kept waiting for a long time in the drawing room. He surmised that she was rehearsing her role as a bereaved widow. Even though she'd never married Mark Bowerman, she was behaving as if she'd been his loving wife. Paul wished that Hannah had been with him. In the presence of a real actress, Laetitia might wilt into the patent impostor she was.

When she eventually appeared, it was once again in mourning attire. She apologised for keeping him waiting but had a warning for him.

'State your business and leave,' she said, brusquely. 'Since Mr Bowerman's death, I have not slept a wink. A physician will be arriving shortly with a much-needed sleeping draught for me.'

'Oh, I'd wager you've been dozing happily enough,' said Paul.

'I find that remark insulting, Mr Skillen.'

'It will save time if you drop the pretence of being grief-stricken. We both know that Mr Bowerman was an unfortunate gull at the mercy of a clever plot. I've spoken to Sir Geoffrey Melrose and to Mr Winters, disreputable company for a putative lady like you to keep. You are a predator, Miss Somerville,' he said, 'but that's not why I'm here.'

'I've already heard enough,' she said, haughtily. 'Leave at once, sir, or I'll have you thrown out of this house.'

'Your manservant and I have tussled before. He'll need three or four others to help if he's to dislodge me. Threaten all you wish. It's pointless. I'll not move until you've answered the question that brought me here.'

'And what is that, pray?'

'Where is Mr Carr?'

She laughed. 'How on earth should I know?'

'You and he and Lieutenant Hamer are bosom friends.'

'I deny that.'

'Spare me your denials and furnish me with the address.'

'I cannot give you what I don't possess, Mr Skillen.'

'Are you claiming that you've never *been* to his house?'

'I've no reason whatsoever to do so.'

'Mr Carr strikes me as a hospitable man. He must have invited you there.'

'Rawdon Carr is no friend of mine,' she said with sudden force, 'and he never will be. I have no idea where he lives and no wish to do so. Really, Mr Skillen, you and your brother seem to have an alarming penchant for slander. If you persist in making groundless accusations, it will land both of you in court.'

'Litigation will certainly come in due course,' said Paul, blithely, 'and we'll welcome it. Mr Bowerman was my friend. To preserve his good name, I feel duty-bound to contest his will.' She paled visibly. 'I see that you understand my meaning.'

'Get out!' she yelled.

'I'm staying until you give me that address.'

Walking to a table, she picked up a small bell and rang it loudly. Within seconds, a manservant came into the room and levelled a pistol at Paul. The visitor gave a philosophical shrug.

'It seems that I may have to leave, after all,' he said.

Encouraged by the reception he'd received at her hands, Fleet left Hannah Granville to study the new song and went straight to the house where Abel Mundy was staying. He was dismayed to learn that the playwright was not available.

'My husband has taken to his bed,' explained Marion.

'Is he ill?'

'He's exhausted by all this spitefulness and uncertainty.'

'As, indeed, am I, Mrs Mundy.'

'Do you have a message for him?'

'I'd hoped to have a proper conversation,' said Fleet. 'Time is running out. A final decision must be made about the future of *The Piccadilly Opera*. The whole company is imploring me to save it from cancellation. Such a course of action would be a huge disappointment to the theatre-going public.'

'All that I care about is my husband's health.'

'He would surely recover if his play were to reach the stage at last.'

'That prospect seems less likely by the day. My husband has not given me the full details of the latest outburst by Miss Granville. Judging by the state in which it left him, I can only conclude that it was vile.'

'There were, alas, unkind epithets hurled on both sides.'

'I refuse to believe that Abel is capable of descending to outright abuse.'

Fleet thought better of disillusioning her. Marion Mundy had a vision of her husband that featured a reasonable voice and an angelic disposition. She didn't realise that, when provoked, he could lose his temper with violent effect.

'How *is* he, Mrs Mundy?' he asked, probing gently.

'He is in despair, sir. We spent some time praying together.'

'Then I wish the Lord had been more attentive to your pleas,' he said under his breath. 'If this play falters,' he added aloud, 'I stand to lose a lot of money and I'll sustain serious damage to my reputation as a manager.'

By way of a reply, she lowered her head. He accepted that it was no use asking her to intercede on his behalf. Concern for her husband's health took precedence over anything else. In her opinion, he was without fault. The problems all arose from the employment of Hannah Granville. Nothing would convince her otherwise. The manager was about to take his leave when the playwright came into the room.

'What are you doing here, Mr Fleet?' he asked.

'I was hoping to speak to you, sir.'

Mundy turned to his wife. 'You should have called me.'

'I didn't want to wake you up,' she said.

'I can't sleep at a time like this. Sit down, Mr Fleet.'

'Thank you,' said the manager, lowering himself into a chair.

'Do you wish me to stay, Abel?' asked his wife.

'Perhaps not, my dear,' said Mundy. Waiting until she'd left the room, he looked warily at Fleet. 'I hope that you've brought an apology.'

'I've showered both you and Miss Granville with a hundred apologies.'

'It's not *your* apology that I seek.'

'Let us not ask for the impossible. There are times, as you've now found out, when working in the theatre is like a descent into hell. It's a place of fire, fury and suffering. As a God-fearing man, you'll know all about the Devil's kingdom.'

'I've met the lady in person,' growled Mundy.

'Come, come, sir, let's not be vindictive.'

'You are right, Mr Fleet. Please forgive me.'

'I have just visited Miss Granville.'

'I knew that you'd go to her first,' complained Mundy, 'because you always do. She is always given priority over me.'

'I didn't go in order to spite you,' said Fleet. 'It just happens that the house where she is staying is on the way here. Had you lived closer to the theatre, my first call would have been to you.'

'What has Miss Granville said?'

'She simply thanked me for the gift I took.'

'Has she made any fresh demands?'

'No, Mr Mundy, I fancy that she regrets some of the ones she's already made. I didn't even raise the question of her attitude towards your play. I went there solely to give her a song written by Benjamin Tregarne.'

Mundy bridled. 'Why – was it destined for my play?'

'No, sir – as things stand, there *is* no play. You and she saw to that. Miss Granville has only had sight of one song. I'm bringing you something far more important.'

'What's that?'

'Mr Tregarne would like to meet you,' said Fleet. 'He finds your play both individual and interesting. If you accept, I'm to take you to his house.'

'What about Miss Granville?'

'She will not be there.'

'Won't she protest at being excluded?'

'Only if she gets to hear of the meeting and I'm certainly not going to tell her.' He gave him a confidential wink. 'Nor are you, I suspect.'

The brothers met outside a tavern as arranged and discussed what had happened. Both had met with the stout denials they expected and left without the address they sought. Stephen Hamer and

Laetitia Somerville were trying to shield Rawdon Carr from them. It was a sign of how important he was in devising their machinations. Peter was amused that his brother had been expelled with a pistol at his back.

At least I was able to leave of my own accord,' he said, 'though there was a moment when I thought I might have to fight for my life.'

'Leave part of him for me, Peter.'

'Your quarry is Miss Somerville.'

'I can see why she appealed to Mr Bowerman,' said Paul. 'He was enraptured by her because she curled up in his lap like a favourite cat. All that I was shown today were those vicious claws of hers.'

They were holding their horses as they talked. The sound of running feet made them look down the street and they saw Huckvale haring towards them at the kind of speed for which he was renowned. When he reached them, he was able to tell them where Carr lived. Mounting his horse, Peter offered his hand.

'Ride behind me, Jem,' he said.

Huckvale shook his head. 'Follow me – it's not far to run.'

They let him lead the way and trotted along behind him. Situated in a quiet side street, the house was smaller and less ostentatious than those occupied by Hamer and Laetitia. The brothers tethered their horses. Paul crept furtively around to the rear of the house to prevent an escape that way. Peter and Huckvale went to the front door and rang the bell. After a while, the summons was answered by a flat-faced servant with an unwelcoming scowl.

'We'd like to see Mr Carr, please,' said Peter.

'May I ask your name, sir?'

'I'm Peter Skillen and this is my good friend, Jem Huckvale.'

'Then I'm afraid that I can't help you,' said the man.

'In other words, you've been told to keep us at bay. Please take a message to your master: if he doesn't have the grace to invite us in, we'll enter by force.'

'That would be quite unnecessary.'

'Convey the message to him.'

'It's one thing I can't do,' said the man, standing back from the door. 'Come in, if you must, Mr Skillen. There's no need to use force. You'll find that your journey here was in vain.'

'Why is that?'

'Mr Carr has gone away for some time.'

'Has he left London?'

'He didn't tell me where his destination was, sir. My orders are to close the house up. Mr Carr's lease is due to expire. The one thing I can tell you is that he will not be coming back to this property.'

'Are you sure he's not skulking inside somewhere?'

'I'm absolutely certain,' replied the servant, opening the door to its fullest extent, 'but you don't have to take my word for it. I can see that you're very anxious to speak to Mr Carr. But I've told you the truth. He's no longer here.'

Laetitia was so rocked by the information that she flopped into a chair as if she'd been given a firm push. Hamer had called to tell her what his

321

manservant had learnt at the erstwhile home of Rawdon Carr. Without warning either of them, Carr had quit London for some unspecified destination.

'He's run out on us,' gasped Laetitia.

'Rawdon would never do that. He must have heard of the arrests and made himself scarce before the Skillen brothers could catch up with him. I didn't sanction the kidnap of that friend of theirs,' said Hamer. 'It was his idea. Rawdon swore that he'd divert them somehow and that's what he did.'

'But it was only for a short length of time.'

'They must have found Huckvale.'

'Paul Skillen came to ask for Rawdon's address. I refused to give it to him. He knows far too much, Stephen,' she said, twisting her necklace with one hand. 'He even taunted me about being the beneficiary of Mark Bowerman's will.'

Hamer was taken aback. 'How, in the name of God, did he hear about that?'

'Mark must have told him.'

'But you swore him to silence, Laetitia.'

'It must have slipped out.'

'This is serious,' he said, pacing the room. 'It's one thing to use a decoy against those maddening twins, but it only creates a short space of time for us. If they know about the will, they may have to be removed altogether.'

She was hesitant. 'You'd kill *both* of them?'

'If it's the only way to protect our interests, I certainly will. As for Rawdon, I can't understand why he didn't warn me that he was about to fly the coop. We've been in constant touch until now.'

'That's what worries me, Stephen. He came to see me a while ago.'

'I know. I sent him. I didn't want to be caught here again.'

'He told me about the search he's instituted for that mistress of yours, Eleanor Gold. I've been thinking about her. Can she really be the scheming creature of report? Does she *hate* you that much, Stephen?'

'Oh, yes,' he said with feeling.

'What did you do to her?'

'I sent her packing, Laetitia. No woman likes to be discarded. Eleanor disliked it far more than I'd imagined. The others merely called me names and stormed out. Eleanor did much more than that. Of course,' he went on, 'that could be the other reason for Rawdon's sudden departure. He's discovered where she is. He told me that he had men looking for her. They must have picked up a trail.'

'Then why didn't he write to tell you that?'

'I don't know,' he admitted.

'And why did he leave orders to close the house up?'

'That was always in the offing. The lease was close to expiring and he'd been looking for accommodation elsewhere.'

She wrinkled her nose. 'Something is beginning to smell fishy, Stephen.'

'I refuse to believe that Rawdon has let us down in any way. He's been like an elder brother to me. In fact, there was a time when I'd hoped we might get even closer. I thought he might become my brother-in-law.'

'That was never a possibility,' she said, crisply. 'He understood that. It's ancient history. Please don't bring it up again.'

'I'm sorry, Laetitia. You shouldn't be so sensitive about it.'

'That period of my life is best forgotten.' She gave a sudden laugh. 'I've just remembered what I told the Bow Street Runners. I said that it was *impossible* for me to marry you. They didn't realise that any union between us would be a case of incest.' Hamer laughed as well. 'You make such a convincing former beau of mine, Stephen. Nobody would guess that we were brother and sister.' She became serious. 'But I'm still deeply upset about the latest turn of events. Vanishing like that without a word of explanation is so unlike Rawdon Carr.'

'I stand by my judgement of him,' he said, confidently. 'Look back on all the things he's done for us. We'd never have succeeded without his help and ability to organise everything. Rawdon is the most trustworthy man I know. Have faith in him.'

When the carriage drew up outside the hotel, she came out at once. She was followed by a man carrying her luggage. The door of the vehicle was opened from the inside and she clambered into it, falling into the arms of the other passenger.

'We did it,' said Carr, kissing her. 'We did it and we got away with it.'

CHAPTER NINETEEN

Charlotte Skillen was a competent pianist who could read a score and play it with feeling. The song given to Hannah Granville had never been played before by anyone but the composer. Since she was the first person after him to bring it to life, Charlotte was very nervous and she had to wipe away perspiration from her hands before she touched the keys. Hannah was equally in thrall to the achievements of Benjamin Tregarne, a man who could write plays and music with equal facility. What she'd been given by Lemuel Fleet was a haunting love song that would fit with ease into the last act of *The Piccadilly Opera*. Even when reading the lyrics, she was moved. When she actually sang them to Charlotte's accompaniment, they made her glow.

'I *must* sing this,' she declared.

'You just did, Hannah.'

'I got nowhere near the essence of the song. It will take days of rehearsal before I can do that. But it's a work of genius. Someday, and somewhere, I simply must sing it in public.'

'Why not delight the audience for Mr Mundy's play?'

'That's no longer a possibility.'

'The final decision has still not been made.'

'Yes, it has.'

'Only Mr Fleet can call it off, Hannah, and he

seemed to be in no mood to do that when he came here earlier.'

'That's a matter of opinion.'

'I thought I detected a faint whiff of optimism in him.'

'Then you are deluding yourself. When you have a worthless play and a stubborn playwright who abuses the one actress who might actually redeem it, you have a recipe for abject failure. In its present form, *The Piccadilly Opera* doesn't deserve performance.'

'What about Mr Tregarne's song?'

'That does merit a wider audience.'

'Sing it for me again.'

'I daren't do so, Charlotte. It will grow on me.'

'Then I will sing it to you. I don't have a trained voice like you but I can sing in tune.' She played a few bars. 'It's such an evocative melody.'

After clearing her throat, Charlotte began to sing to her own accompaniment. Hannah stood behind her and looked at the music over her shoulder. Though she tried hard to resist the temptation to join in, she soon capitulated and sang in a beautiful soprano voice that gave the song more clarity and resonance. Indeed, she took it over so completely that Charlotte was able to lapse into silence and simply enjoy her friend's rendition. When it was all over, Hannah was exhilarated.

'It gets better each time I sing it.'

'It was a joy to hear you.'

'Mr Tregarne is such a clever man.'

'In his own way,' Charlotte thought, 'Mr Fleet is rather clever as well.'

After their setback at Rawdon Carr's house, they adjourned to a nearby tavern to discuss their next move. Peter and Paul were disappointed by the man's sudden departure but Huckvale felt cheated.

'I wanted to leave *him* tied up in that cellar,' he said, bitterly, 'so that he can see what it was like.'

'The law would have to take its course, Jem,' said Peter. 'We have no right to inflict punishment. I just wanted the pleasure of arresting Carr.'

'We should arrest Hamer and Miss Somerville instead,' suggested Paul. 'They must have condoned what happened to Jem.'

'I don't believe that Hamer did. When we told him of the kidnap, it was clearly news to him. I'm sure that he incited Carr to do something to mislead us but he had no knowledge of the details.'

'What about Miss Somerville?'

'She's too busy pretending to mourn Mr Bowerman's death.'

'All three of them are as guilty as hell, if you ask me,' said Huckvale.

'There's no doubt about that,' said Peter. 'The way that they planned to get rid of Mr Bowerman was despicable. Their plot worked so well at first that one is bound to wonder if it's the first time they've used it.'

'I'm certain it isn't,' decided Paul, 'and I'm even more convinced that the person who first devised it was Mr Carr. He has the guile that Hamer and Miss Somerville lack. Without him, they might never have dreamt up such a cunning way to acquire property and wealth.'

'Why has he run away?' asked Huckvale.

Paul chuckled. 'He heard that you were looking for him, Jem.'

'I'm serious, Paul.'

'Then the serious answer is that we don't rightly know. It may be that he was aware of the two arrests we helped to make or it may be that he decided to quit London for a holiday somewhere. There are all kinds of other reasons as well.'

'He's a deeper man than we thought,' said Peter. 'If he's bolted, we need to track him down, though I can't imagine how we'd do that.'

'Can I make a suggestion?' Huckvale piped up.

'Yes – go ahead, Jem.'

'Why not ask Hamer?'

'We've no guarantee that he'll know where Carr is. Didn't you say you watched his messenger arrive with that letter from Hamer?'

'Yes, he held it out but they wouldn't take it.'

'There you are, then,' concluded Paul. 'Hamer didn't know that his friend had left the house or he wouldn't have dispatched a letter to him. He may be as surprised as the rest of us by Carr's sudden departure.' He downed his drink. 'I'll go back to the house and question his servant more closely.'

'He doesn't know where his master went,' warned Peter.

'That's not what I was going to ask him.'

'What else can he tell you?'

'I'd like to know a little more about the kind of life that Carr has been leading. Clues are bound to emerge,' said Paul. 'Mr Bowerman's destiny was effectively settled at the dinner party where he met Miss Somerville. I'm sure that Rawdon Carr was involved in that somehow.'

Yeomans and Hale were sickened by the lack of appreciation shown for their work in making two arrests. It was true that they had to be led to The Black Horse by the Skillen brothers but they then came into their own. Their reward was to be berated by the chief magistrate yet again.

'He's always praising those twins at our expense,' said Hale.

'It annoys me, too, Alfred.'

'They only take an interest if a murder is committed and a large reward is on offer. We handle all sorts of crime.'

'We manage to make a profit out of them,' Yeomans reminded him. 'Some of it is spent on our informers but that's a cost we have to bear.'

'Our informers have been of no use in this case, Micah.'

'That's why I've been kicking their backsides.'

'What did Mr Kirkwood mean when he said that Peter Skillen was ahead of us in the race to catch the killer?'

'Forget about him and his brother. Concentrate on *our* investigation.'

Feeling that there was more intelligence to be gathered there, they were on their way to Laetitia Somerville's house. Their earlier call on her had resulted in an ignominious departure. Yeomans was determined that they would not be sent on their way so easily again. The Runners had a stroke of good fortune. When they reached the house, Stephen Hamer was about to leave and was holding Laetitia's hand. The newcomers moved in quickly.

'We've caught you,' said Yeomans, triumphantly. 'Last time we found you together, you swore that Captain Hamer had only come to apologise, yet here you are showing every sign of affection for each other.'

'Our private life is our own,' insisted Hamer. 'Miss Somerville and I have come to composition. That's all I'm prepared to say.'

'The captain has stated my position as well,' said Laetitia. 'May I ask what brought you to my door again?'

'You've aroused our suspicions,' replied Yeomans.

'We still think you're in league somehow,' added Hale.

'A moment ago, we had clear proof of it.'

'I'm more than entitled to kiss a dear friend,' said Hamer, defiantly.

'We feel that you know a lot more about Mr Bowerman's death than either of you are prepared to say.'

'The only thing we know is that it appalled us, Mr Yeomans. That's why we are so keen to catch the killer ourselves.'

'Why not leave that task to someone more suitable?'

'I don't regard either of you in that light.'

'We're not the only ones taking part in the search,' said Hale. 'Peter and Paul Skillen have taken an interest as well.'

'They always do,' moaned Yeomans.

'We've been pestered by them from the outset,'

said Hamer, angrily. 'If you wish to help us, find a way to keep the pair of them tethered.'

'Someone else is trying to do that. We think it might be you.'

'That's an absurd accusation,' said Laetitia with a gesture of dismissal. 'Take your ugly suspicions elsewhere, Mr Yeomans.'

'The captain still hasn't explained why he's here.'

'Nor do I intend to do so,' retorted Hamer.

'We thought that we were visiting the home of a woman who is mourning the death of Mr Mark Bowerman, yet what we find is that she's receiving a kiss from the very person who tried to kill the gentleman in a duel.'

'He challenged me. I could hardly refuse.'

'You need never have incited the challenge in the first place.'

For the first time, Hamer looked unsettled and exchanged a glance with his sister. They'd been caught in what appeared to be a compromising situation. Realising that they could not browbeat the Runners as before, they adopted a different approach. Laetitia introduced a note of apology into her voice.

'I'm sorry if we've given you the wrong idea,' she said, manufacturing a smile for their benefit. 'We should not be bickering out here on the doorsteps like fishwives. Why don't you step inside the house for a moment? The captain has to leave on business,' she went on, 'but I will answer any questions you put to me.'

'It's true,' said Hamer, taking his cue from her and softening his tone. 'I have an important meeting to attend. Miss Somerville will speak on my behalf. What you saw when you arrived was misleading. You will learn why.'

The Runners were not hoodwinked by the sudden change of attitude. They stepped into the house with their suspicions intact.

It was a revelation for Abel Mundy. During their long discussion of his play, not a single voice had been raised. Instead of being compelled to defend his work, he'd been given praise and encouragement. The gathering doubts about his future as a playwright were soon dispelled. He was given the validation for which he'd yearned. Benjamin Tregarne's comments were not without criticism but they were put to Mundy so politely and presented so persuasively that they didn't feel in the least like censure or disapproval. They were sensible suggestions for improving something that already had great value.

The three of them were in the room in Tregarne's house where he'd worked for so many years. It was in a state of chaos: books, newspapers and sheet music were scattered everywhere. The desk was awash with correspondence. Shelves groaned under the weight of dusty tomes. Only the two pianos and the harpsichord were free of clutter. Given the fact that his comic operas were events of continuous merriment that catered unapologetically for the coarser elements in the audience as well as for the more discerning, Mundy had expected Tregarne to be a man of Falstaffian girth and gross appetites. In fact, he was a small, skinny, wizened creature with a gleaming bald pate and an expressive face. He had a pleasing West Country burr.

'There you have it, Mr Mundy,' he said in conclusion. 'You've created something that will delight a London audience and live in its memory for many a day. Congratulations, my friend!'

'Coming from you, sir,' said Mundy, 'that's high praise, indeed.'

'We playwrights must stick together.'

'I find that writing is a profession that isolates me from everyone else.'

'That's a mistake,' warned Tregarne. 'The bustling streets of London gave me my material. All the characters I brought to life were based on people I'd actually met or seen walking past me. I'd had enough of isolation in Cornwall. Our cottage was ten miles from the nearest village. I couldn't wait to find an excuse to come here. It was a form of liberation.'

'I'd find a cottage in the country very appealing.'

'Stay close to human beings. You can't write plays about cows and sheep.'

'That's true,' said Fleet, chortling.

He got up to signal that it was time to leave. After effusive thanks to their host, the two men left the house with a sense of satisfaction. Mundy felt that he'd achieved most. His play had been applauded by a master of his craft and Tregarne had even been kind enough to suggest changes and refinements that the playwright accepted without a murmur. Incorporated into *The Piccadilly Opera* along with some new ariettas, they would add pace, definition and spirit.

For his part, Fleet was trying to conceal his excitement. Without realising it, Mundy had agreed to almost all the changes first mooted by Hannah Granville. Since they were voiced by a famous playwright, and couched in extravagant praise, Mundy didn't recognise them for what they were. The strategy was the last throw of the dice for the theatre manager. Tregarne might yet be his salvation.

Rollo Winters had an existence that suited him perfectly. Since the House of Commons was well endowed with supplies of alcohol, he was able to drift from one place to the other to exchange gossip and relish the latest scandal. When he was not in Parliament, he moved through a succession of favourite watering holes, always ending up at his club in Albemarle Street. It was there that Paul Skillen found him for the second time. Nursing a brandy, Winters had sunk into his favourite chair.

'Good day to you, sir,' said Paul, sitting beside him.

'Goodbye is more appropriate,' said the other, tartly. 'I've no wish to talk to you, sir.'

'But I bring you news of a friend of yours.'

'And who is that?'

'A gentleman named Rawdon Carr.'

'Yes,' admitted Winters. 'I know him well.'

'I've just come from his house,' explained Paul. 'One of the servants told me of his devotion to his club. When he'd celebrated rather too much, apparently, Mr Carr sometimes spent the night here.'

'We've all done that. It's a privilege of membership.'

'Then it's strange he should abandon it so lightly.'

'What do you mean?'

'Mr Carr has left London for good, it seems, and nobody has any idea where he went. Is that the kind of eccentric behaviour you expect from him?'

'No, it isn't. Rawdon is a sound man – intelligent, reliable and generous to a fault. I've spent many a happy evening at a dining table with him. Where can he possibly have gone?'

'I was hoping that *you* might have some idea of that, sir.'

Winters became cautious. 'What's your interest in him, Mr Skillen?'

'You might say that it was financial.'

'Rawdon owes you money?'

'Quite the reverse,' said Paul. 'I'm in a position to put some his way. Last time we met, we talked of Mr Bowerman's murder. I've been informed by his lawyer that his client named me as one of his executors. I therefore had the chance of an early peep at his last will and testament. Mr Carr is a beneficiary.'

'How much will he get?'

'It's a tidy amount, Mr Winters. I wanted to confide the good news to him but I can't do that if he's left the capital. The lawyer will be unable to get in touch with him as well. If the money is not claimed by a certain time, it will be forfeited.'

'We can't have that happening,' said Winters.

'I agree.'

'And it's a substantial amount, you say?'

'Mr Bowerman was a wealthy man.'

335

'Let me think for a moment...'

The politician had another drink to stimulate his brain, then began to pick his way through a veritable forest of memories. Having expected to be thrown out of the club, Paul had done better than he'd hoped. Winters had actually believed his story. After a lengthy period of meditation, the man sat up and jabbed a finger.

'He did once say something to me.'

'What was that, sir?'

'Well, we were talking about places to which we'd care to retire. I cited this club because it fulfils all my needs except that of ready access to amenable women. Rawdon wanted to go much further afield. He told me that he was always drawn to Scotland.'

'Why was that?'

'Rawdon was born there. His parents brought him south when he was five and he's always nurtured a fondness for his birthplace.'

'Where exactly was it?'

'Edinburgh – he thinks it's the most beautiful city in the world.'

When the boat left the Thames Estuary, it came out into choppier water for a while. It hugged the coast as it sailed northwards. It was a relatively small vessel but large enough to carry its two passengers in comfort and complete safety. Relaxing in their cabin, Rawdon Carr and his companion were still heady with success.

'When will they realise what's happened?' she asked.

'Letters will reach them tomorrow. I gave orders

that they should be delivered first thing. I want the information to bring them fully awake.'

'That was very naughty of you, Rawdon.'

'I've had a lot of time to plan this, my love.'

'Oh!' she cried, embracing him. 'Is there anything sweeter than revenge?'

'They both deserve it, Edith.'

'I'm just glad that I was able to do my share.'

Edith Loveridge was also glad that her real name had been restored to her. While she enjoyed posing as Hester Mallory or as Arabella Kenyon, she was happy that she was now with someone who knew and loved her as Edith Loveridge.

'Your contribution was unparalleled,' he told her. 'I was able to trick them into letting me invest all the money we got from the last time Laetitia used her charms on someone, leaving Stephen to kill the man in a duel. They trusted me completely. But only *you* could have forged their share certificates. Neither of them realises that they have worthless pieces of paper. I'd love to be there when they discover that their investment never actually existed.'

'That will wipe the arrogant sneer off Stephen's face.'

'Laetitia is the one I'll enjoy wounding most. There was a time when I adored that woman, Edith, and she gave me to believe that my attentions were welcome. When she turned on me so viciously,' he went on, 'I was mortified. From that moment on, I was thinking of getting even with her one day.'

'It was the same with Stephen. His treatment of me was not simply cruel. It was downright bar-

baric. He led me on with a promise of marriage then tossed me aside when he found someone else.'

'We should be grateful to them, really.'

'Never!' she decreed.

'Because they rejected you and me, they actually brought us together.'

He kissed and caressed her for several minutes and they forgot all about the lurching movements of the boat. Carr then told her that the most difficult part of the exercise was to convince them that she had died in France. He'd also had to replace Edith in their minds with another possible suspect.

'Her name was Eleanor Gold and Stephen cast her brutally aside.'

'That's exactly what he does.'

'I claimed that I had men out looking for her but that was a lie to deceive them. Because of the way I'd served them in the past, they believed me. For two intelligent people, they were so easy to manipulate.'

'What if they follow us to Scotland?'

'There isn't the slightest possibility of that, Edith.'

'Are you sure?'

'Yes, we've covered our tracks far too well.'

'Stephen might have heard you talking about Edinburgh.'

'I took great care never to mention my love of the city,' he said, 'and besides, neither he nor that venomous sister of his will be in a position to follow us. As well as sending letters to them, I've been writing to someone else.'

'Who is that?'

'I've sent word to the chief magistrate in Bow Street. Playing down my own part in the affair, I told him what Stephen and Laetitia had done between them to Mark Bowerman and to his predecessor. That should be enough to hang the both of them.'

'You've thought of *everything*, Rawdon.'

'I did it all for you, my love. As a result of hard work, I've accumulated a large amount of capital and your forays into the banking system in London and elsewhere have brought in even more. We'll be able to live in style, Edith.' He kissed her again. 'Meanwhile, Stephen and Laetitia will be dangling from the gallows.'

Charlotte had played the piano until her fingers began to ache. Though it was the same melody time and again, she didn't complain. The song never lost its appeal. Over her friend's shoulder, Hannah studied the notes once more and looked for ways to improve her rendition. She now knew the lyrics by heart.

'Let's try it again,' she said.

'You've already sung it fifteen or twenty times, Hannah.'

'I'm still feeling my way through it.'

'But it sounds wonderful to me.'

'Play it once more.'

'If this really is the last time, I will.'

The moment her fingertips touched the keys, however, Charlotte was forced to stop. After a tap on the door, one of the servants came in with a small parcel. She handed it over before going out again. Charlotte opened the parcel and marvelled at what she found inside.

'It's *another* song from Mr Tregarne,' she said, 'and it's dedicated to you.'

Back at the gallery, Peter Skillen explained what his brother had done. Ackford was quick to praise Paul for his enterprise but less than enthusiastic about the conclusion drawn by him. He wrinkled his brow before speaking.

'Just because he likes Edinburgh,' he said, 'it doesn't mean that Mr Carr has actually gone there. I've spent the last twenty years wanting to live on the north Devon coast but the closest I've ever got to it is here.'

'You don't have the same urgency to leave, Gully.'

'I agree,' said Huckvale. 'Mr Carr must know that those two men have been arrested. He'll realise we've guessed who hired them.'

'In that case, he might flee from London,' conceded Ackford, 'but why make for Scotland? It's too far and too uncivilised.'

Peter laughed. 'They're not all wild and hairy Highlanders.'

'I rubbed shoulders with a Scots regiment in America. They were very wild and very hairy, Peter, and they fought with real ferocity.'

'What about his friends?' asked Huckvale.

'What friends, Jem?'

'Mr Carr's friends – will they make a run for it themselves?'

'They won't see the need,' said Peter. 'As far as they're concerned, they're safe enough. Paul gave

340

Miss Somerville a nasty shock by mentioning Mr Bowerman's will. What she doesn't know is that we've worked out the murderous game she and Hamer have been playing together. They'll stay where they are because they think they're safe. It's only Carr who has to get out quickly.'

'I still think he'd go to ground here,' said Ackford. 'That's what I'd do.'

'No, it isn't. You'd run off to the north Devon coast.'

They shared a laugh then continued to speculate on Carr's likely movements. Huckvale had the strongest motive to catch up with him. He could still feel the ropes eating into his wrists and ankles. He was about to recount his ordeal yet again when Paul arrived. They looked up hopefully at him.

'Well?' asked Huckvale. 'What did you find out?'

'I was right,' said Paul. 'He's gone to Scotland.'

'How do you know?'

'I first thought that, if he was making a permanent move, he'd have a lot of luggage and travel by coach. But there's another way to go such a distance. That's why I scoured the docks for details of any vessels sailing for Scotland. In the end, I found one.'

'Was Mr Carr aboard?' asked Ackford.

'The old salt I spoke to didn't know his name but he described a man who sounds very much like Carr. He gave me a more detailed description of the woman who accompanied him,' said Paul, 'because she was very striking.'

'Was it Miss Somerville?' asked Huckvale.

'No, but it was someone equally beautiful and well dressed. Like him, she was travelling with a

341

fair amount of luggage. The two of them are sailing all the way up to Scotland. I'm sure they gave false names to the captain of the boat. I'm also sure that the man must have been Rawdon Carr.'

'What about the woman, Paul?'

'I haven't a clue who she might be.'

'I have,' said Peter, thinking about the forged letter that had lured Bowerman to his death. 'I'd never have connected them before but I can see now that they might be well suited. Carr is travelling with Mrs Hester Mallory or Miss Arabella Kenyon or, to be more exact, with both of them simultaneously.'

The pleasure of meeting Benjamin Tregarne had inspired Mundy. Throughout rehearsals, he'd had his talent called into question and it had sapped his strength and confidence. The time spent with Tregarne had restored both. When he returned to his lodging, he wanted to tell his wife all about the meeting but she was not there. Instead, therefore, he sat down at a table with his copy of the play and began to go through it line by line. There had already been a number of minor modifications. It was only when he went through each scene that he realised that what Tregarne had proposed was really quite radical. It involved cutting favourite passages and even losing some characters. The points where ariettas would be introduced were well chosen, he could not dispute that, but some of his beloved dialogue would have to be sacrificed in order to insert them.

The spirit of resistance was slowly awakened in Abel Mundy. Willing to make some changes, he had been lulled into the belief that his play needed structural alterations. While he refused to believe that it had been a deliberate trick on the part of Tregarne, he was not so ready to exonerate the theatre manager. It was Lemuel Fleet who'd contrived the visit, knowing that suggestions from an eminent dramatist and composer might be more acceptable than if they came from a strident actress.

Mundy closed the last page, picked up the whole play then slammed it down on the table. He would refuse to allow something that was tantamount to butchery of his work. His wife, he was certain, would endorse his decision. Together they would stand firm against the deviousness of the manager and the demands of Hannah Granville. Within minutes of reaching his decision, he was able to confide it to his wife. Returning to the house, she entered the room with great solemnity.

'Where have you been?' he asked.

'I went to church, Abel.'

'Do not waste time praying for the success of my play. It is beyond help.'

'I needed to talk to the vicar,' she explained. 'The load I've been carrying is too heavy to bear so I sought his advice.'

'There is no load now, Marion. It is all over. We can kick the dust of London from our feet and return to gentler pastures in the provinces. They like me there.'

'You don't understand.'

'What I understand,' he said, placing a gentle hand on her shoulder, 'is that I have a wonderful wife on whom I can depend in a crisis. Without you, I'd surely have crumbled by now. You have fought valiantly by my side.'

'I fear that I fought *too* valiantly, Abel.'

'In marrying you, I found myself a saint.'

'The vicar did not think me very saintly,' she said. 'He said that my secret would fester away inside me if I didn't tell the truth.'

'But you have no secrets from me, Marion.'

'Yes, I do.'

She looked him full in the face. Taking his hand from her shoulder, he stepped back a few paces. He opened his mouth in horror as he realised that the dear, devoted wife with her Christian virtues had struck back at the person who'd been plaguing him. It was Marion Mundy who'd hurled a stone through the window.

The second song composed by Tregarne was even better than the first. It left Hannah in a state of pure joy. Having sung it through several times, she took pity on Charlotte for spending so long at the piano and went back to her own house, singing both songs to herself alternately. Eager to tell Paul her good fortune, she was dismayed that he was not at home. In his place, waiting impatiently, was Lemuel Fleet.

'What did you think of the song?' he asked.

'Which one?' she replied. 'They are both delightful.'

'I'm so glad that you approve of them. I had a meeting with Mr Tregarne earlier on and he asked me to send you his kindest regards.'

'That was very kind of him.'

'He's looking forward to seeing you in *The*

Piccadilly Opera.'

'How can he do that when it will never be performed?'

'There's been a change of mind on Mr Mundy's part.'

'What provoked that?'

'I've no idea, Miss Granville, but he sent me this missive a short while ago.'

He handed over the letter and Hannah unfolded it. What she read was at first unbelievable. Mundy was acceding to every demand she'd made. Written in a shaky hand, the letter was polite and respectful. It made a point of praising Hannah's talent and apologising to her for any aspersions cast upon it. There was no explanation of why the playwright had withdrawn all his objections. His surrender was complete.

'This is wondrous,' said Hannah, returning the letter.

'It is, indeed,' he said, chortling. 'It's truly miraculous.'

Having seen so little of her husband all day, Charlotte was delighted when he came home that evening. When he told her of his plans, her delight turned to dismay.

'You and Paul are going to *Scotland?*' she asked.

'We'd go much farther for the chance to catch Rawdon Carr.'

'But you've no guarantee that he's actually heading there.'

'We have enough evidence to convince us.'

'What if you don't find him?'

'We'll keep searching until we do, Charlotte.'

345

'He's an evil man and he deserves to be brought to justice,' she said, 'but you seem to be taking such a risk, Peter. If he *is* aboard that boat, he has already stolen a march on you.'

'Sailing can be hazardous at the best of times,' he told her, 'and boats can easily be blown off course. Paul and I will travel overland and reach Edinburgh well ahead of them. As the two of them get off the boat, we will be waiting to arrest them for their part in the murder of Mr Bowerman and for a number of other crimes. Seeing the look of surprise on their faces,' he went on, 'will be ample reward for the effort it will have cost us.'

CHAPTER TWENTY

When he got to Bow Street early that morning, Micah Yeomans was still trying to wipe the sleep out of his eyes. A long night drinking at The Peacock had taken its toll. Alfred Hale was in slightly better shape. The summons had got him out of bed instantly. To the mutual disgust of the Runners, the chief magistrate was bright and alert. He seemed to be able to work for twenty-four hours a day without any sign of strain. When he explained why he'd summoned them, Kirkwood emphasised the need for speed and decisiveness.

'Strike quickly and strike hard,' he said.

'What exactly is in Mr Carr's letter, sir?' asked Yeomans.

'It's a denunciation both of Captain Hamer –

who never actually held that rank, apparently – and of Miss Somerville. In reality, he is her brother.'

Yeomans goggled. 'That's *immoral*. He can't marry his own sister.'

'He had no intention of doing so. He simply pretended to be her suitor in order to provoke someone into challenging him into a duel that he knew he could win.' He held the letter out to Yeomans. 'Read it for yourself. It's important for you to know the full details of their villainy before you arrest them.'

Standing side by side, the Runners read the letter simultaneously. It drew gasps of amazement from both of them. They were embarrassed to recall how easily Laetitia had allayed their suspicions on the previous day with a series of plausible explanations. When they'd left her house, they'd actually apologised. Yet, they now learned, their earlier assessment of her had been quite accurate. She and Hamer were heartless criminals. When the letter was handed back to him, Kirkwood was contrite.

'I need to offer you both an apology,' he began. 'When you interrupted that duel and prevented Mr Bowerman from being shot dead, you had your suspicions of Hamer. In the wake of Bowerman's murder, you arrested him.'

'He would not have come here of his own accord, sir,' said Yeomans.

'And you released him,' recalled Hale.

'You released him and you reprimanded us.'

'That's why I'm tendering an apology to both of you,' said Kirkwood, almost choking on the words. 'You were right and I was wrong. You smelt corruption and I did not. If everything in this letter is true, Hamer and Miss Somerville are monsters. They may not have killed Bowerman but that was their intention when they trapped him into challenging Hamer to a duel.'

'Why is Mr Carr telling us all this?' asked Hale.

'You've read what he said. He wants to salve his conscience.'

'But he collaborated with them, sir.'

'We'll deal with him in due course,' said Kirkwood. 'What we have here is a damning indictment of two individuals with perverse ambitions and a ruthlessness to achieve them. I writhe in disgust at the notion of Miss Somerville inheriting the bulk of Mr Bowerman's property and wealth. It's unseemly.'

'And it's criminal,' said Yeomans.

'Arrest them both at once.'

'Yes, sir.'

'And be on your guard. Hamer is likely to put up a fight.'

'We'll go armed, sir, and show no mercy.'

'To be on the safe side,' said Hale, 'we'll take plenty of men. Mr Yeomans and I have been rebuffed by the two of them time and again. The tables are now turned in our favour.'

'We know the shocking truth about them now,' said Yeomans.

'And we have a huge advantage, Micah.'

'Do we?'

'Of course,' said Hale, airily. 'We can take them completely by surprise.'

Laetitia was aghast when she read the letter from Rawdon Carr. Her maid took it up to the boudoir where she was reclining on the bed. The moment she saw the opening paragraph, she leapt to her feet. She couldn't believe that she and her brother had been so comprehensively taken in by a man they thought was a true friend. Laetitia was shocked to learn that she was being punished for her rejection of Carr's suit. More astounding, however, was the news that Carr was speaking on behalf of himself and of Edith Loveridge, a woman supposedly dead. Looking back, she saw how cleverly Carr had persuaded them that Edith, reeling from the blow of being spurned by Hamer, had gone abroad and contracted a fatal disease. All the time, in fact, she was Rawdon Carr's partner and an accessory to the murder of Mark Bowerman.

It was several minutes before her head cleared enough for her to make a decision. Running to the door, she opened it wide and called for her manservant. He dashed upstairs as fast as he could.

'Go to Captain Hamer's house and bring him here at once.'

'Yes, Miss Somerville.'

'If he's not yet awake, rouse him out of his bed.'

'What shall I say?'

'Tell him that it's a matter of life and death.'

Expecting far more resistance from Hamer, the Runners went to his house first and deployed their men around it, impressing upon them that the former soldier would try to fight his way out.

Yeomans and Hale approached the house warily. It held some uncomfortable memories for them but they now had a chance to expunge them. The chief magistrate's apology had given both of them a fillip. Their pride had been restored. Whichever way it developed, they felt capable of handling the situation.

Yeomans gave his friend the honour of ringing the bell then let his hand slip to the pistol concealed under his cloak. The door was soon opened by a servant.

'We've come to see your master,' said Yeomans, pushing past her.

'But the captain is not here, sir,' she said.

'Don't lie to me, girl. Where is he?'

'He left the house not ten or fifteen minutes ago.'

'I don't believe you.'

He signalled to some of his men and four of them came running. They searched the house with noisy thoroughness from top to bottom but they found no trace of Hamer. Yeomans rounded on Hale.

'What happened to the advantage of surprise?'

The sudden departure of the two brothers had thrown Charlotte and Hannah together. So excited was the actress to pass on the good tidings that she called on her friend before breakfast. Charlotte was thrilled to hear that rehearsals of the play would resume and that it had been changed largely in accordance with Hannah's wishes.

'Did your arguments finally prevail?' asked Charlotte.

'Something happened to change his mind.'

'He was so adamant at first.'

'I think he recognised that I have the stronger will.'

'Does that mean he'll attend rehearsals?'

'No,' replied Hannah, 'that was the other concession. Mr Mundy promised to stay away until the latter stages so that he wouldn't be tempted to interfere.'

'What did Mr Fleet have to say?'

'Had he been able to do so, I fancy that he'd have turned somersaults. He told me that he'd met with Mr Tregarne yesterday.'

Charlotte smiled. 'I had a feeling that *he* might be involved.'

'It's marvellous news,' said Hannah, 'and it will help to console me during Paul's absence. I slept in a very cold bed last night.'

'So did I, Hannah.'

'He told me that it was all in a good cause.'

'Peter used the same phrase to me. I still think that they're putting themselves to a great deal of effort on the basis of a hopeful supposition.'

'Paul's suppositions are usually proved right.'

'Scotland is so ridiculously far away.'

'If I was in Mr Carr's shoes, that's exactly the sort of place I'd choose. He's betrayed his friends. They'll want his blood. He needs to put hundreds of miles between himself and them.'

'I'm worried about the dangers they might meet on their way there.'

'Peter and Paul love danger,' said Hannah. 'When I first discovered that, I demanded that Paul should find a gentler way of life.'

351

'That's like ordering the sun not to shine.'

'I soon learnt that.' She glanced towards the dining room. 'Have you had breakfast yet?'

'No,' said Charlotte, 'and I'm famished. Do please join me. Afterwards, I suppose, you'll want me to accompany you on the piano at my house.'

Hannah laughed. 'How did you guess?'

Placed side by side on the table, the letters looked identical. Hamer pointed out the crucial difference. At the bottom of his missive the letter 'e' was written so faintly as to be almost invisible.

'Edith is showing off,' he said, ruefully. 'Rawdon wrote your letter and she copied it for my benefit. She has an extraordinary gift.'

'It's more like a supernatural power, Stephen. How many other women can come back from the grave and exact their revenge on someone? It's your fault, really. You didn't handle Edith properly.'

'I had no complaints at the time.'

'You dallied shamelessly with her when what she expected was marriage.'

'Rawdon had the same fantasies about you, Laetitia.'

'They were foolishly unrealistic. That's why I had to shun him.'

Stephen studied his letter. 'Can those investments of ours really be bogus?'

'We won't get a penny.'

'What about Bowerman's property?'

'That, too, is beginning to recede before my eyes,' she said. 'Paul Skillen knows about the terms of the will. He talked of contesting it.'

'Then he'll fail. It was made in good faith by a man who loved you.'

'I thought that Rawdon Carr loved me once.'

Their anger was intensified by the searing pain they both felt at being cheated. Large amounts of money on which they'd depended no longer existed. The person they'd willingly allowed to control events had proved to be treacherous and, worse, was in league with a woman who'd turned forgery into an art. Their whole world suddenly began to rock.

'What are we going to do, Stephen?'

'My first task is to go after Rawdon and kill him,' he said. 'He's not only duped us, he's mocking us for our stupidity. Edith is probably sniggering beside him at this very moment.'

'You don't know where they've gone.'

'I'll find out somehow, Laetitia. They're bound to have left a trail.'

'Are we in danger?'

'I don't think so.'

'What if Rawdon decides to betray us to the authorities?'

'Even *he* wouldn't stoop to that level.'

There was a tap on the door and a servant entered nervously.

'Excuse me for interrupting,' she said, 'but people are surrounding the house.'

'Who are they? cried Laetitia.

Hamer ran to the window and peered out. He saw Yeomans and Hale with a dozen or more men in support. They were closing in on the house.

'It's the Runners!' he yelled.

Having slept fitfully all night, Abel Mundy and his wife lay side by side in silence. Neither of them dared to speak or had the urge to move. Though they were within inches of each other, they seemed far apart. When a window was shattered within feet of Hannah Granville, he'd been moved to sympathise with her. It never crossed his mind as even a remote possibility that the person who threw the stone was his wife. Now that the truth had finally come into the open, Mundy had weathered the immediate shock and sought for an explanation of why she acted as she did.

It was his fault. His bitter feud with a capricious actress had brought him such patent misery that Marion, a woman of great kindness and forbearance, had been driven to administer punishment on his behalf. He couldn't blame her because it was he who was really culpable. Instead of bringing his worries home, he should have kept them to himself. In sharing his anguish with his wife, he'd painted Hannah Granville in the garish colours of a destructive madwoman.

When Marion eventually found her voice, it was only a meek whisper.

'Do you think that I should confess?'

'You've already done that before God.'

'The vicar said that I should tell the truth to Miss Granville.'

'That would be humiliating to you and upsetting to her. The incident is over and is already fading into the past. Now that the play is back in rehearsal, she has got what she wanted. I hated having to cede victory but it was unavoidable. Because of what you told me,' he went on, 'I had to make amends.'

'But it's your play, Abel. You shouldn't have to surrender it.'

'Part of me has done so willingly, my dear. To tell you the truth, some of the demands she made were very reasonable. It was her hostile manner that made me so defensive. Mr Tregarne endorsed her views. Between them,' he said, philosophically, 'they added to the strength of my play. I should be grateful for that.'

She stretched out a tentative hand. 'Do you forgive me?'

'I can do that easily, Marion. But there's someone I can't forgive.'

'Miss Granville?'

'No, my dear,' he said, penitently. 'I can't forgive myself for turning you from the true Christian you are into a vengeful harridan. That's a terrible thing for any man to do to his wife.'

Yeomans waved an arm and the ring tightened around the house. He could catch both of them together now, he thought, and return to Bow Street to bask in the approbation of the chief magistrate. When everyone was in position, he and Hale walked slowly up to the front door. After ringing the bell, he stood back, one hand fingering the butt of his pistol. The door was opened by a manservant. Thrusting him aside, Yeomans charged into the drawing room with Hale. They came to a sudden halt. Laetitia was sitting calmly in a corner, reading a book. She looked up with interest.

'Good morning, gentlemen,' she said. 'Did you

want something?'

'We've come on police business, Miss Somerville,' said Yeomans, gruffly. 'You are under arrest.'

She arched her back. 'On what possible grounds, I pray?'

'Mr Carr has given us several to choose from. We've received a deposition from him regarding you and your brother.' She was startled into jumping to her feet. 'Yes, we know who and what he is now. Mr Carr's letter told us everything.'

'Rawdon Carr is a notorious liar,' she said.

'You'll be able to make that point in court.'

He nodded to Hale and the latter moved to stand beside Laetitia, holding her arm. Though she tried to shake him off, his grasp was too firm. Yeomans took the pistol from his belt.

'Where is your brother, Miss Somerville?' he asked.

'Stephen is not here.'

'Yes, he is. We've been to his house. He received a summons from you and rode here at a gallop. Where are you hiding him?'

'He left before you arrived,' she snapped.

'Take her out to the carriage, Alfred. I'll lead the search.'

Struggling in vain to get away, she was almost carried out into the street then shoved into a waiting carriage. Hale got in after her. Yeomans, meanwhile, called in four of his men and began a systematic search of the house. If Hamer was there, he reasoned, he was likely to be armed so Yeomans kept his weapon at the ready. The search, however, was fruitless. Since they'd been over every inch of the property with excessive care, they had to accept that Hamer was not there. Going back out into the street, Yeomans climbed into the carriage and it set off.

Stephen Hamer watched it from his hiding place behind one of the chimneys. It was a precarious refuge but it had helped him to evade arrest. The Runners had gone and the members of the foot patrol went after them. It would soon be possible to descend. While he was waiting, he wondered how he could possibly rescue his sister.

Peter and Paul Skillen had put urgency before comfort and travelled in a bumpy coach for most of the night. The recent dry spell of weather had left the roads hard and rutted, making the vehicle rock from side to side and, every now and then, plunge into a deep pothole that jarred every bone. It was not until they stopped for refreshment at a wayside tavern that they could talk properly. During the journey, the presence of other passengers had made any meaningful conversation well-nigh impossible. The privacy they now enjoyed was a relief.

Peter harboured doubts. 'This could be a calamitous mistake, Paul.'

'They're going to Scotland. I'm convinced of it.'

'That may be so but are they going there *directly?* What if they stop off for a few days here and there? Scarborough, for instance, would be one of many agreeable places to stay at this time of year. They might not get to their ultimate destination for weeks.'

'In that case, we wait for weeks.'

'That won't make us popular back at home.'

'You were away for longer periods during the war, Peter, and so was I. Are you prepared to let Carr and his accomplice commit murder and remain unpunished?'

'No, I'm not.'

'There's a secondary reason why you should want to arrest his accomplice and take her back to London. She'll be carrying the money she swindled from the bank.'

'I'd forgotten that. Mr Impey will be overjoyed if I return it to him. She was using the name of Hester Mallory at the time. I daresay that she's passing herself off as Mrs Carr at the moment.'

'She's an interesting lady. I look forward to meeting her.'

'So am I,' said Peter, looking up at the clock on the wall. 'Well, I know what Charlotte is doing at the moment. She'll have had breakfast and will be setting off for the gallery very soon.' He looked at his brother. 'What about Hannah?'

'She's so pleased that the play has been rescued that she won't even notice that I'm not there. When I took my leave of her last night, all she could talk about was the fact that rehearsals would start in earnest this morning.'

'It looks as if we'll both have to miss the first performance.'

'Don't give up hope. Carr's boat may reach Edinburgh sooner than you think,' said Paul. *The Piccadilly Opera* has caused so much turmoil that I despaired of it ever being performed. Now that it will, I promised Hannah that I'd be there on the opening night and I fully intend to honour that promise.'

The sense of relief was palpable. As she walked into the room, the rest of the company not only gave her a round of applause, they rushed across to thank her individually. In their eyes, she'd saved the play and ensured that they'd be paid for its duration. Fleet explained to them what changes would be made and how they needed to extend the length of rehearsals in order to make up for lost time. None of the actors had a complete copy of the play. All they were given were the pages containing their respective scenes. It was only when they watched the drama unfold before them that they realised how radical some of the alterations had been. The play began to flower for the first time. Freed from the glowering presence of Abel Mundy, the actors felt able to breathe properly at last and it showed in their improved performances.

During a brief pause, Fleet took the opportunity to speak to Hannah.

'What do you think of the play now, Miss Granville?'

'It's a work of genius,' she replied.

'That's what I said from the very start.'

'Its genius was too well hidden, then. We've brought it out and let it shine. I'm so gratified that Mr Mundy finally saw the wisdom behind my criticism.'

'That isn't quite what happened,' said Fleet.

'Oh?'

'But it's close enough to the truth. Mr Tregarne's

intervention was a great help to us and his ariettas will provide an additional sparkle to the play. However, I bought the rights to stage *The Piccadilly Opera* with you in mind, Miss Granville. I have every confidence that, in its new form, it will even win unstinting applause from the man who first conceived it.'

Laetitia had had to suffer the indignity of being squashed between the Runners as the carriage rolled towards Bow Street. Having woken up in a fragrant boudoir and been surrounded by domestic luxury, she'd been arrested by men whose breath stank and whose clothing smelt of the beer carelessly spilt over it. At a stroke, she'd lost her wealth, her position in society and her prospects. She was fearful that her life would be forfeit as well. When they reached Bow Street, she was formally charged and locked in a small, dank, fetid cell with barely room to move. It was insufferable.

Rawdon Carr, their friend and mentor, had been responsible for her arrest but his wickedness was too appalling to contemplate. She therefore fixed her thoughts on her brother. Her one hope was that he would somehow come to her rescue. He would certainly not let her down. As long as he was at liberty, there was a chance of escape for her. Holding her nose to keep out the stench, she perched on the rough stool in her cell and closed her eyes.

It was the best part of an hour before they came to fetch her. The cell door was unlocked and she was hustled along a corridor and into the chief magistrate's office by Yeomans and Hale. They made her stand in front of the desk while Kirkwood read out the letter he'd received from Carr. It made her pulse with fury. The charges against her and Stephen Hamer were all there, laid out in chronological sequence.

'What have you to say for yourself, Miss Somerville?' asked Kirkwood.

'That letter is nothing but a farrago of spite, hatred and lies,' she said.

'Given what my officers have told me, I'm inclined to believe every last word written here.'

'And will Mr Carr be in court to justify his calumny?'

'I'm not sure that he has to be. Certain facts are irrefutable.'

He was about to deliver his standard homily to a person guilty of serious crimes when he was diverted by the sound of a commotion outside. Crossing to the door, Kirkwood opened it wide, only to be knocked back into the room by the solid frame of Chevy Ruddock.

'I'm sorry, sir,' said Ruddock. '*He* made me do that.'

Held by his collar, he had a pistol pointed at his skull by Stephen Hamer.

'If anyone so much as moves,' warned Hamer, 'I'll blow his head apart. My sister is leaving with me right now. Stand back, all of you!'

The Runners flattened themselves against the wall and Kirkwood squirmed his way into a corner. None of them doubted that the newcomer would shoot if necessary, and they were all too aware that he had a second pistol thrust into his

361

belt. After killing Ruddock, he'd shoot one of them as well.

Thrilled by her brother's daring, Laetitia ran to his side. They began to back out of the room with Ruddock as their hostage. After finding their way to the main door, they went out quickly. A gig was waiting for them. Hamer helped his sister into the vehicle then clambered up beside her, snatching up the whip in order to crack it. The moment that Ruddock was released, however, he came to life. Instead of letting them ride off, he jumped on the gig from behind and got an arm around Hamer's neck. There was a fierce struggle and Yeomans and Hale came out to watch it. Ruddock was bravely trying to wrest the pistol off Hamer. For her part, Laetitia was screaming abuse and using both fists to pound away at Ruddock. The Runners moved in swiftly. Hale grabbed the bridle so that the horse could not bolt and Yeomans joined the fight with Hamer. As the three of them twisted and turned and threshed away, the pistol suddenly went off and Hamer let out a howl of pain. He'd shot himself in the leg. Yeomans relieved him of the other weapon and dragged him uncaringly from the gig. Ignoring her imprecations, Ruddock soon overpowered the hysterical Laetitia.

The attempted rescue had failed. They were doomed.

The rehearsals were not always conducted in a spirit of jollity. There were inevitable setbacks. Minor squabbles broke out between actors, the scenery did not at first conform to the original designs and there was further upset when costumes didn't fit. Lemuel Fleet presided over it all with avuncular tolerance. The main thing was that the play itself had acquired real quality in its new form and the contribution of Benjamin Tregarne added a wonderful operatic sheen. Words and music blended perfectly throughout. It was a pleasure to take part in it.

'It's very tiring,' said Hannah, 'but, at the same time, very refreshing.'

'Don't tell me too much about it,' warned her friend, 'or there'll be no surprises left for me. Are you happy with the ariettas?'

'Oh, yes. No disrespect to you and your piano, Charlotte, but the songs are so much better when sung in the auditorium for which they were written.'

'Have you seen any sign of Mr Mundy?'

'We've not had a peep out of him.'

'He's keeping to his promise, then.'

'He's finally realised that we work best when he's not there.'

It was almost a week since rehearsals had started again and they were dining together at Charlotte's house. They'd heard of the arrests of Stephen Hamer and Laetitia Somerville and were shocked to discover that they were siblings. Charlotte had saved a newspaper that carried a full report of their arrests.

'Peter will be so interested to read it,' she said. 'I know that we ridicule the Runners sometimes, but they have their triumphs just as we do.'

'My triumph will be on the stage in ten days. Paul swore to me that he'd be there on the first night to support me but he could be marooned in Scotland for ages.' Hannah clicked her tongue. 'Why did he have to go all that way?'

'He wants to catch Mr Carr – and so does Peter.'

'But they have no idea if and when he'll actually go to Edinburgh.'

'Paul is certain of it.'

'What about Peter?'

'He's less certain, to be honest,' admitted Charlotte, 'but he knows that his brother's instincts are usually very reliable.'

'I don't like what I heard about this Mr Carr. Paul says that he's a cold and calculating man. He's the one who stabbed Mr Bowerman in the back.'

'That tells us everything about him.'

'He's going to be slippery.'

'Mr Carr will be off guard,' said Charlotte. 'When he sailed from London, he was confident that he and his accomplice had escaped justice. Who would bother to go such a long distance in pursuit of him? That's what he'll ask.'

'And he'll get his answer,' said Hannah.

The voyage had been relatively untroubled. As the boat sailed up the coast, they got a fascinating view of the geography of their country. The captain put into port now and then to buy supplies and to give his passengers the opportunity to feel dry land beneath their feet for a while. Then the vessel was soon on its way again. Expecting some discomfort, Carr and Edith were surprised by how well they felt. Their appetites were unimpaired and they remained in good health.

'How much further is it, Rawdon?'

'The captain says that we should dock early in the morning.'

'Would that be Captain Hamer?' she asked with a teasing smile.

'No, it's the skipper of this boat, as you know only too well. In any case, Stephen was never really a captain, remember. The court martial disposed of that ambition. It meant that he was blackballed at his club so came as a guest to mine.'

'Where do you think he and Laetitia are?'

'They'll be awaiting sentence,' said Carr, complacently. 'The letter I sent to the chief magistrate was their death warrant. They're no threat to us now.'

'And what about those other men you told me about – the twins?'

'Their names are Peter and Paul Skillen and they were embarrassingly clever. I'm glad we've sailed away from their clutches. Their chances of catching us are non-existent because they don't have the slightest idea where we're going.'

Neither of them was temperamentally suited to a long, tedious wait but it had to be endured. For day after day, Peter and Paul had lurked in the harbour and watched vessels coming in or setting sail. Even at night they didn't relinquish their surveillance. Taking it in turns to stay on sentry duty, they checked each boat that docked in the darkness. As a new day dawned, they were seated beside the Firth of Forth once again. Peter was fretful.

'It's a crying shame,' he said. 'Carr was right to say that this is a beautiful city but we've had no time at all to appreciate it. All that we've seen is water lapping the wharves as the fishing boats bring in their catch.'

'It's only a matter of time, Peter.'

'You've been saying that for days.'

'I say it and I believe it. They'll come soon, mark my words.'

'Edinburgh's a fine place but some say that Glasgow will soon be bigger. 'What if Carr decides to go there instead?'

'*This* is where he was born,' said Paul, 'and this is where he'll come.'

Buoyed up yet again by his brother's certainty, Peter returned to his vigil. They'd come prepared. They'd brought a telescope with them. Since they'd been in Scotland, it had enabled them to study boat after boat as it approached.

The first gestures of day slowly gave way to a rising blanket of light. As their eyes scanned the water, they saw two vessels heading their way. The larger was clearly a fishing smack and, even from that distance, they could pick out members of the crew moving about the deck. The second boat was the one that interested them. By using the telescope, Paul could see a man standing on the deck with his arm around a woman. He handed the instrument to his brother.

'What can you see?'

Peter peered through the telescope. 'They're here at last!'

Legs braced against the swell, Rawdon Carr was

pointing out some of the distinctive silhouettes of Edinburgh. He was thrilled to be back in his home town again. Edith listened to him patiently but there was far too much information to take in at once. What she was looking forward to was stepping off the boat for the last time. The excitement of the early stages of the voyage had palled and she needed something more stable beneath her feet. Because the boat was moving at only a moderate speed, there was plenty of time to admire their new home. Carr had told her so much about Edinburgh that she couldn't wait to explore it. When the boat finally reached the wharf, it bounced against the timbers. While one of the crew tossed a rope, another jumped nimbly ashore to secure it to a bollard. When a second rope was in place, the vessel was safely moored. Carr and Edith thanked the captain and left a generous tip for him and his crew. They were then helped carefully off the boat.

A few carriages stood nearby. Two men in large hats and long capes stepped forward to pick up the luggage that was unloaded from the boat. They carried it up to the vehicle at the front of the queue. Opening the door and keeping his head down, one of the men helped Edith into the carriage then stood back so that Carr could climb in beside her. The couple looked weary but contented. Holding hands they sat back in their seats. As he barked an order, Carr was imperious.

'Take us to the Grand Hotel!'

'Oh, we'll take you much further than that,' said Paul, removing his hat and grinning at them through the open door. 'Welcome to Edinburgh,

Mr Carr! I've been waiting for you.'

Carr was horror-struck. 'How the devil did *you* get here?'

'My brother came with *me*,' said Peter, opening the other door and doffing his hat. He smiled courteously at Edith. 'I'm pleased to meet you, Miss Loveridge,' he went on. 'I bring you greetings from Mr Impey, though he knew you as Mrs Mallory, of course. He'll be thrilled to attend your trial in London.'

'What's going on, Rawdon?' she cried. 'Who *are* these men?' But Carr was unable to muster an answer. The plan he'd so carefully drawn up had just vanished before his eyes. He offered a token resistance by trying to push Paul aside and get out of the vehicle but he was easily punched back into his seat. All that Carr would get was a fleeting glimpse of his birthplace before he was taken back to London to meet his death.

Fired by the promise of an exciting new play and the opportunity of hearing songs written by Benjamin Tregarne, people came in droves to watch the first performance. All seats had been sold and the auditorium was buzzing with anticipatory pleasure. Peter and Charlotte had the privilege of sitting with the composer and with Lemuel Fleet in the manager's box. Paul preferred to be in the pit so that he could be close to Hannah. Abel Mundy and his wife stayed at the rear, nursing their misgivings. When a fanfare sounded, the hubbub died down slightly and *The Piccadilly Opera* made its first appearance before an audience.

It was a sensation. The plot had been tightened, the characters defined more sharply and the humour scattered more freely throughout the play. Tregarne's ariettas were inspiring, each one greeted by an ovation. Costumes and scenery were superb, flooding the stage with colour and drawing gasps of wonder. The real surprise was Hannah Granville. Those who'd marvelled at her in tragic roles now realised that she had comedic talent of the highest order and a voice of operatic power. Following her lead, the cast surpassed themselves. A new play had been transformed from its earlier version into a brilliant piece of theatre. When it met thunderous acclaim at the end, nobody clapped louder than the playwright himself. Applause signalled acceptance. In the course of the evening, against all his earlier predictions, he'd become famous.

Back at Paul's house, celebrations went on long into the night. He, Hannah, Peter and Charlotte toasted the success of the evening. It had obliterated all the problems that had bedevilled the play at the start. Everyone involved had been beneficiaries of an unqualified triumph.

'Before long,' said Paul, introducing a sombre note, 'another performance will take place and it's one that can never be repeated. There'll be no love story and no songs when Rawdon Carr and Edith Loveridge step onto the scaffold.'

'There will, however, be a baying mob,' said Peter.

Hannah grimaced. 'I think such a spectacle is grotesque.'

'I couldn't agree with you more,' said Charlotte,

sadly. 'Both of them deserve to be executed for their crimes but it shouldn't take place in public.'

'Yes, it should,' argued Paul. 'It sends out a grim warning. I'm proud that Peter and I brought the pair of them back to London to answer for their crimes. They showed no pity for their victims and they deserve none themselves.'

'That sounds rather harsh.'

'It's meant to be, Charlotte. What we saw this evening was one of the finest entertainments ever put before a London audience and Hannah must be feted for what she did on that stage. It was pure magic. If I hadn't loved her already,' he went on, leaning across to kiss her, 'I'd have been bewitched by her. Yet the truth is that it was all make-believe in front of painted scenery. The execution will be an example of real drama. Peter and I are its co-authors. In a city as beset by crime as London, I'm afraid that it won't be the last time we have to take up our pens.'

The publishers hope that this book has given you enjoyable reading. Large Print Books are especially designed to be as easy to see and hold as possible. If you wish a complete list of our books please ask at your local library or write directly to:

Magna Large Print Books
Magna House, Long Preston,
Skipton, North Yorkshire.
BD23 4ND

This Large Print Book for the partially sighted, who cannot read normal print, is published under the auspices of

THE ULVERSCROFT FOUNDATION

THE ULVERSCROFT FOUNDATION

... we hope that you have enjoyed this Large Print Book. Please think for a moment about those people who have worse eyesight problems than you ... and are unable to even read or enjoy Large Print, without great difficulty.

You can help them by sending a donation, large or small to:

**The Ulverscroft Foundation,
1, The Green, Bradgate Road,
Anstey, Leicestershire, LE7 7FU,
England.**
or request a copy of our brochure for more details.

The Foundation will use all your help to assist those people who are handicapped by various sight problems and need special attention.

Thank you very much for your help.